ASSISTED LIVING

ASSISTED LIVING

a novel by Nikanor Teratologen

TRANSLATED BY KERRI A. PIERCE
AFTERWORD BY STIG SÆTERBAKKEN

DALKEY ARCHIVE PRESS
CHAMPAIGN // DUBLIN // LONDON

Originally published in Swedish as *Äldreomsorgen i Övre Kågedalen* by Norstedts Förlag, Stockholm, 1992

Library of Congress Cataloging-in-Publication Data

Teratologen, Nikanor.
[Äldreomsorgen i övre kägedalen. English]
Assisted living / Nikanor Teratologen ; translated by Kerri A. Pierce ; afterword by Stig Sterbakken. -- 1st ed.
p. cm.
"Originally published in Swedish as Äldreomsorgen i Övre Kägedalen by Norstedts Förlag, Stockholm, 1992."
ISBN 978-1-56478-682-1 (pbk. : alk. paper)
I. Pierce, Kerri A. II. Title.
PT9876.3.E73A79 2012
839.73'74--dc23

                    2011040673

Partially funded by the University of Illinois at Urbana-Champaign, as well as by grants from the National Endowment for the Arts, a federal agency, and the Illinois Arts Council, a state agency

The translation of this work was supported by a grant from the Swedish Arts Council

www.dalkeyarchive.com

Cover: design and composition by Danielle Dutton, illustration by Nicholas Motte
Printed on permanent/durable acid-free paper and bound in the United States of America

CONTENTS

"Schizo-laughter or revolutionary joy, that is what emanates from great books, in place of the anguishes of our little narcissism or the terrors of our guilt . . .

"An indescribable joy always rushes out of great books, even when they speak of ugly, hopeless, or terrifying things."

—Gilles Deleuze

"Even if your home lies at the gates of hell, you still long for your birthplace."

—Norrlandish proverb

"Fairy tales live here yet, and tell us what you were in days past— home to great deeds and virtue."

—"Västerbotten," printed in the newspaper of the same name, 1921

I want to thank the prince of this world (John 12:31), without whom this book couldn't have been written.

TRANSLATOR'S NOTE

Assisted Living is written in Skelleftemål, a dialect found in northern Sweden. This presents the English translator with yet another version of the eternal question: how much of the original text does one try to keep, and how much does one allow to be "lost in translation"? After careful consideration, and a few failed experiments, I decided to translate the book into more or less "good English." After all, I asked myself, and speaking as an American, what could approximate a Swedish dialect in US English? Should I try to make the book sound "regional"? Should backwoods Swedes talk like stereotypical southern "hicks"? Even if I could pull off an authentic sounding text—no mean feat in itself—why should someone from Sweden sound like they're from south Texas? (As a Texas native, a Texas drawl was foremost in my mind.) But, no. Translators must always walk that fine line between the original text and their new translation. In creating something new, something will always be lost—and perhaps gained. As Nikanor Teratologen, reviewing the English text, recently put it: "What we have here is a good Luciferan read."

If I've done my job, the reader will agree.

KERRI A. PIERCE

ASSISTED LIVING

Or, Caring for the Elderly in Upper Kågedalen

NIKANOR TERATOLOGEN'S PREFACE

A dear friend with exquisitely cruel tastes entrusted me with the text you now hold in your hand.

This friend, a man of both honor and lust, strongly insists that he retain his anonymity.

I, supervisor of all sovereign creatures, chronicler of dead voices, guarantor of the world order, thus place myself between him and the other human animals. Thus do I say to cocknibblers and assassins alike: come to me . . . we'll see if the masterhand won't clench itself in the right orifice . . .

I've always preferred pick-up sticks to chess anyway . . .

A DEAR FRIEND'S FOREWORD

Last summer I murdered an eleven-year-old boy. He said his name was Helge Holmlund from Hebbershålet in Upper Kågedalen, North Västerbotten. We met at a urinal in Tivoli just as Men's Night was closing in on Children's Day. He struck me as the quiet, frail type—and it was love at first sight. I took him home, and after he'd performed certain services, I tied him up and locked him in the soundproof cellar I use for such occasions.

For six whole days he gave me exquisite pleasure. After that, I hacked his body into small pieces, wrapped the meat in plastic, priced it, and distributed the packages to a number of different display cases in and around Skellefteå.

I kept his head for my little collection.

While I was burning the boy's clothes and other things, I found a hefty stack of old wallpaper samples tucked in his ratty leather backpack. Each sample was scribbled over in a child's erratic, immature hand, the words all written in different colored pencils. As I made my way through a few of these fragments, words utterly failed me. A brave new world opened before my eyes—one of vile pleasures and terrifying abominations—with the power to touch me in ways I no longer thought possible. Chuckling at his impudence, weeping at his tender sentiment, trembling with sorrow, paralyzed by hate—I sorted these rough fragments and organized them into a number of offensively seductive stories, each one presumably written by the dead boy.

My philological training proved extremely useful in tackling the difficulties posed by these unusually precocious recollections, which the boy had misleadingly entitled *Assisted Living*. I also made discrete inquiries into the poor boy's past, a quest that took me far off the beaten path and into the dark and brooding Northland nightwoods, home to more terrifying legends than any one person is capable of taking in. I wandered down what seemed to me contaminated paths through a hazardous landscape. On both sides of the Kågeälven, the dark river, the earth is fertile and the view open. I could see dirty-gold barley fields, resilient swaths of hay pasture, fallow fields, and hopeful new patches of almond potatoes, all stretching away before me; there were graying Västerbotten farmhouses in various states of decay, though clumps of willow trees and stands of birches try to hide the worst of it. Each of these farmhouses is set well back from the road and has a long approach leading up to it. It's obvious that the people in these parts want to know who's coming; they keep to their own. However, you can still find a few beautiful old Västerbotten farms scattered here and there: dark red timber houses with white doors, small porches, and shingled roofs. For the most part, though, pale and dull dwellings, each one identical to its neighbor, have taken over the region. The empty cow barns (which the locals call *fusen*) yawn empty. Now they use silos. In these parts, there's a chapel for every ten homesteads. Everything's modest and respectable, people pride themselves on their rancor and cunning both. Only old people are left now, out in the country, though in the sparsely populated regions of Ersmark and Kusmark a few communities still try to scrape by: making condoms for Skega and crying outside their closed church. Mystery has vanished from the forests surrounding the riverbed. Winter in these parts is hard. Blizzards numb all human feelings; one's gaze turns inward. During the long winter, people do their best to forget. Imperceptibly the valley fades away, the colors change. Spruces and pines cover the gently descending hillsides. A spiderweb of woodland roads (leading nowhere) spreads throughout the forest. Everything is condemned to be cut down and carted away. The trees are taller and darker here; their melancholy is more powerful than life. The fact that the valley has no visible borders makes escape impossible.

Farther up, the scene remains unchanged. In fact, the character of the dell becomes even more pronounced where Kågedalen nears its end—until, finally, it becomes transcendental. A large power line running from Svartbyn in Norrbotten to Jälta in Ångermanland splits the countryside in half. The forest here draws close to the rugged dirt road; the same is true of the humble homes in the small villages. Every now and then you catch a glimpse of cultivated land: forest-clad ridges crisscrossed by brown swaths of clear-cutting; forgotten, outworn meadows—once worked, now overgrown—boldly marching down toward Hebbersbäcken's shallow watercourse. At Slyberget this creek joins the north-ward-bound Kågeälven, before proceeding alongside the road to Bottenviken. In short, the landscape in Upper Kågedalen is nerve-wracking, bewitching, and pristine. People here aren't too concerned with planting and harvest time; something else fills their minds. The observer is overwhelmed by the mood of sorrow, severity, and loneliness that pervades the atmosphere. The air here is clear, you see all too clearly, but the forest holds an eternal darkness. Human hands could never rob the countryside of its austere grandeur. The old people in these parts are cut from the same cloth. When the time comes, they hang themselves—silently, calmly, expertly—from the rafters of the abandoned cow barns. Grand gestures have no place here. No one even talks about it. What would be the point?

Naturally, I questioned the people in the villages of Upper Kågedalen under false pretenses. Still, they met this polite and scholarly stranger with silent gestures meant to ward him off; and, more often than not, with curses or the evil eye. I preferred concentrating on the shier old men—frail and soft, infant-voiced and doe-eyed—who, after a litany of stops and starts, would finally start rooting around in their own overwhelming oblivion and return with what they found there, which they would pronounce in voices like the newly weaned. Hebbersfors, Hebbersliden, Hebbersholm were all familiar. However, no one knew anything about Hebbershålet. People insisted they'd never heard of, much less met, an old man with a little grandson. It seemed Holger Holmlund was an unknown party. The same was true of Helge. Names from their circle of acquaintance likewise turned up nothing. In the end, banal reality threatened to bury myself and my fantasies beneath its everyday offal.

It began to dawn on my, by this time, that not even the national registry could help me. I'd just about given up. One day, however, just after I had radiated my colony of Necrophorus investigators to death, someone came pounding on my door. When I opened it, there was no one there—just a letter nailed to the doorpost with a dagger. I wrenched the dagger out of the wood, made sure I was alone, and relocked the door. The letter was typed and didn't have a return address. I've reproduced this letter below, though I've edited out certain insulting comments regarding my lifestyle choices:

". . . The old man, may Old Nick's poisoned piss rot his guts, was born on October 7, 1900, the same day as Heinrich Himmler. His mother was a peddler and a whore. Of course, her life was short. When she died, her father took in her little urchin. He'd been a widower for many years, he was used to going his own way. His property lay off the beaten path. No one went there if they could help it. Neither critter nor cretin was safe in Hebbershålet after dark. People say he was a tall, pale chap, a beanpole with glasses, as queer as the day is long. He put on airs, walked quick and proud, thought he was better than everyone else. 'Better to be tall and dangerous than short and lame, he'd say.' Or: 'A devil in the flesh is better than ten in the bush.' He raised the boy to take his place. Holger Holmlund was the old man's name and he baptized the boy 'Holger,' in wolf's blood. He never had a word for anyone. He could've said a mouthful, though, if he'd had a mind to. Black sheep and goats were the only animals he kept. He looked human, though that was just for show. He had books of black magic, and my own

Grandpa told me he could flay your skin off with a look. Holger the Elder died on Hilarymas Day, 1910. The minnows were spawning in Hebbersbäcken, and everyone had joined in the catch. Folk said old Holger had been looking green about the gills, but no one thought much of it. That evening he took his usual enema. What happened next is anyone's guess. The old devil you're looking for, the one who lived to be ninety-one, till someone offed him last fall, said his Grandpa fell asleep at the table with his head on his hands. Suddenly, the old man jumped up and screamed:'*Smaajj å utajj!*' [Geld and destroy! my translation]. Then he grabbed the boy by the ankles and bashed his head against the wall. The next Sunday morning, three days after Hilarymas, the congregation came shuffling to church in their Sunday best, the boldest chewing tobacco and gnawing on licorice strands they'd stolen from murdered, hair-collecting Jews. And there on the steps of the chapel, what do you think they saw? Old Grandpa's cold, dead head whistling tunes from *Parsifal*! When the congregation was within earshot, he greeted them like nothing was amiss. Then he offered to suck dick in exchange for a smoke. For a drink he'd be happy to lick a woman, but only in the ass. People hissed and shook their fists. But the head just laughed and aped them, doing freakishly accurate impersonations, and spouted out all sorts of other foolishness beyond belief. He made animal sounds, howled like a soul in hell, moaned like a virgin in heat. But the worst of all was his laugh . . . Finally, a group of dogged sextons rushed the thing with crowbars. They thrashed his skull as hard as they could. Its pate cracked and blood dribbled from the wounds. The oldest sexton, a man called Epileptic Martin, even poked one of old Holger's eyes out. Then he picked up the head and spit on it. But old Holger—he went on the attack! He bit off Martin's nose and overlip! At that the sextons grabbed a snow shovel and used it to scoop up the head and toss it in an oven. They could still hear the old bastard jabbering, though, even as the fire was scorching away his flesh. And when they finally took the head out, what do you think they saw? The skull was white and shiny, impossible to scratch or crack. No one knows what happened to the head after that . . . Little Holger recovered and learned to take care of himself. No one would have anything to do with him. He was a miserable little bugger; no one even noticed when he left his Grandpa's house. He came back years later carrying Spanish influenza in a pig's bladder. He was something fey, you know, something that shouldn't have been. He certainly wasn't human . . . But you won't find anyone around here who'll tell you about him—not enough time has passed, the wounds are still too fresh. No one wants you here, you don't belong here. The less you know about the old man, the better. Give up now—it'll go bad for you here . . . We're your worst nightmare . . ."

Signed: "Momus."

In this, our blessed extrauterine season, wherein all thoughts and feelings are but memories, if that, I took this letter to be a decree. It was meant to silence me, but it had the opposite effect. It put all my doubts to rest. With the kind support of my good-hearted friend Nikanor, I decided to publish these stories, which are like screams from the heart of an inferno. I know there'll be an attempt on my life, but I'm not afraid of it.

The stories were originally written in the country dialect of North Västerbotten. I've translated them into "plain" language, and when necessary I've provided a glossary at the end of the boy's texts. The following resources have proven invaluable: T. Marklund's *Skelleftemålet*, E. Westerlund's (ed.) *Folkmål I Skelleftebygden*, and M. Hellqvist's *Bättre grå kaka än ingen smaka*. *Assisted Living* follows the organizational principle used by the dead child: each little wallpaper sample is numbered. However, it's fairly clear that the numbering system has nothing to do with the date on which the fragment was written. It's also apparent that several fragments have gone missing.

I've entitled the appendix "Memories of Grandpa." The testimonies it contains, which were supposedly written by Holger Holmlund's "friends and enemies," are almost certainly fictional—fantasies the boy used to try and dull his grief at his beloved Grandpa's death. Any further interpretation we'll leave to the feeble-minded.

As for the character of Grandpa: I picture him as a disreputable aristocrat whose knowledge of the classics would bore you to tears; an amiable and well-mannered man with biting wit, pampered flesh, and perverse energy. A hundred and ninety centimeters tall, fifty-five kilos light, appallingly beautiful. To my mind, he combined a satanic, sado-Nazi latrine-type vulgarity with the despondent devotion that can only come from the beaten and mangled sensitivities of a truly delicate soul. He might as well have been the founder of a new Teratology. He strove for the miraculous and the monstrous; it was this quest that kept him going. As befits an absurdist nihilist, he lived life freely . . . his path to the numinous took him straight through the scabrous . . . His adventures belong to the oral tradition. They should be read aloud in the cellars of haunted houses by the light of a dying fire, making sure to disguise the voice.

A child should read the little kid's story, including his spoken lines. It's important to remember that these are stories written by a child for his fellow children.

Furthermore, Grandpa's sacred sentences should be read by only the oldest, meanest, ugliest creature in the group. The rest will fraternally share out the parts of the women and other minor characters.

May Grandpa's voice drip with spite, derision, and scorn! May it creak with depravity and be oiled with bile! Don't forget that he can adopt a genially cringing tone when it serves his purposes! May Hildingarna hiss with extinguished voices! May anarchic freedom reign!

Bitch like an angry old geezer! Fuss like fretful old farts!

Throw your cares to the wind, become a stranger to yourself!

Everything is permitted!

Do what thou wilt shall be the whole of the Law!

———————————————————

Momus—god of censure and slander

I

Grandpa's tall and he's got a strong smell . . . a foul taste . . . His body is like a skeleton's, but his face is handsome, even though it's all wrinkled . . . He has thin, slickedback white hair and blue eyes that never blink . . . He's the world's best Grandpa, and I'm the only mite he's ever loved . . .

We live out on the taiga . . . Life lurks around the corner . . . the world's vast and ominous . . . we're not too far from the tundra . . . it's dark almost the whole year 'round . . . cold blasts and the soul's penury . . .

> mi ritrovai per una selva oscura . . .
> che la diritta via era smaritta . . .

I might be a jabbermonkey, but I'm no ape.

MI RITROVAI, ETC. "I found myself in dark woods, the right road lost." Dante (Pinsky trans.).

II

Winter woods . . . It had been a clear crystal night and the stars had almost glittered like back in the old days. The day that followed was like the survival instinct itself: resilient, dark, and merciless. The sky was a distant presence, the sun a hostile, gray eminence, a selfdestructive nuclear ball that had turned away its face to give us some peace . . . The woods seemed dead and so unchristianly beautiful . . . it just made you ache inside . . . Spruces watched over us, dreary despite their blankets of snow, and we walked a path that no one ever treads.

When the first snow falls in great white flakes, sealing yet another year of need, we trample a winding path down to the village and back to avoid having to put on snowshoes or snowskis . . . in case someone down there needs a talking to, or we just feel a bit cuddly . . . It's about five kilometers to Hebbers, but we take another way home . . . otherwise you get so fucking fed up with the route . . . They won't plow, just blow big gaping holes in the gravelroad to finish the job begun by the groundfrost . . . They don't want anyone to find their way out here . . . Me and Grandpa were on our way to the village to teach someone a lesson . . . and then, when they least expected it, we'd come back and give them a pop quiz.

When you get closer to the village, everything changes . . . They cut down foresttrees and let them lie, just to have something to do . . . Snowmobiles barrel around like pregnantcows, mowing down everything they come across . . . Logharvesters and foresttractors ramble back and forth, bellowing like crazedkillerbears, destroying as much as possible before the ultimate clearcutting to come . . . There are traps and snares for all sorts of animals, from willowtits to Siberian tigers, but no one has the time or urge to empty them . . . the rotting cadavers have a rich smell . . . Whole trees lie where they fall, if it's worth it they take them to the sawmill and chop them up . . . Only gulls, crows, and magpies can stand the stench of people in the village . . . Closer to us it's more like it used to be. . . like it was meant to be . . . The snow has lulled the greenblack firtrees into a mild stupor . . . it's utterly still . . . There's a merciless beauty in everything, a slumbering fury . . . On both sides of the path the snow is deep and heavy . . . it doesn't support you, but it doesn't give way . . . Treacherous shadows tempt you to lie in wait, or offer yourself up . . . Our path took us through frozenmarshes and groves of young trees bearing the mark of death . . . Up scraggly pineridges and down blessed sprucevalleys . . . The forest is the only thing that can keep them out . . . Animals leave tracks and shit behind . . . A snowleopard on the trail of some huldra had crossed the path . . . A capercailzie, which had been fucked to death, lay on its side with sleeptousled feathers and a film over its horrorblackened eyes . . .

It was so pure and still you could hear God breathe . . . So cold the spit froze on your lips and your eyelids stopped working . . . Grandpa had on Predator Camouflage gear, white with a black-twigpattern, and a werewolffurcoat. He had on camelhairpants, roughluxury homespunshoes, a guineapigfurscarf and an NKVD hat. My own head was wrapped in toiletpaper, and I had on an orange Helly Hansen sweater and khaki Beaver Mountain pants tucked into Graninge hikingboots. I had mittens, but Grandpa had lemurfurlined ballskingloves, which cost more than most houses on the blackmarket. We creakedsqueaked as we walked, both because of the snow and Grandpa's knees. He looked lowspirited and weigheddown . . . just stumbling along, not even managing to smoke . . . Suddenly he veered off the path . . . brushed the snow off a treestump . . . spread out his heatingpad and sat down . . . his head trembled . . . Two huge ravens landed in trees to either side . . .

– Hurts like hell to breathe, he gasped, I need to rest a while.

His breath steamed like he was smoking, and I went up to him.

– How are you, Grandpa?

– Not so good . . . Lately my body's all bitchbitchbitch . . . every second's a struggle . . . it'll be over soon. . . I think I hear the death rattle in my throat . . .

– Are you sick, Grandpa?

– Just old and tired, kid . . . I've outlived myself . . . Now come here so I can hug you . . .

He did that and it warmed me to the crotch.

– My boy, my boy . . . I love you so much it shames me . . . and it's not your fault that Grandpa is sad and has to croak soon . . . whatever else happens, remember that . . .

– You can't die, Grandpa! If you do, I don't want to stay here either!

– Then who'll keep the trolls at bay? Grandpa asked and punched me in the gut.

When I'd caught my breath, I was crying.

– I'll follow you wherever you go, Grandpa . . . even straight down to hell . . .

– Ah, that's a path a man has to walk alone, kid . . . no point in leaving before you're finished here . . . life isn't made of shortcuts and it doesn't have boundaries . . . and there sure as hell's no coming back . . .

– No coming back!?

– There's no such thing as ghosts, you poor little bastard . . .

– You can't die, Grandpa! you just can't!

– There comes a time in every man's life, boy, when sight goes dim and orgasms are nothing more than bladdercramps . . . the people you love are gone and nowhere much feels like home . . . when that happens, it's time to break yourself of the habit of living . . . you've made your peace . . . you're ready to seek the light . . . because you've stopped fearing the dark . . .

– But I want to be with you! I want you to always exist!

– There'll always be a Grandpa, mite, Grandpa soothed. But you have to be brave . . . your Grandpa isn't dead and derided yet . . . time enough to learn to take care of yourself . . . before I'm gone . . . But we won't talk about it anymore, you're getting too worked up . . . Come here and sit on my knee and I'll tell you about the good old days . . .

I sat on Grandpa's knee and he put his arms around me.

– Aren't you cold? he asked.

– Nah, I lied, though I was freezing to death.

Grandpa sat quiet a moment while he sorted his feral thoughts. Then he hawked, spit out a bloodyclump, and began:

– There was a time before everything went wrong, boy . . . it was an age of magic, myth, and ecstasy . . . nature was lavish with his gifts . . . animal life was purely teratological! The first Aryans landed in Garaselet 8,000 years ago and found the thirteen commandments of God carved into the flesh of livingseacalves . . . we were nature's children, baptized by the Devil, and all of Norrland was an orgy in woodland, darkness, and silence. . . trees wore flesh, rivers flowed with blood . . . excess and waste . . . it was the natural order of things . . . no more than 5,000 men in all of Västerbotten and Norrbotten . . . God's sons' highest culture. . . there existed truejoy and eternallove . . . honor and nobility. . . We lived life to the fullest, hardly slept a wink we were so happy . . . beside the current's wild rush . . . though we knew our dreams would be delightful and boundless . . . full of future conquests and heroic deeds . . . Life was an absurdity! Pure chaos! Men laughed in the face of death, lifted their glasses and ran berserk . . . A man's pride and joy was in his cock and ass. The world was brand-spanking new every morning, we woke laughing to tears with bedpissing fear . . . Dionysus was our god and our corporacavernosae told us it was only a hundred yottameters to the universe's edge . . . No one ever talked about doing their part! Au contraire! Woe to those who weren't a deadweight around someone else's neck . . . Work was taboo! We wandered around and simply hung out . . . saw things that weren't there . . . chewed the cud and shot the shit . . . didn't give a damn, because that's how life was supposed to be . . . Sometimes we worked a little, if we had a mind . . . But slobs and slackers . . . that was us to a tee . . . Of course there was work for everyone, because it was the forestfuckingprimeval, but we thought, to hell with that . . . A guy might get down to business for half an hour or so, as long as it was easy and fun . . . Not like now . . . there's a heavenwide difference between then and now . . . it made decent folks of us . . . There were woodcutters, charcoalburners, and logfloaters . . . hunters, meshuganas, and eggheads . . . peddlers, gypsies, and tramps . . . daylaborers, ditchdiggers, and zingaros . . . fortyniners, shamans, and hucksters . . . Lapps, Finns, and Northmen . . . fauns, satyrs, and centaurs . . . urnings, albinos, and matricides . . . mamasboys, clods, and berserkers . . . treehuggers, bushkissers, and turffuckers . . . There were bonesetters, legtwisters, and skullcrushers . . . peacemakers, executioners, and pencilpushers . . . dreamdukes, fantasymarquises, and foolkings . . . pixies, naiads, and screwballs . . . eremites, graybeards, and necromancers . . . hoteliers, whalechasers, and holy bedlamites . . . teethgnashers, nazguls, and Grandpafogies . . . dykepluggers, brushburners, and backyardflooders . . . kiddiediddlers, mischiefmakers, and rabblerousers . . . soothsayers, knifegrinders, and vulcans . . . There were naturalists, navies, and shrinks . . . bravados, turncoats, and tramps . . . neanderthals, grailknights, and dilettantes . . . claqueurs, seers, and skizzos . . . gourmands, narcofiends, and sots . . . flashers, brownnosers, and indiangivers . . . desperados, manolitos, and lotitos . . . rednecks, bushwackers, and backwoodsmen . . . snipers, pushers, and trappers . . . fairies, hustlers, and diehards . . . There were fannyboys, voodoomen, and coalbiters . . . rumrunners, arsonists, and groupies . . . butchers, tanners, and crybabies . . .

sweepers, keepers, and reapers . . . gigglers, grumblers, and grousers . . . topographers, houdinis, and hungerartists . . . battlecocks, fistfighters, and nailbiters . . . sorrowsmokers, pussuckers, and bingeeaters . . . democrats, dryskins, and babyfarmers . . . applicants, elders, and supplicants . . . There were followers, hollerers, and swallowers . . . camptramps, stallmuckers, and fortunetellers . . . tumblers, rumblers, and blunderers . . . conartists, onehandedtypists, and quislings . . . fakiers, brahmins, and maharadjas . . . moguls, sheiks, and khans . . . emirs, imams, and muftis . . . shahs, sultans, and caliphs . . . pashas, tsars, and mandarins . . . massas, sahibs, and tuans . . . There were gigolos, whoremongers, and bookmakers . . . wankhers, dirdirs, and pnumes . . . haruchai, skest, and jheherrin . . . robberbarons, luckyshots, and nightwatchmen . . . There were howdydoers, nitpickers, and runemasters . . . birdsofafeather, backseatdrivers, and blowhards . . . grimreapers, machinejockies, and sanitytakers . . nutcases, testosteronejunkies, and cherrypoppers . . . woodcutters, wormgrubbers, and horselovers . . . buttholesurfers, secondcousins, and raggamuffins . . . There were sufis, zenmasters, and naguals . . . devils in the flesh, wolves in sheep's clothing, and lumps in the pudding . . . freeholders, sharecroppers, and homebodies . . . gravediggers, graverobbers, and cannibals . . . chickenlivers, wayfinders, and bargainhunters . . . shysters, oracles, and tricksters . . . storytellers, timekillers, and supraterrenes . . . birds on the wing, foxes in the henhouse, and cats on the prowl . . . grandstanders, philanderers, and pottymouths . . . loveletterbearers, horsetrackriders, and engineidlers . . .

For myself, I was convinced that Grandpa was jockeying for membership in that last group . . . the engineidlers . . . it was pretty hard to remember everything he said . . . even though my memory's real good . . .

– There were shylocks, buncos, and hypocrites . . . vitiators, vilifiers, and backsliders . . . cobblers, barghests, and dildomakers . . . pickpockets, dogooders, and castlestormers . . . firebrands, troglodytes, and manhandlers . . . ne'erdowells, have-nots, and hitmen . . . megastars, metalogicians, and abhumanists . . . linelickers, spurtphantoms, and gymjunkies . . . lepers, elephantmen, and kurucarriers . . . hydrophobicgeezers, bubonicplaguespreaders, and all sorts of cancers . . . There were nazis, sadists, and satanists . . . demiurges, vulcanists, and consulates . . . ophites, carpocratians, and paternines . . . Bach, Mozart, and Beethoven . . . Brahms, Händel, and Bruckner . . . Russians, Huns, and Turks . . . Helusians, Oxioners, and Finlanders . . . bushcrickets, shelljumpers, and auctioneers . . . pitworkers, bloodletters, and misanthropes . . . trendsetters, spoilsports, and livingfossils . . . princes of peace, masks of death, and objects of ridicule . . . sons-in-law, brothers-in-law, and miraclerabbis . . . There was Gobineau, Klages, and Evola . . . Ortega y Gasset, Jünger, and Pound . . . trailblazers, crackwhores, and bigtalkers . . . conjurers, foresters, and monsignors . . . matroses, monks, and miscreants . . . dockworkers, stevedores, and logjammers . . . torpedoes, duds, and moneygrubbers . . . captainsofindustry, electoralprinces, and royalpains . . . jugglers, inkslingers, and gladiators . . . loosecannons, cockmakers, and coppersmiths . . . friseurs, servitors, and masseurs . . . Rafael, Rembrandt, and Rops . . . Scorsese, Greenaway, and Kurosawa . . . rollingstones, bootleggers, and hobbyists . . . staggeringdrunks, flounderingfish, and eightysixedclerks . . . And many many more . . .

Grandpa took a fistful of snow to cool his burning mouth.

– Back then it was no big thing to be simple and chaste ... or dull and brooding, if that's how you wanted it ...

– Must've been nice ...

– Nothing doing ... we trusted our luckystars ... saw to ourselves ... we were raciallypure and cleanshaven all over ... we propagated with style and taste ... slow and steady wins the race ... We men knew how to enjoy each other ... liked being together ... there weren't too many of us ... five thousand at most ...

Grandpa swallowed, he was having a hard time going on.

– But evil was brewing ... something was coming ... something that would destroy our world forever ...

– Was it women?

– It was women! The inferior race! three openings! Snakeless crotches! ... Darkness covered the land ... troubling rumors reached us from the south, but no one believed them, at least not at first ... They started down in Ume ... something about long-haired creatures making land ... spinning the heads of tried and true buttfuckers everywhere ... of course, everyone thought the rumors were just cockandbull ... balderdash ... But as we were to find out, those stories held a terrible, grim reality ...

His voice sunk even more.

– They spread like the plague ... like gangrene ... before long they'd reached the vicinity of Vindeln ... between Trollberget and Häggnäs ... they were sly ... didn't come up the coast via Bygdeå, Ånäset, and Lövånger ... the shriekingbuggers there should've finished them off! But those inlandfuddies were too slow with the whip ... we were used to having things our own way, no regular mealtimes ... letting it all hang out ... minding our own business ...

no curfews, no responsibilities . . . just whim and will and almighty nature . . . God in heaven, if only the coastguard had blown them out of the water! before it was too late . . . They spread to Pompej and Sirapsbacken . . . lamias and harpies had nothing on them . . . they got beneath our skin with gooeyeyedloveydoveyness . . . they made their way to Gorkuträsk . . . Lossmen . . . the picture was becoming clearer . . . stumpylegged, narrowshouldered, steatopygic monsters with repulsively swollen breasts . . . coldblooded and heartless as vipers . . . they'd swoon on command if they didn't get their way . . . we tore at our hair! went about in a daze! pinched ourselves hard! How could respectable barbarians soil their cocks with that?!

Grandpa trembled with the effort his story was taking . . . The woods brooded over his dark saga, the eternal struggle between evil and good.

– One word, the foulest word there ever was, began to make the rounds: Cunt . . . they had cunts, people said, like little furry animals, smoother and softer than anuses, not as heathenishly narrow . . . All who tried it were sold . . . Amfooorrrtasss!!! That's what it was, all right, the Wound, the gaping, bloody, festering sore that wouldn't close . . . They used cunts to take Norrland from us! Eyes full of bittersweet treachery, tongues agile as squirrels . . . Unlucky love walked among us, burning and pillaging . . . The bitter fate of Enkidu! They croaked in our arms, begging forgiveness for their desertion . . . The whores closed in on us, they were merciless . . . just snuck into our rooms at night and started gobbling . . . the vampires . . . coaxing ever-more perverted, bewitched cavaliers into their entourage . . . not to mention their wagonloads of brats! their knickknacks and householdparaphernalia! . . .

They got off on cheapthrills and expensivegifts . . . had lowtastes and shrilltongues . . . daughters of Lilith and Circe . . . O Tertullian! o Juvenal! Jean de Meun! the godly Earl of Rochester! They made it to Fraukälen . . . Mensträsk . . . we prepared for the last battle . . . drugged ourselves with soma . . . They broke through our defenses . . . Gumboda! . . . Kankberg! . . . they rushed over us! We fought toothandnail, spit in death's face . . . did all that was manly possible . . . raged in silence . . . we were like grandpa beasties protecting our young against devils and trolls! The best of us fell, bleeding from a thousand and one mortal wounds! we didn't call retreat in time! better to be a stuckhog than a lapdog! There was a hundred of them for every one of us! they were like lemmings! Modern men with realjobs and soundminds! fawning, prudish, lecherous cunts! They kept on pushing and pushing, like they were floating logs! Vercellae and Camerone! Maldon and Roncevaux! Culloden and Liegnitz! Poltava and Stalingrad . . . We marched against them from the endless, godforsaken forests . . . We had axes, broadswords, and spears . . . we knew how to use them . . . The ground shuddered when it drank our Aryan blood . . . We fought like Teja, chanted laments like Gelimer! We fell with Aryanogrecocks pointing straight towards heaven, took twenty enemies for every one of us, but they just kept on coming . . . Animals came to our aid, but Mausers took them down . . . Giantbears, arcticwolves, sabertoothtigers, mutantrabbits . . . We protected our grandsons with all we had, no one would touch them while there was still breath in our lungs! They slaughtered us by the thousands! mutilations and outrages! bloodyshame and meatyshivers! they were sly as Phoenicians! horny as Etruscans!

merciless as Israelites! They brainwashed wounded prisoners of war and little boys alike! Taught them to love pussy! and everything else that makes life a living hell! Work! Sobriety! God and church! Law and order! King and country! Offices and factories! Clerks and critics! Bureaucracies and marketeconomies! Majorities and institutions! Parliamentarism and massmedia! Intellectuals and popularopinion! Legibility and literacy! Slave mentality! Slave morality! Creditors! By God! If only they'd killed us! spared us the sight of warriors turning into pigs! Down and Piltdown! After the invasion of the caitiffs and shrews life became what it is now . . . predictable . . . mundane . . . soulless . . . where your only thanks is a fist in the gut and shame is your only reward . . . They killed fantasy, honor, and ecstasy . . . Grubbs and mildew took the cow pastures and crops . . . The Colorado beetle and the Spanish slug did it for the potatoes and other vegetables . . . They domesticated animals . . . began to slaughter them . . . A few of us got away . . . refused to be tamed . . . planned our revenge . . . the last splinters of a shattered nobility . . . Like Milton's demons . . . and I am Satan himself . . . Accusing mankind before God . . . We make our home in the hidden places . . . as close to death as possible . . . outside of reality . . . the beastmen of deserted farmhouses . . . backwater marauders . . . hoochplied wolfhounds . . . depopulation's wackjobs . . . Our time has come . . . let the battle cry sound . . . the lycanthropic revolt can begin . . .

Grandpa fell quiet, kissed me hard on the mouth, put me down, and stood up.

– It's getting colder, he said, gathering up his heatingpad and trudging on.

The ravens launched themselves heavily, silently, into the air. I followed after, and it was like I was walking through a mist . . . into that darkness, silence, cold and loneliness . . .

This is where we come from, that is where we're going, so we might as well start breaking ourselves of the habit of living . . .

HULDRA—an elusive forest nymph in Scandanavian folklore

ZINGAROS—gypsies

URNINGS—homosexuals

BEDLAMITES—madmen

NAVVIES—day laborers

CLAQUEURS—hired clappers

QUISLINGS—traitors to ones' country

LOTITOS—Michel Lotito, the famous metal-eater

WANKHERS, DIRDIRS, and PNUMES—see Jack Vance

HARUCHAI, SKEST, AND JHEHERRIN—see Stephen R. Donaldson

COALBITER—idle youth

BUNCO— fraud

BARGHESTS—legendary, giant black dog with huge teeth and claws found in the north of England, particularly around Yorkshire

ABHUMANIST—see Jacques Audiberti

KURUCARRIERS—kuru, also known as "laughing sickness," is a neurological disease made famous by an epidemic that broke out in Papua New Guinea in the mid-twentieth century; the disorder is believed to have been spread by endocannibalism, or the eating of the dead of one's own tribe

HELUSIANS, OXIONERS, and FINLANDERS—Helusians and Oxioners are the tribes that Tacitus found "beyond existence," where the known world ended; they "have heads and faces of men, but the remainder of the body is a wild animal." As sharp-featured Cornelius concludes: "quod ego ut incompertum in medio relinquam"

INKSLINGER—tattoo artist

COCKMAKER—maker of bridges or pallets for watches and clocks

TEJA—Last of the Ostrogoth kings in Itay, led the desparate fight against the Byzantine army in the years 552–553.

GELIMER—last king of the Vandals

III

– As long as you can make others suffer, there's no reason to throw in the towel, Grandpa exclaimed jovially.

He sat in a rocking chair sewing on a Confederate flag. *Ein Heldenleben* was playing in the background and Larri Isokyrpä and Torsten Murkström were just saying thanks for the coffee— kind of ironic, since Grandpa had mixed strychnine into it and it was just now starting to work. You have to find something to do, you know, when things get slow. Anyway, Larri lived a while longer, looked me in the eye, tossed his head, kicked a bit, but it didn't help. That guy was a loudmouthed jerk who'd rearrange the face of any kid he could catch, making their two nostrils into one. And now they lay there, blueberryblue about the lips, and Grandpa put aside his handiwork and came up to them.

– We are here today to mourn my two dearest friends, who've up and left us with raging hardons . . . Let's start with Torsten, he said, kicking the corpse hard in the ear . . . Torsten Murkström signed off at the unrespectable age of sixty-nine . . .

Grandpa folded his hands in mock solemnity, he was wearing a pink nightshirt and fuzzyblack poodleslippers.

– His arrival into the world was a nasty surprise to his parents. His family scraped a living by making scenes in public . . . Torsten was known early on for his slowwit and charmingservility. At a young age, he'd already learned to fart on the sly and smoke ciggibutts . . .

Grandpa struggled to keep his face serious.

– He spent his whole life trolling the cabins of charcoalburners and logfloaters, trying his best to satisfy them all . . . He'd suck cock for a spoonful of fishentrails and an oldfashioned spanking . . . It was his life's calling to make a bad situation worse. He sowed oats and reaped sourmash . . . He enjoyed strumming on his kantele and sipping motyl . . . When he was stripped of his commission in the Cock and Cassock Society, he got old real quick . . . he had a habit of sitting with his head in the oven . . . he finally worked up the courage to ask Tellemar: How the hell do you do it? . . . he looked for the answer in the Siikavaara Bible . . . in vain . . . Torsten never married, but remained faithful his whole life to Upper Kågedalen . . . His chief mourner is a walkingstick . . . Torsten wants his headstone to read: "Thanks for nothing" . . .

Torsten was laying on his stomach on the tiles. Grandpa grabbed his head and twisted it so hard his neck broke.

– Look at me when I'm talking about you!

Then he turned to Larri.

– Dowser Larri Isokyrpä was finally allowed to peterout after a long and weary struggle with that terminalillness we call life . . . Larri was squeezed out of his Grandma's womb under an uprootedtree in Myskträsk . . . He was the first in a long line of stillbornsiblings and he learned selfsufficiency early on . . . A procession of oddjobs and shortgigs passed him by . . . He was a THX-doctor, a Quaker, a rathawker, a puppywhipper, a snow-man's trunk . . . He married Ms. Glädis Noppa . . . and later on the nationally celebrated onanist Hardy Honkala from Gråliden . . . Frau Hardy kicked it at fifty-three . . . Life was often like a Rubik's cube . . . Nonetheless, this remarkable man somehow found the strength to teach himself dipsomania! His vocabulary swelled to the tripledigits, he discovered words had more than four letters, then came his big, fat chance: a temp job as an outhouse asswiper in Råslyet, a kilometer and a half south of Västbäck . . . Larri worked hard at his many highly desirable jobs until his body finally failed him . . . he devoted his last seventeen years to outliving his children . . . He was a lifetime Jagoda's Witness . . . His interests were many, but to name a few: stroke, pogroms, the lambethwalk, kiddie's diddles, Siberianroulette and *Hylands hörna* . . . As a society member, he was unparalleled . . . his courses in bedwetting and gangrape were especially popular . . . The burial will take place under chaotic conditions . . . Donations can be made to the Dirty Geezer Fund . . .

Grandpa grabbed me by the neck and cackled Grandpalike at his own creativity.

– You know what we're going to do now, child of mine?

– O no!

– First I'm going to take a long, hot manbath . . . And you're going to make me coffee. Then we're going to go outside and get a little fresh air. Why don't you take out the Iron Crown of Lombardy and my Ripper suit . . . Methinks I want to look nice today . . .

EIN HELDENLEBEN—"A Hero's Life," tone poem by Richard Strauss
MOTYL—expiremental mixture of petrol and alcohol used to power
Swedish military vehicles during World War II

TELLEMAR—Hasse, Swedish radio host of the show *Ring så spelar vi* (Call
us, and we'll play your tune) from 1969–1988.

SIIKAVAARA BIBLE—The Siikavaara sect, or Korpela movement, was
started by Toivo Korpela in the 1920s

THX-DOCTOR—THX, or thymus extract, was a natural remedy developed by the Swedish veterinarian Elix Sandberg; he claimed that THX
could help with immune disorders and could even fight cancer

HYLANDS HÖRNA—"Hyland's Corner," a popular Swedish TV program
that ran from 1962–1983

IRON CROWN OF LOMBARDY—crown worn by Lombard rulers

RIPPER SUIT—hunting clothes

IV

– "Yet she became more and more promiscuous as she recalled the days of her youth, when she was a prostitute in Egypt. There she lusted after her lovers, whose genitals were like those of donkeys and whose emission was like that of horses" . . . Ho there, boy, Grandpa winked bawdily and dunked a sweetroll in his ginger-beer. Looks like we need to hop down to Egypt to troll for some real cock. Around here there's hardly enough to live on.

The old Grandpaclock rumblewaggled eight.

– Ezekiel's lips were uncircumcised. His mamma worked at Goethe's Pipe and Peg in Jörn. She was a godpardoned, slipperycunt who'd howl so you could hear it over all of Kvarken when she got some deaddrunkcock stuck up in her rosette . . . Ezekiel and I were the same age, but he only smoked filtered. In my wildest dreams, I never thought he'd end up in the Good Old Shilly-Shally Book.

Grandpa threw his Bible aside, lit an Alte Reiter, and opened the newspaper.

– Sträng and Helén are engaged . . . Archbishop Värkström and Ulf Ekman broke up . . . An oldboy in Risböle pissed himself in the chapel . . . intestinalvilli are wreaking havoc in daycarecenters throughout lower Skelleftecounty . . . Wilt the Stilt Chamberlain, the basketnigger, has fucked twenty-thousand loose cunts . . .

He took a nip of insulin, licked his fingers, and blattered on.

– Five hundred and fifty liposuctionsurgeons discharged in Pite . . . the fourteen-queerold Kicki throatfucked by rimthurs . . . bald, logomanic demon terrifies Uppsala with blasphemies . . .

He fell silent, blanched, swore.

– Cottoneyedjoes and festeringnewborns!

I hardbraked in the middle of dunking a fibroidtumor in witch's milk and waited for more. Grandpa glanced up with an expression that reminded me of a buzzard poised over a mouse.

– They've got Jeffrey, he whispered.

Then Grandpa told me all about Jeffrey Dahmer, who had drugged, fucked, and killed blackhomos in some place called Milwokey. Apparently, he'd called and asked for Grandpa's advice before starting the whole dirty business. Grandpa told me he'd expected a lot from him, because he had grit. A few days went by, and then we heard Nikolaj Dzjumagalijev, the womangobbling funster from Alma Ata, was going away. And when Donald Leroy Evans, who had sixteen-or-so juicy murders to his name, got nabbed, it was like Grandpa had been sent eastward out of paradise. For three whole days and nights all he did was sing the praises of massmurderers everywhere. He seemed to know most of them personally. He was smackdab in the middle of a sentimental harangue down memorylane, something about Kuno Hofmann, the "Vampire of Nuremberg," when he began coughing blood. I helped him lay down on our pegsofa's brightred cushions. Then, my arms around my Grandpa, I was out in a flash. Seventy-five hours among A-list murderers really does you in.

RIMTHURS— in Nordic mythology, rimthurs, or Hrimthurs ("rime giants" or "frost giants") live in Niflheim, the land of eternal ice
LOGOMANIC—logomania, diarrhea of the mouth
WITCH'S MILK—secreted from the breasts of newborn babies, both male and female

V

– Who the fuck's Sara Lidman? Or Torgny Lindgren! I've never heard of anything so moronic! Do they even exist?!

Grandpa was fighting with the bookbusguy, a little graybrown Zionist with glasses, egg in his beard, and a slut with a ponytail and a nervouscough. Grandpa had asked for a book by a bonafide Norrlander. Now he was going on and on about how downright vile, even sinful it was to waterdown fine words.

– What kind of titles are these, anyway? Blatherers and busybodies! Users and abusers! Fuck your motherfucking mother!

Their voices carried very well.

– *Naboth's Stone, Merab's Beauty . . . Husak's Harmonica! Horthy's Exhaustion! Conan's Tears! The Elders' Protocols!*

Sullenly, he lit a Philip Morris and waited on the officiousinstigator. He was gulping down Jim Bean when the latter came bustling up with a new book.

– What about that guy Torbjörg Säve? You read anything by him? He lives out in Lule?

– He a homo?

– Nah, I don't think so . . .

– Not him, he likes women! the cheekygirlie quipped. And he wears black boxers, she sighed longingly.

– Oh, for fuck's sake. Is that all you've got! I'll never be that hardupandhorny for something to read! Never! Throw it on the dungheap! Flush it down the toilet! Obscure wannabes, breadandbutter authors, coffeeshop poets! Marxistoid-apopleptic songs of enforced celibacy! Mediocrity's apotheoses! Rookycliques! Habilehacks! Clever pauses, tedious passages! Not worth lickaspit!

Sharp gusts of wind echoed Grandpa's ire. Fall was in overtime, though there was snow at the door. It was a transitiontime, neither fall nor winter, and that's how it can be around here for months. When Grandpa's mad, he gets stubborn. Now he was refusing to set foot in the yellowbrown bus, but just stood outside, threatening everyone inside with a flogging.

– Do you have anything by Nikanor Teratologen?

– Who?

– Teratologen of the Ten Thousand Tortures? The Misunderstood Genius! The Desktop Murderer! Locked away for life for one repeated offense: the serialrape of language! His words go down a rawcraw like butter! The Slayer of Euphemisms! Scurrilous Church Father! The Confabculprit! The Blasphemer! The Enemy of Mankind!

– So what does he write?

– The worst smut a dirty penny will buy! Bizarre baroque comedies! Downandout orgies! Repulsive yarns! Reptilian jokes! He's morbid! obscene! makes you want to hurl! gets you going! I don't remember any titles! By the devil's pimpledass, though, he belongs to world literature!

– Never heard of him . . . Sorry . . .

– That's not the kind of thing we buy here. We're only interested in serious authors. Cleanly written, clearly stated, with an ear for language's subtleties . . .

– Adorno and Horkheimer! Pöhl and Greenspan! Torquemada and Savonarola! what a blessing it is to be stark raving mad! When I want to read something that gets downanddirty with mankind, it won't be those fucks! That's all I'm saying.

They went back and forth like that for a long time.

Finally, Grandpa borrowed two volumes of *FUB-Contact* and a colorfully illustrated book about "the life of the field digger wasp" by Gottfrid Adlerz.

SARA LIDMAN, TORGNY LINDGREN—Swedish writers from Västerbotten whose work was heavily influenced by local dialect

NABOTH'S STONE—by Sara Lidman

MERAB'S BEAUTY—by Torgny Lindgren

FUB-CONTACT—journal for children with developmental disorders

VI

Grandpa stood at the pulpit and read Max Ferdinand Sebaldt von Werth's racemystical *Sexualreligion* for about ten seconds; then he took up Frodi Ingolfson Wehrmann's *The Germanic Tragedy: Divinely Created Women and the Fall* . . . that lasted for about half a minute; then he tried to read René Fülöp Miller's *The Holy Devil* and Otto Rahn's *Lucifer's Court* at the same time.

In the last five hours he'd gone through about 300 books, reading a couple of sentences, sometimes a full page. Now he was exhausted . . . He came over to where I sat with my Armeniangenocide coloringbook, lifted me off the floor, and shook me like a sackofpotatoes.

– Lanz and Wiligut! By the Devil, they could dance! They're the ones who stood their ground! Why don't you write that down in your dirty little diary, you Satan's pegatu!

– What do you mean, Grandpa?

– Fuck me with a spoon, you little asswipe! Halfwitting nincompoop! Not another word out of you, you yapping old granny!

He tossed me like a stevedore into the thrashingposition, and I lay where I fell. If you don't, you've sown your last seed . . . danced your last dance . . . He calmed down, though, enough that disappointment colored his words. He wasn't dangerous anymore, now he was just depressed and scared.

– I've suspected for a while now that you've been writing on the sly, sugarboy, he announced, and I was just about to say we can't have that . . . but you're one crafty little bugger, and next time I'm sleeping you'll just hide your trash somewhere else . . . I bet you've been spouting a lot of highstrung nonsense, something like Ludwig Derleth's *Proclamations* . . . and I'll tell you something, the thought shames me like a suckwench being questioned by a parishpriest . . . You're too weak to indulge in swearing and bloodshed, blasphemy and some goodoldfashioned Kiruna violence . . . I bet you've got a nice little chapbook going there, you aren't capable of much more . . . You'll be the next Brecht . . . an asswipe who singlehandedly declares creation null and void . . . And publishers, you know, shriek like babies roasting on an openfire for more gangsters and psychos and allthatjazz . . . all you've got to do is pickyourpoison . . . But I've hit on the right medicine for an estruspumped little junker like yourself . . . Before I sleep, I'll see you nailed to the World Tree, so help me I will . . . that'll put an end to your writing . . . once and for all . . . It's for your own good! . . . what do you think Husserl's and Derrida's Grandpas thought of their little grandsons?! They should've blown their kneecaps off from shame! but instead, what did they do when their weetykes first started jacking around with words? They spared the rod, that's what! . . . Me—I couldn't have lived with the shame! A child's faith and the Pearly Gates have always been good enough for me! and they'll do for you, too, oh yes they will! now's the time to get hard! and cocky! but there's gotta be some fuckin' moderation! once you start writing, you're hooked! once you start thinking, you're through! Just promise me one thing, boy: don't come home one day all oozing with feeling! because once that happens, life's over! Leave the writing to the sexmaniacs! the berserkers! the teeming, writhing masses! The hordes and legions! trying to crush each other with their own filth! the raunchier the cunt, the better the story! that's how they think! and if I have to poke your eyes out with my own thumbitythumbthumbs, I'll see to it you never become one of them!

SEXUALRELIGION—describes the sexual religion of the Aryans; von Werth argues this was a form of eugenics meant to maintain Aryan racial purity

WILIGUT— "Himmler's Rasputin," in September of 1933 was appointed under the pseudonym of Karl Maria Weisthor to head up the Department for Pre- and Early History, located within the Race and Settlement Division's Main Office. Wiligut claimed to be the last descendent of the prehistoric Uiligotis of the Asa-Uana-Sippe's seers and priests. Around 78,000 B. J. (before Judas), his forefathers ushered in true history by founding the second Boso culture and erecting the city of Arual-Jöruva-lis. And so forth . . . Himmler was quite interested in the aged "clairvoy-ant," who left the SS in 1939 at seventy-three years of age. Among other things, Wiligut helped design the Death's Head Ring of the SS

PEGATU—a beast-man in Lanz von Liebenfel's conceptual universe (and Strindberg's?)

KIRUNA—Northernmost city in Sweden

VII

Fall was trying to ambush old summer, but August was putting up a fight. We were on swivel chairs in the hunting tower we'd climbed into the evening before. Grandpa kept watch through the flygutsplattered windows towards north and east, and I took south and west. There was a forestroad running right below us. Grandpa had wanted me to shit myself and I'd just done it—and man it felt good. Baal knows it had been a cold, dark night . . . Grandpa had slept curled up, but his chthonic body wouldn't leave well enough alone. He'd kept babbling in his sleep, something about Schuler and bloodlust and honeysweet Nero. He knows a whole mess of things by heart.

– "Das Herz der Erde als Hölle der Christen . . . Morde den Vater, eh' dass er dein Kind, deine Seele frisst, und entfessle die Urknäuel, das hundertspeichige Feuerrad! Die Hölle, das Herz der Gaia, wird dich helfen . . ."

Grandpa's German's so bad it makes you weak in the knees . . .

Later he lit some stormlanterns and comfortmunched all our provisions: schoolgirlfricassé and two balls of yarn. Then he laughed that ghoulish laugh of his, and whipped up some coffee and schnapps.

After that, he toyed with my fudgepacker and rambled on about anything that came to mind.

– Mossad, he said, going hard all at once, Mossad can pull the wool over anyone's eyes. For all I know, you could be sent by Mossad . . . or Wiesenthal . . .

His decrepit risiblemuscles twisted impishly, but there was no emotion left in his eyes . . . empty as a promise . . .

– But it'll be a cold day in hell before those asses get their claws into me, that's all I'm saying! If they get cocky, they'll just have to cry it out, if nothing else works! he declared darkly and fingered his favorite rifle, an eleven point six millimeter .460 Weatherby Magnum built to take out buffalos and elephants.

– When I die, I'm taking all of you with me! The whole goddamned planet! Everyone'll probably be glad it's over! You'll be roasted in Sákar! in Hútama! Omphalus, the World's Navel! The hub of evil! If you get your way, the whole goddamn universe will explode when I'm gone! And you'll give out shouts of rejoicing! You can't even imagine how topsyturvy things will get when I'm upupandaway. Darkness is coming, and how! Pah! Don't you understand? When I finally lay myself down to sleep, and thank God for it, it all stops! I'll hush the animals to sleep with a lullaby and the sun will put on mourningcrape and shroud! Yes, boy, when your collective will has been done and I lay there with a shit-blessed grin on my face, delighted to be with my Father Who Art in Heaven, it'll be too late for tears! It'll be over and done! Over and out! Hasta la vista, baby, and good night!

Grandpa was so worked up I had to blow him then and there, and then we slept until about eleven o'clock. Now we'd been sitting still for about three hours and keeping watch out over the clearcutting. Every now and then Grandpa broke the silence with some phrase he'd just then pulled out of his ass.

– The only Semites worth mentioning are the ones that founded the cult of Moloch. Or: – *Swine and Sex Objects in the Semitic Tradition* by Reichsbauernleiter Diarré is absolutely the worst piece of drivel I've ever set eyes on! Or: – Is there anything more appealing than a sick and hopeless old man pounding on a locked door in vain? Or: – The greatest thing you can give your fellowdemon is an intercession . . . and then a sudden, painfree death . . . Or: – A Dutch explorer, Adriaan Kukkurloom, was the first of the grayraces to describe a thoughtful girl, a creature as rare as God's mercy! Or: – Sigvard Thurneman was a fine lad, just a little persnickety . . . Or: – Soon I'll have devoted ninety years to Nothing, feeling Nothing, thinking about Nothing . . . Or: – The only animals worth hunting anymore are wolverines . . . in a pinch, a polecat . . . every now and then a squirrel will do! But from the depths of my tooty-fruity innards, you'll never catch me taking a lynx in the morel! Or: – The cargocult is the religion closest to my heart . . . In a previous life I was an ascarid in Timur Lenk's gut . . . a pleuralsackparasite in Benedict of Nursia's windpipe . . . he got me by boning a pheasant . . . The USA is the great Jahveh . . . evil's domicile . . . vulgarity's nexus . . . a festeringboil . . . We'll give them a neutronbombshower . . . just as soon as we've founded the Fourth Reich . . . A final solution to the American nightmare . . . Four of the seven mouths of hell are there . . . on

Wall Street, in the Pentagon, in Las Vegas, and in Hollywood . . .
There's one in Rotorua and one in Bangkok . . . The seventh I'll
reveal in the decay of time . . .

Grandpa had on a Barbour oilskin coat and a mossgreen Patagonia jersey. He had girlskinpants and a pair of creamcolored, highheeled, otterskin boots. I had on rough lightblue trainingoveralls, sailor's boots, and a steelcollar: a rosary with shortbarbs for hard obedience training. I'm Sargon the Great and you're Lugalzaggesi, Grandpa had said as he fastened on the chain.

– Hell is other people! Grandpa suddenly exclaimed. That's the only thing he'll quote from Sartre. Otherwise, he hates the guy like sperm hate it when you've got to piss. Then Grandpa switched tracks and launched into a story about a chessmatch between Moses Uritzky and N. A. Fraenkel that had ended in a draw and, finally, in heavypetting. After that he angrily questioned the wisdom of contracting the Kegel muscles for the sake of drier orgasms.

– Depends if you get a shot off, I commented, for lack of anything better to say.

– Shut your yap and keep watch, devilcolt, Grandpa said and jerked my leash so hard the tower shook.

– "What of it then if I warble, babble out a string of verses, if I sing in every valley, wail about in every firwood?" Grandpa väinämöined. You can accuse me of being a local patriot, but I still contend that ethics is the art of cheating, Grandpa snarled in confused conclusion.

The clearcutting was as shittybrown as a partyrally in Myrberg. Rotten brown logs, fallen deciduous trees . . . Large, graywhite stones lay exposed in the darkbrown of the road that ran behind the machinepark. The bog was burntred and frozenblack. Immobile stumps, lichen and moss, a couple of driedout spruces, some raspberrybushes and a mass of halfdead birchtrees. What's the point of sowing anything, plants just die . . . they put up a struggle and end up choked in plastic . . . The forest edge was a long ways away, lots of empty ridges between us and it . . . The wind let up and I thought I heard someone coming down the path. On the horizon a little Jap clunker suddenly appeared. It was yellow and seemed to be struggling. The road here's uneven and rocky, so the going gets tough. Grandpa narrowed his eyes. He began to hum "Headhunters and Headgivers" by the Corpsefucking Crybabies. Then, peering through his Aimpoint 3000 red-dot sight, he started to cackle soundlessly.

– A bull, a cow, and two calves . . . damn berrythieves . . . novembercrooks . . .

The car stopped about a hundred meters away. Our quarry tumbled out and got ready to follow the path leading through the clearcutting towards the meager blueberrybushes five hundred meters north. I used the sight on the other rifle. It was a large Tasco, and the rifle was a .416 Remington Magnum loaded with Swift Bonded Core bullets. They were coming toward us. The bull walked with a manlyman's swagger. Next came the female, her calves swarming around her ankles like sicklebacks around a rotten bullhead. The bull was big and mean, he had the face of a tadpole. The female looked like a dumb bluelightspecialwhore. The calves were nothing but skinandgristle wrapped in bright clothes.

– I'm going to wait a moment before I shoot, Grandpa whispered, carefully opening the window.

– Which are you going to take first?

– The bull, for fuck's sake . . .

They only had eyes for each other, those two: mutual irritation is the only enduring passion. They were as quarrelsome as only your runofthemillskinflints can be. They didn't even look up at the tower. When they were about twenty-five meters away, we had a stroke of good luck. The smallest calf had to take a shit and everyone was forced to participate. The bull tore at his hair and huffed to a stump. The cow ground her teeth and yanked the boy's pants down. But the boy decided he didn't wanna anymore. He howled, struggled, dug in, put up a fight. Grandpa laughed derisively. The bull laughed bitterly. The cow called him a drycock, said she wished she'd gone ahead and fucked every single person at the office party. The bull said she could shove whateverthefuck she wanted up that loose, stinking pussy of hers. He was just itching to do them all in. Start with Magnus then, she shrieked, shoving the now shitsoiled calf away from her, you fuckingidiot, you dumbcow.

Grandpa fired. The crack was deafening. He had an ingenious gadget that minimized kickback. Hilding Marlene holds the patent, but he stole the idea from the Japs. The first shot grazed a hand holding an empty yellow berrybucket. Grandpa reloaded and empty casings turned smoking somersaults in the air. The second shot missed completely and so did the third. The bull jumped up, waving his arms and cussing like a missionary in a cannibal's cookpot. He had an aha moment then and realized Grandpa wasn't finished with him yet, not by a longshot, and sprinted for the car. He was wearing a blue parka with winered corduroy pants. The fourth bullet got him in the leg, the fifth shot like a prayer straight up to heaven. I handed Grandpa the other rifle. It was obviously going to take a while to shut these fuckers up. The woman was tottering on the brink. Hyperventilating, she grabbed her Kanken backpack and took off down the tractor path, herding her calves before her. But one of them still had his pants down around his ankles, so her brilliant plan went up in smoke.

– You failed to read the fineprint, beastcunt, Grandpa hissed and sent two shots into the rosemarybushes around her boots. I can read lips, you know; I learned back when I had an ear infection.

Grandpa began to swear so it curdled the air and startled the birds. The cow collapsed, legs splaying. Her hair was a mess; she'd scratched the Satansbait. The third shot entered her pecadocastigo, the fourth burst her womb, the fifth took her in the mouth. By now the calves had caved in. Grandpa took the reloaded Weatherby and let fly. Big Brother ran around in circles, bedeviled and befuddled, tugging at the cow's leg and making a hell of a ruckus. Grandpa, for his part, emptied the whole magazine. Unfortunately, he missed. After that, he shouldered the Remington, while I reloaded at top speed. One of the five bullets took the calf in the knee, he rolled around and stayed down.

– Hurryhurryhurry! Climb down, we'll show them what we're about!

Through the door and out onto the platform. I slipped on the top step, fell, and got a branch stuck deep in my armpit. I couldn't help myself; I moaned. Grandpa laughed and shot me in passing with a boltpistol that took off my left earlobe. Trying to staunch the blood, I limped after him. The bull was pulling himself through the mud toward the car. He cast terrified eyes over his shoulder, clearly reckoning up all his amortizations. He'd lost a boot and blood was pumping from his beautifully injured leg. Grandpa stopped, legs apart, and gripped his Baby Nambu Onskimodel automaticpistol like an afroamrocop. It took him two tries before he bullseyed the bull's eyes. The larger calf had already passed out. Grandpa swept him up in his arms, kissed him passionately, and slung him belly first into a mudpuddle beside a fallen tree. That just left littlebrother, and he fell to me, since Grandpa thought I needed the practice. He didn't even get up, the little twit, just screeched and shit some wicked sausages onto the grass. He was a stubby kid who'd probably thought he'd grow big and strong and learn to smoke Borkum Riff. I bashed his face in with a thick pinebranch. He didn't have any more tricks up his ass, he just lay there and took it. So I straddled his back, forced his head up and slit his throat with my Ka-Bar Grizzly knife. After that, I puked up the bunch of nothing that was in my stomach. Grandpa immediately set to with the hacking and the carving. – "Beware the melancholy, for they will destroy the earth," he said. He cut fillets from the calves and took a trophy from the bull. Then we headed home.

– Ah hell, we're going to miss *Emmerdale Farm*, we've got too far to go! Grandpa exclaimed. I just know Mr. Wilks is going to rape and murder Amos Brearly some episode or other . . .

Grandpa carried the Weatherby, and I slung the Remington over my shoulder and the shitsmeared meat onto my back. After a few minutes, I started to get my hearing back. We crossed a mild browngold marsh with vomithued hillocks, watching for the darker spots where you don't want to step. Time was, these marshes were bottomless and treacherous, they reached far and wide . . .

Later people drained them just because they enjoyed the challenge, and to give the wetland fowl a hard time. Now the marshes were trying to get their own back, right in step with depopulation . . . we squelchedsucked as we walked . . . Grandpa sang: "So weit die braune Heide geht gehört das alle wir!" The trees were sparse, hunched over like rheumatics trying to avoid a beating . . . they were poor, hiding nothing . . . not even worth a mercykilling . . . There weren't any cloudberries to make jam with . . . that's the one thing I remember about my dad's mom, her making jam while she lifted her skirts to let the snake in . . . "jamming and juicing, Satan's shitwork" . . . We didn't even see a forest bird . . . not a soul was stirring . . . We walked through the trees for hours . . . when it started getting dark, we rested. Evening was coming on fast.

– There isn't nearly enough evil in the forest nowadays, Grandpa complained and shoved a stubborn squirrel back down onto the grillstick.

We sat next to a lazy flame. I tried to brush the cobwebs off my face, souvenirs of a walk through the late summerwoods. Dark-green sprucetrees were closing in, pines swayed stiff as corpses in the wind. The wind and the dark cast doubt on everything you think you understand.

– Once upon a time, mankind was a demonic sort of phenomenon . . . back in the goodolddays, no one knew what mercy was . . . We'd toss furry critters onto the fire, just to watch the greedy flames devour them alive.

– Back in the goodolddays, women and Christians didn't dare leave the highroads . . . If they did, they'd be raped and slaughtered by forestdemons . . . We called them Leshy or sippers, further inland they were known as the overprivileged lips . . .

As we sat there, Grandpa spun stories about terrible powers, secret societies and Satan's commandments. Exhaustion finally conquered terror. Me and Grandpa both fell asleep. When I woke, I was cold as ice inside and out. The sky was sullen. I rested my head on Grandpa's crotch and listened to his sperm gathering themselves for their next pointless assault. As usual, the day had promised more than it could deliver.

MOSSAD—Israeli secret service

WIESENTHAL—Simon: famous Nazi hunter

SÁKAR, HÚTAMA—Muslim hells

WHAT OF IT THEN IF I WARBLE . . .—from the *Kalevala*, the Finnish epic (Friberg trans.)

VÄINÄMÖINEN—Hero of the *Kalaevala*

MYRBERG—town in Västerbotten, Sweden

SO WEIT DIE BRAUNE HEIDE . . .—An SS song: "As far as the brown heath goes, it belongs to us . . ."

LESHY—from Slavic mythology, a male woodland sprite

VIII

– Fuck me, soccer again! Grandpa complained, thumping down on the sofa bed's bright red quilt. He'd just placed a tray holding a stack of danishes and a flask of Black Velvet onto the Perstorptable's slick oilcloth.

– Goddamn game . . . who's playing?

– Barcelona and PSV Eindhoven. Spaniards are in bluepurple. It's the cupcupercup finale.

– Bunch of assgoblins, if you ask me, Grandpa frowned, pointing to the Dutch team. Satan's bedlamites, that's what they are! Couldn't distinguish ciggifilter from ciggibutt! he exclaimed, getting riled up when a kick was blocked.

All Grandpa was wearing was a strawberrycolored T-shirt with the words "Korova Milk Bar" on it.

– What about those Dagos? Where are they from?

– Turkey, I think . . .

He dunked a pastry into his glass of whisky.

– That bear of a man, that bonnieblueeyes, that damn Frankenstein, where did he come from?

51

– You mean Cowman?

– Yeah, that guy!

– No idea . . . they probably bought him off some other team . . .

– What a whore!

Grandpa simmered down for a few minutes, simply sat there muttering to himself. Barcelona had the ball but wasn't doing much with it. Just beating around the bush, while the Dutch just beat . . . off. No one, neither the players nor public, seemed to be having much fun. The ball just got kicked back and forth, while the crowd made faces and booed loudly. Finally, the teams slunk home, tails tucked; the commentator called them fucking homos; the judges on the sideline muttered their agreement; no one knew what the whole mess was good for. Watching a soccer game's a little like life itself. You have to get gone before it starts to feel right. No matter what, everyone's a loser. Clear goals and finesse are as rare as creativity and courage . . . And even then, once set in motion, they usually fall short. That's life, Jack; most everything's a disappointment.

– Ajax is a damn Kiketeam, Grandpa declared. And Tottenham! Hell, it's all money and sex! No one has mercy on me! There's been nothing worth cheering for since Heysel and Hillsborough! These aren't big matches! They're neutrinos! Mites! Nits and gnats! A bunch of fucking nonsense!

– That's just how it is sometimes, I worked up the courage to say.

– So you have an opinion, do you! You who don't even know what dry humor is yet! You're so fucking smart it just fucking makes me want to fucking puke all over your fucking smartass face! If only I had something to puke up!

He farted disdainfully, Zsa Zsa Gabor style, and tossed back another glass of whiskey. I was drinking beer out of an old Bavarianstein with a lid. The stein had scenes from the traditional Lenthunt of little girls: big men ripping up rosy bellies and so forth. Now and then I took a fistful of chips from the washtub. But Grandpa was right, soccer is a surefire path to senility. For the emptyheaded among us, though, it doesn't really matter.

– The World Cup has fifty-one matches! fifty-one! and not a single shot at a goal! just backwardpasses! throwins! gamestoppages! Give me just one serious injury, for the love of God! But no! There are no stretchers in sight! Of course, they carried out that fogy with the grandma hair, you know the one—

– Valderrama—

– But he was up-and-at-'em again in a flash! Why do they bother with that sort! John Eldritch and Bo Jälefors!

– You know what I think is neat, Grandpa?

– Blowing a rabid hyena! Eating me out of house and home!

– No, that soccer demonstrates how a destructive defensive strategy is best. Maybe that could be useful someday . . .

– Useful! That you of all creatures in the galaxy dare to use that word! You were never of any use to anyone! and you never will be! not if you live until the sun falls from the sky and cowboys are walloped by Indians! I'll tell you what useful is! useful is being happy! and happiness is to soar! There's something to think about! you narcissistic little Hitlerjew!

At least Grandpa didn't talk to me like he did when I was small. Back then he sounded like Heidegger, and sometimes like Artaud or Char. Him, the world's worst backward hick. The wind stopped when he opened his mouth; he had an answer for every riddle. No one listened to him, though, so he gave up. When he did, God on high muttered a curse and breathed a sigh of relief; after all, his cover had nearly been blown . . . Back then, Grandpa liked to cram me full of all sorts of things. I remember him telling me how the Sandman was going to jump out of the closet and throw sand in my eyes. There was Plupp, Klas Klättermus, Babar . . . Prince Vibescu, *Naked Lunch* and *Last Exit to Brooklyn* . . . *Curious George, The Satanic Bible*, and Manu's lawbook, naturally in Sanskrit . . . *The Book of Dzyan* . . . *Beowulf* . . . Froissart . . . Borel . . . Sorel . . Przybyszewski . . . Nechajev . . . Rathenau . . . Brehm . . . Codreanu . . . some old editions of *Der Stürmer* . . . *Das Schwarze Korps* . . . He really liked boring me to death . . . with Robert Müsli's *Mom Without Qualities* . . . Hermann Broch's *Death of Svebil* . . . It made him hot when I started to cry, I was so goddamned tired . . . I wanted to sleep and never wake up . . . he just kept on torturing me . . . kept on kneading and kneading. . . the same boring, fucking old shit . . . again and again and again . . . people came and went, said their piece and did their thing . . . chokechains around their tongues . . . they had serious shit to offer, these guys, but I didn't give a damn . . . I wanted to play on Death's team . . . Ordinary match time ended, score's nillnill . . . naturally . . . Too many overtimes, though, you can't use them all.

Grandpa tottered off into the kitchen to get some snacks. He came back with an octagonal nickeltray piled high with coffeebeans, an eggcup with a lightbulb, roadsalt, castoroil, TetraMin, some slices of ryebread smeared with Oil of Ulay, a few Arlanda pastries, and some silverfish. He sat down and immediately found the right tone. He was never long in venting his displeasure.

– Nancy and Raisa! Cunt versus cunt!

Grandpa rumbled on like Bruckner, his tailpipe hissing.

– An uphill struggle against a headwind for ninety years! Bridges and boats all burned! And yet the whole goddamn thing ends here! This here is nothing! It's ghostshit! Satan's ass, the things you're forced to do! It's like swapping feet with a loon! Like a mosquito pissing in the ocean! Like climbing a pinetree to fuck a knothole! Like fucking a juicy boytuft!

Varicose veins were swelling, arthritic joints were aching. Grandpa's legs are chalky, white and spindly, worse than Åsa Lundgren's, the guy who wrote *The Microcephalic Lappish Boy*. There was a good chance the fun was about to end.

– PSV is keeping their team together, the announcer said . . . Chiquita hasn't gotten much done . . . we'll see if they can't step up the pace . . . coming back around the side . . .

– Laudrup is on his side of the field . . . against Roberto . . . Beguiristain . . . Salinas coming to his aid . . . Cochones back to Zubizarreta . . . who hammers the ball . . . signals . . . kicks . . . the Dutch defense has gotten organized . . . van Aerle back to van Breukelen . . . They're playing like they've got Alzheimer's, don't you think?

– They like to feint, especially at the start . . .

– Yeah, but it's been about a hundred and thirty minutes!

– They like to gather in a group and keep a close watch on their own goal . . . the match becomes something like strategic warfare . . . the most important thing is that your team has the ball . . . you'll get your chance . . .

– It's dullsville! It's too goddamned slow! At least we had that brutal tackle from behind . . . we'll get to see it in slowmo . . . hooboy! He knew what he was doing . . . could it be, will it be a meniscus tear?

– It looks like it's Laudrup . . .

– Hope his tendon's toast!

By this time, the commentators were just about foaming at the mouth.

– He's out for at least three months!

– Could be a pulled ligament!

– For the love of God, it looks serious . . . he's being carried off the field . . . looks like he's in pain . . .

– Here comes the freekick . . . the perfect setup for Koeman . . .

– The defense is playing for time . . . they've gained a meter and a half . . .

The referee waved a yellowcard. The freekick struck the defense's wall. End of the first half. Grandpa began to boil over, they were all talk and no action. The universe, on the other hand, runs on adrenaline and testosterone.

– Talk about people who have it bad! A single Grandpa with a scamp hanging from my neck and another on the way! Broke and sick and with a mass of freetime on my hands! It's all downhill from here! It's too much! Comeoncomeoncomeon! It's so fucking painful! God, it hurts! Aoouuuuuu!!!

He banged his head on the edge of the table again and again as hard as he could. While he did that, he rubbed his cock, which refused to stand up.

– Moremoremore! Ah—ahhh—oahhhhhhhh! Fuck it hurts! I'm dying! Don't stop! So fucking good! Harder faster oaahhhhh!

He fell dizzily to the rug. I didn't give a fuck about the next over-time quarter. I dragged my Grandpa onto the sofa and wiped away the blood. Then I puked up my chips, collapsed onto the Almas fur rug, and dreamed sweet dreams about my murderer.

PLUPP, KLAS KLÄTTERMUS—Swedish children's book characters

DER STÜRMER—a weekly Nazi newspaper

DAS SCHWARZE KORPS—official newspaper of the SS

SVEBIL—Olov Svebilius, Archbishop of Uppsala from 1681–1700, who wrote the popular book *A Simple Explanation of Martin Luther's Little Catechism*

ÅSA LUNDGREN—Swedish author who wrote *Långa Lappflicken* (The Tall Lap Girl)

ALMAS—Mongolian for "wild man," a mythical creature similar to Bigfoot

IX

I was in the process of lathering and shaving Grandpa's asshole when the phone rang. He swore so the air sizzled and started groping around for the receiver.

– Reichsführer-SS, he answered weakly and lit a Rothman. Well, hello there, lovey! he chirped next and dug bloody furrows into my skull to make me to stop. Thanks, I'm doing fine, and how are you? . . . Hunkydory, syphilis, and HIV!? . . . You're yanking my chain! . . . What? . . . Don't get all huffy now . . . I know it's no fucking joke!

Grandpa was laying on his stomach on the beanbag. He listened in suspense for a long moment. All he said was: – Mmm . . . hrrmm . . . damn! . . . but isn't that just too bad!

Then he started talking.

– You've got your work cut out for you. I hear you . . . Precisely. This business makes me sad as Appomattox! . . . What the hell's wrong with people these days! . . . mmhmm . . . yeah . . . mmm . . . nah . . . sucking uakari cock's all he's good for! . . . the Jewbeast! . . . you're kidding! . . . bullshit! . . . just think! . . . It's like Pudas's box! . . . precisely . . . No quarter!

He finally shut up, but it cost him. His head nodded and shook incessantly. His nervous tics increased. He began rocking feverishly back and forth, crinkling up his wrinkly brow. When there was finally silence on the other end, he took a deep breath. He didn't sound as much like a hick when he started talking again.

– What can I say! I'm absolutely dumbfounded! You couldn't find words to describe it! not if you searched high and low! . . . Genscher will probably join up . . . maybe Baker . . . perhaps Moammar, too . . . maybe, just maybe Delors . . . I have my claws in him, you know . . . yeah . . . you heard it right here! That only leaves one person! He's not worth a baht, and that's no exaggeration! . . . Getting the truth out of him would be the greatest miracle since Claus Heim massacred 5,000 pigs with two knitting needles and five meat thermometers! It's sad that it's to come to this! . . . that one chromosome can make so much difference . . . I have some influence over Donner and Schein, they owe me a favor . . . thunder and lightening will do what they can . . . Malm is my man . . . We can count on Nicolin . . . Markus Wolf and Horst Herold, too . . . We'll get it together! That can't be allowed to stand! Trust me! You devil . . . you can thank me with a really sexy Mass, okay? . . . what? . . . you've misunderstood me! I believe in God! I just think He's so ashamed that He's gone and hidden Himself! Our universe is just one among the countless batches of sperm that God in His narcissistic isolation jacked off and spewed out, just so He could put His stain on the Nothingness! Galaxies are sperm, you know! . . . I know you take a Near Eastern viewpoint on the matter . . . but we can still be friends, right . . . hmmm? . . . well? . . . that's it exactly . . . that's what we'll say then . . . you'll be hearing from me when I know something . . . the older you get, the gayer you go . . . and when you're getting close to death . . . But you . . . you, too . . . take it easy, suck me sleazy . . . sure, you too . . . byebye now . . .

He hung up and gestured for me to continue my barber work. Grandpa's asshole is huge and grimy and it tastes like sulfur. It's wrinkled around the edges and unbelievably hairy. It's ringed in red, so I think it's infected. I have to shave it every couple of weeks, or it can't be fucked.

– That was the Pope . . . he's afraid the chimney's about to start smoking . . . got in over his head with some narcotraffickinggig . . . Papa Escobar just called him to gloat . . . The Medellin Cartel are a bunch of fucking crybabies! Milksops! And just like always, I have to make everything right . . . If only Terre Blanche hadn't called yesterday! You know what I told him . . . he wants me to come down there for the action . . . things are heating up, the orks are getting cocky . . . Fuck it all, I don't have the time! Satan's hairy ass! Khun Sah had a time of it, too! It's like dancing a jig on crackedheels . . . like chasingmoonlight . . . Now I have to talk some sense into Schalck-Golodkowski and Gerrit Et Wolsink . . . it'll take care of itself, though . . .

I finished shaving and greased his ass with babyfat. In the meantime, Grandpa was stuck remembering the past.

– I've fought in twenty-seven wars on four continents . . . I've personally assassinated thirteen heads of state and helped start forty-nine coups . . . I'm an honorary member of every counterintelligenceoperation, criminalsyndicate, and terroristgroup worth mentioning . . . I've wiped out seventy-one plant and nineteen animalspecies . . . and two whole races of men . . . I've trashed priceless cultural artifacts . . . demolished economies . . . impoverished language . . .

Grandpa pulled on a Ghillie suit GS 1, which made him look like a compost heap. We were going purschhunting for depressives.

– But how does it all end ... dypsnea and congenital biapathy ... vexation and grief ... sometimes I think I don't even exist ... it feels like someone dreamed me up ... like all I am is swearwords and sorcery ... like amlet, dr aust, and don uixote ...

He drained a flask of Old Crow and tossed me a tip.

– All the greats have fallen, one by one ... the greenbloods ... Stroessner! now there was a man with blood in his cock! God have mercy on those who stand proud! And Pinochet, of course ... Papa and Baby Doc ... what's Haiti without them! a firstrate climacteric resort is what! ... Somoza ... Noriega, the old rascal ... Refaat and Penser ... Poor Marcos ... now Khomeini's gone, too, his eyes were out-of-this-world. . . Pol Pot was a godgifted statesman, but what good did it do him? ... Idi, Haile, Ian Smith ... Bokassa and Mengistu ... Enver Hoxha ... Glistrup ... Ceauşescu! He shot at least four thousand bears! What do you say to that!

– I don't know what to say ...

– You'd be wise to say nothing. The world just isn't itself anymore, boy ... There's Amnesty International and Greenpeace yelping like bitches in heat ... It's just about impossible to be an honest, oldfashioned tyrant anymore ... But the battle against peace and prosperity marches on ...

PUDAS's BOX—Folke Pudas protested the loss of his chauffeur's license by spending three months on hunger strike in a box in Sergel's Square in Stockholm

CLAUS HEIM—a leader in the "Landvolkbewegung," a farmer's movement in Weimar Germany; he single-handedly slaughtered 5,000 pigs on a Brazilian farm to protest worsening economic conditions that made ongoing operations impossible

DYPSNEA—shortness of breath

BIAPATHY—bia (Greek for "violence") + apathy = apathy to violence

X

Grandpa was having a splashing good time in a waterbed filled with urine when someone rang the doorbell. He was soaked in sweat and sucking his own dick. He once told me it's the most diabolical pleasure of all, but that it gets harder when you get old, even if you've got the right body for it. His back might crack at any moment, but that probably just makes him hornier. I've tried it on myself, but can't even come close. You've got to be tall and skinny as a scarecrow. You've also got to have loads of selfconfidence. The real pros are more than eight feet.

– It works better with your eyes closed, I remember Grandpa saying, and that's how he was doing it.

He was also listening to Carl Orff's *Carmina Burana*, or rather, *De Temporum Fine Comoedia-Vigilie*, while a different speaker was pumping out Venom's "At War with Satan." Our room's packed with books, mostly history and philosophy. They're in random topsyturvy stacks that reach as high as the bed, and if you want to you can crawl across them. Every now and then Grandpa picks up a book, but he instantly gets sick of it. That's when you get to hear what he thinks about those pussyscribblers . . . someone should drink them under the table! lightweights! gutless breakwinds, miserable assholes, windbags! Off with their hands and feet! just for the fun of it! like in Karaganda! you write a book! a single sentence! and you've waived the right to live! God forgives everything you do to wordwrenchers!

And so on and so forth.

– I'm the one and only consummate Thelemite, because I shit on Crowley's life and piss on his work!

Grandpa's bitter he never got to scrap with Aleister . . . Sometimes he flaunts the dirty letters Stefan George, Proust, and Wittgenstein sent him when he was a strapping young buck . . .

– Now you can see what they go in for, those Aunties Green, Brown, and Violet. Why, those hoitytoity spinsters have only got cockandass on the brain! Marcel stuck nails in rats and came on his mama's picture! And Boy George, what a primadonna! "Als sieger dring ich einst in euer hirn, ich der verscharrte . . ." Hotdamn, that's for me! A great horny owl in a magpie's skirt! I'm not even going to tell you the sorts of thing he wrote! No one would believe me! It's just too, too revolting! And Ludwig! no point in trying to outtalk an idiot or outlumber a calf! Here he writes that he wants to meet me in his nasty Norwegian cottage! I'm supposed to bring two weeks' worth of shit in my bowels! without a hair on my body! smeared up with resin and covered in horsehairtufts! then he'll whip me until I'm just a bloodystain! leave me for the skuas! There you have it! Genius in all its glory! Bighead, smallwit, spread your legs and take a shit! I'm finished with the likes of them! Poppycock and tommyrot! Hefty tomes full of difficult words! A million shittyass viewpoints! Culture's only cockandbooze! if you just scratch the surface!

But now Grandpa was contorted like a sandflea and sucking for all he was worth; his body shone like lead against the oxbloodcolored sheets. Homemade comfort. Some people call that position thirty-four and a half, since it's half a sixty-nine. Grandpa's cock is average, just a little thin and worn. It was holding its own, though, that's for sure. He was sucking so hard his stomach was growling. He has dainty lips, a strong tongue, endless spittle, and his eyeballs rolled behind their greenpainted lids. It seemed to be going good for him, selfmade is wellmade, so I took myself down the stairs and through the hallway to the outer door. I unlocked it and looked out. Standing there was an old man no one had seen before.

– Is the head of the house at home?

He had a voice like Mr. Bean's, you know: constipated and Biblethumping.

– Yeah, but he's giving himself a blowjob.

The man didn't waste any more words, just pushed me aside, rushed in, and yanked off his caracul and galoshes. He showed himself into the living room, plopped down on a rockingchair, and stayed quiet. He looked like a normal guy, just kind of old and serious. Most of them are like that, quiet their whole lives, slaving away, faring ill.

I'd like to be one of those.

Aunties Green, Brown, and Violet—figures from a book by the Swedish author Elsa Beskow

Als sieger dring ich . . . —From Stefan George's poem "Der Gehenkte" (The Hanged Man)

XI

I was reading Grandpa the personals from the Västerbotten *Volks-blad*. I made sure to skip the really perverted ones, though, where someone was advertising for a person of the opposite sex. Those'll make you sick after only a few lines.

"A slightly bitter woman is waiting for you. I'm 19 and have 3 kids. I look 40. It all feels so strange. Why did they do this to me? I've done my best, but I simply can't go on . . ."

Or: "Skinny white guy, 24 years old, short, with everyday interests, seeks girl with special interests. I don't think I've ever done it, but I'm willing to give it a try. I've got a pretty secure job and I'm happy to share. Everything we've pent up needs to come out. I'm living with Aunt Sigris right now, but am looking for my own place . . ."

But Grandpa was only interested in the homoads. Unfortunately, all the ones who wrote in to *Gay Guy Contact* were too far away. Southerners seem to be gayer Nonetheless, the locals did seem to be getting gayer by the hour. Grandpa was lying on the ribbackedsetee and sucking down some Johnny Walker Black Label, and I was reading the ads in the order they were printed.

– "Shy, incontinent Sävarbugger, who's usually a wallflower at dances, wants to find a fellow he can snuggle with. You are laidback, nice and sweet, inmates preferred. I'm bald and nervous and only smoke at parties. I work at a daycare center. Desire is driving me wild. Especially interested in illegal immigrants! Respond to: 'Got that spring feeling down in Obbola.'"

– Damn, what a repulsive pig! Onto the next one . . .

– "Horny guy, 39 years old, small and dark, looking to find a sex-hungry backseatjockey in a preppy cardigan and berretta. You are 67 years old, deaf and dumb, suffer from psoriasis, and preferably live in Vuollerim. Extra plus if you're bitter, angry, and have a chronic smoker's cough Reply to: 'We two in in the old jalopy, Wilmar.'"

– Go on . . .

– "Crabby sanatorium dweller, 29 years old, with a thin blond mustache wants to be slapped around by a wellhungguy. I have an appetite for most things that make life a party, and I've hung out with Etienne Glaser and Hans Werthén, to name a few. Interests include: casualsex, emptyshells, the vermiformappendix. I've got AIDS and the guardianship of an autistic child. Respond to: 'If there's no time, there's no time.'"

Grandpa sighed dejectedly, and I knew what he meant.

– "Sallow, fat, cowardly man in upper middle age seeks contact with a flexible snugglebunny with huge manboobs. I'm bulimic and want you to cum inside me while I puke. Respond to: 'Churchwarden who believes in truelove.'"

– We'll cut the dick off that one, Grandpa swore.

– "I am who I am and I've been paid back with interest. It's good to walk a straightline. How we can meet. Take a car if it's too far. I live alone. Drink and jack off. Us men should stick together. Like those young guys too shy to try a smokesucksmutyourselfup session in Kusmark. What's the big deal. That's all. Respond to: 'Bertil.'"

– That must be Hilding Henning up in Sälgdal. He hasn't fucked anyone in over fifty years. And he isn't going to fuck me, none of them are . . .

ETIENNE GLASER—actor, producer, and scriptwriter
HANS WERTHÉN—Swedish industryman

XII

– Sweden's only had one writer worth his salt and that was Elfred Berggren from Furuögrund. I've read *God of Robots* over a hundred times. He was the same age as me and Himmler, but died at thirty-two when he was raped by a ringedseal . . .

Grandpa poured himself some more smallbeer. He was trying to crush a whole bottle of Veronal into his mug, and he was stirring with the stick normally used for mercykillings. He was wearing a T-shirt with the words "Adolf Hitler European Tour 1939–1945," a warharness, and Israeli commandoboots with Hushalongs. I was wearing my culturalrevolutionary outfit and a black skimask. We were getting ready to go out. We'd made quick work of newlyhatchingeggs, newbornkoalas, and teutoburgers. For dessert, Ibiza cream and Patpong dates. Grandpa had spent the morning reading Deschner's *The Criminal History of Christianity* and Villeneuve's *The Torture Museum*. Now he was going on and on about the stagparty literaturi.

– A knife blow to an old woman's back's got more culture than anything those scribblescrabbling morons will ever come up with . . . belleslettresloving cuntlickers . . . that's what they are . . .

XIII

Yesterday we played games until our eyes bled and our brains boiled: the first World Cup in sprinting, eighteen teams in three divisions, twelve branches per year; then the World Cup in skiing with twelve legendary competitors in different places around the world and with different distances and styles, also with eight teams, four from each team in the individual runs; then a little boxing and wrestling to wind down. All it takes is dice, a will of iron, some schizofantasy, and paper and pen. Then we played soccer with a hundred and twenty-eight teams; a hockey tournament with sixty-four teams—tabletop, of course—then the World Cup '90 and tennis on the Sega; then Risk, chess, and Beat the Homo; and, finally, a homemade game involving exterminationcamps, where each of us plays a different commander. And now for the rest. We played Dragons and Demons, Lords of the Rings, and an awesome wargame Grandpa dreamed up about Diadochi. Now that I think of it, a few days and nights must've passed . . .

   We heated up sandwiches in the microwave . . . with tonsils, two jars of bustedappendices, and the dailynews . . .

We drank beer from casks and then pissed in them so we wouldn't have to get up . . . To play like we played, you've got to forget everything else . . . You've got to have a nativebestiary, a true cornucopia to populate your teams with . . . You have to like protocol . . . talking big and talking small . . . simulation . . . When Grandpa and I play together, I feel there's a bond between us . . . No one else could've done it . . . When we play, it can sound like this—it was the ninth-year A-division, I had cerebralpalsy-women, Kåge-Suburbs, and Schools, and Grandpa had the Bush, Kåge-women, and Finland . . .

– Who's running for the CP-whores in the marathon?

– Who ran last year?

– Let's see . . . They were in B then . . . Konda Forssell . . . time was three hundred and fifty-six . . . three points . . .

– Nah, I don't trust her . . . Has "The Ant" run yet?

– Nope . . . she's just sitting there scratching the skin off her nose to make it smaller . . .

– Then we'll take "The Ant" . . . she's a fighter . . .

– I'll take a wild stab . . . I'm bringing in "Sinbearer"!

Then Grandpa took his sweet time telling me about "Sinbearer," a nasty old tramp who'd lurked around Skellefteå in the '20s . . .

– He was big and fat and popeyed . . . not to be confused with "The White Boss," who was another guy entirely, had dandruff for eyebrows . . . but everyone was terrified of "Sinbearer" . . . he wasn't right . . . He limped along with a sack bearing all the world's sins . . . He didn't say much, but when he talked, his words were both timid and perverse . . .

– "You don't eat pork, witch?!" he'd laugh, or: "Badluck and pigslop! that's all I've ever met with!" or: "Best meat's between the legs, best sausage between the stones!" That's what he'd say, when he got someone alone. He had a coarsemade pillory and testes like pitepalt. Grandpa told one tramptale after the next . . .

– A good story is always sterile, monotone, he liked to say. Spleen and ennui are all you can hope for . . . Then it got even more longwinded . . .

I got to hear about "Five-Penny Jonas," a sullen little caramel and thimblehawker, who liked to eat live colts . . . about "ByeBye," also known as the "Gypsy Dancer," who was beautiful as a näken and liked to seduce young men with his accordion and then slit their throats . . . about Åkerström, who drank more than a hundred liters of water per day and had a habit of suffocating snakes by sticking them up his ass . . . about "The Hobo King," who worked the roads and never stopped crying . . . about "The End Times," who ran steelwire at faceheight across the road and killed forty-three cyclists . . . about gypsy Karlsson-Tydén, who made whisks but couldn't bear to part with them . . . he wandered between Skellefteå and Ume his whole life and never got anywhere . . . about Lejonberg, the frowner, who fenced with pigs using his stiff, naked cock . . . about "Ne'erdowell Fredrika," who had more lice than all the Croats in the Thirty Year War combined . . . about "Sitting Pretty," a rickety bowlegged tramp who liked to enjoy a smoke dangling over a great height . . . about "The Big Scare," "Finn-Pavola," and the sweet and mild Sehlstedt, a fervently religious tramp with a holy medallion around his neck . . .

Later he talked about Augusta Hamberg and "Poas," who wandered around Storberget in Lycksele . . . about the English disease, about huge, hairy warts, and about the poisonous tallowcandles that were used to get rid of stomachparasites . . . a driedup old mocassin if ever there was one . . . about "The Black Girls," Jonas and Johannes Södermark, who played bedandbordello with every gypsy to cross their paths . . . they were dark, had rings in their ears, and blowjobs dancing in their eyes . . . and in their mouths and their bellies, by God . . . they'd sell out their own grandpas . . . so long as they didn't quit. . . yes, Grandpa realized he'd lost contact with the trampworld . . .

– Who wants Sub in the marathon?

– Johan Westermark . . . he got full points with three hundred and seventy-eight last time . . .

– And I have Kåga-Women . . . by Satan . . . for lack of anything better, it'll have to be "The Stork" Sundqvist . . .

Then we were finished with rolling dice and writing stuff down . . . the marathon was played with ten times ten dice, you start at the top of the list and go down one roll at a time . . . At three throws, "The Ant" Greenland slipped . . . she was thirty points behind the nearest challenger . . . The others were close, between a hundred five and a hundred ten . . . After five throws, half the marathon, the positions were:

"The Ant" Greenland	160
"Sinbearer"	193
Johan W.	178
"The Stork"	189
"SATO"	166
Rockojärvi	175

It looked like I had two losers to deal with . . . "The Ant" and "SATO" were the haircurdling showstoppers . . . Moronic Greenland threw a 24 in the seventh. The tramps and "The Stork" caught up to the leaders. It was starting to look like a triple for Grandpa . . .

– Noooo! Looks like Johan, the bastard, can't even get his cock blue! I groaned when he threw 27 in the ninth.

Grandpa took the ten small white dice with black pips and rolled them imploringly over his open palm . . . Then he tossed them onto the felt cloth with a sly look . . . A quick glance revealed: 36 . . . fair, but nothing to holler about. The last roll was anticlimactic. Grandpa rolled a three-double: The Bush 6p., Kåge-Q 5p., and Finland 4p., Sub. 3p., CP-q 2p., and Skola, the old masterteam, 1p. "Sinbearer's" winning time was a nice 384 . . . 6 of 10 rolls of 40 or better . . . But the ten-time runner scored over 400, so he'd averaged above 40.

The World Cup ran two "days" with six meets per day. A runner could only participate in one race a day.

100, 400, 1500, 5000 marathons and 4x100 the first day . . .

3x3, 4x4, 4x5+1x3, 6x8, 10x10 and four stretches with 3x3 dice . . .

The second day: 200, 800, 3000, 10,000, half-marathon and 4x400 . . .

2x6, 4x5, 5x6, 8x8, 9x9, and four stretches with 4x4 dice . . .

When we played "Lord of the Rings," Grandpa wanted to be Sauron. When I said it was against the rules, he beat me with *Bolshevism from Moses to Lenin*. He refused to trade down to a balrog, and waved his hands dismissively when I read the racial descriptions of the Uruk-hai, Huorns, dragons, and Nazgûl. On a whim, he let himself be persuaded by what I read about the Nazgûl in the rulebook: "If revealed with the aid of magic, they appear in the guise of great, haggard kings with cold, evil eyes . . ."

– Okeydokeysmokey, I'll be a ghost, then . . . and I'll be a black Númenórean. . . and an Uruk-hai . . . You'll be a fallohidehobbit . . . a hummerbagge. . . a buggerwoser. . .

We made up our own rules this time . . . We said you didn't have to die if you died in the game . . . Grandpa won . . . he always does . . . he makes the rules . . . he pulls the strings . . . he's behind it all . . .

NÄKEN—a water sprite

XIV

Grandpa was in bed with his cock wrapped in a wet, warm towel, reading aloud from *Geronto-Eroticon* by Ernst Carson, the Skråmträsk devil.

– "... let men protect their sweet flesh from sexual intercourse with sundrenched whores—hair like frostbitten chaff, asses like rusty, sooty, greasy burntout ovens" ... bring me my munchies, you little rat!

I sat in my dogcrate gnawing on the corn growing on my largest foot.

– Bring me my special brownies and buttermilk!

I went to get his snacks. Down in the kitchen, a feral cat was raping a cacklingtease of a laughinggull. I walloped them both with a firepoker and went back upstairs with Grandpa's evening snack. When I got there, his hoarse wheezing voice washed over me like the scent of pigs roasting near Smammarn.

– "... Augustine already wrote about how nasty, dirty, sleazy, and queasy a woman's embrace can be ... Kill the firstborn of her loins! Let a cry be heard from every sty! For every killing-blow, a man goes free! As long as a single motherwomb exists, we'll never find our way back to Our Father! We'll be nothing but wideeyed little boys when Doomsday's Bloody Sunday strikes! On that day, magisters will roll up the starry skies! The earth will swaddle us like a rotten mummy's bandages or a stinking, unchanged diaper, hail big as horseballs will beat the recreant earth blackandblue . . . Copperbright bikers with awful hygiene will wander cold waiting rooms with shaking voices: 'How odd that mommy's late . . .'"

Grandpa put the thick leatherbound book away when I crept close to the bed.

– Ernst was a fellow with the right attitude, he said. He could tear the throats out of a hundred and fifty chickens a minute and never show a trace of remorse . . . the guy was icecold . . . But his writing is as bad as a cop's.

Grandpa opened the box and crammed his mouth full of special brownie. I poured his buttermilk into a mug.

– I could tell you things about Ernst and his life that would make Unicef and those Save the Children queers look for a nice quiet corner to curl up in and die . . . But I think I'll give you an oraltest instead!

His sharp, level gaze turned Latinate.

– What are the sevendeadlysins?

– Humility, generosity, chastity, modesty . . .

– More!

– Uhhhohhh . . . bulimia! meekness and productivity!

– Bravo, boy, you're the slowest of them all . . . And my totem is . . . ?

– The brown rat.

SMAMMARN—small lake in Lappland

SKRÅMTRÄSK—village in the Skellefteå region

XV

– I owe all I know to the Herrey Brothers, Grandpa said, looking embarrassed and taking a drag from his Kent ciggibutt.

– All too often the all too many assume it was Nietzsche himself who transformed me into nature's stroke of luck, which is what you could say I am. But no! it was the Herreys!

– What about Basedow and Bekhterev?

– I met them when life had already used and abused me until I felt like Sigge Fürst trying to blow Satchmo. Of course, Hegel's *Phenomenology* and Schreber's *Memoirs* served their purpose, when I decided to dynamite my brain so it became as small as a strandloper's. Think and feel as little as possible, always be happy and kind! he commanded and speared a titmouse with a dart.

Herreys—a Swedish pop group made up of three Mormon brothers
Basedow—Karl Adolf von, a German physician who studied Graves' disease (also known as Basedow's disease)

BEKHTEREV—Vladimir, Russian neurologist who studied what came to be called Bekhterev's Disease

SCHREBER—Daniel Paul Schreber, author of *Memoires of My Nervous Illness.*

SIGGE FÜRST—Swedish film actor, known for appearing in the films of Ingmar Bergman, among others.

STRANDLOPER—Afrikaans, "beach walker," name for a native bushman

XVI

– You may think you're a boy, but you're just a fuck, my own dear Grandpa said, laying it all out for me. Anyway, the one measly adventure I remember was taking the bus to Auntie Eskil's out in Tåme. He was gentle as can be and always offered you a mixedracejuice and priestscurfpowdered kannibiscroissants stuffed with livelampreys. Weather willing, we'd look out onto his grisly little courtyard. He'd also turn on the radio, which must've gotten screwed up somehow, because it was always playing the same program.

– Andthenwhat?

– Uncle Sven would force his commando rod deep into some creep named Nils, who lived out in Rykhyttan. Auntie Eskil was small and plump and sugarysweet, but he was a terrible talker. He never said anything you expected, his voice stuttering and limping along. He was so deranged and dejected it was a wonder he was allowed to roam free. He kept up an erotic correspondence with Eugén Andersson, the busty cherubchef from Burträsk. He had an original copy of *Death and the Maiden* by Hans Baldung

Grien up on the mantel. He'd written a forty-thousand line epic in alexandrine verse about the Emperor Caracalla. But Auntie Eskil couldn't stand other people's eyes and voices for long, so after coffee he'd get hotheaded and give us the coldshoulder. If we were lucky, he'd teach us to drown cats and geld mice. Fuck me, how we'd bug him to show us his cock! Then whoever wanted to could touch it . . .

XVII

I tried to creep up into Grandpa's lap, but he wasn't having it. Then he saw how sad I was, so he relented.

– Come on up here, then.

The canechair creaksqueaked and outside the windows, which were all nailed shut, twilight creatures squawked out their foolish desires. The TV is homemade, it's round and square, and usually all it gets is shit. Above the TV—to one side of the Mandela poster and the postmortem photographs of Rosa Luxemburg, Béla Kun, and Benno Ohnesorg—there's a rabbit strung up by its back legs. Stuff is starting to grow on it, but Grandpa doesn't think it's time to throw it away yet. On the other side he hung up a velvet portrait depicting the popular motif of "chainsmoking infants." The wallpaper in the sittingroom is a patchwork thing and curls at the edges. That's where I'm writing now. That day the north wind was huffing and puffing away, it was a normal evening, where everything that exists seems like it's over and done, and the autumn night was busy destroying every tie that, oddly enough, still bound. I was in the mood to get cozy, but Grandpa put a stop to it. No wiggleroom for me tonight.

– Sit like a real person, parasite!

If I'd pushed my luck, I would've seen a rampant bull . . . I would've found out why Zarathustra burst . . . he would've made a Spanferkel of me . . . I had one knee hooked over the arm of the chair and my whole upper body was unsupported, but I had to stay stockstill and couldn't twitch a muscle. Grandpa fussed restlessly with the controls. All at once, Gyllenhammar was sobbing and begging forgiveness for his "pitiful vermin existence" . . . On Channel 2, Lena Liljeborg was red, bloated, and bursting with laughter as she talked about the teeming animal life in Jane Björck's blondebush . . . He fluttered between one flickering channel and the next. Afrosport was showing the tongueswallowing championship in Djibouti, Screamsport reported on a qualifying match in propheticdreaming, MTV was featuring the Headbanger's Ball, and RTL Minus a long cavalcade of deathjumps, mostly from rooftops and bridges. The Children's Channel was playing Transsexual Videos, Hyper Channel was running an installment of that autopsy series called *Bibersmut*, the Loser Channel had a special report on stuffedanimals demanding tribute from their owners. Here in Hebbershålet we also get the channels you can't find in other places. One runs shows by Swedish TV personalities like Jan Lindblad, Nisse Linnman, and Bisse, but without sound; one specializes in fiascofucks caught on hiddencamera; one exclusively shows garroting and grannieporn. Grandpa's windpipe rattled, the channel needed changing. He didn't have the energy to throw a fit, though. I pretended I was asleep.

He turned off the TV and carried me into the bedroom, crawling over the bookstacks as he went. Then he gently lowered me onto the urine-filled waterbed, kissed my forehead nightynight, lay down, and sent up a thanks for all we had received. Outside, everything continued as it was. It's worse than you can ever imagine. No matter how deep you sleep, no matter how good you've got it, tomorrow always comes.

SPANFERKEL—suckling pig
GYLLENHAMMAR—Pehr G. Gyllenhammar, well-known Swedish businessman, CEO of Volvo for many years
LENA LILJEBORD, JANE BJÖRCK—Swedish TV hosts
JAN LINDBLAD—Swedish naturalist and writer. He was also quite a virtuoso when it came to the art of whistling

XVIII

– You know you're a man when you can tell the difference between having to take a piss and wanting to fuck, Grandpa declared and took a big honking swig of Jack Daniels.

– Geiserich's fimbuleyes and fistulousdick! he swore, after he'd downed half the bottle. They must've let a nigger jerk off in that.

That meant that Kvasir's Blood was especially potent today. We were sitting in a nettlebower with Eilert and Petunia. Summer had cum a few hours ago, but was good to go again. The sky looked like a rotten cloudberrycompote, the wind brought with it the ripe aroma of the gypsymassgraves up north. The only mixer we had was rosehipsoup; all we had to munch on was a thick slab of St. Lucia cake and a few soggy, lukewarm loinglands.

But: – They'll be the main course, won't they, Momma? Eilert had said when they turned up on the road leading to the caste villages and the Yehuda Triangle.

– Hellandhighwater, Grandpa, don't you think a boy becomes a man when he kills his first Jew? Petunia asked, sucking on a Rio Brasil.

– Hosianna, but you sure can talk shit, woman! Grandpa exclaimed.

– Killing Jews is about as difficult as gaying up Foucault!

– But Globocnik said . . .

– I shit on Odilo! fumed Grandpa. And on his compassion! And on his scythe! And on his spatula!

– Shit, we're so comfy here, Eilert broke in, can't you two stop fighting?

– You better think about just who you're dealing with, Grandpa warned him.

– Oh, we are, Eilert said, planting a kiss on Grandpa's veiny, shriveled hand. Grandpa's eyes narrowed dangerously as he glared at Petunia from beneath his forelock, but then he cast himself back into the Neapolitanyellow and Berlinblue hammock. Beneath the driedout layer of sperm and vomit, you could still see the bestiality motif from Suleiman the Magnificent's rape of Europe in 1530. Vera Renczi had embroidered it with newbornbabies' intestinalvilli.

– Hey there, boy, Eilert said, faking a laugh and trailing a finger over my neckshotdimple, don't you have anything clever to say? I think you're too silent and sullen for your own good.

– I don't know about that, I said, dropping my eyes to my cock. Not that there was much to see. They'd made that clear enough.

– Tell them about your noobproofs! demanded Grandpa.

– Okay, I've thought up three lazy and logical proofs for God's existence. They come from how things are.

– Let's hear them, you snotty windbag! Petunia quipped. Auntie's a beast, she'd just as soon smoke a ciggi with her cunt as her mouth. She's ugly as a walrus and she's fat, foul, and knocked up to boot.

– The three proofs of God's existence are: I. Pain and shit (even though that's how we like it). II. Everything's so cunningly made (though there's no point to it). III. Everyone's nice to me (even Petunia, who's usually nasty as an octoberotter).

First there was silence. The grasshoppers were chirping hard. That, combined with the garbagesparrows' frosty cheapcheap, were the only sounds in the world. Everyone was elsewhere. Petunia shook her head and speared me with her eyes.

– You little demon, have you been sneakreading Jewdevil mysticism?

– They're mine! I thought them up!

– But that sounds an awful lot like the concept of *tikkun* from the Lurianic Kabbalah, Eilert observed, a frail grin touching his vapid face.

– I don't know anything about whatever you just said! It's all mine! I haven't snuckread anything!

– The only things he gets to read on his own are the Pnakotic Manuscripts and O'Donnell's *The World's Worst Women*, Grandpa reassured them. Besides, there's only Shabbetai Tzvi, and Nathan of Gaza is his prophet!

– Galut and Kelipot! swore Petunia, eyeing me skeptically, that boy deserves a worse fate than your average chainsmoker could think of!

– What are you going do about it, eggbrooder!

– Let it go, Eilert said, stroking Petunia's plowhorse flanks soothingly. She'd sprung up from her Bergen-Belsen lawn chair with murder in her eyes.

– Let's see what he's got, he doesn't have an easy life, you know.

She plopped back down on the deck chair, though, which collapsed beneath her. Grandpa started laughing like Czardas's Princess, but at least he tried to smother it. With Eilert's help, Petunia settled into an overstuffed chair. By now she was positively crackling with rage.

– Fucking Satanspawn, she growled. You can only take so much before your womb falls out! She plucked a thumbscrew from the trashpile and lobbed it at me, but it missed.

– I'll spraypaint you with eggliquor! I swore in a thin voice.

– Not now, boy, soothed Grandpa. Don't force us to go bashing heads. Besides, every once in a while Petunia fucking snaps and runs around like a berserker until there's no one left breathing. Like that time in the bookbus. She was like Cú Chulainn . . . Or like a Yanomami warrior who inhaled ebene and sang about flesheating hornets . . . You'll have to excuse me, Petunia, but it isn't the mite's fault. That Bergen-Belsen isn't meant for someone as fullskirted as you.

– It's nothing, Eilert answered for Petunia, who was hooting like a capercaillie in a freezer.

– Anyway, let's quit harping on the Jewish God, Eilert begged. It's making my stomach sick and my dick limp.

– Here here, Grandpa proclaimed. Mr. J.V. Sabaoth isn't even worth a consolation prize. And you know what, by George, I just remembered that that boy I bit to death last Sunday is still in the cellar. Why don't we slap him on the grill? A bite to eat might stop us from squabbling like littleoldladies!

– Shouldn't we have a nice game of croquette first? Eilert fretted.

– Nah, too *Alice in Wonderland* . . .

Eilert agreed and Petunia nodded, but she had a look that said, it might be nice if . . . so I was sent away with a lash for my pains. I felt as outofplace as an outlander inland. I'm always getting in the way, but I can never get *with* anyone. Love seems like something chemical and technical: hard to come by and then painful when you come by it. I'm too ugly, though, for anyone to really want me. I tried to stroke my dick, but it hurt. I took a shortcut across the stubblefield toward the cellar, which is on the far side of the yard. The earth was black, the grass gray. The clouds squirmed. The woods pressed close. It was gloomy and stuffy and shot through with gusts of cold wind. I jumped over the sausagerack and tzimzummed between the Germanmaple and the dragonbloodtree, the snakebranchspruce and the bokglobules. The hillside was covered in mushrooms: death caps and bleedingconifercrust, tremblingmerulius, devil's bolete, sickeners and many more. They were varying shades of ochre, rust, lampblack, and terracotta. When I got there, the cellar door was already open. Something gurgled and chuckled, it sounded too gruesome to be human.

– Who the fuck's there? I asked aloud.

– *Iäääh! Shub-Niggurath!* the terrifying thing howled.

– You'd better haulass back to Kokkola before I call Grandpa!

There was a shriek and then the sound of something writhing and pulsing down a tunnel. Then all was still.

– That's right—you don't get to play in our backyard, I sighed in relief.

Then, feeling so-so, I sank down onto the brown grass. Being Grandpa's child is like playing Russianroulette. Fear was doing a number on me, but there was no point in asking for help. I'm more afraid of Grandpa than anything else; that's because I crave his love. I drained the two mammothbeers I'd nabbed from some strangers. That put a little hair on my chest. After a moment, I was able to enter the cellar and turn on the gas. A flame leaped up, sending flickers pitterpattering down the passageway. It was sticky and rank. Most of what was down here had been hanging so long it was inedible. Whatever they'd once been, they'd definitely returned to their origins. A gooey string of grease snaked its way towards a hole in the floor. The meatlocker held a lot of crimcram: boysroomsmokers, greeneyedlouts, kwashiorkors—in other words, a lot of nipplesuckers were hanging from the dripping ceiling. After a moment, I found the kid Grandpa had jumped while the dolt was out trapping woodpeckers on Flakaberget. He was dangling from a meathook and wasn't especially pretty. He was about my age, only bigger. I had a hell of a time trying to pry him loose because the hook was caught in his ribs. Finally, though, I worked him free. It happened so quick that I fell backward and he landed on top of me. I couldn't drag him by the head, because Grandpa had taken such big hunks out of his neck that his skull would pop off. So I grabbed him by the ankles. When we finally made it out of the cellar, I turned off the gas and locked the door. Then I dragged him across the yard the same way I had come. I went as fast as I could, because I knew the others would get tired of waiting soon. I nearly got stuck in the hedge, but I pulled myself free. Exhausted, I finally tumbled into the bower. They all fell silent and stared at me. Grandpa twisted my nose without a word. He was cold and hard and I knew he'd been hitting the hooch. I tried to explain, but he pressed his death's head ring into my cheek until it drew blood.

– That's what a thirst for adventure and a hunger for knowledge will get you, he quipped.

– This meat looks ready to cook, Petunia said, drowning herself in ethanol. As long as he wasn't shitting himself when he died.

Fear makes the meat tough and bitter. Better to roast them alive, before they know what's happening.

– I'm sure he'll be fine, Eilert said.

– Just let me light the grill, Petunia said, wanting to show how capable she was. She emptied two fifty-kilo bags of walruspubes onto the two-meter-long grill. Next came a bottle-and-a-half of mouthwash. She downed the rest, since it was still "firewater." Good plan, except she lit the grill without taking her cigarillo out of her mouth. That's when the show got good. The fire leaped off the grill and landed in Petunia's tangled mane. She stumbled around, arms waving wild, while brightred blisters blossomed all over her face. The fire cackled merrily and the oldhag howled to highheaven. It probably hurt, but it was fucking hilarious to watch. Petunia's fiery blouse was itself a joy to behold; also the way her piggy flesh cracked and spit like fryingbacon. Grandpa looked on indifferently, but Eilert sprang up and pushed Petunia across the bricks and into our morayeelpond. He held her under the water until the fire was out. Good move, except that when Eilert pulled her up, she had a schweinfurtgreen, thighthick Beriamoray dangling from her chin. That didn't last long, though. With a little cooing and coddling, Grandpa got it to open its jaws and sink back into the fermenting pond. Then Eilert smeared ramlotion on Petunia's face and shoulders, and soon she was unconscious.

– Ah hell, complained Grandpa, making her down a few tins of a hundred-and-twenty-proof fermented Balticherringbroth.

– You look like hell, of course, but not really any worse than before. At least that's something.

– Goddamn you, Grandpa, whined Petunia. What happened to me? Why is my face so hot?

She was completely out of it. All we could do was play along.

– It was heatstroke, Momma, Eilert lied suavely. But I greased your burns with butterandhoney, and everything'll be fine again soon.

– I have to lie down, Petunia gasped and took a few tottering steps toward an inflatable Babar with three lubricated openings. At that, Grandpa played the good host and helped her down onto the squeaking plastic.

– I hope Frau Tjut gets her stiff and stately boxerman before her turn comes, she babbled and shut her singed eyes.

– No way, no how! Eilert exclaimed anxiously and flipped through a racingform.

– She'll be fine, Grandpa assured him. Petunia is about as perverse as a Khmer Rouge in a gospelchoir. She's cheated life, now she'll cheat death. But I have to get on with my boycarving.

– Do you need help? asked Eilert.

– Nah. The mite'll pitch in.

Buzzing like a drunken fly, Grandpa tossed the boy in the air, gripped him around the middle, and danced a Finnish gypsytango. We clapped time. Then he heaved the corpse onto the cuttingboard and broke the pelvis and shoulders so it would lay right. I helped him lash the body to the grill with steelwire. Then Grandpa gutted him. The bellystroke was nobly done. Small intestines welled out like lava or like a writhing mass of snakes. His large intestine was pale bluegreen, his stomachsack was shriveled. With dash and daring, Grandpa flipped out the liver and kidneys; he dug out the heart with true flare. Or maybe it was the pancreas and spleen, I can't remember. He rinsed the cavity with reindeerpee. Then he filled the little cretin up with Psilocybe cubensis, grannycream, and manastuffed diaperrolls.

Eilert and I helped sew the kid up and light the grill. The fire beat at our eyes, hot as a Papuan sauna.

– Spice to taste with gunpowder and wormwood, Grandpa instructed. Whip together some cayenne pepper and absinthe and splash it on. Turn him as much as you like, use the grillbrush to apply all the oil you want. By the way, the oil's made from a secret recipe I got from Emperor Bokassa. For the sake of longsuffering Jesus, though, don't burn the food or I'm not responsible for what'll happen next.

I volunteered for the job, even though I knew I was clumsy and weak. Grandpa took a piss, whistling something from *Madama Butterfly*. Then he settled himself into the seat of honor, lit a Morgoth and splashed half a liter of vitriol and tequila into a flowervase made from Saxon porcelain. Eilert stuck to sodawater with verdigris and morphine. He only smoked when he forgot himself.

– That jerkoff in the other division, what do you think about him?

– Who do you mean?

– Jim Klick, behind Speedy Blowjob.

– A laughingstock, Grandpa declared, utterly selfassured.

– What do you think about Sune P. Limpas saying that in the coldbloodedheat he'll finish between Breker and Poor Dobbin?

– Onguard with Perrudja for sure. Last I heard, he cannonballed twenty-nine-and-a-half down the track and did it hoofless and with a drunk jockey.

– North Swede horses are fucking thickdicked, Petunia said suddenly, not bothering to open her eyes. Negritos in nigredo . . .

– They just insist on having their Filly Division, Eilert complained. At sixteen hundred and forty . . . It's so fucked up, you wanna weep blood.

– Verily I say unto thee, Today shalt thou be with me in paradise.
I snickered to myself and oiled the boy up as if my life depended
on it. I knew that Grandpa had never backed a winning horse. But
he wastes ten thousand a week on it, sometimes much more.

– Messalina might be a possibility, but her form is as questionable as Celan's.

– Jewdevil, snuffled Petunia.

– I prefer Céline, admitted Grandpa. And Petiot . . . Unfortunately, I think that Simian Cunt will overtake her on the inside,
so Brazar might as well run himself off a cliff. He's cooked . . . Pa-
siphae will do okay coming up the rear and Stig H'son's Stig H'son,
so Color Queen's got a shot at the finish, despite her handicap.
Semiramis has been in rut, so there's no telling about her. Like as
not, Shekhinah will turn out to be a thorn in everyone's ass . . .

– You don't like Steaming Snatch?

– Not a bit. Can't hold out on the inside.

– Who would you put your money on, then?

– Fat Fuck from Gärdsmygsmark is riding Kolli, but his position's terrible. It's a fucking shitrace that ought to be totally covered with Dazed and Confused, Hog's Dong, Lobotomy Lobell,
and Freak Show.

– And Bronze? I'd pegged Katyn Forest myself!

– You're on the right track! He flew from sixteenth position
on the outside to get past Oradour at sixteen to one! The third
track behind the starting car goes smooth as a nippercock into a
lubed toiletpaperrole. If he flounders, Åke Svinstedt and Zyklon B.
might do something. Of course, Sharpeville, Shatila, My Lai, and
Kolyma Vacation all might have beginners' luck.

– Class III against Class I then?

– Gamble on every horse you can afford and then some! Oracular Orifice has class, but he does his best work at the head, which he'll never get to, so. Olle Boop will trounce the Gobbler, you mark my words. He's been gone six weeks, though, and the fourth track's the worst imaginable. Mau-Mau, Nice Rape, Chicken's Bladder, Potlatch Poodle, and the Coroner have all got the same chance. You can't dismiss the rest, either.

– All right, I took your advice, Granpageezer! We'll see just how psychic you really are.

– Thanks to me, handsome, you'll hit so hard, you'll be able to buy all the love on the market.

For shits and grins I checked the results on Sunday:

Sec. I. Filly Div., nr. 2 Bum Pus.

Sec. II. Class II, nr. 6 Gangrene.

Sec. III. Coldblood., nr. 1 Hairybeaver.

Sec. IV. Gold Div., nr. 9 Package

Sec. V. Bronze Div., nr. 5 Jasenovac.

Sec. VI. Class III against Class 1, nr. 1 Aiwass.

Grandpa had done it again. V-6 paid out two hundred thousand, but Eilert never brought it up.

KVASIR—God of poetry and wisdom in Norse mythology, created from the combined saliva of all the gods; his blood was used to make the Mead of Poetry

Vera Renczi—A Romanian socialite, who in the 1920s seduced and murdered thirty-five men, and then stored them in zinc-lined coffins in her cellar

Shabbetai Tzvi and Nathan of Gaza—Shabbetai Tzvi was a manic-depressive self-proclaimed Messiah who in the 1660s started large-scale uprisings among Jews the world over; it was through Nathan of Gaza's preaching that Shabbetai first became convinced of his mission

Galut—in Kabbalistic terms, the world in exile, deprived of God's mercy

Kelipot—the realms of darkness

ebene—hallucogenic drug used by the Yanomamo Indians in the Amazon

tzimtzummed—tzimzum: the idea that God contracted and withdrew Himself, in order to "make room" for creation

Bok globule—dark cloud of dust and gas where stars are formed

Shub-Niggurath—read old H.P. . . .

Kokkola—town in Finland

Psilocybe cubensis—a hallucinogenic mushroom, probably identical to the Indo-European Soma, the source of holy ecstasy

Petiot—Marcel Petiot, Parisian doctor, three years younger than Céline; murdered by injection around seventy people who were trying to flee Nazi-occupied France; Petiot told them they would need to be vaccinated in order to emigrate, injected them with cyanide, and then took their belongings

Jasenovac—World War II Croatian concentration camp

XIX

Today we went into Kåge and tried to prostitute ourselves at the foundry. But the proletarian bullocks wouldn't play along.

– It's the dogdays of summer. It makes them priggish, Grandpa said reassuringly.

– Doesn't matter anyway, you fucking pricks! he hissed at the foreman, who was throwing us out.

Down in front of the foundry, goldbrown, frothtipped wavelets lapped at the river's rough black boulders. Thistles and nettles lined our path, which led to the bridge. As we crossed the river, I looked between the boards at the black vortex that gurgled and churned away below us, a skinny, washedout kid, naked from the waist down, wearing an oversized cardigan patterned with vipers. Life's a ghastly affair—I'd never make it without Grandpa. I only wish he'd say he liked me every now and then. The water at the bridge's base was calmer. A newborn intestineshimmering Lapp baby in a birchbarkbasket was floating there. It'd probably made it all the way from the Kågeälven's unknown source. A miracle. Not that it was much longer for this world. A hundred-kilo pike awkwardly glided up from the river's muddy bottom and crunched basket and newborn between its divinely beautiful jaws. It was fucking hilarious, but Grandpa was in one of those moods. He punched me in the small of my back and started yelling.

– What the fuck are you looking at?! Keep moving, or I'll give you something straight out of Brueghel and Bosch!

I kept moving, since I'd rather keep it like Bauer and Beskow. From the bridge, we could see the ravaged village square. Overhead the sun was blotchy, the sky was watery, the earth was the color of old skin. Summer was wheezing its last, and the soursweet dusk of a late summer day closed around this smokeeating town like an ulcered mouth around a cankersore. The sky was a chamberpot upended over an embonpoint landscape. The area around the church was overgrown with weeds, but the bush down by the river was tamer. Roots hung helterdeeskelter over the gouged-out, ratinfested bank. In Kåge, the grass is always yellower; the buildings look like they were built in the blink of a blind man's eye. Every house is a different color, they're built wherever people get the whim to build them. Kåge's a boil on the butt of the Bay of Bothnia, and the folk in these parts are a homicidal bunch. They've got ostisch and fälisch strains in them, most of them think that the meaning of life's in spreading garbage around and polluting as much as possible. They're vultures, most wear kerchiefs to parties. They love dirtyjobs, and in their freetime, they like to lay back and gobble dicks. They begrudge everyone everything, they're quick to anger and quicker in bed. Bigmouthed, but small between the legs. They're coarse and mean. Rude and prude. In Kåge, existence is an open saltandpeppered wound, and they kill joy wherever they find it, no one has the cowballs to do otherwise. The true Kågeborner is slackjawed and secondrate, content to go behind his neighbor's back and talk trash. They fuck women, but never redheads. And their faith in bwana Namnam is highly adequate.

– Kåge is an udumucavern blessed by Satan, Grandpa said during the trip from Helvetesliden, and there's something to that. The most remarkable thing Kåge ever produced is Margot Wallström, and that's saying a helluva lot.

When we were approaching the river's north bank, Grandpa pointed out one of the area's main attractions, which was located about a hundred and fifty meters upstream from where we were standing: over the years, around two hundred suicidecorpses had gotten stuck in the barbedwiretangle that borders Eelspit, and there they stew to this day.

– My old flame's down there, Mauritz Hamilton, Grandpa reminisced. He went down into the river sometime in the mid thirties, thought he was going hetero. We had a honeysweet romance in old man Wonkowaara's loo. You see, being laidback and easygoing is its own reward.

We strolled nonchalantly toward Sällberg's Meat and Gristle, hoping to run across Pulli and Nyllet. When we knocked, though, all we got was Vivo, wrinkled as a wet ballsack and with a ciggi dangling from each nostril.

– Wherethehell's Pulli and Nyllet? Grandpa demanded.

– Hooked up to respirators. Suicidepact. Tried to suffocate each other with their dicks.

– Ooh, that's horrible! Grandpa screeched, lighting a ciggibutt, whatever could've gotten into them? Nyllet was so fucking sugarysweet, he had peachfuzz inside of him! And Pulli, Godforbid! he was just made to suck you deep!

– Too true, Vivo smiled.

– How long have you two been married? Grandpa croaked, ashing in Vivo's hair.

– Don't really know. But now it looks like I'm all by my lonesome, she said, scratching her crotch.

– But Vivo, you old bonedry cowcunt, you wouldn't happen to know if Ditti or Amos would be up for a little harmless flirtation, would you? said Grandpa, warbling like a fucking swingkid.

– I heard Ditti was shitting himself after he let himself be duped into some gang hankypanky with a group of Polacks down by the docks, all for a keg of beer. And Amos just moved in with Björn-motherhexer. As of now, he's only got eyes for one.

– What about Gammsagge Ahlgren, the organgrinding queer?

– All he wants to do nowadays is pretty up young Mormon boys, cackled Vivo. But you can try it with Tattar-Torsten up in Högsen, I hear he's like a cat in heat.

– Hell no, I'd rather diddle a woman, Grandpa blasphemed.

– You sweet man, I've always said there's no finer gent in all of Kågedell than old Grandpageezer, Vivo lisped and licked her lips. That got Grandpa shaking in his boots. Just to be safe, he beat her with his cane until she swayed, lost her wig, and collapsed. Then we hauled ass back across the bridge.

– Hell, that Vivo's nasty as Old Nick, I squeaked.

Grandpa was trembling so bad he'd pissed his snowboots.

– I thought it was all over, mite, he finally stammered. Did you see her eyefucking me? I never thought I'd live to see the day when it was so hard to drum up a little action around here.

– We can hide in the bushes around the kindergarten and snap up a boy or two to fondle, I suggested.

– Nah, I've lost the urge, Grandpa sighed. Women—they just make me limp. But pull up a chair and listen here. What say you go and nab us some bacon and old Swissrolls and then we'll surprise Hilding Dahlgren at the old folk's home. Oh, and if they've got issue twenty-nine of *My Life's Novel*, grab it. Meet me at the church afterward, I like to shit in peace! He was still yelling as I made my way to the supermarket to nab what we needed.

I watched out for the girls making faces at me, but then I almost got lost. Behind the parish house a tobaccopug was tonguing a kidneystone buyer from Istermyrliden. At that same moment, a tbs. of people came dripping out of Kågebadet's gates and shrieked and laughed at me. A few of them picked up rocks and gave chase. When they caught me, they punched me in the stomach and kicked me in the head.

When I woke up, they were gone. Luckily, the church was close by. I went inside and immediately got hot. Grandpa was sitting on the altar chainsmoking. His pants were down around his knees, those long legs of his were hanging loose, and God's house was chockfull of his uncleanness. But he was pissy and kept his distance.

– You took your time! he exclaimed, coughing a Dzerzhinsky cough and boxing my ear.

– I had to suck J.O. at the hardware store to get some of this paint thinner, I said defensively.

– Is that right? Grandpa asked, clearing his throat. Now clean me.

I tonguescrubbed his sweetspot until he started to protest.

– Okay, cowboy, enough with the fine tuning!

He pulled up his pants and snuffed his ciggi out on Jesus's left nipple.

– Now we'll see what Hilding's good for, Grandpa declared and spit in a churchwarden's eye on his way out.

The river murmured in heat. Kåge's center spread itself out. There's no library anymore, instead there's a video store. They also have a paint store and a newskiosk. We passed a reservebarracks where the future of the town had left weekendengravings and spatterpaintings. . "Luge sucks shit" . . . "Kåge by night, full of fight, Kåge by day, girlie and gay" . . .

People Against the Missionary Position had set up a snuff- and splatterfilm booth directly in front of the Belial office of the local Demonsbureau. Homo-Lage and Wanker-Helge were working the counter. We joined the group of inbred apemen listening openmouthed to the pompous bullshit spouted by the lot from Skellefteå. I recognized "Cowberry," "Wolfman," "The Quack," "Chevve," and "Moans a lot" in the crowd.

– Raoul Wallenberg's alive, his death's a conspiracy, Lage was grandstanding. He lives! I know it! Sure as Jesus Christ shot his wad on the cross! As he babbled, he lit a licorice ciggarette. Me and Helge met him in Finlandferry on Pentecost. He was calling himself Inez and making a living blowing pens through a straw with his ass, and telling fortunes by consulting balls.

– But Lage, Bjuuv interrupted, with a becoming hint of feeblemindedness in his voice, how the hell can you be sure it was Raoul?

– Because he was him! shouted Lage, starting to get riled up.

– I've been with tons of guys who claimed they were Raoul Wallenberg, old tumor-for-a-toupee bragged.

– You're way too pretty for that, Helge said mockingly, screwing up his chloasmically blotched face. By the devil, you AIDS-riddled swine, if you sucked cock as well as you lied, what more would we need? That doxy we met was the Grauballe Man, though, you can believe Lage the Lip when he says that it was Raoul. And you know what Wallenberg told me, just between us four balls: Nothing can match a foul, fleshy Finn feeling peckish for a good old slaughtertango. Then he taught me gutter Finnish and got Lage and me to like lappwaltzing with our lappcocks. He was so sweet I felt like a little girl all over again!

– Aw, you've got so much love in you, Wanker-Helge, said Frusse. But what was he like? How did he look?

– Well, Raoul's scrawny and nervous, but he's got motherofpearl skin and eyes like amber. He has bite marks on his chin and forehead. He doesn't have any feelings, but he cries at the drop of a hat.

– And the guy has tried everything, continued Homo-Lage. One day he was a mongoloid, then an absentminded professor, and after that he really needed to take a shit.

– Limpcocks and dryfucks! Grandpa said in a halfwhisper. Come on, mite, let's leave the whores to their filthy jabbering.

We walked past the supermarket with hate beating down the back of our necks. As we passed, I read some of the headlines.

"Queen Bee Silvia: Fuck it all!"
"New Hope for Bisected Seamstress"
"Ingemar Stenmark and Björn Borg Having Love Child"
"Ibrahim, the Centipede, Dead"
"Shocking pictures: Loffe Breastfeeding Hagge!"

"Oldsberg and Melander No Longer in the Running"
"Tumba Refuses to Jerk off King!"
"Dalai Lama Has Great Faith in Stig H. and Nasty Faggot"
"The 100 Poorest Swedes: Pictures and Facts"
"Barbro of Surahammar: I've tried to commit suicide 110 times"
"Bengt Westerberg Single Again: I love loving to the sound of a heartsick, squalling babe."

Our brains were buzzing like bees in a macramé pie when we finally snuck into the old age home and knocked on Hilding's door.

– Who's there? he rattled.

– Erik O., grunted Grandpa, disguising his voice.

– And someone else who wants to talk to you, I said, playing along.

– Whatdoyouwantwithme, you demons? Hilding whimpered, cracking the door and peering out with bloodshot eyes. I didn't order no meatwagon.

– Just Mengele and Streicher here to play a little game of two on three.

– Nonononono, grimaced the ravaged face, not gonna happen!

– God Hilding, you poor scoundrel, don't you recognize me, Grandpa cackled and forced his way in.

– We used to be joined at the hip, he continued coaxingly.

When we entered the room, Hilding Dahlgren, who was stark naked, wobbled and staggared around in a wet, oozing morass of shit and vomit.

– But what on earth, he clamored, rubbing his pupasack, his nipples going stiff with fear.

– Get a hold of yourself, have you gone schizo? Grandpa asked, embracing him. Hey there, Grandpa soothed, don't you remember me?

– But is it possible that you've really come to visit after all these years, Hilding snuffled. It just makes me want to cry, he went on in a smokeychokey voice. God bless you, Grandpa, for thinking of a poor old man! he moaned and grabbed Grandpa's chainlinksuspenders so hard he pulled him over.

– You've become kinda chubby, but otherwise you haven't changed a bit, Grandpa choked out.

– And you're a consumptive, wasted fuck, just like you always were, cackled Hilding. But plop yourself down, welcome to my rathole, make youself at home, he said and pulled himself off the floor. Black coffee's all I've got, if that'll do.

– Don't bother about coffee! I said politely.

– And who's this little shit? Hilding glared, suddenly enraged.

– I brought my calf with me, Grandpa explained and pinched my ass. In case you're in the mood. You still got sauce in that old bag?

– Don't take this the wrong way, Grandpageezer, but these days they ring the churchbells for a miracle if I happen to get blood in my cock. Now that I'm old, I shrivel up when some tyke grabs my fly and puckers on up. And that's the truth.

– I know just what you mean, the same thing's happened to me, Grandpa lied and started telling him what we'd been up to.

– Hell, you need a drink! Hilding exclaimed. And I could use a nip myself, he said. You know, I was sure it was the crimcram coming to take away my nearest and dearest. I thank God for the day that He gave me Leatherbeaver here, Hilding proclaimed sanctimoniously and fingerfucked the pulsing mooseass that had been his only sexpartner for countless years. I hit him over by Twelve Meter Basin, and no devil alive's going to take him from me. Over my dead body! Anyway, get ready for a smoker, he said, rooting around in the mountain of bottles in the living room.

– You know, Kosken and Explorer are for old aunties. Give me Hormoslyr and antifreeze any day, Hilding babbled. But you'll see! Drink your fill, don't be shy, he called out.

The two old men took swigs that made their bodies shudder and thrash. Me—I dipped my blanky in paint thinner and enjoyed the sweet, sweet aroma.

– Hilding, my friend, Grandpa said, as he stretched, we brought along some snacks we'd be willing to share.

– Show me what you've got, Hilding hiccupped, staring glassy-eyed, as I opened the basket and displayed the goodies. Rotten vealbrawn and pickled pigdick! And an old Swissroll! All this tasty stuffy for me? Thanks, thankyouthankyou, he stammered. But for the life of me, I don't know how I'm going to keep these treats down, since I can't even stomach dumplings, he complained and pointed to some enormous throatpuslumps, which had gone right through him. Each of them was as big as two clenched fists, had been swallowed whole, and were smeared with grease.

– Once a wackjob, always a wackjob, Grandpa sighed.

– Yeah, you are what you are, you can't fart freely and be anal-retentive all at once, Hilding agreed and scratched at his head of German hair.

– Que será será, sweety, Grandpa muttered, taking a long drag from his ciggi and flicking ash on my fontanelle.

Señor Dahlgren set the table and Grandpa blessed our meal.

– Hold up, boy, you're like a magpie over entrails, Hilding yelped, when he saw my mouth start to water.

– Big eyes, small gullet, Grandpa said sarcastically and rammed a fork into the roof of my mouth.

– The eyes say yes, the shithole no, Hilding declared, joining the fun.

Grandpa went at it like he was starving, but Hilding's rotten piehole played it delicate.

– I have to take it slow, he admitted shamefully. Back in the day, oldfarts didn't even have the heart to eat when food was actually plentiful. They'd have rather seen it go bad.

– The higher and mightier you get, the harder you fall, Grandpa chirped and wiped his mouth with the same rag Hilding's guests used to dry their diarreacunts. You got anything stronger than this damned babypiss? he snorted, sending Hilding back to the pile of bottles.

– How about a schnapps, you old devil, Hilding coughed, wrapping a shitsmeared fist around his limp cock. Landrucognac, Kürtenvodka, and Druittgin!

– What the fuck? Have you gotten yourself saved? Grandpa asked in astonishment.

– Yessiree.

– God's a man with marrow in his bones and sunshine in his eyes, Grandpa testified. He's got bad breath, worse skin, superior manners, a delicate voice, and glasses. He's ugly in a cute way, insanely funny, and pretty old for his age.

– Half of what you say excites me, the other half scares me, Hilding said, sweettalking his guest.

– You choking up, you old codger? Grandpa asked and mixed himself a misogynistdrink. We're sworn bloodbrothers, remember? How about that time we spread ourselves open for Tore Hedin?

– I remember it well, Grandpa, and I bet you remember how pretty I was back then!

– You were sweet as a dead girl, Grandpa lied sourly and sipped at his drink.

– Right you are, Hilding proudly declared, smearing his infected ballsack with a salve of mashed pissants. But Tore Hedin was a real wackjob, he continued. He wanted me to do stupid, perverse stuff to his junk, so I put a stop to it.

– Tore was a queer one, easy to piss off, Grandpa reminisced.

– But when he hooked up with that old cow, that was just too much. But apples and oranges, different strokes and all that, he nodded sagaciously, inflated by his own wisdom. Then his tone turned maudlin. I told my boy, though, that no matter what life throws at you, don't you take up with any girlypigs, because by Satan that'll be the death of me!

– Too fucking perverted! Not a word more! shrieked Hilding in drunken terror, covering his ratgnawed earflaps with shaking hands.

Grandpa took him on his knee, hushing and cooing until everything was good again. Hilding crawled across the compostfloor and took a swig of something or other.

– Too bad daddy's not alive today, he flung out. He was so fucking horny he brought home the village idiot. And one time he fucked Palo Spanish-style and pretended she was a he.

– Old Hilding was too much, chuckled Grandpa in nostalgic appreciation. "How long, how wide?" he nagged like the devil's own idiot. He was like a broken record: your member should be short, thin, white, knotty, and supple, that's what he'd say every time someone admired his own huge, redeyed donkeyballs.

– Papa's back was always straight as a board, Hilding said, plopping down on a messy taboret. Poor guy always had the worst luck, he gasped. But by all the possessed wretches who sucked Jesus Christ's bigone, do you remember the time we decided to rape Miller-Olle?!

– Oh, you! cackled Grandpa, getting goosebumps. You should know, you little shedevil, he smiled spitefully and caressed my ass, that even when I was a girlylad licking the cream from my own Grandpa's cock, sex without violence was like thumbing a numb lappdick. So you can believe that I was all ohsweetLordhavemercy when whatthefuckshisname Hilding said: let's go and get our claws in old Mill-Olle. That was back in the good old days, when we were still nubile and sly.

– You're fine the way you are now, Grandpa, I piped up tactfully.

– Go suck cunt! snapped Grandpa, mostly for the sake of appearances.

– It was a Sunday evening in a morbidly obese summer and I was perky and Hilding was all dolled up. We were crawling on all fours through Brylle's yamfields, deadly afraid of aging dancingslags. We had blueballs that ached like the nails through Christ's hands getting nailed to the cross. By Satan, old Olle was going to get a shot in the rathole! When we got to the mill, we heard him humming and acting busy, and that was his mistake. I knocked on the mill door and, suddenly, it went quiet for a long time. He was probably hiding his dirty magazines, he liked *Donkey Love and Daisy Chain*, near as I remember. But the coward was cunning and he put on airs.

– "Who are you?" he squeaked. "The three little pigs!" Hilding rumbled. "Are not! You're just teasing me. Say who you are!" "The good Samaritan," I giggled and then Hilding broke into the floursack room. I followed him, prancing pony that I was. I was already loosening my belt and old Olle looked like he was about to cry.

– He hadn't been such a fraidycat since Folke Bernadotte came to town, Hilding cut in with a slippery grin.

– "Who are you? I gotta get my hair cut!" the miller boy gasped, eyes like ashtrays, Grandpa continuined. "Don't get your panties in a wad," I said and that was it for the pleasantries. Hilding kicked him in the stomach so hard he puked up a waterrat and a catechism. Then Hilding dragged off his hopinbed jersey and pinioned him, while I pulled out his teeth with a pair of pliers. We threw him in a seedtrough and started loving him up. Hilding fucked him in the mouth and I took him in the ass and then we switched holes.

– Mother Teresa, you dryteated sow, we sure whored it up in Olle's virginflesh, Hilding gushed, laying his arms around Grandpa's neck. We sure raised the roof! And I think it was good for old Olle, too! Because, Lord bless me, how he howled!

– That's what we came for, all right, Grandpa said, and that's why, after a smokebreak, we decided to torture him. "A sour stab follows a sweet scratch," as I used to tell Grandma when she was alive. But Olle's squealing and groaning was starting to give me a headache. But since he was a real classact, he got the beating he deserved.

– Is there anything sweeter than forcing someone, who's begging to die, to go ahead and live? sneered Hilding and put Grandpa's right hand on his Jewscrew.

– We crowned him with a Tyrolese hat, just for shits and grins, laughed Grandpa. Then we fried his dick in a pot of boiling syrup. Hilding frenched him and bit off his tongue, right in the middle of a leechkiss, surely you remember that?

– Mmmhmm, Hilding said, amused. Suddenly he vomited up a meter of his intestines and had to push them back down his throat, bubbling blood.

– He got a broken bottle up his asshole, and then we fucked him in the eye until he died, Grandpa said. Miller-Olle was a repulsive devil all right, he jeered and lit a Rönnskärsciggi. The spitting image of Mikhaylov. People said his own Grandpa's ass was an open invitation for Schuvaloff when the Russians played army with the Kåge boys during the old war, Grandpa continued, talking trash with an epicurian glint in his deadeyes. The Satancunt probably had Ruskyblood in him.

Hilding snorted blood and rubbed his rotten cock with an alcoholsoaked strip of bacon. He was bitter that neither Grandpa's dirtytalk nor his spotted hand could make his kidbeater stand up straight. Grandpa saw how it was and knew that pretty soon Hilding was going to lose it. He put his arms around the upchucked skunkboa's skinny shoulders and began buttoning up his crowhued blazer. Finally, he brushed the ash off his pink linen pants and fastened on his SS cap.

– Hilding darling, he whispered and held Hilding's scabby hand against his sunken chest. I'm afraid I'll be called home before we get the chance to mess around again. We could've had a good time, but you've gotten too fine for me. Now, now, he soothed when Hilding began to roar like a boar, you're not long for this world, either. Be a good boy, Hilding, promise to take care of yourself.

We left Hilding Dahlgren foaming at the mouth and crawling across the floor with a nice piece by the GöingeGirls playing on the radio. The summer evening was soaked in sweat. Kåge's air is always saturated with a primatefear. Grandpa unbuttoned his pants, squatted down, and took a shit. He caught the two gleaming sausages before they could drop, pulled up his pants and smeared the crap in some àlamoder's hairdo as she walked on by with her nose in the air. When she yelped, he suckerpunched her. Then we strolled on . . .

– You got a light? asked a skinny young drunk, and Grandpa doused him with ethanol and lit a match. We waited at the bus stop while he burned. Grandpa began to tell a story.

– It was a raw February morning in the Whoregod's year of 1945, and me and Dirlewanger were partying in the orphanage's ruins. "You know that Himmler's balls taste like apricots, right?" he asked.

– "The fuck you say?!"

– "I swear. I heard about it when I served in" . . . But wait, is that Jalle driving the bus? He'll probably make a pass at us. Hurry up, boy, let's see if he's hungry . . .

BAUER AND BESKOW—John Bauer and Elsa Beskow were Swedish children's book artists

OSTISCH AND FÄLISCH—East European and Phalian respectively, from Hans F. K. Günther's studies on race

BWANA NAMNAM—Jesus Christ

UDUMUS—a beast-man race that Jörg Lanz von Liebenfels identified on the Assyrian King Salmanassar's black obelisk: hairy, half-stooped

MARGOT WALLSTRÖM—former vice-president of the European Commission

MY LIFE'S NOVEL—Mitt livs novell, literally "The Book of My Life," a women's magazine in the 1970s that gave sex advice

DZERZHINSKY COUGH—hacking cough, named for Felix Dzerzhinsky, first director of the Soviet secret police

KOSKEN—Koskenkorva Viina, a clear Finnish spirit

EXPLORER—a popular Swedish vodka

HOMOSLYR—a pesticide

GERMAN HAIR—soft, pliable wooly hair is said to be German, in Sweden

LANDRUCOGNAC, KÜRTENVODKA, AND DRUITTGIN—Henri Désiré, Peter, and Montagu, respectively: renowned killers of women; Druitt was even suspected of being Jack the Ripper

TORE HEDIN—Sweden's worst mass murderer

FOLKE BERNADOTTE—Swedish diplomat and nobleman

I GOTTA GET MY HAIR CUT!—said Red Rudi Dutschke, reportedly, after Josef Bachmann sent three bullets into him in 1968

SCHUVALOFF—commander of a Russian army division that operated in Västerbotten in the war of 1808–1809

XX

The monthly mail had come . . . which annoyed Grandpa something fierce . . .

– Bunk and drivel . . . demands, threats, summons . . . collections
and distraints . . . preliminary investigations and surcharges . . .
seven thousand in back taxes . . . Flat-out rejection of my applica-
tion to be fancyfree . . . A certificate from NAMBLA . . . a premature
Christmas cards from Leuchter, Swaggart, and Schwarzkopf . . .
and Gudrun Schyman . . .

He poured more Cheetos onto a Kefir plate and sprinkled them
with Ajax. Then he continued ripping open his letters, already disappointed beforehand.

– Norstedts wants me to describe my longsuffering death . . . two
million in advance . . . then ten thousand kroner a page . . . Extra
bonus for ultraviolence and hypersex . . . The devils are asking for
a "concise backwater tone" . . . Who do they think they're dealing
with . . . Burroughs and Bukowski! Writing's like masturbating
without fingers . . . But look, I'm being honored for my article on
Baudrillard and Bataille in *Merkur* and *La Quinzaine littéraire* . . .
A white flag from the world's Jews via Mordecai Gottleben . . . An

offer of credit, three billion from Dai-Bitching Kangyo Bank . . . if I stop abusing Japs and Jews, that is . . . A check for twenty-five thousand, because I'm so sad and lonely . . . from the Sigrid Visent Memorial Fund for Indigent Bastards . . . The latest issue of *Boy Butcher* . . . Two books: Segev's *Soldiers of Evil*, that's about the worst concentrationcamp commanders, and Tankred Koch's *History of Executioners* . . . Bonniers isn't interested in my translation of the *Bibliomystikon* into Lappish . . . But here's something nice . . . Gunnar sent a bunch of newly discovered bugs from the Upper Xingu River . . . We'll look at them later . . .

Grandpa set the rhombusshaped piece of cardboard aside and sighed.

– An invitation from Michael Aquino and the Temple of Set . . . They want me to come to Wewelsburg and lead the ceremonies . . . I guess I could throw something together about the battle of the birch treeorsomething...AthankyoufromArtosPublishinginSkellefteå... "Without YOUR participation the collected Meister Eckhart sermons wouldn't have been possible!" . . . blahblahblah! who the hell cares . . . They should've been nice and sent me a rosycheeked cherub instead . . . I could've played Tiberius and the little fish . . . that little game Suetonius gossiped about . . . The cops want my expert expertise on an investigation into sexual attacks on children . . . An inquiry about whether I want to defend my S&M title . . . An offer to lead a course called "Trashing the Swedish Language" . . . The usual private weekly update from Peter Arnett . . . And last and certainly least, a picture postcard from Astro Lindgren . . . "I don't know where I am . . . life sucks and I'm scared . . ." And here we have the latest diagnosis from the hospital . . . they've called in the bigguns from Jerrold Post's Center for the Analysis of Personality and Political Behavior to help them . . . I really worked up all the psychiatrists they sent to "help" me . . . They think I'm "an evil, phallic narcissist" with "necrophiliac tendencies" . . . A "schizophrenic solopsist" filled with "demonic rage, an insane thirst for revenge, and a wild contempt for the entire human race" . . . They talk about "total alienation," "paranoid and sociopathic tendencies," "sexual psychosis," and "a fetishization of violence" . . . Poppycock and twaddle! . . . Up one side and down the other . . . contradictory bullshit . . . The only thing wrong with me is that I never got enough beatings or love . . .

Grandpa lit a Salem, took it out of his mouth, and stuffed in a horde of marzipanpiggies. He seemed apathetic and absent-minded. I slurped up the last of my oatmeal from the shallow bottom of my lucky plate. I'm not allowed to take milk or butter, but there was a little gunoil left, so I smeared it on a piece of sweetbread. Then I drank some Salubrin.

– Every letter, every telephone conversation, every visit, just another nail in my cross, Grandpa said, when he'd finally swallowed. People exist only to be corrupted and killed . . . I've spent my entire life leading the battle against humanity . . . The humananimal has had his time in the spotlight . . . Now he'll have to eat what he's puked up . . . He's done the best he could . . . haircare and guidance on language usage . . . charters and therapies . . . cuntbrains . . . sisnadevas . . . orgasmaggregates . . . I'll see their backs against the wall, I promise you that, Lustolito . . .

Grandpa exaggerates, but most of the time there's something to what he says. Unfortunately, what came next made me want to laugh. Some say he's fickle, but I don't buy that . . . I know his game. He doesn't always mean what he says.

– Grief, hate, and shame . . . They're the pillars of the Krishnan throne . . . Life's got three billion years by the scruff of the neck . . . Our screwball Creator's great idea . . . Always the same old song . . . Kill, fuck, eat, shit . . . Hate, howl, carcass, fetus . . . Cum, blood, flesh, death . . . Struggle, bluff, fear, nausea . . . How strange we never get fed up . . . Long to get away . . . Look for something a little less garish. . . Life just leaves you hanging . . .

He smeared grease and snot on a rotting scab, glanced up, and saw that nothing ever changed . . . All was lost . . . Blueblack clouds were piling up, the wind shook the grumbling Worldtree. Evening here is always just around the corner. We don't see the sun until it's on its way down.

– Nasty looking clouds, I said. Looks like it's going to be one hell of a folkstorm.

– Evil's dark spirits, hosts, and principalities infecting the sky! Coming to take away the Philistines and Pharisees . . .

Grandpa moistened his thumb, gathered up a few golden breadcrumbs, and licked lips that would never be clean. Then he took some dirty swigs from a flask of Polish robberrum.

– Kids should be raised by animals . . . Jackels and baboons . . . otherwise, you just end up with crybabies . . . Sade's the only writer who knew anything about love . . . Read, laugh, and enjoy . . . Laban and Åby are traitors . . . Piss is good . . . Hegel's easy . . .

Grandpa's hopscotching thoughts had stopped confusing me a long time ago. Logic is the first thing you've got to let go, if you want to be a Grandpa. "Logic is for whores, lawyers, diplomats, bankers, technologues, and professors . . . the earth's damned!" he once said. "What's more logical than an emancipated pussy?!" he liked to joke. "You should only use the genius God cursed you

with for tirades and diatribes . . . persiflage and pejoratives . . .
interjections and imperatives . . . impulses and intuitions . . . id-
iosyncrasies stewed in internalsecretions . . . Just blasphemy and
abuse . . ."

– I hate everything . . . Everything I know and everything that
exists, everything I've dreamed and everything that could've been
and wasn't . . . I despise all the rest . . . Sweden's cultural heritage
would all fit in your average cunt . . . and that's where it belongs,
too . . . we're gakis . . . wimps . . . archaebacteria in our festering
sulphurate are our ancestors . . . World history reached its high-
point with the Indian Thuggees . . . the Children's Crusades of
1212, the Black Death and the Taiping Rebellion were good times,
too . . . "Memoirs of the Kalda Railroad" was Kafka's best work . . .
On the Jewish Question was the best the eldest Marx brother had
to offer . . . And so the apodictic linedance continues . . . The day
should just surrender . . . it usually does, if you just wait a bit . . .
windblasted and feckless, no thought for Papa Death . . . The days
are getting harder to get through, though . . . they cling like bur-
docks and ticks. . . it's worse than Surt . . . I surveyed the remains . . .
the world is out there somewhere . . . so they say . . . This can't be
the real world . . . I'm sure of it . . . This is the evening county . . .
Octoberland . . . night's domain . . . the heart of darkness. . . The
world is full of beasts in cages. . .jigaboos and gringos . . . No doubt
they're quick and bold . . . tightfisted and hardpressed . . . busy as
bees and hard at work . . . Nothing but ninetofive, thedailygrind,
productivity and stress . . . They love doing business . . . breeding
and traveling abroad . . . sure, there's a lot of hustleandbustle going
on, but part of it must be goodnatured . . . They're also progressive
and prominent, emancipated and renowned . . . Quite a few know

quite a lot . . . they've got real purpose . . . good looks . . . They're different than me and Grandpa . . . Sorcerers and organgrinders . . . crooners and streetcornerperformers . . . Everything in the big wide world just goes its own way . . . a lot of strife . . . A hullabaloo jamboree . . . Once you've got the devil in your boat, all you can do is row to shore . . . And there's a cunt in every harbor . . . That's a given . . . But if you come from the wild country, you better think twice about venturing out . . . into the world . . . the city . . . I mean, it'd be pretty ridiculous . . . just look at Samsara Lidman and Poas Enqvist . . . This here is more than enough for us . . . The fact is, it's almost too much to bear . . . I cleaned up and then went to the john to see if I could shit . . . Grandpa came to the door and watched me work . . . he didn't say a word . . . what the fuck's there to say . . . he just shook his head and went to lay down . . .

LEUCHTER—Fred: author of the Leucther Report, which denies the mass murder by gas of the Jews during the Holocaust

SWAGGART—Jimmy: TV evangelist

GUDRUN SCHYMAN—Swedish politician and feminist

NORSTEDT—Swedish publishing house

TIBERIUS AND THE LITTLE FISH—according to Suetonius, emperor Tiberius played this lascivious "game" in his self-chosen "exile" on Capri

SISNADEVAS—phallus-worshipppers, possibly temple concubines (among numerous other conflicting interpretions of the word)

LABAN AND ÅBY—Former coaches for the Swedish national soccer team

SURT—a figure in Norse mythology who will play a major role in the events of Ragnarök

BIBLIOMYSTIKON—Lanz von Liebenfels's Bible commentary

MICHAEL AQUINO—Colonel in the United States Army who helped to found the Temple of Set

TEMPLE OF SET—Satan worshipping Nazi cult

BATTLE OF THE BIRCH—an old Westphalian legend tells about a sheepherder's vision of the BOB, in which an enormous Eastern army will be stopped and slaughtered by a devoted mass of Europeans. On Wiligut's advice, Himmler decided that the town of Wewelsburg, not too far from the Teutoburg Forest, where Arminius's tribesmen defeated the legions of Publius Quinctilius Varus, was a probable stage for this world-historical event. Therefore, it became SS headquarters. Under the influence of Wiligut/Weisthor, the commander, Manfred von Knobelsdorff, attempted to revive the religion of Irminism. Irmin (Chrestos) was crucified by schismatic Wotanists in Goslar around 9,500 years before Thomas the Doubter walked the earth

PETER ARNETT—legendary English-language foreign correspondent

SALUBRIN—a disinfectant

GAKIS—hungry ghosts in Japanese Buddhism

WIMPS—Weakly Interacting Massive Particles

SAMSARA LIDMAN—Sara Lidman, a Swedish author whose work was heavily influenced by dialect; Samsara is the cycle of rebirth, death and decay that Buddhists believe will be ended by enlightenment.

POAS ENQUIST—P.O. Enquist, a canonical Swedish author who grew up in Västerbotten.

XXI

– I'm Buddhist to the bone, Grandpa joked. I want you all to die for your desires, stop hating me, and let St. Lucifer dispel your errors.

– Oh Grandpa, you're too much, Myrtle said carelessly and set out a round tray with seven different kinds of desserts: night-marefudge, Jewishbread, Dr. Ottaw's Swedish Spritz, rectorynuts, Strassburgers, pretzelsticks, and chimneysweepcookies.

We were sitting in Signar and Myrtle's kitchen, planning the next worldwar. It's always transition time there: not winter, not spring, not this, not that. It was like life had stopped. Signar and Myrtle are peabrained, but popular. Meanwhile, Grandpa continued his wild ride on this latest cockhorse.

– The only thing that's kept my engine running all these years is the dream of a neverending love! From Ascension Day to All Saint's Day, my eyes have been locked on one prize, on our Savior's pristine, white, unspeakably sweet Godcock! Great will be his anger at those who don't lube their assholes against the day of his return! Mighty are his hips! And his voice—sexy as shit! Like old Blue Eyes himself . . .

Grandpa came up short, he was running on empty. He fell back in his seat, suddenly dull and lifeless.

– Who knows if He'll ever come back, at least not while the Social Democrats are in office, Signar continued.

His skinny, naked body was trembling in a cold watertub. He's short as a seven-year-old and is on probationary discharge from the madhouse. His only hope, though, is a mongolstorm.

– Wherever you get people, you get trash, Myrtle threw out haphazardly.

She was busy as a whirligig in the kitchen, a ridiculously tiny person with limbs like toothpicks.

– Stop growing up if you want to find truelove. The others, the ones still growing, have no time or energy for their fallowman. It happens again and again. How many times have you seen someone throw out a judgment here, a complaint there, only to end up drawing the shortstraw? No one's too little to love.

She hopped to the stove and jumped on a stool so she could reach the coffeepot. She had on a dirtygreen jacket with Elvis's or maybe Kaltenbrunner's face embroidered in purple on the back. Her clothes were made from crowskin and she had on a crepepaper hat decorated with deadflies and kittenpaws. Finally, she clomped up to the table on mismatched clogs, climbed onto the rented sofa so she could serve us coffee, and then scowled over the dented brass mugs. Signar dried himself with a scouringpad and pulled on a pair of darkblue Landmann overalls. Instead of diapers, he used a copy of a newspaper called *Land*. Then he joined us at the table. Myrtle had set out flatbread and buns; with feigned irritation, she urged us to dig in. I had at it and came away sticky, but Grandpa just sat there and stirred sugary lump after sugary lump into his coffee.

– We're vegetarians now, Signar said. We only eat fallenfruit and animals who died from natural causes . . .

– How do we know a man's soul goes up to heaven, but an animal's goes down to the earth? Myrtle asked cryptically.

– That from the Salter?

– Nah, the Preacher . . . We love all living things here . . . especially the AIDS virus . . .

The kitchen was warm and cozy, you had to give them that. It was papered with obituaries from North Västerbotten. They had an ironrange and an electrichotplate, just in case. On the windowledge were the twelve apostles, a clay Gorgon with a candle, and half a dozen Mochica statuettess showing different acts of bestiality, most of them involving vicuñas. There were handmadebags and cornsacks everywhere. To the right of the refrigerator were a couple of pictures: *Dog in Agony* and a Flemish sketch of hobos on the gogo. To the left was a slightly retouched photograph of almost all the king's family. There was a prayer on a nail above the sofa. Embroidered gold on red, it featured the familiar words from the Sermon on the Mount: "Suffer the little children to come unto me, so I can fuck the shit out of them." Over the sink, where a grouse sat still in a bottle, Signar had taped a naked picture of Upper Kågedalen's soccer team. They were pink, hairy, and fleshy. On the wall behind Myrtle were her parents' mummified hands and a few nailriddled dolls; they looked like neighbors and friends who had suddenly become ill or died. Outside the window, a roughhewn old man in a peaked cap struggled forward on a tricycle.

Something was wrong with him, he was missing both neck and eyes. Plenty of people are like that in Kusmark: obese and blind.

Grandpa didn't say anything, so I edged on in. I tried to be pleasant, but I had too little confidence to be convincing.

– Soooo . . . uhhhh . . . how's the harvest coming? I asked in an unnecessarily serious voice. Not because I really cared, but just for something to say . . .

– What's that?

– How did the crops do?

– What the fuck are you babbling about?

– Farming!

– Do you know what pimpleface is saying?!

– How did your seeds do?

– Owwdjrseedsdo! mocked Signar. Thanks for asking, but our shoots and sprouts got all froze and drowned!

– We shouldn't be like that, Myrtle said decisively. I'm not one of those . . . So how's school going? she asked, just so I'd be at a loss for words.

– I don't really go . . . I'm out sick at the moment . . .

– You'll sure have to repeat a lot . . . Probably too much . . .

– So what's your problem?! yelped Signar.

– Pretty much everything, I guess . . . my stomach . . . my head . . .

– You're telling me! you look like you're at death's door!

– And me, I'm just your ordinary whiny rheumatic . . . so it's not going great for me either, Myrtle sighed and dug a maggot out of her rotten nose. It'd been bitten off by a badger last fall and resewn.

Grandpa ignored us and kept on stirring in sugar.

– Grandpa's gone beddybye . . .

– Headed for the hills . . .

Signar heaped a couple of tablespoons of snuff on a piece of bread and scratched a scar that ran from ear to ear. That was a souvenir from the time he and Grandpa had come to blows, long before I was even a gleam in the world's eye. Grandpa had said that of the four stooges in the *120 Days of Sodom*, he was most like the Duc de Blangis, at least in character. Signar had insisted he was more like the Bishop or Curval.

– Curval's an old drunk, a filthy bag of bones with two inches of shitcrust around his immense assholecrater . . . *Tat tvam asi*! Signar had shouted.

When Grandpa gets mad, he turns red, white, or blue, just like Torgeir Håvarsson: "For his heart wasn't anything like a bird's crop. It didn't hold blood, it would never tremble in terror, since it had been hardened by the best smith on earth." So Grandpa had hatched a plan. He'd plied Signar with porn and snuff. When the miscreant was finally out, Grandpa had jumped him in bed, slit his throat, and headed for Finland. But Signar wasn't done for . . . He woke up in the morgue when someone fingered his anallobes. Since Signar was so short and he didn't actually die, Grandpa only had to pay a sixteenth of a weregild: a half kilo of coffee and a packet of sugar . . .

– It was just a goddamn accident, he'd complained, and Signar had bided his time.

A couple of years later, Signar had jumped out of a drainageditch and tried to shoot Grandpa. Good plan, except that the gun exploded and Signar lost a thumb and an eye. At that point,

Grandpa declared them even. Signar wasn't handsome, but he was a greedy little bugger and Grandpa wanted to keep him around. After all, you can fuck everything that shits . . .

– Have more, Myrtle urged, and I made it a point to praise the pretzelsticks and strong coffee.

– Is it just me or is this a little surreal? Signar asked.

– Nahhh . . . just a little strange, I said.

– Goddammit, you've gotta stop cioranizing! Think pussyteev! demanded Myrtle. Life's a goddamned fine thing! Live modestly, talk honestly, you'll be alright! Think of what a blessing it is to wake up every morning with a sob in your throat!

– I dreamed the strangest thing last night, Signar began. I sat beside the river of Babel and cried . . . I was thinking about Zion.

– Did you hang your harp on a willow tree?

– Yeah . . . how the fuck did you know that?

– §§§ . . .

– I saw a man with clear eyes and another wearing a muzzle . . . They were shrewd as snakes and harmless as doves . . .

– Matthew ten sixteen . . .

– The cleareyed chap said his name was Aappo Kiimainen and the other one was Jyrki Muostalainen . . . Then he read from a big book called *Finnish Bad Behavior from Mommilakalabaliken to Mainilaintermezzot* . . . It was printed on babyskin . . . After that, he fucked me every which way . . . And while we were loving it up, he made me tell him my favorite sex fantasy . . .

– Which is . . . ? I snooped.

– It's not that one about being raped by miners, is it? cackled Myrtel, lighting a lazaretcigarette with Gandhi's platinum lighter.

– Nah, I never had the guts to talk about this one before . . .

– Tell us now, because our warcouncil is over if Grandpa doesn't come around soon!

Grandpa, however, showed no signs of returning to earth. He'd already emptied the sugar bowl. Now he sat with downcast eyes, stirring so thoughtfully that it echoed.

– So here's my hottest, girliest fuckfantasy . . .

Signar blushed at his own daring.

– Lanz von Liebenfels's *Theosofy and the Assyrian Beastmen* talks about a twobodied, fourarmed, fourlegged Hindu named Lalao . . . I'd like to fuck a freak like that . . . mercilessly . . . He'll croon folk love ballads in a shrill, cracked voice while I'm pounding him . . . At the same time, he'll fuck Bhagwan in the mouth, while the guru is being devoured by a Komodo dragon . . . When Bhagwan is all eaten up, Reagan will take his place . . . then Thatcher . . . Schwarzenegger, of course, will be pounding me from behind . . . it'll be an honest-to-god Apachefuck! And I'll look, and before my eyes I'll see a thousand newborns carried away by condors, eaten up by wildpigs, drowned by barricudaswarms . . . Legions of godlygirls and pregnantwhores will be caught in lavaflows, quicksand sinks, and ratinfested bunkers . . . they'll have to stroke themselves and talk dirty till their dying breath . . .

Myrtle was smoking and obviously enjoying herself, and I was listening like a wideeyed peeping tom. Grandpa was as lost to us as before.

– A cheeky old Soldier of Christ will lash my back and ass with a cat o' nine tails . . . When I'm one bloody weepingwound, he'll be decapitated and I'll open my mouth and receive his last repentant shout while I kiss him deep, deep down in the gaping wound where the blood's already starting to congeal . . . Cities will burn, hydrogen bombs will explode, cultures will go kaplooey . . . Tom Jones and Julio Iglesias will gnaw off each other's cocks . . . "Plura" and Thåström will sliceanddice each other with chain saws . . . Me and Arnold will come . . . And an that very moment, the universe will explode . . .

Signar's fantasy had brought him to a boil. Now he wanted a straightup, nofrills fuck. Myrtle obediently went down on all fours and shut her little peppercorn eyes, the better to fantasize with. Signar called his pinkyfingersized cock up from the underworld and chose door number two. He spewed after a dozen repulsive little rabbitjerks. Myrtle grunted in disappointment. Signar wiped his bloody cum on his sister's wrinkled chin. She lapped at it greedily while she came. The fire died down and they resumed their places. Signar started in about an overlyserious Betaniaboy in Byske who already spewed blood instead of sperm. Myrtle told about the triumphant moment when she'd finally emptied a boiling pan of toffee over some swankpot's head at her sewingclub.

– She was an old gossip, she said, explaining the why of the enterprise, which had been short and sweet. Do you remember how pious and pure you were before we got together? she asked flippantly, reversing course midway.

– We lived like catandrat when I was a drooling and panting twenty-one year old . . .

Signar's eyes were distant and uncertain.

– I'm still researching the Kusipoho Ritual of the Bikomoloise Tribe . . . They're native to the corrugatedcardboard regions north

of the Ngorongoro Crater . . . and they worship Harri Tularemi . . .
When their oldest innocent gets his first morningwood, they get
the lowest geezers together at a seedy pub . . . and then they draw
lots to see who gets to give the boy what he wants . . . They begin
with a Chimbú handshake . . .

– We've heard it all before!

– Yeahyeah . . . so, anyway, you're wanting me to remember how
unsexy I was . . . God help me! I was more of a prude than Aloysius Gonzaga and Johannes Bermanns put together! Selivanov's
chastity was my polarstar!

– And now it's just the opposite: you want it so bad it shames
you, and when you get it, you die! I busted out, right to the point.
I don't know what had gotten into me . . .

– Be polite, boy! the tetchy little man exclaimed and slapped me
with a flyswatter. You only have a voice on Holy Innocents' Day,
and then the crows will drown you out!

– The younger the child, the worse the devil, Myrtle recited as
she bent over, grabbed my hair, and spit a snuffwad onto my forehead. I could feel it sticking there, but I didn't dare to wipe it off . . .
Minutes dragged by like Achilles' cloven heel.

And they just sat there and stared at me . . . they seemed inhu-
man . . . their eyes weren't their own anymore . . . I couldn't return their gaze . . . I just trembled in my seat . . . pissed myself, of
course. . . fixed my eyes on the linoleumfloor . . . piles of ratshit . . .
a moldy smell getting stronger by the minute . . . until it became
unbearable . . . The gaslamps dimmed . . . it got dark . . . they only
got clearer . . . though they were the last things I wanted to see . . .
a Christmascandle burned on a shortwick . . . it was epileptric . . .

They were in my head . . . screwing around . . . trashing the place . . . feeling me up . . . laughing . . . on their way through to my innermost parts . . . lurking around the outermost of my defenselessness . . . needing to hurt me . . . to make me beg . . . To force me to see myself clearly . . . the boy behind the babble . . . the face behind the wankoff's fist . . . OhnoohnoohNO! . . . I struggled . . . put up a fight . . . they weren't expecting resistance . . . they pressed harder . . . but I was defending the most precious thing of all . . . the thing you never surrender . . . no matter how bad you've got it . . . it's the primal thing . . . in you before the beginning's beginning . . . I'm talking about boyhood . . . the magic seed . . . the thing that makes you a Grandpa . . . It may be small and warm . . . but when it counts, it's the strongest stuff of all . . . I didn't want them to get their filthy hands on my hidden treasure, my boyhood . . . the Godgiven heart of us all . . . protected and sealed within us . . .

Signar and Myrtle growled and spit . . . they were used to getting their way . . . a mere boy couldn't defy them . . . but the harder they tried, the worse it went . . . They redoubled their efforts, brutaled up their attack. . . he came in through the eyes, she through my fontanelle . . . They wanted to reach my psyche . . . but my heart's root is somewhere else . . . farther in . . . I didn't surrender . . . I called on all my love for Grandpa . . . I called on him, too . . . "Help me . . . I can feel myself disappearing . . . soon your mite will be gone!" . . . The demons were certain of victory . . . they wanted to defile me, to drag me away where no one would find me again . . . forever and ever . . . ruin me for all time . . . I called on Grandpa . . . I could feel my head splitting . . . I bled from my nose and ears . . . and I told them again and again: "I'll always be a boy, since I have to become a Grandpa . . ."

"you're not a boy any longer," they mocked . . . their voices like a swamp in winter, all ice and sludge . . . "you don't have what it takes to be a Grandpa . . ."

"i'll be both and much much more," I said . . . "i'll hate and love and live and die . . . I'll be animal and man and angel and demon . . ."

"all you'll ever be is a demon, the most useless demon there ever was" . . .

They'd broken through the outer layer . . . turned my fear to selfloathing . . . I'd never really liked myself, but this was a thousand times worse . . . I crumbled up . . . hunched down . . . began to break apart . . . but still I resisted . . . didn't give in . . . put up a fight . . . they raged and burned . . . brought all their strength to bear . . .

"see how pathetic you are, taste your bitter failure, your defeat, your wickedness and lies . . . you've betrayed what you were, there's nothing left in you that's pure and true . . . aren't you disgusted by your thoughts, sickened by your feelings, shamed by your actions . . . you're no germinating Grandpa, no, you're too cowardly and fragile for that . . . but you'll never be a boy again, either, not after what you've thought, said and done . . ."

"my boyhood's still there, deep and buried . . . it's hidden and only the power of love can call it out!" I shrieked, trying to drown out the tumult in my psyche . . . "Grandpa has always been there for me! . . . he's coming to rescue me!"

"your Grandpa is Satan himself! who do you think ordered us to rip out your guts! break your back! destroy your heart's root!"

"i don't believe you! deep down I know Grandpa's good!"

An inferno . . . a firey darkness churning beyond time and space . . . Primeval forces bent on annihilating everything . . . And then I was back in the moldy kitchen, back in the sor-takinda, the scare quotes of reality. My head was heavy and my nose was bleeding. Signar and Myrtle trembled, almost like themselves again . . . Flies swarmed around Grandpa, he woke up and speared our hosts with his eyes. The coffee was cold, the clock had stopped.

– Yeah, well . . . we'd better be off . . .

– Hey, Grandpa . . .

– How are you feeling?

– Not too good . . .

– Who the fuck feels good? Afzelius and Lundell!

Signar and Myrtle put on a real show, obviously trying to smooth everything over.

– Stay and have a cozy chat! You've hardly had a bite!

– Your chair isn't covered with nails, you know!

Grandpa shook his head, firm and masculine.

– Nah, we've got to shove off . . . we're pressed for time . . . our day is packed . . .

– Come back soon, you hear!

– We've still got a war to plan!

– Stop by when you're in the neighborhood!

– And for the love of God, take the boy with you!

We got up, I was dressed in a flash. I stood uncomfortably by the door, hand on the knob, letting in a breath of fresh air that quickly made the rounds of the room.

– Byebye, now . . .

– Thanks a million . . .

–See you later, alligator. . .

– Thanks for the coffee, Myrtle!

When we reached the mailbox, I turned around. I wiped the snuffwad off my forehead. They'd climbed onto back of the couch and were staring after us. The Adventcandle cast a dismal sheen. I could've sworn they transformed right then and there. Hairy . . . pointed ears . . . red eyes, sharp teeth . . . Fell . . . We stole an Ockelbo snowmobile and drove home, even though it was only September. When he'd locked up behind us, Grandpa said in a choked voice:

– You know what I find really appalling, boy?

– No . . .

– That I have to deny all my doubt and worry . . . always be funny and drunk and dangerous and horny . . .

We went to bed with our clothes still on. In the middle of the night, we woke up and made love. It was soft and sweet. I didn't tell Grandpa what had happened. The next evening the braintrust was meeting at Ove and Siv's. We wanted to come up with a way to destroy the universe.

KALTENBRUNNER—Ernst: Austrian SS officer

VICUÑA—camelid found in the South American Andes

TORGEIR HÅVARSSON—one of two main characters from the Icelandic *Saga of the Sworn Brothers*

"PLURA"—Per Malte Lennart "Plura" Johnson: Swedish singer, songwriter and author

THÅSTRÖM—Joakim: Swedish rock star

HARRI TULAREMI—tularemia is a zoonotic disease also known as "rabbit fever"

AFZELIUS—Björn: Swedish singer and songwriter

LUNDELL—Gerhard: Swedish singer, songwriter and author

KIIMAINEN—lecherous

MUOSTALAINEN—dark person

CHIMBÚ HANDSHAKE—gripping each other's private parts in greeting (on Papua Nyou Guinea)

ALOYSIUS GONZAGA AND JOHANNES BERCHMANNS—terribly chaste, mortification-seeking, beatified Jesuits who died young

SELIVANOV—Scoptsy leader, advocated cutting or burning off one's penis

XXII

– Keep Sweden weird! Ninety-nine out of a hundred drivebys are committed by immigrants! Two thirds of all fatties are foreigners! More than half are over sixty quadratmeters! They cost us more than all unstandard emissions put together! No matter how I add it up, it doesn't add up! It's not right! Satan's hellfire, I've never been a weight around anyone's neck! That ought to be worth something! I can't allow more of them in now! It won't work! not all at once! They'll overrun everything! Both small and large! Everyone, young and old, forced to slave away! Settle the debt! Mush, by God! Set your nose to the grindstone! Trample the ordinary pusher into the ground! Into the shit! That's how the system works! So the fine gents can cruise down easystreet! So the wifey can have it cozy! It makes me frightened for myself just thinking about it! How can it go on! How can they take it lying down! The Kooperation's behind it all! that's who we have to thank! Thanks for nothing, fucks! Thank them and blame them! It's their fault things are the way they are! They're pulling the wool over everyone's eyes! All for the sake of new members! all for the bottom line! Makes me dizzy just thinking about it! You keep at it until the fat lady sings! and what do you get in return! a mobilebingo doorprize! Every ten years! But my luck's held out! compared with the least! the tonguetied! the heartburned! or the ra-ra-railroad workers! What's become of them! Can you answer me that! They're gone is what! Presto! Just like that! And why do you think that is! Immigrants, of course! All the oldfarts are dropping, too! like flies! You think they'd keep dying if the immigrants would stop coming! Are you stupid enough to believe that Sweden would actually lose the Melody Festival if we were rid of them! No more accidents! year 'round sunshine! sweetsweet air! fatter wallets! No more leaving the table hungry! no more impotence! incontinence! intelligence! no more! It eats at you that no one ever listens! Watch out! Otherwise it'll just slip through your fingers! out onto the sand! Every damned word I say is true! It's crystalclear, if you just stop to think a second! a nanosecond! Do you think children want to throw fits! Hell no! They're just scared of the darkies! That's why they're crying! But seriously, and this isn't bullshit: it's the worst of it! it's the whole fucking cranedance! It's their fault! They can't undo what they've done! They can't do any better! Their plots were successful! their sly, gutless intrigues! and here wc sit! devils in green! you're stuck! there's no going back! neither a softtouch nor mouthfuck will help you now! you're finished! adios! *spassiba*! it's nothing less than the *Untergang des Anuslandes*! Just like Semmelweis predicted!

 – Spengler, corrected Grandpa, winking at me with arioheroic irony.

 – Yeahyeah, old hindufucker Oswald! Whatever: weeds and vermin! lice and mice! that's what we're dealing with! Whatdoyouthink! tell me if I'm wrong! we're the ones saying foreigners should have to draw the shortstraw! and yet here we are! just scrape and bow! curtsey and blow! with cap in hand and pants pulled down! Who fucking said it should be like that! I mean, the average, savage worker has never had it so bad! He doesn't even get mustard for his hotdog! Higherwages and shorterhours, that's the lie they've shoved down our throats! I spit on their taxreform! The only ones who'll profit are the furriers! and the immigrants! Are you proud about having it bad, just because you're Swedish! The devils! They sat down! made a pact! stole our jobs! and then our fucks! They give us crewcuts and then here comes the straightjacket! and freestylejazz! and rap! nonstop! da capo! You can't hum along, when it's reggae! calypso! whatthefuck! hiphop! voodoo! tutu! all meant to drive you bonkers!

Benny drew a deep breath, then sat lost in thought. Gasping and panting, totally exhausted. His fattyflesh was the same color as a Västerbottencheese. Peppered with the kind of acne that never matures. He looked like a lesser Bert Karlsson. His hair was white and thin and tassled. He had a nice paunch. His mommy sewed all his clothes. Grandpa whipped out a joint and lit it stylishly and recklessly.

– You must have diabetes, the way you're going on.

– Or pepsilepsi, I threw out.

– Shut your mouth, mite, if you ever want to become a man. But Benny . . . if I may ask . . . what's weighing on your heart? . . . what's got your dander up?

– That's easy! foreigners! they're taking over! multiplying! being left in peace!

– You ever seen a live nigger?

– No, but they're out there! I know it! I wasn't born yesterday!

– Ah, you poor little punk, Grandpa playcoddled him, I sense you're not being honest with old Grandpa . . . there's something else going on . . . tell me what it is! Is it really so bad, my boy?

– I don't know . . . I think it's just the world . . . and everything in it . . . I mean, what will become of us . . . how will it be after that . . . there aren't too many stories about that . . . I swear, if you didn't have to grinandbearit, you'd always be cryingyoureyesout . . . I don't know up from down . . . and I'm too afraid of heights to hang myself . . .

– Benny, my friend and lover . . . You know I respect you for your galliant fight on behalf of the pinkrace, but lately you're just too much to take . . . So I'm going to loan you a couple of books, and then I don't ever want to see you again . . .

– What do you mean?

– Offing yourself is the only way to come out on top . . . look at it as a necessary step in the evolutionary process . . . depopulationing . . . nature's progress . . . Now this book, he said, fingering a worn text with bite marks on the spine, was written by Saddam Hussein's Uncle Kairallah . . . it's called *Three Things God Never Should've Created: Persians, Jews, and Houseflies* . . . The other, he said and held up a gleaming hospitalwhite book, explains how to commit suicide deftly and expertly . . . it was written by two Frogs, Gyjo and Le Boniek, I think they were called . . .

Benny humbly thanked Grandpa for the books, but begged him for his help.

– I'm so damned close to the edge . . . I can't do it anymore . . . help me, Grandpa . . .

– Sorry, I've already got plans . . . we're having company . . . Hilding Skivling has some things for me . . . you know how I get

139

when I've got the chance to cum in an unkissed mouth! . . . And tomorrow Schönhuber and Le Pen are stopping by for coffee and cookies . . .

Benny shoved off after a few more buts and ifs, his face hanging like a hound's. Then me and Grandpa went on a walk down to the river and then over the flatstones.

– My old Grandpa wasn't much for talking, said Grandpa. But he wrote up a storm! . . . On deadleaves, fishscales, the loamy sand down by the troutstream . . . Yes, us Grandpas are handy with words, it comes from our homeland . . . But I want to hear them taken by the wind . . . scattered by echoes!!! eeechooo . . . eechooo . . . chooo . . .

The word rolled around, suffered, died, and vanished.

– True knowledge is powerlessness, mite . . . hotair is your legacy . . . First you play tricks with words, then it's words playing tricks on you . . . Words are like barnodors, once they've taken root, they're there forever . . . Then they make the rules, they drive you out of your mind . . .

He laid both hands on my shoulder.

– Promise me one thing, mite . . . Read as little as possible . . .

– I promise you, Grandpa!

– This is probably how my brain looks, Grandpa said, picking up a handful of lichens.

– Dry and airy . . . *Das Gehirn ist ein Irrweg* . . . Once thoughts and images are in your skull, it's impossible to protect yourself against feelings . . . Feelings are like scarletfever and measles and mumps . . . a child can survive them, but once you're a man, it's your life on the line . . . I think I had feelings once, mite, even if

I can't remember what it was like . . . They vanished, fell out like babyteeth, because when you grow up you need something else to bite with . . . When you're grown, when you're a Grandpa, for example, feelings just make you want to die . . . you want to laugh, puke, and hug someone, but there's no doing any of that . . . It's like being eaten up from the inside . . . a sorrow not even death can remove . . . and you know deep down you can't tolerate it! nowaynohow! Then you'll prefer living life freestyle!! You get along somehow! thoughtless! emotionless! careless!

We went home arm in arm, and I stifled my every passing fancy so zealously I got a stitch in my side. Two weeks later we learned that Benny had gone straight home and shot himself with an old Mauser. Instead of getting down to business, though, the bullet had just played ringaroundtherosy in his head, and now Benny was completely paralyzed. He still had his sharp wits, he just couldn't talk.

– Pity, he was a honey of a man, Grandpa said and sent a "Get Well" card showing a coalblack nigger fucking a lilywhite virgin's tender asshole. She looked like she was enjoying it.

———————————————

BERT KARLSSON—Swedish entrepreneur, politician, and founder of the reality TV show *Fame Factory*
KOOPERATION—Swedish cooperative union and wholesale society
THE MELODY FESTIVAL—annual Swedish music competition

XXIII

The Marleners slithered in. Hilding is nice and warm, he tastes like maranathasmegma. His son, Royal, though, is a little too good. He'll do whatever you want if the price is right.

– Damn, you got all scrawny! Grandpa complained, putting his claws in front of his smokedried face.

– Take it for what it's worth, but you turn me on, Hilding wheezed and frenchkissed my Grandpa. Then he gave him a smoke.

– Your tobacco is blasphemously good, darling, Grandpa twittered, taking a drag and moaning like a dollarstorewhore.

– You've got a nice head of hair, boy, Royal joked. But that's one fat dick—what's wrong, you got cancer?

– I think you're starting to go soft, mousling! You want me to tame you?! Hilding shouted and hoolahooped with his lovehandles.

– Uh, thanks, I think, I babbled.

– You smoke like a girl, Royal bawled and fondled my crotch. Then he stuck a wad of burning Greve Hamilton between his fuckready lips.

Grandpa stared me down, eyes gone wild, what was going to happen next?

– You're not scared of me, are you?

– What's that you've got, Grandpa? I stammered.

– A guanobat to plug the ass of a nosybrat! Grandpa howled and forced me to asssmoke a cigar. Then he shoved it up wrongways, so the room smelled like burntintestine.

– That'll teach you to get cute, you little nervousnelly.

– Damn, what I wouldn't give for a fuckhungry toddler about now, Hilding chuckled. My old man, you know, seduced Abd Ur Rama when he was still a giggly young cockteaser and you know as well as I do that he was the devil himself. He was devilishly fond of ramming nails through our balls. Of course, there wasn't any point in crying to mommy or hanging on her apron strings. When that happened, the old man would just make a pitchhat from squirrelcunts and wrap it around the pissmakers of us whoresons. When he ripped it off, we'd be smooth as babes between the legs. But it made men of us.

– I remember how my old Grandpa did it, Grandpa said. If some little mama's boy started bitching and moaning about this and that, he'd slice their belly open, wrap their intestines around their head and neck, and bite them like Satan himself until the little tyke had learned to keep his fretting to himself.

– You're full of shit, you old geezers, Royal declared and took a flask from his partybriefs. This'll put hair on your tits.

Grandpa threw his arms around our guests and showed them into the living room. They made themselves comfy on the sofa, and I crouched on the floor like a curdog.

– A shot of brandy is good for the loving, Grandpa told them, taking a slurp from our homemadedistillery's mainhose. The Marleners guzzled turpentine and chainsawoil, and I sucked on a rag soaked in paintthinner. No one said anything for a few minutes, and I started to feel goodlooking and goodforsomething.

– The boy should be guzzling mongoloidpiss! Royal suddenly shouted, and Grandpa kicked me down to the cellar for the pissbucket.

– This is premium grade piss, you know—only the best village idiots have been invited to make a contribution, Grandpa bragged. And then he hooted: Bad behavior will earn you a calfweaner!

I went down on my knees and drank piss until I choked. It tasted like a lovesick girl's mouth. Then Grandpa took me on his lap and brought me back around.

– Everything is all good now, he cooed. You know how I hate it when you whine. But it's all over.

He squeezed a gluetube onto my tongue and gave me some ethanol to wash it down with.

– That's right, scrub that foul taste right out of your mouth, he said. Go ahead and cry me a river, while I ram your shithole with a candlestick.

He hummed "with lovely lips you'll always have a baby in your arms." Then Hilding struck up a Lappish tune, "The Song of Kuckumaffen," and Royal whistled "you've got your red meat here, you've got your meathole there, your red meat, your meathole, right up the fucking asshole . . ."

– Now let's have a bite to eat! Hilding shrieked in falsetto.

– It's BYOB, kids, Grandpa declared, he's always a real scrooge. So what have you brought?

– Grandpa, you know I've had it rough. When I was young, we came in a souppot to make dumplings. We'd bite slivers from the inside of our lips for bologna. It was a real feast when Daddy brought home some pubichair. Creepycrawlies made a banquet, indeed. We ate dandruff for desert.

– You going somewhere with this? Grandpa interrupted him.

– Your mouth. Anyway, we ran after wagons on their way to buggermass and caught the spitblobs the uppityupps sent flying our way. In winter we wore gasolinebarrels and in summer we dressed in tires. We filled our bellies with stones and sponges. Every year Dad begged for shavings and splinters so we could have Christmas dinner. When someone took a shit, it was dogeatdog for who got to have it. We suckled each other and ate what we spewed up to get by. But let's be clear about one thing! he yelled and waved Royal out to their old clunker, we've brought a whole trashbag just chockfull of goodies!

Royal struggled in with a trashsack that reeked like the mouth of the Kåge River. Making a show of it, Hilding rooted around in the sack and brought out: earloberinds, burntsausage, outiesandinnies, and psoriasisbroilers. Royal cast about with prinskorvfingers and found: pimplephlegm and dingleberries, livingcandles, some ear-nose-throat runoff, and an Algotseamstress' torso.

– I see all that, Grandpa grunted. But you know, Hilding, my lamb, I'm just craving something sweet.

With a dangerous glint in his eye, Royal drew a flask of Bukuttingismegma out of the skinfold of his inguinal hernia.

– Fire up the stove for coffee, Grandpa ordered, while I cleanse myself.

– Don't you scions of the masterrace have a gasoven? Royal laughed.

I lit a fire in front of the pneumaticchamber Grandpa had gotten from Uncle Rascher. The pot boiled so fast it gave me blisters along my hairline. In the meantime, Grandpa dug out a yetipastei and a bucket of sheep's wool soaked in lubricatingoil. He opened up his IV bag and emptied everything into the fagragout.

– Waste not, want not, he declared.

The pot simmered for a few moments and then Grandpa ladled the mixture out of the Gundestrup cauldron with a toiletbrush until everyone was satisfied. Royal started to look green about the gills. He retched, took a leak, and puked a hairball right onto Hilding's burntyellow pants.

– That's nasty, Royal, Hilding exclaimed.

– Do the nasty, Royal shot back.

– Do it, just do it, when you want to go to it, I babbled, trying to make everyone smile.

– Shut your yap while you eat, piglet, Grandpa yelped. Stuff your gut today, because tomorrow we'll skin you raw. Of course, now he probably won't be good for cleaning up or getting dirty, he complained peevishly.

– A meal in a million, said Hilding, downing a twittering critter.

For dessert the Marleners had brought sundried kiddieweewees and a package of Donald Duck cookies. After we'd finished, Hilding patted his pigbelly and Grandpa snorted blood.

– Now we'll have a smoke, I said, trying to sound like a Big Boy.

– Sweetpussy, he's all grown up, Hilding bleated.

– Real smooth, fartface, Royal screeched.

– It is what it is, Grandpa laughed, and now I'm ready for a carton of ciggis.

We smoked like the rectalrabbis from Wankdorf and Hilding told us about a sanatorium patient in Bure who could take a grown cock in both nostrils at once.

– Now we're going to have ourselves a raw assfuck, Grandpa exclaimed, putting his ciggi out in my nose.

– Or maybe a fistfuck? he asked, tousling Royal's curly, red, scurvy hair.

– Let's get on with it, then, Hilding said, trying without much success to hide his enthusiasm. We're going Dutch, after all.

Royal wriggled like a worm on a hook and howled so loud we had to cover our ears, when Grandpa rammed a wrinkled fist up his sphincter. Grandpa gave it to him hard, using his fingernails and his fist. He also kept an eagleeye open for fakeorgasms.

– Cut the apeshit, Royal, you're so willing it makes me blush, he crowed. Now go and molest Hilding, Grandpa said to me, and make sure you bump back real hardif he rams your ass. You know how polite and helpful you can be when you let your feelings out. If I remember right, old Hilding's a hard bugger to milk and he sweats like a pig. He's easypeasy, but hardtopleasy. Squeeze his tits while you suck his lolly.

– You're so sweet I could just eat you up, Hilding said, gnashing his teeth and dragging out his maypole. Then I got ready to do my part.

– Suck until you drop, Hilding moaned and I could see the whites of his eyes. Time stretched as I massaged his balls with what you might call a publicservant's devotion. As I was working him, though, I heard something heavy hit the glass. I immediately knew it was those afterbirthmunching suicidebent owls trying to break their short necks against our mirrorwindows. After I'd finished, there was hardly a drop on top and Hilding didn't even seem to notice he'd spewed. Grandpa drew his bloody fist out of Royal's ass. Royal, for his part, was out cold with a thumb in his mouth. Then Grandpa took a shot of something, unbuttoned his washedleather pants, pulled down his underwear, and lubricated his hairy asshole with pigfat.

– I'll tell you something, Hilding Marlene, and it's this: I'm a no-good woman, he sobbed. I want you to take me just like Joseph did baby Jesus in the manger in Bethlehem!

Hilding's blotchy, weathered face lit up and his meatsack got all stiff again. Grandpa went down on all fours and stuck his ass up in the air.

– Good Lord, what big hemorrhoids you have! Hilding laughed.

– Blood's the best fucksauce, Grandpa retorted bitterly.

– You don't have to feel dirty or nothing, Hilding reassured him.

With a firm grip on Grandpa's Biafrahips, he drove his chimneybrush deep into Grandpa's wildstrawberrygrotto.

– O-Oh-Ohh! Grandpa panted. Satan, it's good to have my clock cleaned! Hilding, pound me with that croolcock of yours! make me feel like a flayedbaby!

Marlene humped him like a naughtygaycentaur.

– You want to fuck my bones until they crack, don't you? Grandpa howled.

Just to be wicked, Hilding put an oldwomanheadscarf on him, but Grandpa didn't notice. The tempo picked up, Hilding went at it like a murderous troll with Old Testament resolve. Grandpa tossed his head and screeched out loud. It was the worst I'd ever seen, the whole house was shaking. Hilding's cock was like a piston, it was turning blackandblue, and there Grandpa was, begging for more.

– That's it, abscessass, Hilding whinnied at last.

My Grandpa spewed foam and spoke in tongues, it looked like he was in his death throes. Hilding moaned until it hurt, then came so hard it splashed deep into Grandpa's gut, shot right through him and dribbled out the corners of his mouth. It was a good while before Hilding was himself again. There was so much lovejuice it terrified me.

– I think you've crippled me, Grandpa finally growled and ripped off the headscarf. But fuck me if we haven't earned ourselves a cup of coffee.

While we drank coffee, Hilding sang "Greasy Love" by Snoddas: "Long ago when I was young my dick was big and mean / and all the boys for miles around were jealous of my seed / in every house and every town I had a little friend / who'd use their ass to squeeze and squeeze and squeeze me dry again . . . Though man and beast may hate me for my stiff one / I'll rub and love my ogrecock for as long as I'm alive / I'll laugh and cry, my sperm will fly / straight down the throat of a scabby old goat . . ."

Grandpa told us about a failed sixty-nine he'd had with the Stenbergapyromaniac back in the fifties, then he slapped the back of my head for being so giggly. The doorbell rang and I went to get it. Two toddlers were selling gingerbread cookies for the dildomakers in Kräkångersnoret. Both were wideeyed and gullible; at that age they'll swallow anything. Grandpa wasted no time. He seized them both by their hairtufts and dragged them into the living room. At that, they began to shake and whine.

– No crying! Grandpa shrieked.

Then he pounded their milkteeth out with a mortar.

– Suck on God, he grunted and grabbed the kid with the blondest hair. Here's a lipstick for you to chew on.

When he was finished with their mouths, he told me to get him a fistful of steel wool. Then he started playing Open the Locked Door with the first kid. The other one curtsied and bowed to Hilding, but a knee to the face took his breath away. After that, Royal showed him how to smoke Sumatra cigarillos and Hilding forced the kid to kiss him down there.

– Try it, you might like it, old Auntie Marlene grumbled when the kid wouldn't open wide.

– Mind your manners, Royal groaned at the one Grandpa had just released.

– He's nothing to write home about himself, Grandpa said, winking meaningfully at the urchin and swallowing a fistful of Oxazepam. I mean, his meat is all rotten, he continued, squeezing Royal's doughy manhood with a look of disgust.

– What did you say about my boy? Hilding demanded.

– The worst thing about you, Hilding, is that you howl when you shit. You don't even know when it's over. Get out of my house, asscunt, and take the buggerbitch with you.

– You're real pissy all of a sudden, Hilding laughed and fondled himself.

– Start walking, Grandpa ordered. Don't let the door hit you in the ass, you old gypsydevil.

– You know, people talk too much, Hilding said spitefully. And you know what they've been saying about you, Grandpa?

– I don't give a rat's ass.

– They call you and the boy Pimplejuice and Soursprout, and they say your asshole's so dogeared it wouldn't sell at the dollarstore, and that your boy's so ugly he has to suck invalids just so he can afford the next issue of *Korak, Son of Tarzan*! You've sucked your last dick, Grandpageezer, that I can promise you! Hilding went on cockily, grabbing an old rifle out of the trashbag.

– What the hell are you talking about, Grandpa hiccuped. Have you no sense of decency in you?

– You're about to find out, old sport. Get ready for a bullet in the twat! Prepare yourself for your last good pounding!

I flew at Hilding and started biting his neckrolls.

– What are you doing, you garbagegrub? he screamed and punched me where it counts.

In the meantime, Grandpa had knocked Royal out with a piece of firewood. Marlene was what you might call a hardened fighter, but I grabbed his dick and squeezed until he laid down his weapon.

– Leave off, mite, Grandpa said, clutching his heart, you'll be the death of me! You know, Hilding Marlene, you're the worst thing I've seen since Olga Korbut and Ida Nudel sang "Dancing in the Streets" in Babi Yar! plus you're a real balltwiddler when it comes to the old pushandshove!

– And you're fucking sick in the head, snapped Hilding.

– Nah, I just got a foul mouth, but I want you to do something for me, Grandpa told him. I want you to clean my hiney. And then I want you to take it all back.

– Tell your funboy to drop my rod first, Hilding sulked.

– As if you'd get off so easy. No, it's Holmträsk justice for you.

Hilding proved to be a good asskisser, and Grandpa began to purr with enjoyment. But Marlene was tired and hot and got into trouble when he burst Grandpa's favorite boil. It was the one he'd got the Pekka Langer Medal from PRO(c) for.

– Go get him!

I went to town on Hilding's nuts like there was no tomorrow and that stopped him in his tracks. He was too drunk to really feel pain, though. Without a word he dragged Royal out the door, through the empty hall, out the front door, past the trashpile, through the sewerpit, and into their car. Then they wobbled and jerked away.

– Byebye now, and if more like you turn up, we'll say byebye to them, too! I yelled after the Marleners.

– Now, I knew Hilding was a bastard, but I never thought he'd go and make such a fool of himself. He can't fuck, he can't fight, what a fucking buggerbeast! But you did good, boy, he told me, giving me a thumb's up in just the right spot.

– Let's kill the kids, I said, mainly because I wanted Grandpa to myself.

We went in, leaving the starry sky to cast its spell over the ashgray landscape. One kid was already dead, but the other tried to fight back. Grandpa knifed him and let him bleed out.

– Tomorrow we'll put them in the trashbag and toss them out with Hilding's gun.

Grandpa went around and turned off the lights and then we went to bed. Grandpa washed up with jewfatsoap and gypsyshampoo. I gurgled with ammonia. After that, we were almost ready for bed.

– Say a prayer to my old Grandpa in hell, Grandpa ordered, pulling a poliosweater over his head.

– He who knows what a child is, fuck me because I'm small, wherever I go in this world, fill my hands with shit, Satan comes, Satan goes, he loves sheepdick, that's all, I recited.

– I don't have any energy for flirting and fondling, mite, Grandpa said after we'd crept under the pigskin. Stick a cherry-bomb up your ass and light it.

I had to do what he asked, because he's a hard man. Afterward, he licked my sweetspot.

– Fall nights are like a kid's ass, always wet, he mumbled before he slept.

He snored like a hornytoad. Softly, I stroked his beautiful head and dried the tears off his dry, cracked chin. Then I crept as near him as I could, pressed my body close and shook with silent sobs. I hadn't been this horny since my dad's mom died.

GREVE HAMILTON—Swedish pipe tobacco

ABD UR RAMA—a fakir who turned up in Skellefteå in the 1930s and liked to stick long, coarse nails through diverse body parts

PITCHHAT—a gummy leather cap that sticks fast to a child's scurfy, lice infested skull; when it's pulled away, it takes both hair and dandruff with it

WEANER—anti-suckling device used on calves

METHO—denatured alcohol

PRINSKORV—literally "prince sausage," a small Swedish sausage

BUKUTTINGI—literally "high hill," one of the largest cities in West Sumatra

RASCHER—Sigmund: Nazi doctor who carried out altitude and cold experiements with deadly results in the concentration camps

GUNDESTRUP CAULDRON—Celtic archeological find

GOSTA "SNODDAS" NORDGREN—Swedish singer and actor

OLGA KORBUT—Belarusian gymnast

IDA NUDEL—Soviet-born Israeli activist

HOLMTRÄSK JUSTICE—the way of the fist

MEDAL FROM PRO(c)—an award instituted by the breakaway faction of the Public Retiree Organization, PRO-cocksuckers; given to the cocksucking fogy with the fattest and ripest assboil

XXIV

The one thing I remember about living with my dad's mom is that she liked to keep an even tone. She had a habit of suppressing laughter . . . I think Grandma was obese . . . complex . . . addicted to smokes . . . she knew what people were about, gave them all they could stand . . . she never talked to me, what would be the point of that . . . not that it made any difference . . . she took me in so she'd have someone to blame . . . she was enough and more than enough . . . she knew a thing or two . . . folded up toward the finish . . . she'd have had plenty left to take out on other people, if she hadn't been so goddamned horny . . . everyone said so . . . they were right, though it sounds strange . . . we had it good, though . . . I and she . . . she and I . . . we just shut each other out . . . nothing was ever planned in advance . . . she wrung each day by the neck . . . sometimes she was sick . . . nothing to do then but starve . . . she'd sit with her head under the faucet . . . running cold water for hours . . . for days . . . she never told anyone what was wrong . . . she had a nose for slaughtersites . . . good grub to be had there . . . it was enough . . . since I received, I kept my mouth shut . . . she was a midwife once . . . when people got all upset at her, she just stonewalled them . . . she didn't give a fuck . . . no point in getting your dander up . . . let them keep on keeping on, if that's how they wanted to play it . . . that's just how she was . . . I was safe . . . nothing ever changed . . . day and night, summer and winter . . . there was just a kitchen and a Grandma . . . a silence like outerspace . . . she did the best she could . . . it was the way she was made . . . it was all she'd ever known . . . she wouldn't tolerate baloney and hogwash . . . if things weren't normal, she made them that way . . . order and manners never killed anyone . . . she didn't want to be a bother . . . didn't want to make a fuss . . . just wanted to keep an even tone . . .

When she died, I didn't know what had happened . . . All I know is that Grandpa came and got me, and it started to tingle down there, and my heart started to pound . . . That's where it started, the thing that will soon be ending. I decided to ask Grandpa if he remembered what it was like to be little.

– Not a damned thing! Lucky me!

– Can't you remember anything?

– My old Grandpa ordered me not to remember . . . He was stout and proper . . . Carnap and Frege, they were his poison! He was stylish and popular! down to earth as you could get! strict with all and sundry! it wasn't worth it!

– But how did you have it?

– My life was sunny! rosy! huddlycuddly! What a childhood . . . Fondled and coddled by all and sundry! If I didn't have time to play, my friends would off themselves assemblyline style. Everything was grand, I was so fucking happy I don't even want to think about it!

CARNAP—Rudolf: German-born philosopher who embraced logical positivism

FREGE—Gottlob: German mathmatician and philospher, he's considered to be a founder of modern logic and analytic philosophy

XXV

I woke up to Grandpa emptying his balls on my face. He made me slurp the trickle from his head, and then he lay back down and read a Bamse story, the one where Little Hop meets Gut Twister. Grandpa cackled, struck a match on my eyelid and lit a ciggi. When he finished with the paper, he snubbed out his ciggi, shut his eyes, and stopped breathing for a few minutes. A gradufly crept into Grandpa's cocainepitted nose, drawn by the soursweet scent of brainrot. I felt weak and wobbly, all I'd had to eat for the last few days had been a Saintpaulia.

Mumbleslumbering, Grandpa dug up a lecture about Henry the Fowler's winter campaign against the Hungarians in the year 920—according to the criminalchristiancalendar, that is. I let him talk, but I didn't listen. Then he hummed a Grandpa original, a hymn to Basil II, the famous Bulgar-Slayer: "The Lord gave me thirty-thousand eyes to put out . . ."

BAMSE—in this case, a reference to "the world's strongest bear," a Swedish cartoon character

158

HENRY THE FOWLER—German king from 919–936

GRADUFLY—an insect drawn to curious or questionable smells

XXVI

We were in Skellefteå on our way to Etage, a nightclub, but the townies there were all worked up.

– Fallrot makes them anxious, Grandpa said reassuringly.

So here's what happened next . . . We went down to Bastuliden and stole an old Opel coupe. The owner came rushing out and grabbed hold of the bumper. He managed to stay with us a good long while. Then we drove up to Kågedalen again to see if Eilert and Signar could hang out, but they bailed on us. Fall was going strong, there was a riot of color wherever you looked. Just the right time for having a little fun. As usual, the old Kåge road— torturous curves paved with gravel—was too hard for Grandpa to take. He was all excited to try it anyway, though, so he put the pedal to the metal right where the road begins. At Twelve Meter Basin, we went into a ditch doing a good hundred-and-thirty. The car flew into a copse of trees, rolled once, and burst into flames, but we weren't hurt. No, I just went through the windshield and bit clean through my lip. It only goes to show that even when we're taking a falsestep, we've got fallenangels watching over us.

– Now you don't need lipstick to pull a good pout.

We had to walk the last few kilometers. On the way, Grandpa speared some hedgehogroadkill with a stick and began to munch. Two cars tried to run us down; they honked and gave us the finger. We saw a bullelk with bloody antlers crushing a toddler in its jaws. He disappeared into a copse of young, white birchtrees that—slender and attractive—were being stroked brusquely by the east wind. Out toward Torp Road, we spied a nice ride parked off in the trees. It was a winered Saab Turbo. It was bumping and jumping, so we knew something funny was happening. We crept forward and Grandpa quietly opened the passenger door. The scene that greeted our eyes was enough to make a midwife blush: the shirted back of a man no longer in his prime, and pimpled asses moving like they had minds of their own . . . heaving and bucking . . . His tie was slung over his shoulder and he had on wrinkled, damp socks . . . his feet jerked when the door opened . . . Beneath him was some kind of animal . . . red, bloated, and panting . . . it looked like a caughtrabbit . . . whimpering and moaning in fearful ecstasy . . .

– What the fuck, the guy managed to say, but it was too late for prayers . . . too late for tears . . .

Grandpa put his knee against the guy's back and mechanically wrapped a pianowire noose around his throat. After ten seconds the guy was ripe . . . he choked . . . drummed his feet . . . his dick jerked and spurted cream onto the stomach of whatever was beneath him . . . he shuddered and went still . . . It turned out the survivor was a woman. During the fuck, she'd been looking back over her shoulder . . . she looked tired and annoyed . . . didn't know shit was going down . . . just thought he'd cum too soon again . . . Then she saw Grandpa . . . who'd dared to disturb the great sacrament . . . she drew a breath to spew a bunch of filth . . . Grandpa wasn't fazed . . . he just knelt on her whalebelly . . . seized her dirtyblonde, cheapoperm curls and fastened the noose behind her head. She didn't put up a fight . . . that was smart . . . she was a fat cow . . . rolypoly . . . pigglywiggly . . . Hissing, Grandpa tightened the noose and she strangled herself trying to ease the tension . . . She was married, had long nails, a short lifeline . . . Her eyes had seen their share. . . her tongue was unbelievably long . . . bluish red . . . in between her chalkwhite teeth and fuckmered lips . . . she tried to claw at Grandpa, but couldn't do much . . . so she just struggled . . . Grandpa's grip wasn't that strong . . . he asked her if she'd read Bram Dijkstra's *Idols of Perversity* . . . she shook her head . . . slowly suffocated . . . her eyelids fluttered . . . the pianowire cut through her flesh . . . sliced her larynx . . . she finally twitched and went limp . . . her last breath was a pussyfart . . . Grandpa climbed out, wiped the sweat from his forehead with a piece of rubberfoam, and then washed his hands in a puddle. He lit a Dunhill and took a few swigs from a half Ballantyne's.

– Holy Sebastian's martyrium, I hope you didn't see too much of that, kid . . . What they were doing reeks in God's hairy nostrils. It's every macho/maso-man's duty to slaughter every copulating-couple he comes across.

– I hardly saw anything, Grandpa.

– Then we're sitting pretty! You know, Montaigne says that nature gave us pain to honor and serve pleasure . . . Someone who's got three or more fuckable openings just isn't human . . .

Remember, we're Norrlanders, not fucking Westerners! Didn't gaunt Tacitus say in his *Germania* that even back then blond beasts had a hard time tolerating impudent whores?—"The pale and darkly dressed Harierna force their immoral women to shove vipers, burningbranches, and mouldymazarines up their diseaseinfestedswamps. Then they hang them by the ankles from the stiff branches of deadtrees and militaryrecruits get to use them for punchingbags. Publicatae enim pudicitiae nulla venia" . . . Also keep in mind that in his festive *History of the Franks*, Gregory of Tours tells the story of a synod in Macon in 585, where the declaration that "mulierem hominem vocitari non posse"—that is, "cunts ain't human"—was met by a deafening roar of applause. Furthermore, Friedrich the Great says at the end of *Ecco Homo* that "All creative Dionysians are tough and live for destruction." Even Jesus Christ shouted out: "I've come to destroy the work of women . . . As long as they exist, conception rules death's dominion . . ."

– Amen.

– Now, my little cuddlemuffin, let's go find the Grail! or at least Sampo!

We dragged the pair out of the backseat . . . they'd both shit themselves . . . Grandpa took out half a dozen goldfillings with a pair of pliers . . . the man had bitten his tongue off . . . We climbed in, buckled up, and burned rubber. Before we came to Dalkarsliden and the outskirts of town, we'd already run a Volvo off the road and squashed a racoondog flat.

– This is called The Sinking Valley . . .

I understood why. Grandpa tossed an empty bottle out of the window at a hundred and ten MPH, and pinged a small child's dad right in the head. A sign warned us to beware of "Living Dead Children." Skellefteå's a huge disappointment . . . All roads lead to black decay. It's not a real city by any means. . . just barracks and bivouacs . . . if you have too much zest for life, that's the place for you . . . People who stop in Skellefteå have nowhere else to go . . . the descendents of a worthless race . . . Suffering from the Skellefteå Blight . . . a deadly disease that saps the muscles, nerves, and will . . . the nasty Västerbotten Syndrome . . . a slight mentalretardation and skinrash . . . More people die in Skellefteå every year than in the rest of Sweden combined . . . The death struggle is longer and more painful . . . Skellefteårs are mean, when they get their courage up . . . sheltered . . . ingrown . . . Good at keeping things quiet . . . holding themselves aloof . . . making things easy for themselves . . . Pigs in men's clothing . . . the legendary nineteenth century townies "B. C.," "Lord Grogg," and "Hin Håles Juvel" used to live here . . . Now the town is just a mishmash of debris . . . apemen . . . A Skellefteår knows everything in advance . . . understands how everything works . . . carries a big stick . . . is quick on the draw. . . He's got conviction . . . everything he touches and sees shrivels and turns gray . . . one hand washes the other . . . industry and information . . . money and sex . . . pollution and trash . . . Skellefteårs are zombies in limbo . . . freezedried . . . frostbitten . . .

The biggest thing to happen in Skellefteå was when AIF won the hockeybockey gold in '78 . . . They're still high off it . . . going on and on about their smackdown . . . slapdown . . . uprising . . . Skellefteå is Sweden Sports Central . . . everything else is lower on the totempole, there . . . sometimes the Sunnanå tribaders even make it up here . . . there's no baseball, because there's no competition . . . Sports are useful and important . . . they don't wear out your brain . . . Skellefteå has hatched two world-class balltalents . . . Jocko Nyström and Erika Norberg . . . that's something to be proud of . . . not everyone has seen Wilander and Malmsteen dangle balls . . . People are shorter in Skellefteå than in Kågedalen . . . they're quicker, even though they're fatter . . . they're good with the analphabet . . . In Skaeliptom, which was the old name for the place, most people are welfare cases and minimumwageworking socialautocrats . . . Though there are a few mongotheists who own their own shops and eat their meals with a knife and a fork . . . they're considered highclass . . . They go to the theater . . . they're experts in selfdeception . . . the hollow pillars of society . . . if you cover your eyes, you don't have to see how things are . . . In Skellefteå, it always pays off to stay poor in spirit . . . people are mean and soulless . . . It's always good to be around and about yourself alone . . . to gossip about others . . . People here have narrow eyes and forgettable faces that are hard to get used to . . .

"Furthermore, since they did not think it worthwhile to retain the knowledge of God, He gave them over to a depraved mind, to do what ought not to be done. They have become filled with every kind of wickedness, evil, greed and depravity. They are full of envy, murder, strife, deceit and malice. They are gossips, slanderers, God-haters, insolent, arrogant and boastful; they invent ways of doing evil; they disobey their parents; they are senseless, faithless, heartless, ruthless . . ."

– Time they realized Jarry and Vaché have come to town! Grandpa exclaimed and screeched to a halt before a climactericcrossing.

– Molloy and Malone! Caiaphas and Judas! I shouted.

– Hooboy! Trying on Grandpa's shoes, eh!

When the pedestrians thought they were safe, Grandpa did a burnout and hit two old women. They arced through the air, clutching their handbags . . . Then Grandpa drove up on the sidewalk and hit a carriage. Mother Cluck threw herself into the street. "Crazed Driver" is what the headline will say, but what's wrong with having a little fun so long as you're only hurting other people? We were doing ninety when we passed the Kaplan School and made our way down to Kyrkholmen.

– Hophophop! shouted Grandpa and we threw ourselves out of the car.

The car was thundering toward the river while we were rolling in the grass. Grandpa laughed until he choked and I had to thump him on the back. Then we trotted up toward Bonnstan, where the farmers used to hold booze- and slaughterfests during church holidays. Gray and dullred sheds made of leaky wood.

– This summer we'll burn the whole stinking shithole down!

Two girlygirls dressed in pastels came cycling along. They were about my age and ohsosweet. Grandpa whipped out some scissors and attacked one. She had long, wheatgold pigtails, which he hacked off at the roots. When she yelped, he cut a hunk of rosyflesh from her cheek and popped it in his mouth. She was so shocked she fainted. Dolly number two shrieked and peddled away, but I hopped on the second bike and chased her down. We both fell, and I punched her hard enough that she sprang a leak and shut up. About time. I went back to Grandpa . . . he read me a eulogy . . . Then we went down to Nordanå . . . publicpark . . .

historichouse ... museum ... playground ... There are huge trees
there, lindens and I-don't-know-what-the-fuck else ... Thrushes
and sparrows lead doomed lives ... They've got the Swannery ...
a few ponds with ducks, geese, and swans . . . we wandered
around . . . Grandpa chuckled . . . Satan's cruel as a child . . . It
was a Sunday, so families with small children were showing their
faces . . . who are they trying to fool . . . birds are icebound in
winter . . . then they thaw out again . . . old railbirds and young-
scamps threw half loaves of bread into the gasbubbling water . . .
creampuffs . . . busschedules . . . the birds ate it all . . . I adjusted
my snuffwad . . . even my fingernails had frostbite . . . We stopped
at a fence . . . ducks waddled and quacked . . . I heard voices . . .
A swan glided forward . . . it was knobby and huge . . . Grandpa
picked up a sharp rock and took aim . . . He threw it as hard as he
could and hit the swan in the head ... The bird screamed, flinched,
forgot itself . . . tried to fly though its wings were clipped . . .
blood ran down its neckfeathers . . . people gasped . . . looked at
each other and started whispering.

– What the hell did you do that for? some nappyhaired family-
man asked.

– He looked at me funny, Grandpa said and slouched away.

At the next pond, unsupervised kids were hanging out . . . a
mess and a fuss, nothing to do but get pissed off . . . Grandpa
grabbed a little kid in pink rompers, slurped down its juicyjuice,
and tossed the kid into the water.

– Sorry, kinky cherry . . .

Several mammalian lifeforms rushed at Grandpa, hooting
and hollering . . . Grandpa shyly defended himself with knife

drawn . . . The kid floated on its stomach . . . splashing listlessly . . .
woolcap bobbing . . . One of those big crocodiles Grandpa had
planted there in the seventies, graygreen and grinning broadly,
took the kid in its jaws and rolled him down to the sewers . . .
Meanwhile, the old bitches weren't playing nice . . . they'd decided
to teach us a lesson . . . fucking PMSers . . . screeching to highheaven . . . Grandpa cut a couple down to size . . . Then we hauled
ass toward what passed for a downtown.

   – We'll have to visit the museum and alter history some
other day!

   We ran . . . they were still chasing us . . . Grandpa isn't exactly Bikila . . . they were gaining on us . . . snapping at our
heels . . . breathing down our necks . . . three sturdy boys in real
bluejeans . . . Grandpa couldn't catch his breath . . . he was wheezing
like babyhamsters sucked up a vacuum . . . He stopped . . . laughed
at fear . . . they started in on him . . . knocked him down . . . taunted
and threatened him . . . scrapped in the gravel . . . the devils . . . it
wasn't going well . . . they didn't give a fuck about me . . . I found a
weapon . . . a cracked baseballbat . . . I struck without thinking . . .
crushed the skulls of the two who were holding Grandpa . . . the
third kicked out at me . . . the bat was useless . . . I rushed him . . .
butted his crotch with my head . . . he folded . . . I headbutted him
hard and heavy . . . when he lay curled on the ground, I started kicking him with my Doc Martens . . . until he cut the bullshit out . . .
Grandpa finally got to his feet . . . his suit was definitely ruined . . . I
dusted him off as well as I could . . .

   – That was just mean . . . what a fuss, just because I took his
juicyjuice . . . he didn't even want it . . . But now we definitely need
a real drink!

We headed downtown as charliehorses ran races up and down Grandpa's legs.

– Everything's closed, Grandpa!

– Calm down, boy . . . Trust me . . .

Most of what I've written about Skellefteå is stuff Grandpa's told me. I asked him how he knew so much about the town.

– I had a little lover here . . . once upon a time, before I was a Grandpa . . . He was beautiful both above and below . . . but his ass would get so tender, one time I couldn't even get my ringfinger up it . . . If he were still living here, we might arrange an introduction. There are too many dead souls here . . . evilspirits . . . more than I can stand, now that I'm sobering up . . .

We walked watchfully down the street. The buildings pressed together and were several stories tall . . . Shops and more shops . . . They sold clothes, jewelry, and household goods . . . stuff designed to keep up appearances . . . There were beautysalons, healthfoodstores, and sportsgoodsstores . . . so many chimerical promises . . . though a Fridaydoo and a Sundaymanicure will end up rotting in the grave just like everything else . . . There were whores everywhere you looked . . . lots were pushing strollers . . . lips dripping with honey, mouths more slippery than oil . . . I didn't give a fuck about the women in this trashtown, I knew I'd survive . . . I knew that someday the Lord God Almighty would cover their scalps with sores, and expose their nasties for all the world to see . . . baldskin instead of permedhair, sackcloth instead of fineclothes, brandingirons instead of beauty . . . Grandpa put a protective hand on my neck.

– Never let them know what your thinking and you'll be all right! That's the only way to protect yourself!

It surprised me to see so many of those creatures, all thinking they were human . . . I'd never have believed it . . . But they were worlds away . . . continents away from each other . . . galaxies receding at the speed of light . . . These days people don't have anything to say to each other . . . if they'd just sit down and think about it, though . . . that's what they should write about . . . They think they know where they're going . . . know where home is . . . placidly go to school and travel abroad . . .

They have names, jobs, pets, and securityblankets . . . friends and dependents . . . you can do without all that . . . just look at me and Grandpa . . . Traffic honked and screeched when we approached the crosswalk, but we made it across unscathed . . . The buildings got bigger . . . I fingered the upsidedown silver cross around my throat . . . comfort and security are the things they value above all . . . but that's the last thing the world will give you . . . Up until now, all the world ever gave me was something to think about . . . a rawfuck every now and then . . . chronic heartburn . . . The people who bothered to notice us smirked and grimaced . . . people only have two reactions when they meet a Grandpa's boy . . . indifference and contempt . . . Grandpa took off his Bogarthat and dried the coldsweat from his Sydowforehead . . . then put it back on . . . they tittled and tattled . . . Shriveledaunties, puffedupuncles, snottycocks, insatiablecunts . . . Persians, Arabs, poodles, clones . . . Dummies, labrats, internalcombustianengines, sexbots . . . Consumers, mutants, patients, lemurs . . . "The Count," aka "Martin Bormann," greeted Grandpa heartily and paraded next to us, lifting his legs a little too high . . . A retired, germaphobic driving instructor whose name Grandpa couldn't remember passed us clutching a tissue and looking desperate behind his poindexter glasses . . . "The King" and "Sweaty" had apparently taken a break from bingo and the lottery . . . they looked you in the eye and found you wanting . . . "Gypsy Rickard" and "Gypsy Allan" were heavilypetting two fat constables . . . Leif and "Moddan" were squabbling like so many times before . . . Leif had just puked on the toystore's front steps . . . Maud looked off balance . . . Sten and Georg met like nothing was up . . . they smiled, victims of the same dullwitted maliciousness . . . "Kurt the Can," who'd moved up in rank after "Little Herman," the graybearded dwarf, died, was rooting around in the trash for something to pawn . . .

– "Little Herman" was the better man . . .

– Yeah, he had a certain something . . . Called everyone idiot, thought animals were smarter than people . . . fought assholes with his cane and made himself a cardboard hat . . . His cynical little brain didn't even weigh a halfkilo . . . he was like a windup toydoll . . .

Tempo and Domus, the department stores, were right in front of us . . . but we weren't welcome there . . . Grandpa had pinched a lawnmower and a freezer, once . . . The building was so tall that I got dizzy and reached for Grandpa's hand . . . but he didn't tolerate that kind of touching . . .

– Let's go down to the citypark and look around . . . if nothing else, there's probably someone sleeping it off on a bench . . . a stolen fuck with a comatose drunk can't go wrong . . .

Video Lime had moved . . . it probably hadn't gotten any better, so we spared ourselves the headache . . . they never had what we wanted . . . The best they ever had was *Saló, Caligula, The Omen, The Evil Dead, The Silence of the Lambs*, stuff like that . . .

a little on the light side, but not half bad . . . You'd never find *Suspiria*, *Trauma*, or *Tenebrae* by Argento . . . no *Cannibal Holocaust* or *The Texas Chain Saw Massacre* . . . Grandpa had gone in and begged them to buy some quality familyfilms like *The Children from Frostmos Mountain, Shiteating Teenies, Ass in a Virgin's Ass, Carcass Rapist, Grampus Fucker, Marmot Mayhem* . . . But no such luck . . . A photo shop had set out a truly merciless display of color pictures showing ugly mugs and corpses in varying stages of decomposition . . . Sluts in whitegowns and graduationcaps preened coquettishly . . . It was a goddamned menagerie . . . Absurd bridal pairs . . . the last couple out . . . the bride's I-got-the-ring smile, the groom's studied selfcontrol . . . Toddlers with moist, pouting mouths . . . Rundown, dressedup fortysomethings . . . Four generations, each worst than the last . . . All trying to smile and act like everything's normal . . . One photo was cool, but unbelievably gross . . . a little mayqueen with terrified eyes sucking a goldbrown cock so hard she had grooves in her cheeks. . . it looked like Mishima's . . . or maybe Issei Sagawa's . . .

The Bay Leaf Bookstore was advertising the newest titles for fall . . . a stationary display. . . New releases from our folkhungriest graphomanes . . . Ivar LOB Johansson's monumental *Only a Whore* . . . Mora-Martinsson's gripping *Grandma Gets Married* . . . Vilgot Moberg's fit-for-the-fire masterpiece *Your Piece of Ground* . . . And then some stale leftovers they'd oh-so-lovingly left out . . . Jesus Gardell's *Mel Mermelstein's Hen Party* . . . Claus Östergren's *Bleda* . . . Maran Kandre's *Baby's Baby* . . . They had *Povel's and Tage's Love Letters . . . Taube's and Cornelis's Love Letters* . . . And *Tage's and Aina's Hate Letters* . . . They were trying to push Kjell-Olof Fält's memoirs, *All These Fucking Shitdays* . . . and Lazar Kaganovich's childhoodmemories . . . And Traci Lords's *Inside My Cunt* . . . The window on the other side of the door had books that were more to my taste: Boforprizewinner Eliot Cannetti's lively novel *The Confusing* . . . Bruno Skult's crisp *Cinammon Shops* . . . And Robert Walser's cocky *Jakob von Gunten* . . . Sven Hassel's *Kommando Reichsführer Holmlund* . . . Tolkien's *Lord of the Cockring* . . . Lovecraft's *Cthulhu* (a true story) . . . and the Tintin comics, the best thing the worst terror on earth has brought us . . .

– Hergé Bashevis Marquéz puts out some good stuff . . . compared to the folkstuff. . . Humanism's a monstrosity . . . One frightened look in the mirror should be enough to convince you that mankind is an abomination . . .

Grandpa didn't bother to kamikaze his way into the bookstore . . . we're banned from both there and the library . . . they think we lick our fingers too much when we browse . . . make all the pages stick together . . . The library's got us blacklisted . . . we use friedeggs for bookmarks and tear out what we consider to be extraneous pages . . . As we made our way to the city park, we heard some preppy neoliberal grandstanding out on market street:

– Mandatory abortions! Three cheers for female circumcision!

So far so good . . .

– Blinking yellow traffic lights 24/7, let the people decide . . . More girlyman matches . . . Easier to grab a quick one whenever you want! . . . Social Democrats must stop their cuntgrubbing! . . . Tax exemption for highincome fags! . . . Castrate the unemployed! and everyone else who gets a freeride! . . . Sterilize women! Slaughter all underperforming and overage athletes! like we do with race-horses! Ban relapsingornothologists! Grade adults on everyday life! Put it on your todo list: fapp-fapp! . . . All statesofmind to be ratified by the EU! . . . Nip ontological questions in the bud! before they blow up in your face . . .

You caught fragments from passersby . . . a conversation of sorts . . .

– But seriously . . . I think I drive better drunk . . .

– You sure fuck better . . . you feel less, you can hold out longer . . .

Isolated soapbubbles drifting on the breeze . . .

– I think he's just shittysweet . . .

– Too bad his dick's so tiny and *Hard on Hard in Helsingfors* is the only book he's ever read . . .

– Did you really sleep with him . . .

– I think so . . . I don't really remember . . . but I think he was with us up in Piteå . . . dragracing . . .

– You have to trust in the *Malleus Maleficarum* . . .

– When did he say you should come back . . .

– When I feel like that again . . .

– Like what . . .

– Like I did last night . . .

– Do you think so . . . are you ready . . .

– Hey . . . that wasn't yesterday . . .

– Thanks . . .

– Are you out running errands . . .

– Nah, we're just cruising around . . . talking shit . . .

– We've got our plates full just trying to look honest . . .

– We're looking for a jacket . . .

– Fuck Trisse . . .

– Did you just get out? . . .

– So I joined the "Semitic Society for Painful Animal Experimentation" . . .

– Have you tried it on the Old Man . . .

– That guy at the men's clothes shop is never going to die . . . why, he almost looks alive . . .

– So listen here, whatshisface said he wasn't going to do it at first . . .

– Or "Bella," you know, the guy who centrifuges cats out in Getberget . . .

– And "The Skunk" . . . shame about him . . .

– I heard you were going to close up the kitchen . . .

– Yeah, we're going to knock out the bathroom wall instead . . .

– Prison or mental hospital, that's the choice . . .

– You don't say . . .

– You don't get out too much . . .

– You have to stay sharp . . .

– Talk about a fucked-up guy . . . I'm so fucking cursed . . .

– What did he do . . .

– He's bonkers . . . what a moron . . .

– It was then, after we'd had coffee . . . that's when he rolled up a thousandkronornote and stuffed it up my pussy . . .

– Hey there . . .

– Hello . . .

– You going out this evening . . .

– No idea . . . you . . .

– Nah . . .

– Stop on by . . .

– Nah . . .

– Byebye, baby!

– Byebye!

– I always forget how ugly you are . . .

– Right back at you!

– You're going to put your mother in an earlygrave! She won't survive it!

– A blindbitch is the only thing that'll fuck you! One without fingers! And a nose!

– You've got a face only a mother could love!

– You're a miscarriage no mother would want!

– Your mother was a jackal!

– Your mom looks like a dugong!

– We're looking at new wallpaper . . .

– And lightfixtures . . .

– We bought a house . . .

– A fairyhouse . . .

– We're looking for a catheter . . .

– We're looking for someone to talk shit about . . .

Two troglodytes came up beside us . . . one was babbling like an incubatorbaby on laughinggas . . .

– I've thought up a damn good movie idea! Want to hear it!

– No . . .

– So here's the deal! Jacques de Molay (de Niro) and Hermann von Salza (Brandauer) are celebrating their honeymoon on a luxurycruise somewhere in the Caribbean . . . Just picture it . . . alpine landscapes . . . ciggibutts . . . retarded dolphins . . . boys, kulis, and pickolos . . . quick-as-a-whip flashbacks . . . bodybuilders in hotpursuit . . . loversquarrels . . . Pinocchiojokes . . . heartbreaking motoric disturbances . . . Can't you just see it all?

– No . . .

– Anyway! They've got it fucking good! They catch albatrosses and dress them in bikinis . . . one evening they get so shitfaced they start rewriting literary history . . . they bask lazily in the sun making fun of straight, farming Swedes . . . Then, boom! Schleyer (Rutger Hauer) and Moro (Nicholson) turn up with a cocaine delivery and a pair of fat, ignorant fucksluts! They force them to drop anchor! And when Hermann and Jacques try to save the day, they hijack the ship! But a hurricane is coming! They've sabotaged the radio! Don Johnson is hidden in a sack of cocaine, he'll probably sleep forever: a closeup of his shitsmeared undies! They drag him out and throw him to the hammerheads! like a sack of garbage! Cut to the cabin! It's evening and Robert and Klaus-Maria have begun to suspect they've got a couple of scumbags on their hands. I've thought out some nice pieces of dialogue and memorized them! Just listen to this . . . Nicholson's been working a cheerleader's ass with a rhubarbstalk. Now he's having some warm chocolatemilk and liverpaste on toast and he's got that sneer . . . he looks scarier than he did at the Overlook Hotel . . . And so he says . . . think of his Lokigrin and that impudent eyebrowcurl . . . So he says, low and hoarse . . . "I want to torment, humiliate and cut up all girls who refuse to drink the washingwater of lepers and eat lice and shit from poor people's clothes . . . What the fuck . . . It's not too much to ask for that! Like Angela of Foligno . . . and Catherine of Genoa . . . the saintcunts . . . I want to promote Heydrich-worship . . . And the Saint-Justcult . . . Make this fucking world a decent place to live in . . ." Hell yeah, that's cold! ice cold! and just like him, too!

– No, it's awkward . . . Just pathetic . . .

– He's dangerous when he's drunk . . .

– Don't look now, but there's the guy that trashtalks Skellefteå . . .

– I see him . . . the punk . . . the motherfucker . . .

– A coward, that's what he is . . .

– He's got to be totally fucked in the head . . .

– Get a load of that, full SS-gear . . .

– He should be stoned . . .

– Axl Rose . . . now he's a tasty bugger . . .

– There aren't any prettyboys in this town . . .

– They fuck like invalids . . .

– They don't know what a girl wants . . .

– They don't know what a girl needs . . .

– Love and affection . . .

– Precisely . . .

Grandpa led the way with his Merovingian stride. An ostentatious municipal building is next to the citypark . . . the social welfareoffice, not to mention the employment office . . . Stasi and Securitate . . . Local politics in Skellefteå is the battlefield of retired officemachinery . . . The park is small . . . the river is nearby, too few people have drowned themselves there . . . larches and southernhardwoods . . . no drunks, though . . . Something bustled in the hedgerow . . . someone was up to no good . . . we got scared . . . started to sober up . . . we turned around and beat a retreat . . .

– Let's take the bus to Morö Hollow!

We cut across Possibility Square. . . lots of shops . . . Polarn O. Pyret . . . Stor eller Liten . . . got on the number 2 bus . . . Grandpa paid for us both . . . it started up . . . it was ten past two . . . it was nice to sit, even if the bus was full of the dying . . . a pimplefaced teen was reading Delumeau's *Sin and Fear* . . . a poster showed a cleancut retard with the words "handler wanted" . . . we crossed the traintracks and turned towards Lasarettsbacken . . .

– We should've stopped and said hello to Abraham Bessik in the longtermcarefacility, Grandpa suddenly remembered. He could use a little cheering up.

I sat quietly and stared out into hell. Grandpa flipped through an issue of *Siegrunen*. Over the E-4 . . . along Tors Street . . . I saw a little cavalierdog, absurdly happy—being dragged by two washedup old coots who waved at me . . . past Norrvalla and Eddahallen . . . Grandpa had had himself a nice jacuzzifuck there one night . . . or was that someone else? We continued east . . . towards Järnskogen . . . Morö proper was a ghetto . . . apartmentblocks and parkinglots . . . then Morö Hollow . . . a sleepy town . . . houses in rows . . . each one worse than the last . . . blocks of greenhouses . . . hatcheries . . . burning plastics . . . spiraea, hydrangeas, and blue mother-of-pearl clematis, all wilting, of course . . . peace and order, psychosis on Friday . . . A German shepard fucking a dachshund . . . a weimaraner, a papillon dog . . . the busgate was lifted . . .

– Here's where we get off, Grandpa said. This is Dripdrop Street.

We strolled around a bit . . . past gloomy little houses . . . they might've been red and white . . . looked in on other people's wasted lives . . . An old crone glared at us from between a Hoya bella and a busy Lizzy . . . A group of darkies were having a fight . . .

A henpecked husband sucked on a Volkswagon's exhaustpipe and dreamed of suicide . . . A loudmouthed, middleaged, brown-haired whore in a Mickey Mouse T-shirt was getting her Daily Double on the kitchen table . . . she grabbed the balls that were beating her ass and bellowed like someone possessed . . . Teiresias sure had it right . . . Next door the light was dim . . . no one in sight . . .

– Bempa lives here . . . he's Royal Marlene's son-in-law, and Popo Dahlberg's sister-in-law . . . Anyway: before I ring the doorbell . . . Remember on the old TV show, what was it called, *Juttu*? When Uncle Lauri carves a willow pipe for that six-year-old whore?

– Yeah . . . Why?

– No reason . . . just checking . . . Qué será será . . .

He rang the doorbell and knocked. A cautious shrew opened the door a crack . . . Grandpa forced his way inside . . .

– Hellandhighwater, what've you done with Bempa?

– What are you implying!? Get out of my house before I call the cops!

Grandpa backhanded her and she fell down.

– And I politely asked where Bempa was, pissbag! I'm Lieutenant Onada and this is Wiener Sångerknaben! he shouted, pointing at me.

– Bempa's sick . . . he's in the living room . . . he got a brainbleed at Christmas . . .

– No worse than a headache nowadays . . . probably the same thing . . . You aren't exaggerating are you, cunt?

– Bempa's done for . . . he can't even swallow . . . sometimes he doesn't even know me . . .

– I wouldn't know you, either, not if we'd been slaving side-by-side on the same galley for fifty years . . . Who the hell are you, anyway?

– I'm Bempa's wife, Livia . . .

– Wife? If Bempa is fucking crazy old whores it's no wonder he's gotten sick! But I'll put a stop to it, if it's the last thing I do! Grandpa swore, dragging the woman by her hair toward the garage. I helped. And no matter how much she struggled and howled, Bempa didn't show his face.

The TV was shrieking . . . it was *Batman* . . . an old gray Mercedes stood in the garage . . .

– Partytime! Here comes the refrain!

He told me to run and get a hose, and then attach it to the showerhead, so we could have warm water. While I did that, Grandpa held Livia down and pried her mouth open with a hammer. I turned on the hot water and he forced it down her throat . . . liter after liter . . . up her nose and in her eyes . . . up her ass, too, but by then she was already dead . . . Grandpa had hammered too hard . . . We were banged up ourselves, but it was worth it. We went back into the house to look for Bempa . . . have us some guytime . . . he was in a urinesoaked leathersofa . . . entranced by the Joker . . . But Grandpa was the real thing . . . I turned the sound down . . . Grandpa walked in, plopped down, adjusted his glasses, and lit a Cinderella in an ivory ciggiholder . . .

– Hey there, Bempa, he smiled . . .

Bempa, though, was vacationing in the land where lollipops grow on trees and gingerbreadboys dance the hula . . . An inhumanly emaciated figure wearing a yellow collegejersey and sweatpants . . . frightened eyes . . . around fifty or so . . . just a baby, really . . .

– Grandpa's here . . . everything's going to be okay . . .

– Hogomooo . . .

– You've been a real champ, you know that . . . headaches are nothing to sneeze at, of course . . . you're just a little skinny . . . you look an awful lot like that chess guy, Mikhail Tal . . . but never mind that, he's my favorite . . .

– Gaa flaff motamaa . . .

– I'm doing fine! Fit as a fiddle! Fact is, me and the mite are going to paint the town red tonight. You got anything to drink?

– Schwuuu . . .

– That's a no, huh . . . best go on a boozerun, while the boy keeps you company . . . he sticks out a like a sorethumb, I can't be raiding stashes with him along . . . he doesn't know how to behave himself . . .

Grandpa limped out and I was alone with Bempa . . . We watched Robin and the Penguin to avoid looking at each other.

– You know anything about Count Gyula Andrássy of Csikszentkiraly and Krasznahorka? he suddenly asked.

– Huh?

– Noopuulosch . . . Ngugi . . . Humwawa . . . Mangu . . .

– I don't understand . . .

– Mokèlé-mbèmbés are found in Likouala . . .

– Uh huh . . .

– Sickan Carlsson gave Thor Modéen head . . . Ludwig II of Bavaria frenched Sacher-Masoch . . .

– Did she now?

– Kroogoshwiiri . . . Anticimex . . . Baubo . . . Mushoyoku . . .

– Don't worry about it . . . Even Nietzsche ate his own shit and drank his own piss when the going got tough . . .

– I remember when King Filimer ordered us to march through the Pripjet swamps toward the Pontian Steppes . . . and that was after we'd destroyed the Harappan civilization . . . Blubblubbuuuwy! Kaiomortz! Nyarlathotep! Igjugarjuk!

– Take up piano . . . write to Saida in the *Hemmets Journal* . . .

– Hyynokoruta! Waaaaa! Wholottalovv!

– Yeah . . . it sounds like you're the toast of the town, all right . . .

– Craaaa . . . Toush . . . Boohoo . . .

– Yeah, it sucks . . . just be happy there are people in the world who have it worse than you . . .

It was already a quarter to six. Someone had taken a couple of hours and flushed them right down the toilet . . . The front door flew open and an arrogant voice sliced right through us:

– I'm back, fotzelovers! With war spoils from fallen Ilion!

Grandpa clomped on in like a porcelainelephant. He sat three bags holding three bottles in front of each of us.

– Let's see your true colors, Little Boys Blue . . . The Holy Ghost guided my steps straight to a pair of lugubrious butterballs . . . We discussed Sigmund Fraud and then I beat them to death with a coffeepot . . . they had a good stash, too . . . enough for a real boozefest . . . They also had a few amphetamines tucked away . . .

He chugged half a liter of Smirnoff while standing, hurled the empty bottle at the wall, it broke a mirror and a clock, and then fished a scalare up out of the tank and swallowed it whole. He took a seat on the sofa, put his arms around Bempa, lit a joint, and farted contentedly . . . then Grandpa began to fire off his usual fusillade of fustian ideas and cackling harangues . . . he was in his element . . . flying high . . . Luther's and Hitler's table talk had nothing on Grandpa's when he was like this . . . I only remember parts of it . . . his head's a real randomgenerator . . .

– Jesus is the posterchild for animal desires! Peter should've cut off his cock instead of his ear! "Suffer the little children to come to me and don't stop before they're bleeding from both ends . . ." —Matthew seventeen and nineteen . . . A thousand thanks, oh yes! Christianity says it's okay to cast newborns before swine! That kind of talk makes me blush! Same with Luke fourteen twenty-six! And if that weren't enough: you shouldn't make representations of God's likeness. He's too ugly! If God exists, he owes me an apology! compensation for pain and suffering!

Grandpa scooted closer to Bempa and let his fingers shuck and jive a dirtylittleditty down his collarbone.

– We should stay light and transparent like "Mazdaznan-Hanisch" says! Erect a new Aryan high culture, where people sing of me and my adventures alone! Me and Tintin were named on the same day, in the same breath! They'll print my divine mug on T-shirts and posters! like Che Guevara! Humanity's most intimate little critters, crabs, and tapeworms, haven't gotten the praise they deserve . . . Fuck me, but I'm going to devote an epic to those little bastards!

– Or to the brown rats stealing the world from the black rats, I piped up.

– You've hit the nail on the head, sprout! I'll do it after I've finished my psychic war against the vibrators of Tinnitus XI! My other big project is rewriting the librettos to Wagner's musical dramas! Cleansing them of all that unnatural sex! I want happy, girly, loser endings! Let Tristan have Kurwenal! Let the Dutchman be filled with spectral seamen! Let Tannhäuser party with the four nobleboys! Let Lohengrin, King Heinrich, and Friedrich von Telramund wear out other's middleaged dreampipes with their plucky little karatepricks . . . let the fucking swan get in on it too! And I've thought of a fitting punishment for all those virtuous, cuntstinking temptresses, too . . . Elsa von Brabant will be fucked to death by the last group of mountaingorillas! Elisabeth will get knocked up by her father, Landgrave Hermann von Thüringen . . . then the fetus will bite and claw its way out like a bloody little gnome . . . Senta will get a job at a truckdriver cafe in Uganda . . . Isolde will take up with Fassbinder . . . Siegmund and Hunding will hook up and torture Sieglinde to death with rough old kikejokes . . . Siegfried and Mime will live happily ever after in the smithy . . . Brünhilde will burn up on the pyre that Wotan wisely enough tampered with . . . But I won't change a note of the music! It's just devilish!

Then Grandpa switched tracks, took another detour . . .

– Pataphysics, petrochemistry, and pornobiology are the cornerstones of the bestialfaith . . . the secret teachings of saprophytism . . . Apropos: what wouldn't you give to see the Olympian play of expression across the Geheimerat's face while he jerks off into a paraffinsmeared erminemuff?

– How do you spell Goethe?

– G Ö T E . . . like it sounds . . .

– Koroo . . . Sonyhaiku . . . Pobbolollysatori . . .

– I think you've gone around the bend, my sweet . . . tuataras are pinealeyed, but don't fret . . . a third eye is just one more thing to miss . . . during its centurieslong dozerregime, the Sassanidians conducted research in the field of oblivionstudies . . . They were blinded by moonlight and didn't give a damn about appearances . . .

On the news, they were talking about a Bolshevik statue toppling happening in the Baltics . . .

– I wouldn't mind having that Dzerzhinsky statue, Grandpa said with a rare tear in the corner of his eye. You'll never hear me say a word against the Cheka, GPU, or KGB . . . Felix was a gentleman . . . And all the others, too . . . Yezhov, Pavlov, Mikhailov . . . Nijinsky and Stravinsky . . . I could best be described as a proud member of the People's Party . . . What else is there after Mundebo and Jan-Erik Wikström . . . If Bildt hadn't been such a tedious fish fuck, who knows, I might've been a moderate . . . a neoliberal . . . newlysaved . . .

He spit at Anna Lindmarker and hit her between her beady little eyes . . . the blob ran down between her boobs . . . from the way her lips were moving, she was talking about something hot . . . Now Grandpa was telling a story about a sly old fart who'd lived undetected in a dumptruck for decades . . . And another who'd collected a lifetime's worth of piss and shit in big barrels . . . and how his father had done the collecting for him when he was too young to do it himself . . . And about a bigshot farmer in Kågemarken who'd had special cages built for all his fuckable domesticanimals; only their noses and assholes were exposed; that way they could snuffle around and get fucked in the ass, but couldn't put up a fight: he had bulls, boars, foxes, bears, gray owls, golden eagles, and everything else imaginable . . . He gave it up, though, after he installed an aquarium, got drunk, and tried to fuck a fifty-pound pike through the food opening . . . And Grandpa told us how to dig kiddietraps on the beach . . . Catch them with boathooks under the docks . . . And told us how it feels to fuck someone whose upperbody is stuck in a burningoven . . . He claimed that sourcecriticism is only valid when performed by the disabled . . . He told us how you can make a typewriter sound like an Einsatzkommando, just by pressing the right keys . . . He said that Max Stirner's *The Ego and Its Own* is the only philosemitosophistic work worth dragging yourself through . . . that the phrase "Ho Chi Minh sucks dead cocks" in *Apocalypse Now* is the only thing you need to know about the Vietnam War . . .

– Is there anyone else who thinks Bempa is a little down in the dumps?

– Me . . .

– You won't say no to some fish and booze, will you deary? Grandpa asked, tickling him under the chin.

Then he went and got a colander from the kitchen and three tiger barbs from the tank. A last meal . . . He tried to feed Bempa the fish and to force some Bacardi down his throat.

– And now take a bite for Ohlendorf . . . and another for Pastor Paisley . . . and one for Pogonophorans . . .

But Bempa couldn't swallow . . . the barbs came right back up . . . they flopped around on the labialhued broadloom carpet . . . Grandpa dumped twenty centiliters of alcohol over Bempa's head. Then he sat and smoked quietly for a few minutes . . . half-watching TV . . .

– Am I the only one who wants to play Bismarck? . . . Oh well, spoilsport! enough of that! What are we supposed to do now, exchange luberecipes and talk trappingmethods?

– For Robespierre! yelled Bempa. Gmoopoffbaluuu . . .

– Shut your mouth, brainfry! Manu says, he who garbels language garbels everything . . . From his viewpoint, you've been found guilty . . . You're worse than Michael Finnigan's Wake . . .

Grandpa was dreaming up some new devilishness . . . the corners of his mouth were twitching . . .

– I'll admit that my stomach is starting to rumble . . . I'd really like one of your kidneys about now . . .

He got out a Hubertus deerwhistle. It could make both a deer's distress and an old goat's mating calls. Grandpa pipped and squeaked first one, then the other . . . Bempa got confused and sat up . . . Garn howled outside of Gnipahall . . . Grandpa decked Bempa one and pulled off his leather belt . . .

– Before I take a kidney, I want you to blow me! That way we won't wear out your shithole! he said considerately.

He put a Blessed Host on Bempa's dry tongue and pushed in his cock . . . it wasn't easy . . . Bempa didn't have any spit . . . But Grandpa didn't give up . . . the cock goes in, morality goes out . . . life's one giant swing . . . the fun lies in jumping off right when you know you're gonna fall . . . Bempa had come to the end of his long journey . . . he gaped wide . . . barfed when Grandpa's cock rammed the back of his throat . . . weak yellow bile . . . Grandpa raged like he had rabies . . . punched and kicked . . . lashed out with his belt . . . blinded one eye with the clasp . . . He hooted and hollared . . . bent over and bit the carotid artery . . . Bempa crawled toward the kitchen . . . blood splattered across the cheap knick-knacks . . . a strong stream, dark and lively . . . Grandpa drank from the source . . . Bempa had served his purpose . . . Grandpa pulled up Bempa's shirt . . . sliced him with a glass shard . . . carved out the kidney . . . gobbled and slurped it down . . . took a drink . . . started to relax . . .

– Now you can eat, he declared, and I obeyed . . .

Luckily, that only meant that I was supposed to go down on Grandpa . . . otherwise I would've puked . . . I used an Old Norse sucking technique . . . Bempa's bile tasted like French mustard . . . murder made Grandpa blasphemously horny . . . another person's fear of death is the strongest aphrodisiac around . . . when Grandpa came, he shrieked curses at the Yankees and the Russians . . . his sperm tasted like mincemeat . . . then he gave me a quick jack . . . that was nice of him . . . Piglet and Pooh were on TV . . . my cum shot a few meters out . . . ran down the TV screen . . . Grandpa sobbed . . . he felt bad for Eeyore . . . Grandpa's strongest point is his humor . . . his weakest is emotional instability . . . He buried his face between the sofacushions and waaaaahhhhh'd . . . I buttoned my fly, climbed up on the sofa, and put my arms around my Grandpa . . . he calmed down a little, blew his nose on a cushion, took a swig of Renat . . .

– Together with the primedminister, I say: "Faith in humanity's worthlessness is what keeps me going," he sniffed. *Winnie the Pooh* was over . . . I flipped through the TV schedule to see if there was anything else on . . . drank my Lord Culvert . . . program after program . . . *Who's Raping Who(m)* . . . the usual parade of has-beens on *Culture* . . . I turned up the sound, but it was still pretty low . . .

– Have I told you about how we murdered all those Christians in Ostvik? It was me, "Maxin," "Elisha Burr," Ragnar Rök, and

Hilding Lindgren . . . We bound their hands and feet, tied them to a pole, smeared them with syrup, and threw them naked on an anthill . . . mosquitoes, blackflies, houseflies, and gadflies all got some, too . . . Then we covered them with Bible pages until they looked like mummies and lit a match . . . We buried them alive sixty-nine style, two on two . . . Death by orgasm . . . rats in pipes ate out their pussies . . . We rammed crucifixes up their asses and into their stomachs . . . Dunked them in acid baths, which skinned them alive . . . They were selfserving . . . we tore the fetuses out of their wombs and sprinkled them with salt and ketchup . . . We nailed them to hayfences by their kneecaps . . . Of course, we made them all fuck the priest first . . . Pier Luigi Farnese would've felt right at home . . .

He lost his train of thought, but found another . . .

– Oh yeah, mite . . . Next year you'll be able to go on *Vi i femman* . . . What do you think of that?

– I don't know . . . do I have to?

– What the! Of course you have to! Don't you want to show those fancy queers what you can do?

– I'm scared of messing up . . .

– That's the last thing you have to worry about! You've learned loads from me . . . for example, you know it was "Race Günther" and not Dürer who engraved "Knight, Death and the Devil" . . . How many prepubescent sluts do you think know anything about that?! Be thankful you get to participate!! People don't trust their ears! Drops in the bucket! My whole life I've tried to be an embarrassment to myself and a warning to others . . . eking out a shitty little existence for you and yours . . . Charis and metron have been my guiding lights . . . ahimsa and caritas . . . but this is just plain wretched . . . what have I done to deserve this . . . the worst karma in the solarsystem . . . a child so hardhearted it'd give the Devil himself pause . . . you're the new Seydlitz . . . the biggest bluff since Konrad Kujau . . . the worst thing to happen to Sweden since Ansgar . . .

Grandpa finally got tired of this querulation, his thoughts never followed a straightpath . . . Now the train had left without him and he was lost . . . he drank and waited for inspiration to strike . . . It looked like Östen and Svante were having a good time . . . even though they were shitfaced sober . . .

– I know what we can do . . . let's make some prankcalls!

He went into the bedroom and flipped through the phonebook on the nightstand.

– Let's see . . . redactors? . . . nah . . . refectories . . . regulators . . . robots . . . salt, wholesale . . . sand, gravel, shingles, macadam . . . smokehouses . . . here's a good one . . . Tank and Sludge in Skellefteham . . .

He dialed some numbers on the buttercolored telephone . . .

– Howdy! I'd like to order a sludging! that I'll forget right away! As soon as possible! My name's Erling Hardass and I'm stark raving mad! Do you have a penispump! I live in Orrliden! That sounds good! Let's do that! Bye now!

He threw the phone back onto the receiver.

– All they had was an answeringmachine, the devils! I was thinking about ordering a "total inspection of all unsavoury orifices" for you at the Suck and Swallow beauty salon . . . Then Grandpa called the priest on duty and told him that he was about to slit his wrists in a hot bath . . . The illusionist John Houdi landed himself an engagement for tomorrow evening at the old policecommisioner . . . Then he threatened to kill a few old ladies . . . Ordered fifty pizzas from Bel Party service to be delivered to an innocent girl . . . Time had taken a great leap forward again . . . it was after ten . . . Grandpa called emergency . . .

– Something real bad is about to happen . . .

He sounded like an auntie who's afraid she's got a bunintheoven.

– They're going on something terrible . . . they're going to kill each other . . . they're in Dripdrop Street . . . Yes, my name's Nagarjuna . . . and I'm here with Heliogabalus . . . we're on our way out . . . together with Harald and Frank Alexander . . . but we'll wait for you . . . absolutely . . . see you in a moment . . .

The next call was to a taxiservice . . . We stopped to piss in a bucket . . . Then we went outside and waited . . . The taxi roared up like a batoutofhell . . . a couple of cougars appeared from the house next door . . . They weren't exactly kittenfresh. . . dewynew . . . but they'd done their best to look it . . . spackled over the flaws . . . they were sourpussies without a cock to ram them . . . they needed something hard between their thighs . . . they were divorced, single . . . secondhand goods . . . spavined . . . petulant . . . I recognized the woman who'd gotten fucked on the kitchen table, I'd seen her on the back of a milkcarton . . . she was number thirteen in a series of notorious, neurotic bluelightspecialwhores from Gold Town, which the ill-humored liked to call Skellefteå . . . she seemed dull and dense. Grandpa went up and introduced us . . .

– Hi there, I'm Michael Myers and this here is Jason . . .

The two sluts were insolent, giggly . . . their labiallips were swollen with wine . . . When the taxi drove up, Grandpa dumped the pissbucket over their heads ... They put up a fuss ... made a stink ... Their nice evening had been ruined . . . these were women with oldfashioned morals . . . each of them had worked whole citydistricts on their backs . . . they descended on Grandpa, delicate fists swinging . . . he knocked the two shrews out . . . then we jumped into the taxi . . .

– Possibility Square . . .

We passed a police car . . . they were too late . . . The taxi driver's days were numbered . . . you could see it immediately . . . he was depressed . . . unhappiness dripped from every pore . . . he looked like he'd singlehandedly shouldered the blame for the genocides in Equatorial Guinea, Rwanda, and Burundi . . . Ropes and knives, bridges and guns send secret signals to guys like that . . . Grandpa talked about the *Summa Theologica*, asked the driver if he really thought that Socrates blew Alcibiades . . .

– I don't know . . .

– Can you believe that I'm made up of quark-gluon-plasma! I needed *cura* but I got *usura*!

– Uh-huh . . .

– Now you've wounded me! We gotta make it right . . .

– Be quiet, you shit . . .

– Did you just cuss at me?! you devil! How's that for manners! With that sweet mouth, I bet you're just a babyfucking homo! Plebian! Cuckold! Circlejerker! Democrat!

The driver slammed on the brakes, told us to pay and get out . . .

– What the . . . don't you want to kiss and make up . . . ?

– Pay the damn seventy-eight kroner and get out! You've crossed the line!

– I crossed it a long time ago, friend . . . Fuck me, but you look just like Allende . . .

The driver glared at Grandpa in the rearview mirror . . .

– You *are* Allende! Confess it, you devil! You escaped your just deserts! You thought you were safe! But now you've met *Los Novios de la Muerte*!

Just like that the pianowire was around Allende's throat . . . in a flash and a gurgle he was dead . . . We hauled the cadaver out of the car, emptied the cashbox, and then Grandpa burned rubber toward downtown . . . He forgot to brake at a red light outside of Expolaris . . . We hit a Renault with an average Joe inside . . . the cars came together in a tangle of bumpers and trailerhooks . . . we got out and taught the guy a lesson . . . then we beat a retreat . . .

– Let's go to Scandic and have a beer!

It was nearby . . . big and fancy and askew and it had a glassceiling . . . they wouldn't let us in . . .

– Come on, Taisto, Grandpa begged, we're as good as any of them!

– It's got nothing to do with that . . . the boy's too young and you're both drunk . . .

– I'm shitsober! I swear! I just had a beer with my sausage, that's all!

– No point in arguing . . . we've got our rules . . .

Grandpa paused a moment . . .

– Can't we just come in and get warm . . . See, I look just like Twiggy! and the boy here is a carboncopy of Genet! I know that gay hairdresser, Moshe Bindefeld! I participated in "Glaube und Schönheit"! We aren't sybarites, if that's what you thought! I've got pubelocks from both Ulyanov and Jughashvili!

When the bouncer was least expecting it, Grandpa stuck a knife in his belly.

– One side, seacalf!

Grandpa sliced a cyclist across the face, flung himself up on his bike, and peddled away . . . He made the sign of the cross, so I understood we'd meet at the nearest church . . . I raced past the Canal School, alongside Nygatan . . . they were after me . . . two big boors . . . Kodiak bears . . . their legs pumped like pistons . . . their shoes slapped the pavement . . . I knew it was a matter of life or death . . . if they caught me, it was all over . . . they started panting . . . lagged behind . . . I picked up the pace . . . they gave up . . . I kept running . . . came to my senses . . . found my way back to St. Olaf . . . Grandpa was waiting for me in the dark . . . I saw his ciggiglow . . .

– I just knew it, mite . . . You're a little Aouita in the rough . . . now if you could just get rid of those lovehandles . . .

He pulled me under the streetlight.

– Before we go into Etage, I need to have a look at you . . .

Sincerely feigned dismay lit his eyes . . .

– What a sight! The worst I've ever seen! It'd make anyone sick just looking at you!

– What is it, Grandpa?

– You probably look like this all the time! But I never look at you this closely! No wonder they wouldn't let us in! . . . you're Elephant Man in the flesh . . . or maybe the sexhungry monster in Tobe Hooper's *Funhouse* . . . we've got to do something about this . . .

We hid behind the churchyard wall . . . after a little while two blond, nineteen-year-old shebeasts came strolling along . . . in fuckme outfits . . . chatting like naughty kiddos on the way to a Christmastreeplundering . . . Grandpa blocked their path . . .

– Greetings, Judith and Salome . . .

They stepped into the street, to hell with Grandpa . . . Resolutely, he grabbed their manes and cracked their skulls together . . . a few times . . . there was a squishypopping sound . . . their eyebrows and lips split open . . . they fainted . . . Grandpa drew out his Game Skinner and began to scalp one expertly . . . with conquistadorian flair he held up a blooddripping blonde wig . . .

– When you put it on, make sure the blood soaks your hair . . . that way it'll stick . . .

While I did that, he rooted around in the little floozy's purse for her makeupcase . . .

– Let's see, a bit of red and black on your humdrum face and you might reel in a little MS-cock, if you're lucky . . .

He fixed me up under the streetlamp's deadwhite light, and then I caught a glimpse of myself in the case's little round mirror . . . I looked damned . . . in a different way than usual, I mean . . . I changed into the girl's black eelskindress, put on her suedejacket, hose, and pumps . . .

– There you go, now you're a fullfledged whore . . .

We made our way into the city . . . humanity babbled around us . . . A Sunday evening makes you want to trashtalk your country more than St. Bernhard and St. Goytisolo combined . . . Grandpa sang "Der Tod sei unser Kampfgenoss, wir sind die schwarzen Scharen!" We passed a fat, ugly statue . . . stores . . . Kid and Nervefiber. . . Blast-Furnace Bazaar . . . Salamander Optics . . . Inside a doorway, Lars "Humpy" Holmgren was on his knees, trying to

give a pal a blowjob . . . Rönnmarks . . . Thylins . . . Dåmus . . .
around the corner past the Sparkbanken . . . Etage . . . Malmia . . .
Into the lobby, which stank of dirty living . . . ropes formed barriers . . . we took the lefthand path, as we always do . . . the bouncers
nodded their understanding . . . Grandpa shelled out two hundred
kroner . . . they let us in . . . I left my jacket with a humanoid behind
the counter . . . got a little plastic ticket as a reminder . . . We went
downstairs . . . afrojudaic rhythms were pounding . . . the light
was glaring . . . people were playing roulette . . . the room looked
promising, it was packed with boys . . . Grandpa recognized a few
initiates and winked . . . he'd brought me to the temple of pleasure
and love . . . It was dark, smoky, warm, and fleshpacked . . . rotten
and raw . . . idols and progeny . . . Jungle rhythms thumped . . .
waking vulgar desires . . . a shething was singing like she was in
pain . . . why don't you touch me . . . waa-a-oa-a-a-aaa . . . A maze
of stairs led up and down to the dance floor . . . We formed a
Boar Snout and shouldered our way to the central bar . . . scooted
in next to Tomas Sandström and Uffe Samuelsson, who robustly
caressed each other's hardused cocks through their stonewashed
jeans . . . Judge Stäglich was in a heated discussion with Mailer,
Ärkesnärt was looking on, three Greenlanders, Kennet, Rolf, and
Kjell tried to outdo each other in piggishness . . . Grandpa ordered
a drink . . .

– A Fanfarlo and a Horla, please! Those are absinthes!

They didn't have any . . .

– A Mafarka and an Uomo finito then!

They didn't have those either . . .

– Two beers on the house! Just joking!

A skinny, stuckup redhaired primadonna poured the beer . . .

– Ninety-six kroner.

– Couldn't you give Zebulon and Bombi Bitt a break . . .

– No . . .

Grandpa sipped the foam and then took a couple of gulps . . . bared his goldteeth . . .

– Tonight will make the Battle of Catalaunian Fields look like Sunday school!

He had to shout to be heard over the music . . .

– I haven't felt this pumped since they shot Kennedy and MLK!

Grandpa bent toward a shy, sweet boy with a deshimaric expression, the kid looked like he was trying to become a part of the mineral kingdom . . . Grandpa recited Mallarmé's "The Afternoon of a Faun," toasted him, and turned back to me . . .

– I'm going make the rounds . . . Wait here . . .

He forced his way up the stairs to another bar . . . doling out punches and benedictions . . . mockeries and hypocrisies . . . parodies and repartees . . . people eyed him askance . . . I leaned on the rail overlooking the dance floor . . . It was jampacked . . . flooded with bodies . . . they jerked and twitched spasmodically . . . they looked like they were doing jumping jacks . . . it thumped and throbbed . . . some poor bastard was singing: "she has sperm in her hair that only I can see" . . . While I was standing there, a tall, balding man in wirerimmed glasses and a jetblack outfit came up and touched my breasts . . . he didn't have a prayer . . . He smelled like Absolut Citron, insisted he was Ignatius of Loyola, a member of the Leibstandarte, and a necrology student in Uppsala . . .

– Can I give you an enema . . .

– No, thank you . . .

– Abdominal abominations! he shouted. Back off, bitch! Can I at least take your temperature?

– I said no . . .

He folded his hands in a parody of prayer . . . Then he slurred out "lord of silence, supreme god of desolation," wrote "Make love, don't fuck! The soul of a woman was created below Jesus Christ I beg your pardon you indescribable tramp . . ." on a napkin and stumbled on, looking for a woman to love him to death . . .

Grandpa came back from his adventure, elbowed aside some little windbag . . .

– What a drag! I had to lace some glasses with cyanide up there, this place is just crawling with heteros!

Despondently, he examined the rocking and writhing clumps of flesh lit by the flashing lights way up on the ceiling . . . the song ended . . . the next number was a slow one . . . Steers hit cows up for a dance . . . it was disgusting . . . it's only Gere and Swayze who respected gender boundaries . . . they danced hip-to-hip, mouth-to-mouth . . . If I could only find words, to tell you I'm sorry . . . A big, bushybearded, greeneyed man of indeterminate age shoved his way to the railing . . . He smiled a shy, miserly, unpleasant smile at Grandpa . . . he had on a black shirt with a big silver Thor's Hammer around his neck . . . Levi's 503 . . fucking jew-jeans . . . still, he had a nice ass . . . hard to say if he was sad or mad . . . Grandpa went up to him . . . laughed condescendingly . . . kissed him tyrannically . . . they got to talking . . . two of Satan's own . . . they seemed mighty friendly . . . their conversation lasted a while . . . I gave a couple of guys high up on the permillascale the brush off . . . tossed my hair and smoked like a girl . . .

They parted with a handshake . . . Then Grandpa yelled in my ear . . .

– Nikanor's one of a kind! There's no one who can taunt cunt as disgustingly as he! When he was young and soursweet, he sullied his magnificent vandalcock in more than a few rancid hellholes, let me tell you! He likes to think of himself as an intransigent refractor! That is, until the next bout of cuddlesickness hits him! Then he shifts into overdrive!

– God creates work and Old Nick stress . . .

– Exactly! But he's a good guy, just a little weak and indecisive . . . If anyone can describe the way the world works, it's him . . . Odin speaks through him . . . right now he's working on "Lovesong to the Maneating Animal," plus a distortion on "The Biological Abnormality of a Woman's Need to Breed" . . . He's the last true Nietzschean . . . a courteous, lecherous voyeur . . .

The music begin again, "My Home Town" by the Wankadies.

– Time to stir the pot, mite!

Grandpa asked everyone in sight to dance, but they said no . . . then he guzzled their beer . . . a storm was brewing . . . There was a crowd at his heels . . . a bunch of beefyoafs . . . giantbabes . . . youngpups . . . They didn't attack, because he looked so frail . . . but they told him to pay for the beer . . . Grandpa gestured and joked . . . the trashier tramps laughed . . . the swankier skanks drew back . . . the mob closed its ranks . . . drowned out Grandpa with scurrilous words . . . suddenly he was holding a silenced Glock . . . he started with the loudmouths . . . three of them fell with holes between their eyes . . . Grandpa headed for the exit and I followed . . . it was hard to make progress . . . I slit my skirt up so I could go faster . . . Grandpa shot a bouncer in the belly . . . stabbed a pair of leviathans . . . We sprang across the square . . . Grandpa reloaded in flight . . . turned and shot down the two who were chasing us . . . more were coming . . . We sprinted past a kiosk . . . a dark car was making a turn . . . Grandpa wrenched open the back door . . . waved his Glock . . . three passengers threw themselves out . . . we hopped in . . . Grandpa told the guy to drive like Holy Mary was giving birth in the backseat . . . tires squealed . . . past the policestation . . . onto the E4 . . . going the wrong direction . . . north . . . I mumbled the end of the 137th Psalm, the same thing Signar dreamt about: "O Daughter of Babylon, doomed to destruction, happy is he who repays you for what you have done to us—he who seizes your infants and dashes them against the rocks" . . . The driver got into the right lane at the Kanalgate intersection . . . no one was following us . . . we were headed home . . . away from the city of woe, eternal pain, the population of loss . . .

– Well, that's an evening that will go down in history . . . it was so fucking boring . . . Everyone and everything was just nasty and ugly . . . it takes your breath away . . . it bowls you over . . . shocks you to the core . . . They're like the Viet Cong and Hezbollah all rolled into one . . . I'm not used to that kind of reception . . . And you, you asspicker, you'd defend them, wouldn't you, he said to the driver, shoving the gun into his neck.

– Please, I don't know what you're talking about . . . but I'll take you wherever you want to go, just don't hurt me . . .

– We want to go to Hebbershålet . . . You know where that is?

– Somewhere around Hebbersliden . . .
– It's the Land of the Hyperboreans . . . can't be reached by land or sea . . . It's airyanem vaejo . . . swetadvipa . . .
– Just tell me where to go . . .
– To the journey's end . . .
Me and Grandpa sat quietly and watched the darkness race by. The coniferoustrees embraced their lost sons . . . In Hebbersfors, Grandpa hold the guy to stop . . . shot him in coldblood . . . with coldblooded courage . . . a lot is excusable, when you don't get worked up . . . We nicked a couple of bikes and rode to Västbäck's Bridge . . . cross at your own risk . . . Then we went home, just as cold, tired, and loveless as before . . . We crawled into bed, both agreeing it would be a long, long time before we went clubbing or pubbing again.

PUBLICATAE ENIM PUDICITIAE NULLA VENIA—"The loss of chastity meets with no indulgence"
FURTHERMORE, SINCE THEY DID NOT THINK, ETC.—Romans 1:28
BIKILA—Abebe, champion marathon runner from Ethiopia
SYDOW—Max von, Swedish actor
MISHIMA—pen name of Japanese author Kimitake Hiraoka
ISSEI SAGAWA—murdered a Dutch classmate while attending school at the Sorbonne in 1981, eating part of her corpse; having returned to his homeland, he is now free and enjoys a cult following of sorts (books and films have been made about him, rockbands sing his praise)
MALLEUS MALEFICARUM—1486 treatise on witches, by Heinrich Kramer, Inquisitor
SOMETHING BUSTLED IN THE HEDGEROW—see "Stairway to Heaven" by Led Zeppelin

Jacques de Molay—Grand Master of the Knights Templar, burned alive on the order of Philip the Fair

Hermann von Salza—Grand Master of the Teutonic Knights from 1210–1239

Siegrunen—Waffen-SS history journal

Teiresias—seer punished with blindness by coweyed Hera when he claimed that women enjoy the "love act" incomparably more than men

AIF—corruption of AIK, the town of Skellefteå's beloved hockey team

Jocko Nyström—Joakim Nyström: tennis player from Skellefteå

Erika Norberg—Swedish journalist

Mats Wilander—Swedish tennis player

Malmsteen—Swedish heavy metal rocker

Ivar LOB Johansson—Ivar Lo-Johansson: Swedish author, wrote *Only a Mother*

Mora Martinsson—Helge Maria Swarts, also known as Moa Martinson: Swedish author of *Mor gifter sig* (Mother Gets Married)

Vilgot Moberg—Vilhelm Moberg: Swedish author, wrote *A Time on Earth.*

Jesus Gardell—Jonas Gardell: Swedish author

Klas Östergren—Claus Östergren: Swedish author, wrote *Attila*

Maran Kandre—Mare Kandre: Swedish author, wrote *Bübins unge* (Bübin's Child)

Povel Ramel—Swedish entertainer

Tage Danielsson—Swedish author and entertainer

Evert Taube—Swedish author and entertainer

Tage and Aina—Aina Erlander was married to the Swedish prime minster, Tage Erlander, for fifty-five years

Cornelis Vreeswijk—Dutch singer-songwriter, put out a tribute album to Evert Taube entitled "Cornelis sjunger Taube" (Cornelis Sings Taube)

Kjell-Olof Fält—Kjell-Olof Feldt: Swedish social-democratic politician, wrote a memoir entitled *Alla dessa dagar* (All These Days)

Lazar Kaganovich—Soviet politican, known as the "Iron Lazar" for the zeal with which he carried out Stalin's orders

Traci Lords—American porn star

Eliot Cannetti—Elias Canetti: Bulgarian-born author who wrote in German, author of *Auto-da-Fé*); he was awarded the Nobel Prize in Literature in 1981; his loathing of T.S. Eliot is legendary

Bruno Skult—Bruno Schulz: Polish writer and translator

Sven Hassel—Danish author, wrote *Kommando Reichsführer Himmler*

Daddy Cool—Australian rock band

Lieutenant Onada—Hinoo, a Japanese intelligence officer; for a number of years after World War II had ended, he sat isolated on some god-forsaken island, firmly believing that the war was still going on

Count Gyula Andrássy, etc.—the Habsburg Minister of Foreign Affairs; together with Bismark, he negotiated the alliance with Germany in 1879

Ngugi—John, Kenyan, one of the world's best cross-country runners

Humwawa—demon, master of perversion, face made from viscera

Mangu—Möngke Khan, descended from Ghengis, he ruled in the 1250s over the largest state that ever existed

Mokèlé-mbèmbés—dinosaurs still believed to be living in tropical Africa

Sickan Carlsson and Thor Modéen—Swedish actors

Anticimex—Swedish hardcore punk band

Baubo—old woman in Greek mythology; tried to cheer the goddess Demeter up while the latter was mourning the loss of her daughter

Kaiomortz—both beast and man, the oldest of all creatures

Nyarlathotep—read Lovecraft already

Igjugarjuk—Inuit mystic who claimed that the way to wisdom was found through solitude and suffering, far away from men

Saida in the Hemmets Journal—"Home Journal"; Saida Andersson was an advice columnist

fotzelovers—*fotze* is slang for "cunt"

Mazdaznan-Hanisch—Otto Hanish founded the Mazdaznan movement, a synchretistic religion focused on health

the secret teachings of saprophytism—being the teachings of something (or somethings?) living off dead and rotting substances

Mundebo and Jan-Erik Wikström—Swedish politicians, members of the People's Party

Bildt—Carl: Swedish former prime minister and nowadays foreign minister

Anna Lindmarker—Swedish journalist

Einsatzkommando—a Nazi killing squad active in World War II

Pastor Paisley—pastor in Northern Ireland and leader of the Democratic Unionist Party

Garn howled outside of Gnipahall—in Norse mythology, Gnipahalla was the entrance to Niflheimr (the "Abode of Mist") and the wolf Garmr was set to guard the entrance

Renat—Swedish vodka

AMS—Swedish National Labor Market Board

Svante Thuresson—Swedish jazz musician

John Houdi—Swedish illusionist and magician

Svarte Filip—Filip Johansson or "Black-Filip": Swedish soccer forward

Arschberg—Robert Aschberg, a vulgar TV-show personality

Pier Luigi Farnese—black magic made him rape the Bishop of Fano (according to Jacob Burckhardt)

VI I FEMMAN—"We in the Fifth Grade": a Swedish radio question and answer show for children

RACE GÜNTHER—Hans Friedrich Karl Günther, influential Nazi Nordicist

GLAUBE UND SCHÖNHEIT—"the Faith and Beauty Society" was a Hitler youth organization open to young girls ages seventeen to twenty-one

CHRISTMAS TREE PLUNDERING—a Swedish festival that takes place on January 13th (Saint Knut's Day), which marks the end of the Christmas season; Before the Christmas tree is thrown out, it is "plundered"

HARALD AND FRANK ALEXANDER—father and sixteen year-old son, murdered three family members in ritual fashion (the mother and two teenage daughters) with knives on Tenerife in 1970: the women's breasts and vaginal lips were cut off and their hearts cut out; the Alexanders claimed their motive was to "save humanity"

MICHAEL MYERS AND JASON—from *Halloween* and the *Friday the 13th* films, respectively

CHARIS AND METRON—ancient Greek terms: *Charis* refers to grace, light, a joy in simple stillness; *metron* entails a resolve to lead a balanced life; see also the works of Vilhelm Ekelund

AHIMSA—total non-violence (within Jainism)

SEYDLITZ—Walther von Seydlitz-Kurzbac: general, leader of the captured officers who worked with the Bolsheviks following the Battle of Stalingrad

KONRAD KUJAU—claimed at the beginning of the 1980s that he'd found Hitler's diaries

ANSGAR—St. Ansgar, the "Apostle of the North"

CURA . . . USURA—Heidegger-Pound

LOS NOVIOS DE LA MUERTE—a death squadron organized by Klaus Barbie and Stefano delle Chiaie, among others

Aouita—Saïd: Moroccan athlete

boar snout—a Viking charge

Fanfarlo . . . Horla—Baudelaire-Maupassant

Mafarka . . . Uomo finito—Marinetti-Papini

Zebulon—"Zeb" Macahan; see *How the West was Won*.

Bombi Bitt—television character played by Stellan Skarsgård, Swedish actor

deshimaric—Taisen Deshimaru, Zen Buddhist teacher and monk

Leibstandarte—Hitler's bodyguards

"lord of silence, supreme god of desolation"—from Damien Thorn's monologue in *Omen III*

airyanem vaejo—the Aryan Persians' legendary Northern home

swet-dvipa—the region situated in the farthest Northern reaches, where Narayuna (which is light) lives together with uttarakua (the ancient Northern race): according to Aryan-Indian traditions

XXVII

Grandpa was lying down and watching *Father's Little Dividend* with Spencer Tracy. He'd drunk fifty beers, Kaltenberg and Kaiserdom Edel, since this afternoon. I'd just dumped ten cans of maggots into a bowl and was coming back from the kitchen. I also had a flask of Portello and a saucer of unripe gooseberries. The movie had reached the scene where Spencer is in the swing talking to his whoredaughter. She's knockedup and worried about how it'll be between her and the guy who fucked her when the baby falls out.

"How did you feel when you had your first baby?" she asks. "Did it make any difference between you and Mom?"

". . . I remember lying awake that night, thinking to myself: Now what have we got into, here we were, two perfectly happy people, free as the air—now we're trapped, trapped by twenty inches of screaming humanity."

– Whoresongod and Jewjesus! That's exactly how it is! Grandpa exclaimed. If I didn't have you holding me down, I could run like Ratatoskr! up and down Chaos's cock! I'd get back everything I've ever given up! I could've been a diva! a primadonna! Courted by the world's richest, most perverted queers! I would've been worse than Zarah Leander! Farah Diba! Divine! Liberace! ten thousand times worse!

Grandpa sat up and took a fistful of flylarvae and sawdust. It probably didn't taste very good, though . . . Suddenly, he snorted and spit the maggots out all over the table.

– Fuck Satan all the way back to hell! they were hardly moving! I bet my blackguard's knee and tenniselbow you didn't keep them in the fridge! They rot at room temperature!

He cuffed my ear and took the switch with the colorful feathers out of the urn where we kept it.

– You're about to get what's coming to you . . . shitcunt . . .

Grandpa seemed to be getting the sunsetblues . . . Must be in the genes, because I usually feel pretty sour in the evening, too . . . He threw me across the table, yanked down my pants, shouted a few curses, and started beating me with the springy switch.

– How I hate you! Pampers and Semper! *Kamratposten* and *Barnjournalen*! And you actually dared to like them! You actually had the stomach for it! Evilevildevilllll! There you go! And there! There! Everyman! Tusenbröder! Tschandala!

He'd worked up a good sweat by then. But Grandpa wasn't interested in just scratching the surface . . . Not by a long shot . . .

– Lie still! Meir Kahane take me if I can't make you love me like I deserve!

While Grandpa went to the john to get the mulewhip, I thought of the words Jesus spoke in Sirach: "Bend his neck in youth, bruise his ribs while he is a child . . ." It looks good on paper, but death is pretty gruesome when it finally comes to call . . . Grandpa threw himself back on top of me, shrieking in his shrillest shrewvoice:

– You'll never see Uno Myggan's monstermember! because I'm going to beat the life out of you!

I cried and begged for mercy, but Grandpa just whipped out his oneeyedsnake, held me down on the table, and started up again . . . He walloped his heart out, bopped until he burst . . . I bawled until I was blue, promised to turn over a newleaf . . . but he was tired of being tired . . . he lit a Gauloise in the heat of it . . .

– Hushababy! chin up! simmer down! tickletickle! Not enough? . . . Here you go! You want some more?! Hooboy! Uburoi! Sanssouci! You make me sicker than Nathan Ratschild!

The leather left deep, bloody welts in my flesh . . . Grandpa beat me where a man keeps his pride, on the ass . . . the back . . . the back of my head, too . . . Wherever he could reach . . . it was all the same now . . . thin bloody ribbons of flesh . . .

– Littleshit! Pissrat! Frogboy! Nilsen! Berkowitz! Begin!

I hollered so it echoed from Mångberge to Storberge! . . . Grandpa grabbed some coarse brown tape and wrapped it a few times around my neck and mouth . . . then he continued . . .

– Dingbat! Hamhand! Klutz! Notail! Goedzak! Mercader!

He waxed into paroxysms and waned into deliriums . . . Went crazier than Ernst-Hugo . . . He couldn't stop . . . he wasn't just whistling Dixie . . . he changed hands because he's ambidextrous . . .

– Hornboy! Marbuel! Makbenak! Agnus Dei! I'll beat the evil out of you! Troglodyte! Trilobite! Starlet! Sweetthingwithacherryontop! I got the nigger by the toe! You'll cry uncleuncle before I'm done!

Blood sprayed with every lash . . . shreds of skin dripped, too . . . it hurt so much I tried to stop breathing . . . Grandpa threw the whip aside . . . he'd gone semirigid . . . come to his senses . . . tried to rekindle the flame . . . get himself together . . . but it had burned down . . . bled out . . . he'd lost it . . . he told himself the same thing had happened to Stendhal . . . he was indecisive now . . . frazzlehaired . . . worndown . . . upsidedown and insideout . . . he lay back down on the sofa bed . . . sang in castrato:

– *Nur wer der Minne Macht versagt, nur wer die Liebe Lust verjagt . . .*

Snuffling and tearyeyed, I crept to the john to wash my backside as best I could . . . I worked the tape loose . . . bathed in punsch . . . put soaked vealbrawn and soggy bread on the wounds and wrapped gauze around my lower body . . . then I undressed and put on my wet nightshirt . . . I went back into the living room . . . Grandpa lay there reading *The Temptation of Saint Anthony* by Flaubert . . . the TV was still on . . . Bobby was giving JR a blowjob . . .

– Listen here, squirt: "The child is little like a dwarf, short, thickset in body with a miserable aspect, some white hair covered his prodigiously great head, and he shivered under a paltry tunic, guarding in his hand a roll of papyrus . . ." That's your spitting image, boy! he chuckled. Instead of papyrus, though, you're guarding a role of toiletpaper!

I knew it was true. . . I was the most pathetic thing on earth . . . anyone can have me, but no one wants me . . . I was ashamed to exist . . . I received life as a wound and I have forbidden suicide to heal the scar . . . just like Maldoror . . . as long as you don't end up in North Västerbotten when you die . . . I sat down on the small woven rug ... looked at the floor ... I ached ... that was probably the point ... A nature program came on ... bloodred, slavetaking brigandants were lapping up a Lomechusa beetle's shitdope ... the anthill goes down the toilet soon as they get addicted ... Grandpa was jacking off ... it was the idea that turned him on ... insects fondling each other always makes him hot ... especially when it involves interspecies action ... He joylessly spewed a few wet drops ... not long after that he went to sleep ... walking through the valley of the shadow of death ... I didn't budge the whole night ... I wandered lost ... Empty within ... cold without ... longing for someone to put me out of my misery ... Alone in the Milky Way galaxy ... I'm so scared ... I'm going to crash and burn ...

PORTELLO—fruit-flavored soft drink

RATATOSKR—squirrel who scurries up and down Yggdrasil, the World Tree

ZARAH LEANDER—Swedish actress and singer known for her controversial decision to move to Germany and work for the state-owned film studio UFA during the Nazi period

FARAH DIBA—married name Farah Pahlavi, former empress of Iran

KAMRATPOSTEN—Swedish magazine for eight to fourteen year olds

BARNJOURNALEN—weekly Swedish television news program for children

SEMPER—Swedish company that makes baby food

TUSENDBRÖDER—Swedish television series

TSCHANDALA—untouchables in the Indian caste system. Also the title of a novella by August Stringberg

UNO "MYGGEN" ERICSON—Swedish journalist, historian, and author

Nathan Ratschild—Nathan Rothschild, a London financier

Nilsen! Berkowitz! Begin!—two mass murderers, one prime minister

Notail—Pelle Svanslös, or "Peter No Tail," the protagonist of Gösta Knutsson's series of children's books

Goedzak—Lamme; Thyl Ulenspiegel's sidekick

Mercader—Ramón; hacked Trotsky to death

Ernst-Hugo—Ernst-Hugo Järegård, famously temperamental Swedish actor

Marbuel—child-devil in Werner Egk's ballet *Abraxas*

Makbenak—"the flesh falls from the bones"; Freemason codeword

Nur wer der Minne Macht . . .—"Only the one who renounces the power of love, only the one who forswears passion," from Wagner's *Das Rheingold*

Punsch—traditional Swedish liqueur

XXVIII

Grandpa had kept his face to the wall for a whole week. He'd just lain there . . . he hadn't eaten, drunk, spoken, or slept . . . He'd just smoked . . . When I tried to comfort him, he chased me away with a filletknife. It's how he gets when he goes without drugs. I don't understand why he torments himself like that. It's also how he gets when the springsun slits open the curtains and knifes you in the eye. I went outside . . . slush was melting into drunken rivulets . . . pockmarked snowdrifts were wasting away in piles of ooze . . . bare flecks of muddyground were showing through . . . I flooded a few hectares . . . I was conducting an experiment . . . finding out which animals could swim . . . The sun was a shrill presence, more white than yellow . . . it didn't quite have the bite it wanted, though . . . winter was bowing out, the air was filled with the heady sound of horny birdsong . . . clumps of snow tumbled from the evergreens, everything was melting except my heart . . . there the permafrost is perennial . . . sorrow has frozen the vital-nerve . . . The sky contained weak strips of blue . . . they were busy changing the decor . . .

I went into the kitchen and opened a jar of loveravaged hearts soaked in sweet brine . . . I put two on a plate and went into the living room . . . Grandpa was in the same position on the sofa bed . . . his yichudim were done for . . . I took my life in my hands and asked him if he wanted a couple of passionbroiled suicidepacthearts . . . But he didn't give a shit about what I had to offer . . . Just lay there, like that Buddha statue in Polonnaruwa . . . unapproachable . . . unfathomable . . . dead to the world . . . closer to God . . .

YICHUDIM—"unifications"; secret knowledge, divine gifts gained through meditation in the Chasidic, kabbalistic tradition

XXIX

– Damn smoker's cough, gasped Grandpa when I brought him his coffee and brandy in bed. Do me a favor and piss in my mouth, mite.

I opened my fly and lightened my bladder. Grandpa squatted to receive it then gargled with his eyes shut.

– You certainly can piss, little Ficedula hypoleuca, but it takes a fucking sumppump to suck the sperm out of you! he griped and spanked me. Me now, I had sperm coming out my ears when I was your age! hooboy! I could both give and take a squirt! I was their fucking Helen, I swear to God! They were on me like blowflies on syrup spilled over a festeringwound! Of course, I only fooled around with them if they treated me nice, otherwise the narcohomos could go blow themselves! Yes, I frolicked and fell away from the Word of God with a pocket of cocksocks spurted full to the brim, so you can see why some of those buggerfiends got jealous, the devilqueers! I enjoyed myself so fucking much the memory still makes be blush!

– You don't say?

– One day, I got word that the Old King was in Skaeliptom hunting waxwings with gutstring. He was scalding hot, ready to come down on me like a hurricane. But the Little King gave me a sign and warned me. So I prettied myself up as much as I could, shaved my balls and powdered my ass. I remember it was Milky-John who curled my hair, because Frusse was in doing some rehab shit. By the by, did I ever tell you about how I bit Milky-John's cock off on Walpurgis Night all those hebbersyears ago?

Without waiting for my answer he went on:

– That night we were horny as pigs. We'd gone skijoring on a truck bound for Spännarberget, because we were slated to play a game of bumhook with the Gideonites. I was wearing a rough sheepskincoat, rubber snowboots, and moleskinpants, a shagcap and some fancy leathergloves. As luck would have it, though, me and Milky-John were both headoverheels for a sardonic little permobilwarf named Leif. He was one of the chosen few, he could crack a Rosita with his ass. Anyway, we were both assoverend, but you should know that that dollarstorewhore made the rounds kissing and karasarting with the dwarf and frankly it made me a little sick. Plus, he'd always been a burr-in-the-ass knowitall, and you know I can get pretty jumpy when I'm horny. That's something I'll freely admit. So anyway, we started brawling and John took a hunk of out of my back. But we finally agreed on a triangle and I began it by licking Milky-John's chapped flange. But you know what that dumbfuck did next?! He started shouting about bottlefed lambs, hinting I sucked cock like a goitresick deacon. Then he sung in a snotty voice, "who can suck without slurping, who can flay without nails?" so I swallowed his pole whole and gulped his eggs. Then I bit them all off like a rabid badger and ate them up like a bootlegger.

I made my eyes wide and Grandpa lit two black Blends.

– I'll never forget the look on his face when he figured out I'd just severed his salvation, Grandpa giggled. His face was as gray as Auntie Eskil's roughest pube. Of course, I was choking with laughter, but John was so thickskinned he barely whimpered. Since then, though, he's become the worst sort of homebody, a real brownnoser. But you know, it was like Leif and I were meant for each other. It was too bad he had diarrhea most of the time. I sold him to Sixteen Lammby, the trashpeddler, who was into dwarftossing. Poor Leif, it didn't take much to make him puke, but he could tear up a cock like nobody's business. Kissing him was like taking a mudbath, Grandpa reminisced dreamily. His tongue was slimy as a wombat's ballsack and his saliva tasted like catpiss. I'm not ashamed to admit it gets me right here, right in the pants, just thinking about it.

– But Grandpa, what about the Old King?

– Come and sit on my knee, girlyboy, Grandpa said coaxingly, and I didn't have much choice in the matter. It looked like the Old King was just gaga for the Überrace. "I just want one night of your homespun ass," the Old King, Mr. G, croaked as he rammed me with a tennis racket. He drywanked like that for about an hour until his Little Prince wept blood. Then he started to sob. "I wonder . . . might the king blow?" I asked. "You taste like fermented herring," the King said, going all sham elegant and smacking his lips. He gave head like a girl, though, and I didn't know whether to laugh or cry. He was so fucking sweet I just didn't have the heart to cum. So I smeared my cock with ricotta and planted it in His Majesty's fungoidal lovetunnel. "This is one girl who can't take it anymore," Mr. G wept. You know, of course, that he was an archeologist. While I fucked him like a vole, he spouted some papist bullshit about balanitis's conquest of Jericho. Next day, he was so sore he couldn't walk. But did the Old King have the grace to say thank you, my boy, job well done? No sir! He refused to acknowledge me. It seems he was ashamed and regretted our lovely time together. "Don't make a dirty mess of yourself with a woman, whatever you do!" he shouted as he left. The Old King may have been a tatty old sow, but he made me a man. I knew he liked Negro spirituals, so I sang "Give Me that Old Gay Religion" every time he got what he was begging for. But the brokendown old bugger was as ungracious as Satan himself.

As the story ended, Grandpa shook off his sorrow and anger. He let his gnarled pettingfinger glide from my navel to my cock, which stood upright to meet him.

– Now imitate the Little King, mite, he demanded and licked my left earlobe.

FICEDULA HYPOLEUCA—the pied flycatcher

OLD KING—Gustav V

LITTLE KING—Prince Carl Philip

WHO CAN SUCK WITHOUT SLURPING—allusion to a Swedish sentimental song "Vem kan segla föruten vind" ("Who can sail without wind")

SKAELIPTOM—earliest known name for Skellefteå

SPÄNNARBERGET—in Kåge

BUMHOOK—a game like Indian leg wrestling

KARASARA—Swedish, a woman who likes to hop from one man to the next

BALANITIS—inflammation of the foreskin and head of the penis

XXX

Grandpa and I were on our way to Stålberget to burn Siegfried Israelsson to death in his house, and were following the animal trail countless generations of alcoholics had beaten through the brush. On our way, we passed through a jumble of stones dotted with gnarled pines. A goshawk was riding the barebreasted sky. At a bend in the path, we stumbled on an angry fortysomething in a redcheckered shirt and carpenter's pants. Flushed and enraged, he was uncombed and unshaved. He'd been laying in wait. When he saw us, he whipped his pants off. He grabbed Grandpa, who was shedding his skin just then, not a pretty sight, let me tell you, and bent him double.

– Let's see your liceridden ass, you old fogy.

I drew my Lapp knife and got ready for some hand-to-hand combat, but Grandpa shrieked like a stonewalled stockbroker: "Stay back, boy! this doesn't concern you!" I obeyed and backed off a few meters. Still, I couldn't look away. The guy had a huge, unabashadly magnificent cock. He went down on his knees and pushed in until he was up to his balls in my Grandpa's ass.

– You give me any apeshit and I'll fistfuck you with my rough lumberjackglove!

Grandpa had to grab a pineroot with both hands to help him take the rawfuck coming his way. He opened and shut his eyes, lewdly rotated his hips. But the big laborer wasn't into that kind of nonsense. He grabbed Grandpa's hips hard, forced him to hold still, and impaled him again and again with his furious, explosive cock. It was a good plan . . . Draw back and shoot forward, retreat and attack . . . Like Mundelföri twirling his firewhisk in chaos . . . Grandpa's hornjuices squished, he blathered and yodeled . . . You could hear it for miles . . .

– Maaaooo . . . mu-hu, mu-hu, maaah . . . awwa-aw-wa-aw-waaa . . . Jesus . . . Jesus . . . JEEESUSS! A-a-a-aaa! Yeeesss! more! Oh yeaaaahhh! Take me as I am! Straight up! Hole in one! Aah– Hilding–uhh–Hilding–mmh–Hilding! Oohgooood . . . you're so hard . . . you're so big . . . you're so far in . . . I can feel it all the way to my heart . . . Goooddd! Fucking Satan, damned to hell!

Grandpa began to cry it was so good.

– Buuuaaaa! I love your nasty cock! Waaahhh! it's so raw! Boo-hooo! fuck the shit out of me!

The guy was rough and violent, just like Grandpa liked them. He rode the expresstrain for about an hour, pushing and shoving, grinding his teeth and changing his grip and position. He beat Grandpa bloody with his clenched fists and called him everything you call your bosomfriends. For his part, Grandpa called on heaven and hell. He shrieked himself hoarse in the process. By the time it was all over, lust had done him in. The guy came silently and resolutely, pulled up his pants, kicked Grandpa in the tailbone and chin, and marched off. I made my way up to my Grandpa, dressed him, and gave him something to drink.

– Did you know him?

– I don't know his name . . . never asked . . . met him three four times . . . always angry as hell . . . but he fucks like a god . . .

Grandpa was too beaten, bruised, and stiff to continue on . . . Homeburning would have to wait for another day . . . I stole a David Brown tractor and we drove home. That evening in bed, before we abandoned ourselves to our nightmares, Grandpa said: Love's a curse . . . a toil and a trouble, a fence and a farce . . .

– Is there love other than the cockkind?

– Oh sure . . . But the animalmagnetism between cock and ass, or cock and mouth, or, Jewgodforbid, cock and cunt usually gets in the way. Trust me, boy, evil always triumphs . . . Even though sometimes you wish it could be like in *The Amorous Adventures of Prince Mony Vibescu* and those other classic fairytales . . . A love pure and true . . . short and sweet . . . soft and warm . . .

– Ethereal . . . seraphic . . . comic . . .

– You don't know what you're saying . . . you're all tuckered out . . . Go to sleep before we quarrel . . . Nightynight, snoopydoo . . .

– Nightynight, Grandpa . . .

MUNDELFÖRI—a jotun (giant) in Norse mythology; in von Werth's Aryan cosmology, he whisked the universe into being out of chaos

THE AMOROUS ADVENTURES OF PRINCE MONY VIBESCU—aka *Les Onze Milles Vegres*, by Guillaume Apollinaire.

XXXI

– Paul Holm lives here, boy, Grandpa wheezed, sinking down onto a rotten ovarianshaped stump.

– I need a smoke, he panted, completely out of breath.

In front of us a house and a barn were falling into each other's arms like Latter Day Saints on Sunday. Tangles of weeds dug their claws into the dying homestead, which was afflicted by oldboyscurvy and gayrot. It was the stuffiest buggersummer ever, and the town of Lillkågetrask quivered like sourpork in the heatwave. The people around there are nothing but slobs and slatterns, happy—when it comes to the lice in their tangles—to live and let live. Most are fat and blue, not too good at standing on their own two feet, but great at creeping around on all fours. The forest around here is spindly and sparse: driedout old pines, toppled trees, a few stumps. You can't see far, either; it's like everything is obscured by a mist or haze.

– Gabriel's fireygold, cuntsmelling piss! Grandpa swore, letting his reptilian eyes roam over the pockmarked swamp dotted with cowpatties and placentas, covered with branches and shrubs, turnipbeetfields and peatcrofts.

The neighborhood in general was the graybrown of an old gypsy-cock, but around Paul Holm's barnhouse a riot of color was in full swing. In Lillkågeträsk, most of the soil consists of cigarette ash; the only things worth growing there are assbiters and buggerleeks. Around Paul's home, though, abominations flourished in the fermenting mould, the thriving afterlife of shit and cadavers. Grandpa hawked a loogie and swallowed his ciggibutt.

– Hishiryoconsciousness is something you only reach when someone fucks the shit out of your compostculvert, he said and straightened his emaciated carcass. I never thought I'd have the strength . . . It sure ain't like the old days, when you sprang like triggerhappy fool with a portablehuntingblind between church-villages, just to see if anything was going down!

He brushed the maggots from his shoulders. The severe black suit he wore contrasted nicely with his vampiric complexion and those pale blue eyes.

– But fuck my tender asshole, it doesn't help to plead with Jesus! Oh well, let's go brownnose old Paul! he said and staggered to his feet. By the way, you'd better be a nice and polite boy when we meet Paul, he warned, as he pushed his way through the pigweed and scabroustissue toward the farmyard. Paul is harder on kids and animals than anyone I know, he continued and came to a sudden halt. By Satan, what happened to you? Did you see the spermcovered face of God or what?! he exclaimed, eyeing a tortured bogbody wearing a toecap. It's clear as a sneeze in church that Paul has been at this one, he said, poking the broken shitcarcass with his stilettocane. I think Paul is a Jew, he said and blinked, sickened, before heading toward the Holm house.

Grandpa had to use his cane to clear a path, since the going wasn't exactly easy. Down off the hill, it was easy to forget where you were. Everything was bigger than it should have been. Gargantuan leeks and fireweed eight times the height of a man. Ferns as big as back in the days of the dinosaurs. The mosquitoes were especially hard on me. I bled from eleven thousand wounds.

– Bromberg's Bloody Sunday! this is nothing! Back in my day there were winged insects with only one thing on their mind: putting out decent people's eyes! Everyone suffered! Ninety-five percent were blind!

A brusque shove.

– Watch it there, teddybear.

He suddenly lashed out with his cane and carved out a flesheating, cocksucking orchid's gallyellow, naughtyboy snout. Kidneycolored sludge gushed out. Others, their smiles mocking all that breathed, were greedily closing in, swaying forward on thick, hairy stems. They smelled hot and bitter. Finally, though, we managed to fight our way out. Hopping over a feebly trickling stream, we found ourselves in the farmyard. The land here sloped down to a lake. On closer examination, it was obvious this place used to be a respectable Västerbotten farm house . . . But not anymore. Now everything was a confusion of tangledcreepers, mostly ayahuascas. Nestlesnarls wrapped themselves lasciviously around drainpipes, squirtingcucumbers looked for a mug to cum on, stinkhorns revelled in their sunripened, carrionfed bloat. The remains of beasts killed by suicide and emergencyslaughter both were scattered everywhere. It was a crawlingwanker's paradise.

– Are you still daring enough for the riddle of the sphincter? Grandpa asked.

– When I'm with you, Grandpa, I'm not scared.

– Now you sound like something out of *The Brothers Tigerheart*, mite . . . Let's pretend we're Gog and Magog on our way to a smoking hot prayermeeting . . .

It seemed Paul was a gospelsectarian. The fields were victims of neglect. A rusty castrationdevice lay askew in a pansybed, and an old Massey Ferguson buzzed with anger about forgotten to-dos and unfinished tasks. Judas's ears, Wandering Jews, and kohlrabi grew around the entrance to the farmyard. A surly badger was roughfucking a young waitress who, blissfully whimpering, was bent double over a fence. Ruffs clucked, lapwings burred, an elk sampled a poison saltlick and went bellyup. A Gabriel in a gray coat landed on Grandpa, ladybugs mobbed dungbeatles, and a raffsetgrasssnake hauled ass after a mouse running on fumes. It was Eden and Gomorra, baby, and the heavens themselves blushed at what was going down. But mammals were the minority lifeform here. Mourningcloaks and death's head moths darted between clusters of smoke-, butter-, and cartilageballs swaying in a musty breeze. Mouldspattered narcobuggers hissed from a thorny refuge of Satanstickbrush. Scurvyherbs, ringwormeuphorbia, and ileusranunculus shook spastically, burly burntorchids and swarthly wolf's bane rustled their leaves, vericellazosters and oxeyecervicalcollardaisies were about to pass out. Runners and creepers, shooters and sprouters, buds and bloomers! Seeds and spores, pericarps and shrubs, flowers and fronds! Phallos vulgaris, vagina spurius, anus murinus! Smoking- and explodingvines held court, nightlurkers and aeaeaeberries beckoned with poisonous fruit. Devil's weed flourished among poisonnettles, green and white lovage struggled with ruddy witch's herb. Goldbrown birdsfoottrefoil, purpleshavingbrushes, darkblue madwort! Confused rattails were in danger of a Ruskie ambush! Dog tongues panted over hot red tufts of burninglove! Virgin Marys rubbed shoulders with bastardalkanets and lessertwayblades. Rosynorns and fierygold tigerlilies stood out against black slack- and slitstars. Scrapironpiles had given up jammering for attention. A big calf gave its last kick. I was glad to be allowed to exist.

Grandpa took over.

– I bet your bleedingbrain that Paul is in the barn getting himself a raw beastfuck, he said.

He started off again, his shadow proceeding him, and soon he reached the dry farmwell. He bent over the tile rim and saw some emaciated toddlers clamoring for something to drink.

– Well, I'll be damned, he chuckled, whipping out his sweaty balls and pissing on them.

He shook the last drops of piss onto me and slipped his cock back into its holster. We started on the path to the barn, which towered before us like a windowless sepulchre. Bumblebees and wasps burned and stung us, but I taught them to show a little respect. Grandpa always had a cloud of flies buzzing around him, no matter the weather or season. But now all I could see was a black whirlwind; I couldn't even hear what he was saying. Paul had doused the area around the cowbarn's door with Agent Orange. It was also mined, and Grandpa buzzed and whirred. So I crept through the mess of tendrils along the ancient concretewall, which blocked off all light and air.

Finally, I discovered a huge rathole behind a bunch of dandelions; it was so big I was able to fit inside. I found Grandpa, but the flies were so insane I had to drag him by the belt.

I crept forward and Grandpa came after, his nails digging into my cheeks to make sure we didn't lose each other. The barn was as black as the soul of a knockedup woman and the gases made Grandpa want to hurl. We waded without seeing much through a lake of sewersludge; the shit was up to my crotch; finally, we found a ladder fastened to the wall and climbed up. Then we made our way along the rafters. Grandpa's flies fell away one by one. When our eyes had finally adjusted to the dark, we realized we were in a labyrinth. Mutatedcows with whorefaces made their way through the sludge, humming hohum hits. From the stalls off to the side we could hear angry bassvoiced livestock bellowing their two cents worth in a neverending quarrel over Talmudic slaughterrituals. Musk oxen clamored for the right to die, glowworms burned their little hearts out, and a colony of surrogatemothersmothers wrapped themselves in rosy cocoons. In one stall we could see a godfearing, Protestant ram wearing a straightjacket, and in the stall next to it a sow in a harness took the virginity of a crucified, dazzlingly white bull.

– Sri and sa-bdag, Grandpa said, we've entered the holy of holies . . . Eleusis for sure . . .

He gave my cheek a gruff stroke, chuckled and then crept on. Apparently, one had to be agile here.

– It's not worth thinking and feeling down here, bolardwarf, "here time becomes space"!

On the whole, though, I didn't feel much like Parsifal, and I certainly never pictured Grandpa as a Gurnemanz. More like a Klingsor. But something strange was definitely going on. From the outside the barn hadn't seemed so huge, but from the inside it felt neverending. We were in a hallucination, an illusion. It felt like the beams were taking us farther and farther into a dream, and there was always something worse waiting ahead. A smokebelching pit gaped beneath me; you could see black flames dancing far, far below. It was surrounded by a wall that kept back the sludge. Grandpa crawled up beside me. I thought he wanted to make love, so I tried to kiss him. But he gripped my neck hard and pushed me down against the beam.

– Satan's balls, he croaked, calm down, horndog, or I'll throw you head-over-heels into the netherworld!

Then Grandpa pressed his lips to my right eye.

– This, he whispered excitedly, this is one of the seven pits of hell found on that miserable dirtball we call Earth. It's the abode of He Who Has No Eyes, he who calls decent folk home when they're too old and sick to cum anymore . . . Down there no day is ever wasted and the fountains run a hundredproof. Animals are tame, they hop into the pot of their own free will. Everyone dines on stewedadvertisingexecutives and policechieffillets . . . You can babble all you want and everyone tries hard to please you. The words never give out, they never get battered and threadbare. Everything's always orderly, no shab or drab anywhere . . . There's never any reason to be despondent or depressed . . . you can sample hallucinogens from far away galaxies . . . All the bossboys are down there, from Heraclitus to Cioran, but they give you the respect you deserve . . . If you want, you can torture angels . . . You always know exactly what to do with yourself . . . You're always giving tit for tat and they let everything slide . . . You're always right, you're held in high esteem . . . An innocent person dies for every word you speak . . . You get to play poker for entire galaxies . . . interrogate all known lifeforms . . . subvert evolution . . . In Hell everyone is given a cock tough as leather and hard as Krupp steel . . . longer and rougher than the nastiest IdiAmincock! Your balls are always ready to burst and your asshole is as wet as a salivating confirmationpussy! You can have as many fuckbuddies as you want and they always pack it in as best they can! They look like Clark Gable, Errol Flynn, and Adolf Valentino rolled into one! They give head like sucklingpiglets on crack and their assholes are so narrow they screech when you ram them! When they fuck you in the ass, it's so good you see fireworks! you hear the delicious sound of Jewbacon frying! But there's one thing you should know, boy, and it's this: skirtchasers end up somewhere else! they're damned to gospelheaven and they're forced to suck syphilic cunt for an eternity's eternity!

Grandpa let me go, suddenly terrified.

– There's evil in here, boy, I know it in my shrinking bowls! We have to find Paul and get away from here before some demonbastard finds us first.

Grandpa tried to move along the rafters like a sloth.

– This way is faster, easy as a thumb up the ass, he said, voice strained, before he let go and landed on his back in the viscous cowplop.

I dropped after, since the shit was only up to my knees.

– How's it going, durchleuchtigste? I asked and licked his johnson clean.

– Whoredevil, he snorted and laboriously got his skinny legs beneath him, don't bother faking it. It's like intelligence. An old geezer has got a certain something that tells him when someone else is being a smartass. He shuffled off through the mess and kicked up a shrieking thalidomideboy, who he then ground to a pulp beneath his commandoboots.

– If we've learned anything, analnutjob, it's to give them hell. But now I'm going to call to Paul. Something else might hear and come to suck our cockblood dry, of course, but that's a risk we'll just have to take.

Grandpa used his nicest voice.

– Oh Paul! Paul, it's me! Here to tell you that Grandpa from Hebberschhåle hasn't forgotten you! We had the same headmaster, don't you remember?

It was silent as God's conscience.

– We're lost in space and have some goodygoods for you! Grandpa lied.

Something came hurtling out of a corner, but it wasn't Paul. A shitfaced bitch stumbled clumsily up to Grandpa and embraced him. She was bald and blind and had snapping cunts over her whole flabby body. Hydrocholoricacid dripped from every whorehole. She was dead, but wouldn't admit it. Her hornjuices were stickier than life itself.

– Mammaa–a! Grandpa squealed and shimmied like an epileptic. He tossed his head and ground his hips, but she only clung harder and reached for the fearstiffened, cerisehued salami sticking out of its flannelholster.

I knew I had to do something then and there; if I didn't, my Grandpa would be lost. I found a crossbar and tried to pry the thing loose, but it was stuck tight as a chastitycork in a baby's ass. The cuntlady had got her hand around Grandpa's bacon and was licking her chops, trying to decide which hole was the hungriest. Meanwhile, Grandpa was clutching his heart and watching his checkered life flash before his eyes like an ultraviolent pornobio. I pried the crossbar loose just as the oldbag was about to stuff Grandpa's junk into an especially rude-and-crude hole right above her navel. I swung and drove the crossbar straight into the back of the whorebeast's head, so that the two six inch spikes sank deep into her brain. She hissed, loosened her grip, and I was able to pull Grandpa free. She swayed and collapsed and we splashed away through the barn's innermoat. There were at least four different directions to choose from, though, and we were lost in no time. Grandpa's asbestic lungs were whimpering like scalded lemmings, and finally he slipped, arms waving wildly, on some cuddlehungry spermgobbler.

– Aah boy, he sobbed, chasing away the lipmasseur, she was just ghastly. I haven't been that submissive since the Christmas I lay with my broken cock in a Lappish hut and Uno Taikon forced his way in through the backdoor.

He looked at me and those terrible eyes were wet with emotion.

– You may be a hoyden and small as a girl down there, but there'll always be a place for you up Grandpa's exhaustpipe. You might be as useless as a lightningbolt in a woodpile, but when it's a matter of life and death, you get the job done. You're like a pinch of snuff up God's hairy nostril, he finished and told me to unpack the licoricerolls.

– You've got to have some fire in your guts if you want to play with devils, he exclaimed as he dunked a roll in turpentine. That frontloader should've been stripped with a woodplaner! But this sour flame's still smoking, you know, Bejn-Burman won't make glue of me yet. Now take some of the edge off your hunger, this is so good it melts in your mouth.

We didn't dare smoke after our snack, but just toddled along like two rawthighs on their way to Golgotha. Rotten cadavers made insolent advances and a facultyparrot burped up a lecture, "Well-to-do Wankers in an Everyday, Dirty Little Swedish Industrial Community." But then I saw a light weak as a mother's love glinting from a narrow hallway off to our left. We tippytoed along and swallowed our tongues to stop from breathing. Then we peeked through a crack in the door.

Paul Holm lay on a Judebag with his eyes shut. A Mangalitza pig, the bones of its lower back jutting against its flesh, humped him like a jackhammer.

– Oh, ohyeah, Paul shrieked unconvincingly.

The purebred boar was old and timid and had lost all its finesse. Its twitching flesh was covered in sweat, but Paul's haughty face wore a look of complete dissatisfaction. No matter that the pig's cock was doggedly hammering his persnickety asshole. He was as unmoved as if he were offhandedly wanking off to Yanni. Suddenly he whipped around and dug his thumbs into the boar's eyes. The animal jerked and squealed like a sourwoodfire and then went limp. Paul grabbed a pitchfork and rammed it into the pig's soft belly, and the fleshyfuck bawled, like the first time Down-in-the-Mouth Märta sucked babooncock in the People's Park. The pig's rancid snout snapped blindly, but Paul dodged like a bellydancer. Then the captivating old geezer grabbed a gaslamp and brought it down on the pig's twisted back, causing the animal to burn like a Christian at the stake. It tossed and shrieked like a grandma on a zombiecock. Soon the fire died away, leaving a pile of sooty, smoldering bacon. Paul hawked, spat, and then pulled on a pair of khaki shorts and a yellow shirt. After that, he sat down on a bag of Khrushchevbran and lit a tallow candle and a Gitanes. Making the sign of the swastika, Grandpa stepped forward, devastatingly handsome in his soiled cryptsuit.

– *Nilapadhana*, he chanted in a dark voice, his eyes burning like quasars.

Paul looked up, his gaze soiling everything it touched.

– You still alive? he whispered rudely.

Grandpa's nod was like a doll's.

– Why are you lurking around in my barn?

– I'm so fond of you.

Paul's laugh was smooth as a cadaver's caress.

– Cut the bullshit! he chirped. Anyway, I prefer a cock up the ass.

– Too bad you fuck pigs!

– Bo-Lennart humped so bad it's just as well he's dead, Paul said and tore out a blackened hunk of flesh from his lover's smoldering corpse. He took a bite but spit it out again quick. Then he snuffed out his ciggibutt, stood, and took a step toward Grandpa. All at once they were hugging and kissing with filthy, gyrating tongues. When Grandpa tried to grab his ass, though, Paul broke it off.

– Not now, he mumbled.

Grandpa wiped his forehead with a piece of Jesus's shroud.

– Damn but it's hot in here, little gaffer, he complained.

– The animals thrive on it like a cunt in the sink, Paul said. But sometimes you have to rake a few of them over the coals, otherwise they get all strepto-leninistic.

Paul was sweet and delicate as a fairy. His long, silky white hair, which framed an ascetic doperface, was smoothed back. Those old nostrils began to vibrate, though, when his arrogant eyes found the corner where I was crouching.

– I know the smell of a sickly child, he muttered.

– That's just my boy. He's real handy with his mouth.

– So that's how it is, smiled Paul. Come out so I can see you, don't be afraid. I just love little boys.

I crept forward with my balls retracted and my heart in my throat. When I reached Paul, I curtsied and bowed and then stood there with downcast eyes. All I got for my pains, though, was a knee in the jaw that sent me rolling.

– Satan's smelly cunt! Paul gurgled, What a pasty little colt! If you weren't Grandpa's boy, I'd carve your eyes out!

– And I'd ask the Lord to protect me for the sake of Virgin Mary's vaginitis, I threw out.

Paul scratched one of his many liverspots and smiled.

– Good, he said at last, you're more promising than you look, ciggidick.

– I'm trying to turn him into a real crass bastard, Grandpa said. But I think he's got too much cunt in him.

– Should we kill him?

– Nah . . . Maybe . . . I don't know . . .

– Abel Allmonikus and his woolyheaded niggerdogs! Paul cursed. Aren't you man enough to kill a child?

– Tweedledeedee old Paulgeez, Grandpa smiled lifelessly. Now what do you say to shutting off the suctionpump and inviting us in for a little soup and sour milk.

Paul Holm positively dripped with venom, but then thought better of it. Wordlessly he turned toward home, and we followed. The tallow candle quivered feebly as he made his way through the seething passages. Animals fled at the sound of our steps. After about fifteen minutes, we reached the tarpaulin separating the house from the barn. Groundcherries and Judas's coins surrounded the frontporch. Suddenly, Paul grabbed a healthy looking piglet. Stars danced in his eyes as he squeezed the life out of it. The piglet shrieked and shat and Paul tossed the dying corpse into a corner of the dark basement.

– My dear child, here you'll see all the great trophies Paul has collected throughout the years, Grandpa said in a friendly tone and pointed to a stuffed alderman hanging on a wall in front of us.

Paul's reserve melted a little and he lit a sevenbranch candlestick. The rumpusroom came to life like a bloodclot in the heart. The walls were covered with Paul's prey. Every trophy had a brass plaque recording what had been killed, when, where, and how. Next to the barn's entrance a huge hydrocephaluscranium hung alongside a sabbathgoat's darkly gleaming horns. Rows of embalmed cocks, mandrillbutts, and mottled retireehides gave way to mammothparts, doxies in fur coats, an entire sasquatch family, and a mummified *Australopithecus*. Hundreds of alcoholfilled jamjars held cherubic toddlerheads. The real prize of the collection, though, was a manticore—wiry and bloodred with three rows of teeth in every mouth and a scorpion's tail—poised to spring, a basilisk: that huge snakecock with a murderous gaze, a nerveball from a kikeplanet near the horsehead nebula, and a few things I didn't know what they were and a few others I don't want to remember.

– This one was hard to kill.

Paul stroked a stuffed author's unwholesome face.

– I had to crouch in the dungcellar beneath the cowbarn a whole day and night before I got him.

The placard said: "Teratological author. Cryptogerman. 187 cm., 80 kg., 20 cm. cock. Killed the twenty-seventh of October nearly 2,000 years after Christ's inglorious death under my barn with my dear old tencommasixmillimeter .416 Rigby."

Grandpa lit a gray Prince.

– What was so special about him?

– He had some papers on him describing how folks like us live and what we do.

– What did you do with them?!

– I used them to wipe my ass.

– That was the right response: Satan's dysangelium must be kept secret from the uninitiated until the Antichrist's arrival.

– He's close, Paul smiled darkly and led the way into his sick house.

We climbed a warped staircase to the back of the house. A woebegone cryptozoologist impaled on a taxidermist with rigormortis was standing in a niche. Paul kicked open the basement door and led us into the povertystricken kitchen. He moved a stack of beastsexmags and a Möbius and Weininger off the rickety, stained table and brought out two hollow meteorites, which he filled with blacksoup. Grandpa flipped through Abdul Alhazred's original *Necronomicon* and I scratched my scraggly hair. Paul laid out the sooty maincourse and scraped some burnt flakes onto plates for desert.

He sat them on the table and watched Grandpa.

– This spread is a little sparse, Grandpa said in the selfrighteous, vaguely threatening voice that guests tend to complain in.

– You always do this! You're always a pain in the ass! If you were anywhere else, they'd fuck you in the duodenum just for being the way you are!

– But Paul! Grandpa hiccupped, Why are you so pissed off. Has the devil got your panties in a wad!? Tied the duodenum into knots?!

– YouyoudamnfuckinsatandontknowhowitfeelswhenIget- pricklingsinmychestandstomachwheniseeyouigetallmessed- intheheadsomeonecomeandputmeoutofmymisery!

Grandpa's cold eyes were mocking and Paul slunk off to the john to dry his tears.

– He's stingy as a Chinese priest, Grandpa muttered, shoving aside the cupboardcurtain and disappearing inside.

He rummaged around for a bit and then came out with an ELC-brain in brine, a bowl of shredded pigcunts, a tub of Vaseline, and a nicotineloaf.

– Kolyma-Paul's shots are stronger than Karelin's lecherholds, he nodded in the direction of the bathroomdoor, which had just opened again.

Paul came out as though nothing had happened. He threw himself into his chair and began ladling out the black soup. Grandpa dug into the brain with his bare hands, and at his nod I spread Vaseline on a piece of bread.

– Forgive me Paul, Grandpa slurped out, I didn't mean what I said.

– I forgive you, because you're not right in the head.

Grandpa bent over the table and pulled Paul close to him. Then he gave him a sloppy wet kiss. He reminded me of a neighborgeezer comforting a kid who'd just puked.

– Being all anguished didn't help much when old Herod took a shine to babybashing, Paul proclaimed. But all human lives are of equal worth . . . they're not worth a shit!

– Typical Paul! Grandpa laughed, turning to me. You see, Paul here, when he's not being a troublemaker, is one of the finest misanthropes to ever claw his way out of the pateruterine cavity. But since he learned everything he knows from a fellow with a PhD in Cryptic Oncology, don't be surprised if what he says sounds as squirrelly as morals do to a girly.

– Not so unlike yourself, Grandpa, when it comes to the purely intactual, Paul observed. I wonder how some of the other boys are doing, though. I haven't seen hide nor hair of them since our schooldays.

– Whatever happened to poor old Torkel?

– Professer of Processorfelling in Lappbatikhalet.

– And Bulimic-Henning?

– In a psychiatrichospital.

– What about that slanteye with feverblisters?

– Kang Sheng?

– No, the other one.

– Anton Szandor? I heard he founded a Satanic cult in Pissiniemi.

– Thinking of them gets me all tingly.

Grandpa slurped up the Rolandicstrip and wiped his mouth with a bib that Nils Poppe had given him as a thankyou for services rendered. Then he sprawled in the rickety crofterchair, flicked away a gooberdinky, and lit a handicappedciggi.

– But I still say, Paul, my old friend, that you and I were the two the man in black had the highest hopes for. And I hardly think he's been disappointed.

– True, true, Paul nodded sagaciously, a junkie's insectsful wisdom written all over his far too lovely features . . .

– You and I were the only two who followed Baphomet's call, Grandpa declared and took a swig from his pocketflask, which was filled with fermented biturongpiss and spiked with Elie Wiesel's bile.

– Nah, there were a few others just as promising . . .

– Like "Måntengrymmer" and "Jan Orsa Päll" . . .

– Yeah, but they frittered away their evil on mere mischief. It takes more than celebrating Gilles de Rais's birthday or rattling off the peristalticconfessions every night to call yourself Hell's emissary. Most of them didn't make any more splash than a fart in the bath. They lived following Martin Luther's motto, "Live and let live so you won't get mauled," rather than the Lord of the Flies', "Buggering thy neighbor beats the hell out of getting a rattan cane in the ass."

Paul half-heartedly tried to shoo away the persistent flyswarm as he fell into daydreaming.

– Oh, how his dead voice burrowed deep into the mustiest corners of the brain, planting the black seed that changes all you see to gray. "Seek out need and show no mercy," he ordered. Great and terrible, cloaked and cowled, in chronically magnificent condition. He kept shagtobacco, you know, in a real heteroballsack. His rough hands gave the toughest whoreboy caresses. And the sulphurtaste of his slimy grizzlynuts . . . He touched me deep inside . . . He was so hard and went so far in . . . His cock was colder and rougher than the resinous dwarfpines on Ryssberget's baby-barbecueplateau.

– I'm ready to admit he was charming, Grandpa said reluctantly, trying to cut short Paul's gooey reminiscing as politely as possible. But compared to me and my Grandpa, he added, so low that only I heard him, he was a frostyvirgin trying to spruce up his deliriumfrazzled frizzdoo with spermdaubs. Now Paul, he said, louder, the boy here has been complaining that he's never got a fishingpole wet.

Paul's nostrils widened.

– So I was thinking that if you don't have plans for the afternoon, we could cast a few out in the swamp.

– Heeheehee . . . That little ratcunt has you so wrapped around his wormeaten parsnip you don't know inside from out.

– As long as there's strength left in my sphincter, no one farts in my mouth and gets away with it! Grandpa shrieked and sprang up from his chair, knife drawn.

Paul tried to bare his teeth at the same time as somersaulting backward. He smacked his head on the ironing board, but came sickquick to his sockless, ungulatehard feet. He groped after the fireiron and began to hum a potpourri of Gullan Bornemark's lullabies. Grandpa crackled with rage and feinted with his scalpel. Paul circled nimbly around the overturned table, egged Grandpa on, and tired himself out with futile attacks. When I saw Grandpa begin to stumble, though, and heard Paul's maniacal "Wipe wipe wipe that sour face away," I decided to go to the aid of the master of my nights. Paul then knocked Grandpa down with a jab to his right kneecap, but got a kick in the chin for his pains. I didn't need any more encouragement. I started an electricdrill, jumped forward with a sidewaystwist, and buried it in Paul's left temple. He glanced at me irritably as the drill ate into his rotten cerebralcortex. Then the light in his dull eyes extinguished. I shut off the whining drill and wiped the boneshards and brainflecks out of my eyes. Paul's remains, however, were lit by an underearthly light. Clear, white, and glorious against the dingy rug, peaceful as a stillborn in a slopbucket. Grandpa clawed his way across the lambertianarose parquetfloor and drove his scalpel into Paul's alabaster cheeks. After the guy's face looked like a Sutcliffesteak, he sliced open Paul's belly and pulled out the viscera and lungs. He tossed the shriveled heart to me.

– Flush it down the toilet, he growled, foaming at the mouth. Before I could pull the handle, though, the wasted hunk of flesh was drawn into the labyrinthine sewers by a toothy maw that vanished into the seething whirlpool.

When I came out, Grandpa had already downed Paul's testicles and had poured himself a Sevesogrogg.

– It's probably safest if you don't come any closer, you might get chloracne or something, he said goodnaturedly.

Then he examined Paul's mangled remains and rubbed his blue and swollen knee.

– Horrible. Just horrible. How do you get to be like that?

Grandpa sighed like a rejected asskisser.

– Old Paul was stronger than he looked. And tough. But I got the best of him in the end. And now I'm going to fuck him.

He cut the elastic on Paul's shorts and teased out his joystick. Then he positioned himself awkwardly above the corpse and tried to work his lightlysmoked sausage into Paul's seasoned intestinalchamber.

– Dear Satan, but I need salve! he bawled and airfucked Paul's slack stomach. Then he dipped his girlygirl cock in Paul's brainmatter and sprayed lovejuices all over Paul's doxyhair.

– Halledoodane, he babbled softly as he milked out the last few drops.

Grandpa half-collapsed for a long moment and toyed with Paul's eyeballs. His own eyes were half-closed, but he still studied me up and down.

– Fuck me, mite, life can be gruesome.

At that, he chugged a lug from his flask and zipped his fly.

– Time to get gone, he said. But first I need to change clothes and then, as God is my witness, we're going fishing.

He ordered me to find some clean clothes. So I tripped out into the hallway and up the stairs to the bedroom. In the closet, I found two dubious hideshoes, a blouse with an underbodice, a racoonskincoat, a wifebeater, and a walruswrap. Over the arm of the chair next to the bed were two pairs of chaps.

A dead child was wrapped in the black velvet sheets. A tattooed lampshade stood on the bookheavy smoker's table. In a grimy aquarium, two tapeworms twisted and writhed with bleatbreaking, and the black drapes that hid the walls were made of live bats sewn together. I took the clothes down into the kitchen and helped Grandpa into the wheelchair Paul had used for decoyhunting retirees. Grandpa was about a half meter taller than Paul, so the rags didn't fit well. Still, since Grandpa was so skinny it worked in the end. I got the wifebeater and a pair of the chaps and Grandpa chose a dandeliondecorated bonnet and a pair of boots he found in the dirtyclotheshamper.

– These are for you, boy. And don't you look good!

I packed a boozebag with snacks while Grandpa wheeled himself to the indoor toolshed to have a look. I filled the bag with raw rolldough, stewed prurience, pukeshitbread, and Tuaregquenelle.

– Don't forget the booze! Grandpa called, still rooting around in the closet.

I quickly filled a ten-liter can with syrup and phenol and then took a smokebreak astride a roughchair. The kitchen was no cozy place to be. Flies in droves sucked and licked their way across the floor. Palmsized lice performed pirouettes in Paul's cluttered sink, troughs with workingman's ribs and babypurée meant for the creepycrawlies reeked and bubbled. Above the sofa a teflon wallhanging caught my eye. "Vita brevis, ars longa" stood there, red on black, and underneath it the translation: "Life is short, the arse is long." On the windowsill some wilted pigskinbegonias drooped in cracked pots, trying to shut bitter eyes against the abuse of the oncoming night.

– How about some help, fancypants! Grandpa ordered.

The entrance hall was darkly illuminated by the glow from Grandpa's ciggi. He had a Kalashnikov, a flamethrower, and two-dozen nervegashandgrenades in his lap. He was also dragging a trough full of abortedfetuses and a hempsack with fishingequipment. I went out into the muddy yard to look for a wagon of some kind. I found a cobbled-together cart and a timid old ox to haul the stuff down to the pier.

– Well, suck the old geezer's dong! Grandpa swore when he got to the door. Harry Kågström made that cart for the Party

Convention in 1937. I recognize it by the swastikashaped spokes. It'll get nasty if we don't get out of here before the separatists make their evening rounds. Hurry and load up, you SRB-cunt!

With an effort I got the sack, trough, and Grandpa loaded onto the cart. I climbed up onto the runningboard. When I struck the ox on the flanks, it echoed dully. Bellowing, the umber beast began to pull us toward the overgrown path leading down to the swamp. Grandpa egged it on too, lashing out with his plumbbob until all the skin had been flayed off the ox's frothing, bloody hindquarters. The beast lurched through tangled stands of flutteringelm, jaundiceberry, and silverbirch, out onto a level marsh overrun with bogrosemary, sourdock, waxycrust, and a thriving coleopteranclub. There I took out first one of the beast's hindlegs, then the other.

– What the fuck you doing, are you trying to kill me! Grandpa laughed madly and clicked his shithole to goad the ox on, who was bravely hauling itself forward on its two remaining legs.

Slowly we bumped along the last hundred meters to the beach, where brown waves gurgled against the sand. The vanishing shoreline hesitantly sketched itself against a mess of flat, washedout, roughlydrawn surfaces. Ramshackle hovels covered in Maoist graffiti squatted there dismally. The beast stopped and I helped Grandpa down. He limped painfully forward and took the ox by the horns.

– Make him hot, boy, and then hack off his slimy rawballs.

I lay on my side and began to suck. The beast's cock tasted like chervil. Just when the ox was so hard it thought it might have balls after all, I took out the cockshears I keep in my waistband in case a Jew ever touches me. The steer bawled and tossed Grandpa into the nearest boathouse. I deftly broke its front legs so it couldn't escape. Silently, Grandpa staggered back toward the cart and took out a dull, rusty boxsaw. Then we placed ourselves on both sides of the beast and began sawing off its head.

– This is a tough job, Grandpa lifted his voice to drown out the ox after a few moments of hard cutting. It's mostly cartilage, though, so he doesn't feel anything.

Fifteen minutes later we were done. Grandpa sat on an abandoned earthcloset and lit a radioactiveciggi.

– Find a boat, load it up, and then we'll look for some bait.

I splashed my way through the mire to the wharf. A horrible smell greeted me at the water's edge, where a tangle of *Ulva intestinalis* and *Delasseria sanguinea* mixed it up with waterweeds and crabs. The lake looked like lumpy bouillon served on a quivering plate. Fertilizationcanals originating in Paul's barnhouse branched out around the wharf, where two boats were moored. One was a dinghy made of resinsealed cardboard. The other was a skiff made from baobabwood. It had a blackpine keel and was shaped like a Finnish whitewaterraft. Small animals were living it up in the roomy sump. I undid the boatchain from the post and clumsily tipped myself in. Then I found a pole and tried to steer the boat back to land.

– Fuck, it isn't working, Grandpa! I finally exclaimed in desperation.

Grandpa stubbed his ciggi out in the earthcloset, where trashfish chattered greedily. Looking as calm and collected as a priest during delimitation, he pointed toward a promontory about a hundred and fifty meters west.

– Go there and calm down, waif, because by Satan's tumorriden ass I don't want to mess my clothes up!

Grandpa was obviously in a bad mood. He made his way down the beach with difficulty and I followed his directions and rowed west.

– Ruhollah's rough shanks, Paul must've been fucked in the head! Grandpa swore. A few years ago, all he did was send his shit down to Lillträsket. That's a lagoon about three hundred meters southeast from here, he explained irritably, stomping a young penduline tit to death and elbowing his way through creepers and clingers. The terrain became more passable and the fleshy ground played host to cocoplants, opiumpoppies, oralpoplars, groundcherries, and bluegums.

Then the land suddenly flatlined, although a stalk of grain showed every once in a while. Otherwise, it was just mud.

– This reminds me of the Tibetan legend about Lepra-Berit and Leatherface, Grandpa began and recycled an old story from Maldoror's greatest hits.

I think he was just looking for an excuse to rest. After ten minutes, he pulled himself up again with difficulty. He'd been sitting on a shipwrecked timecapsule, which held a multi- and ganglylimbed, minium-and-olive striped visitor from Earth's near future. Grandpa gloomily examined the white and bloated sky, which looked like a dead fish's belly. A flock of beangeese flew into the sun and burned like fallenangels. A waterspout that had started in the bottomless pits below Björnhusberget whisked the calm summer twilight. It had schlepped a rotten house all the way from Träskbacken, and was whirling it away toward Lidträsket. After it was gone, silence rolled over the defiled landscape, stifling the contradictory clamors from both propagationarea and offaldump under the cold weight of indifference. Grandpa carefully studied our darkening surroundings. Nothing really excited him, though, since he was already waiting on the darkest night of all. Still, his looks silenced mayflies and dragonflies in their frantic buzzing over reedclumps and garbagepiles. Becquerelcicadas and other players waited for a sign from Grandpa before starting up again. I wanted to burst into song or something, just to keep Grandpa from destroying the world. His eyes offered a challenge to chlorotics and skeptics alike. At the edge of my vision, I saw the shadowforms of fibromyalgic moose and Samsonfoxes with troll and dwarf kings riding their backs. Sprites were straddling dirty, fattened hogs; sexgorged pixies rode Persian lambs ripe for the slaughter; darkelves perched on twoheaded calves. The world awaited Grandpa's judgment. With a thoughtful expression, he looked over his mangled realm, the sad remnants of his army. Vampires, werewolves, and demons had either found other sorcerers or had died terrible deaths at the hands of modern *Hetero patiens*. Pale as a birch, Grandpa continued to stare into the sinking sun's last lascivious light. The petty gloom was still waiting on his answer. Perhaps all those creatures of the night could re-educate themselves in the fast-growing fields of computing, media, or finance? Grandpa's stiff posture and imperator profile betrayed nothing of what he was thinking. Then he lifted his right arm. At first I thought he was going to perform a *Sieg Heil*, but instead his workshy hand gave a last mocking wave.

– Nightynight, snoopydoo, he sneered to the twilightcreatures, who existed by the suggestive power of his will alone.

The world knitted itself back together at the seams, and when I finally dared to look all I saw were the solid contours of familiar things. Grandpa was staring at me. If he could've sobbed, he would've done it.

– Now we can expect anything, lassie. The everyday world will get its claws into us sometime or other. When that happens, the jig is up. There's no place for the likes of us there.

He walked the last thirty meters to a little pier made from beercans and sillyputty. I tied up the boat and jumped ashore.

– What do you think you're doing? Shove off and get the fishinggear and all our other crap!

I was forced to make two trips. During that time, Grandpa stood alone at the berth. To calm himself down, he talked about the time we shot Palme. The trough and the can made for precarious going, but I managed to get everything onto the boat without its capsizing. Then I carried Grandpa out. Unfortunately, he slipped and fell when he stepped aboard. He crawled to the back, inventing new curses to hurl at me.

– By Ruth, I can't believe we're made from the same gristle and snot! The easiest task in the world, finding a seaworthy boat, is harder for you than getting Pelé to blow Muhammad Ali on live TV! using the pope as a bed to boot!

I knew it was useless to argue, so I jumped in and cast off. Moaning with the strain, I pushed us away from land, carving a path through toiletpapergarlands and barbedwirerolls. The water was like bloody diarrhea until we were a ways from shore. Then it was like peasoup shot through with splashes of quicksilver and strings of oil.

– Steer toward Storholmen! Grandpa barked. You know, it was out there that Terror-Nikanor hooked a Jewishly huge devilfish a handtrolley of years ago . . .

I sat down on the seat and began to row. The slender oars were made of psychomor wood and bit easily into the grainstrewn surface of the water.

– Boy, you've got less vim and vigor than Emil Zátopek when he won double gold at the Olympics in, what was it, forty-four? I was there with Rudolf Höss, Commander of Arschwitz, and the mood was all mob: thirty thousand Hasidic miraclerabbis roaring from the galleries of the amphibioustheater and just as many Checkers and Pollards. And there we were, fifteen reckless prettyboys from the SS's PJ/SE–battalion.

Grandpa suddenly fell quiet, shhshd for good measure, and made the deafmute sign for "If you don't stop now, I'll give you an intestinalparasiteenema." I braked with a splash of the oars and turned to see what had caught Grandpa's attention. A few barkhouses, good for learning how to go numb, lurked around Storholmen. And in front of one cottage, a fatgeezer was fucking a littleshaver. We slowly glided toward the fireblackened shore, making for two burntout oxhuts.

– Stop, Grandpa! It's not fun anymore! the youngster complained in a teartrembling voice.

The guy was standing with his back counterclockwise to us, but well within shotgun distance. He bit the kid on the neck and growled Fafner's and Fasolt's leitmotiv from *Das Rheingold*. His rheumatic loins moved like a piston, and his pockmarked hammer pounded straight into the little blond tyke's plump babycheeks. He'd tossed the kid over the dryingrack where Bogomils used to dry priestdicks. This geezer's cock, though, looked like it had been forged: rough, tough, and crooked, with a steelblue sheen and a rustred head. He drummed like he was young, a panting billows with a fattyheart, and scratched the screeching boy's back bloody. The boy, however, squirmed like a frog on a spit; his shrieks were metallic and wordless now; dirtyblood poured from his defiled rump.

– Cry, cry, honeypie, the geezer muttered gutturally and lit a fatsocigar with his free hand.

At that, Grandpa pointed his Kalashnikov and yelled.

– Karl-Johan!

Without missing a beat, the old man glared back over his left shoulder. At the sight of Grandpa, different emotions ran a relay across his forgettable face. At first he seemed surprised, then spiteful, then cringing, and finally miserable.

– Be nice! he whimpered. Can't you just wait a sec until I've done my thing!

– Pull your dick out now!

– Let me finish! Karl-Johan protested.

– YouheardwhatIsaid!

– Chill out, for fuck's sake!

Grandpa fired. The volley hit him in the back and killed him instantly. He fell flat on his face, but managed to drive his cock in one last time. In a few strokes we'd reached land.

– Get the boy and cut the geezer's right ear off! Grandpa ordered.

I sliced Karl-John's ear off and dragged the brat toward the water. Then I stuck the kid in the back and shoved off.

– Karl-Johan was an idiot . . . he liked disposable Q-tips . . . he also used Daisy Midi, the adult diaper "for those who leak just a little more" . . . I had a few bones to pick with him, but nothing that's worth rehashing now . . . Take us out to the reef by Tegeludden . . . Right at the dropoff where Ki Lu caught himself a Greenland shark. It was back when the summer of lovestories to end all lovestories was nearing its climax . . .

– Here?

– Nah, I changed my mind.

I rowed past Abborrudden toward Räften . . . After a while we reached a little islet. I dropped our rusty anchor, even though the water was mirrorsmooth. Then we rigged the net. Paul had a large tacklebox packed with wobblers, most of them magnum. I saw a waspcolored Swim Whizz, a silvergreen Cisco Kid, a rosy Heddon Tad Polly, a yellow-red Hellraiser, a darkly glittering Heimar Mene; the largest Rapalan was silver and black; the largest Hi-Lon was red and white; a flexible pikecolored Rebel, a bulging and bigspooned, perchcolored Rebel, and hundreds more . . . But Grandpa chose a dull old silver Kaleva. His rod was seven feet long and wicked stiff, crowned by an old crimson Ambassadeur. The line looked fresh, three hundred meters, 0.45mm. I had a limp little gasstation rod and an enclosedreel with no brake. A medium-sized Mörrum-troll was tangled in the worn line.

– Before we fish, let's chew some peyote, Grandpa said, opening his leatherpouch. I got six and he took twelve.

The bitter nubs are gumnumbing and the tough fibers really challenge your jaws. We chewed and spit, blobs splotched where they landed . . . But nothing was different than before, the world was just as hard to make out . . . you sit on *förtvivlans giffel,* the croissant of despair . . . on your way to the Great Attractor in Centaurus . . . the two hundred billion brain cells you have before you drug yourself up still don't know what darkmatter is . . . even though it makes up almost everything in the universe . . . making your way through life is hard, almost impossible . . . it's best to do what Grandpa says . . . Right now he was casting with a practiced swing, swaying to the rhythm, real smooth . . . the line ran out . . . The dark was about to swallow us whole . . . night had come on quick . . . He reeled his line in . . . nothing bit . . . mist came off the cold water . . . everything was calm . . . Grandpa cast again and again . . . in all directions . . . toward the reedclumps . . . the openwater . . . into nothing . . . He let his lure sink and turned the handle in a spunky rhythm . . . I cast with what I had . . . there was hardly twenty-five meters of line . . . I reeled in as good as I could . . . suddenly I felt a bite . . . I pulled against it . . . tried to jiggle it up . . . fear gnawed at my so-called heart . . . I couldn't see anything . . . the line was worn . . . it gave . . .

– Fuuuck!

– Why are you shouting, my unworthy lad?

– I had something . . .

– Got your hook stuck on the bottom . . .

– I don't think so . . .

Grandpa grabbed his rod and came out swinging. The face of an absolute dictator . . . my reel jammed . . . Grandpa's snarled . . . the rebound straightened it out . . .

– Now for some real action!

He emptied the trough of aborted fetuses . . . Skellefteå's romantic trials and tribulations made tangible . . . the whole redish-black, rotten, slimy mess of them . . . the blackwater swallowed them all . . . Grandpa fastened the Kaleva by the scalp . . . tossed the open tacklebox into the water . . . everything was lost . . . most sunk straightaway. . .

– Even Fehmi Varli's twenty-six-kilo pike wouldn't do for bait in this sea! Now let's show them what we can do . . .

Grandpa took Karl-Johan's little fucktoy . . . he'd fainted . . . stuck the kid on a meathook and used five pieces of nylonrope for a line . . . then he swung him twenty meters out . . . used a Tupperwaretub as a float . . . now that's honest-to-god tackle . . . I was in the process of putting the oxhead on an ironhook . . . but I didn't have line enough to get it more than a meter from the boat . . . The summer night had clocked in . . . we sat and hoped . . . The sky darkened . . . puckered up its eyebrows . . . from somewhere we caught the scent of gravity . . . A sheer cliff fell straight into the water . . . we had to imagine the rest . . . nothing's possible, but everything's imaginable . . . Grandpa waited . . . everything was still . . . time passed out . . . we began to despair . . . Suddenly I saw something circling my bait . . . it took a nip . . . a bite . . . swallowed it whole . . . headed straight for the depths . . . Grandpa cackled . . . I fought it . . . it was strong . . . it wanted up . . . no quarter . . . Carolines versus Muscovites . . . it was yielding . . . I fought like an animal . . . it came to the surface . . . it was terrible . . . no one would believe us . . . we moved counterclockwise . . . it seethed and gurgled . . . churned and shrieked . . .

– It's a demon! A devil!

Grandpa threw down his tackle and took up mine . . . he swore up one side and down the other . . . He saw more than I did . . . Resolutely cut the line while I stood and heavyheaved . . . sat back on his seat . . . took a grenade in each hand . . .

– That was the Midgard serpent! Ouroboros! Forget what you saw, if you want to stay simple and true! Fishing time is over! We've got to make for land as fast as we can or we're cooked!

I dipped my oars in the sullen sea.

– Row like your Grandpa was tied to a whippingpost dripping with benzine and Calvin came along clicking his lighter!

The land fell away . . . the water was dark and sullen, but still I dug in . . . Grandpa was uneasy . . . scared shitless . . . finally we were home . . .

– Look here, boy! We're going to go home and sleep it off . . . sleep as long as we want . . . And when you open your eyes again, you'll have forgotten everything that happened tonight . . .

We dragged the boat up on land, shooed the mosquitoes away, and pretended everything was normal . . . Loons ransacked us with their desolate cries . . . a thousand times more worthy than we . . . The devil made himself known . . . mocked our every step . . . Grandpa didn't dare say a word . . . only stopped to mumble a "Sour Father who art in . . ." We stepped into our home's human warmth and fucked standing up . . . quick and easy . . .

Before we went to sleep I asked:

– Can we play Emil of Lymmelberga tomorrow?

– Nah . . . Tomorrow we're going to hold up our end of the bargain . . .

STINKHORNS—*Phallus impudicus*

BROTHERS TIGERHEART—Astrid Lindgren, a Swedish icon of "goodness," wrote a book called *The Brothers Lionheart*

GABRIEL IN A GRAY COAT—a little gray gadfly

RAFFSET—a Swedish word for sexy female undergarments

SATANSTICK—slang for cigarette

AEAEAE—magic

WITCH'S HERB—St. John's wort

BIRDSFOOT-TREFOIL—in Swedish "käringtänder," or "old woman's teeth"

VIRGIN MARYS—seven-spot ladybugs

NORNS—Calypso orchids; also the Norse Fates (Swedish *norner*)

SRI AND SA-BDAG—Tibetan demons

BUT THE SOUR FLAME'S STILL SMOKING—*Men he ruk laing i surom brannom*, an expression referring to someone who's suffering from a long, painful illness, and just won't die

BEJN-BURMAN—bought bones and turned them into glue

NILAPADHANA—some sort of necrophilic-sadistic Tibetan ritual, my sources tell me, wherein a man has to embrace a corpse, convince himself it's alive, and afterward pry open its lips and bite off its tongue (the Chud rite, "the way of the corpse")

JUDAS'S COINS—*Lunaria annua*

ABEL ALLMONIKUS—*Abel* means mischief-maker, joker; *allmonikus* means tired

MÖBIUS—Paul Julius; *On the Physiological Deficiency of Women*

WEININGER—Otto; *Sex and Character*, that fascinating work!

ELC—Evangelical Lutheran Church

KARELIN—Alexander, Russian wrestling champ

GOOBERDINKY—a booger, bogy, etc.

NILS POPPE—a Swedish actor

BAPHOMET—Satanic symbol, often represented by a goat head; also, see Klossowski

GILLES DE RAIS—a Breton knight, companion of Joan of Arc and a serial killer of children

SUTCLIFFESTEAK—Peter Sutcliffe was the "Yorkshire Ripper"

SEVESOGROGG—Seveso is a river and town in Italy; "famous" for the eponymous disaster in which several kilograms of the dioxin TCDD was released into the atmosphere by a nearby chemical plant

CHLORACNE—an eruption of cysts and pustules

SRB-CUNT—Swedish Red Breed, breed of cow

ULVA INTESTINALIS—green sea grass

DELESSERIA SANGUINEA—red algae

DELIMITATION—delimitation period: the process by which parts of the Swedish crown's land was transferred to private ownership; in Västerbotten, delimination can be said to have ended before 1870

PSYCHOMOR—Swedish, lit. "psycho-mom"

PJ/SE—Practical jokes/Special effects division

HEIMAR MENE—Heimarmene: the oppressive cosmic wasteland in Gnostic belief

FÖRTVIVLANS GIFFEL, THE CROISSANT OF DESPAIR—Cioran's first book, brilliant of course, came out in German with the title *Auf den Gipfel der Verzweiflung*, or, literally, "On the Peak of Despair"; the Swedish anti-writer Lars-Olof Bengtsson thought *Gipfel* in this context meant *giffel*, Swedish for "croissant"

CAROLINES—soldiers of Charles XII of Sweden

EMIL OF LYMMELBERGA—"Emil of Lönneberga" is a fictional character in a children's book series by Astrid Lindgren; in Swedish, "lymmel" means villain, whereas "lönne" means maple

XXXII

When Grandpa gets tired of me, I play by myself.

Sometimes I play the quiet game . . . sometimes I play dead . . . sometimes I draw old geezers I've met and then I pretend I'm them . . . sometimes I lay on my back in a September field and listen to the earth hurtling through space . . . to victims shrieking at all the evil-deeds wrought upon them . . . then I try to sink into the light, soft, fluid grass and become a part of its mystery . . . Nature thrives on destruction . . . everything starts soft and small, but ends hard . . . they hound you till you're hard as a rock . . . sometimes I try to figure out how many fucks are going on at a single moment . . . sometimes I think of everything I won't ever get to fuck . . . When I can bear it, I try to look ahead . . . but all horizons are equally galling . . . sometimes I force animals to fight to the death . . . mink vs. weasel . . . rat vs. rooster . . . shrike vs. jay . . . beaver vs. badger . . . ant vs. earthworm . . . sometimes I think I'm going crazy . . . sometimes I play Grandpa-daddy-boy . . . sometimes I'm my own imaginary friend . . .

Most often I play with my plasticsoldiers . . . they're from different WWII militaryunits . . . Grandpa knows all there is to know about the war, since he was one of the ones who started it . . . He knows a lot, but he won't talk about it . . . Every now and then, when things are getting too comfy, I get an earful about Florian Geyer or Götz von Berlichingen, Kharkov and Cherkasy, the Children of Nemmersdorf and Papa Eicke . . . I stole my plasticsoldiers from Grandpa . . . when he thinks no one's watching him he plays with them . . . I play on the livingroom floor or out on the rocks . . . Outside there are cracks and crevices, reindeerlichen and bear's bedmoss, heather and wildrosemary . . . it's all so natural you forget about time and space . . . I have two collections of bluegray Germans, the Afrika Korps and the Japanese . . . they fight the gray Russians, the sandcolored Eighth Armyrats, the Yankees, the Aussies, the Commandoyankees, and the Commandobrits . . . the Rommels and Japs are also khakicolored, so Grandpa's bought me a few special collections . . . some partisan fighters from Prince Eugen's Mountain Division . . . and a handful of Bad Tölz Junkers from the Nibelungen Brigade . . . Playing with my plasticsoldiers has taught me how cheap life is . . . how easy it is to die . . . how soon it's all over . . . When I gather up the victors, and the good guys always win, they seem a little confused . . . the slanteyed swordslinging officers . . . the German machinegun troopers . . . the SS-Junkers . . . When you've killed your enemy, there's only one thing left to do: shoot yourself . . . preferably in the spleen . . .

When I walk home through the tired, brightwhite wildoatfields after having waged a war, I'm numb . . . that's the good thing about life . . . most of the time you don't have to feel it . . .

ROMMELS—soldiers under the command of Erwin Rommel, also known as the "Desert Fox"

XXXIII

– You're the only thing in this life that's never disappointed me, boy . . . because I never expected a god damn thing from you!

Grandpa and I were out on the terrace getting ready for my party. It was going to be outside, even though it was late October and sleeting to boot.

– How old am I, Grandpa?

– Nine or ten, I guess . . .

Grandpa had dressed up in a darkgray suit with a starched shirt, loose collar, and a preknotted tie. I had on a knitted woolsweater, balloonpants, and gummyshoes.

– You're a timesink, a milksop, you're stupid and you suck like a girl! FYI, this is your last birthdoomsday . . . I can't do it any longer! I can't stand the sight of you!

Grandpa squirted Schick's shavingcream onto the Styrofoamcake. I decorated it with red marbles and pennies.

– There now, all finished . . .

– Soon it'll all be over . . .

The time was pushing three and night was storming down. The powersthatbe had cheated the sky . . . the day wasn't worth a plugged nickel. Cold and gray, a foretaste of times to come. Grumpweather.

    – Are they going to show soon, Grandpa?

    – Did you tell them three?

    – Yeah, three . . .

    – Probably on their way . . . can't imagine where else they'd be . . .

We sat down on foldingchairs and waited. Grandpa passed the time squishing the lice he'd grown tired of . . . He spared the artists among them. With trembling underlip, I checked an estrustimetable . . . We'd done ourselves proud, the kids would like it. We'd hung balloons, garlands, and wires. There was popcorn, peppermintcandy, and caramels. Paperplates, plasticcups, and cum—and barfbags too. AROM condoms, Absolut Citron, and blackcurrentschnapps. Amphetamine tablets, cannabismuffins, and burnt gingerbreadbiscuits.

    – Can I ask you about a few words, Grandpa?

    – Is there anything but words in that sick brain of yours?

    – I want some more to play with . . . Just this once, Grandpa!

    – Fine, what are the words?

    – First I want to know what "solidarity" means.

    – Well, solidarity can mean a shitload of things . . . injury for others . . . losing yourself in the herd . . . hating the next guy as much as yourself . . . But it actually means that some people are worth more than others . . . and they have the right to do whatever the fuck they want . . . To be like liliesofthevalley . . . to not give a shit, because nothing's worth a shit anyway . . .

    – What's "stress"?

– Let me see: the Nibelungs had stressgut . . . the LO and SAF-bigwigs arrange a yearly stresshunt of sick retirees . . . Stress is God's foremost quality . . .

– Who's Oskar Ernst Bernhardt?

– The Messiah.

– Why doesn't a creek get tired of flowing?

– All creeks are tired! Don't you hear them sighing that all is vanity?

– What does kal-lukä mean?

– Killdeathkill.

– Why do we talk in dialect?

– Västerbotten's dialect is the language Guido von List talks about in *The Primal Language of the Aryo-Germans and their Mystery Language* . . .

– Is there life after birth?

– No.

– Is there intelligentlife on Earth?

– No.

– Who was my daddy?

– Some *Homo erectus* . . .

– Was it Gazin or Aristov who wrote *Doctor Chicago*?

– Neither . . . It was Kharlamov . . .

– Why shouldn't you write?

– Writing is like pissing truisms into the Pleonastic Ocean . . . Though the Almighty Public, the misshapen crowd, has definitely earned a good pissing on . . .

– What's the difference between Platonic and Aristotelian love?

– The difference is huge! Platonic loves means you can only jack each other off with two fingers while wearing rubbergloves . . . Aristotelian love means you can fuck armpits and kneehollows too . . .

– Why does it feel better when someone forces you to do it?

– Desire is hard to distinguish from nausea and suffering . . . pain, terror, and shame . . . Pleasure is knowing it's not possible to go any further . . .

– Which is worse, a sobbinggrunt or a groaningwhine?

– Both are the same . . .

– What were Jesus's last words on the cross?

– "My honor is loyalty," according to the Synoptics. But the Gospel of Python claims he said: "Life's a piece of shit, when you look at it!"

– Why are there so many people in the world?

– They're practicedummies.

– Why do so few of them give a damn about us?

– I've wondered the same myself . . .

– What are we made of?

– 95% hot air.

– Why are we here?

– To give each other hell . . . shame each other . . .

– What are we really?

– Cenobites.

– Why do we live in a grayzone, a nomansland, a waste?

– That was decided September 2nd, 1809 (or eighty years before my own personal calendar kicks in: when Nietzsche saw the light and Hitler issued forth into darkness), when Sandels and

Kamensky drunk themselves blind at a buggerinn in Frostkåge and agreed to an armistice . . . Russia's main base became Pite and rural Sweden's became Ume. Ever since then, those of us who live in between must exist in a powervacuum, an interstellarvoid, the windblasted and lambasted waitingroom of a Veterinarian that only has one treatment and one syringe . . . Two weeks after the Frostkåge boozefest, we lost the faithful Suomicocks to the Russians. Norrbotten was separated from Västerbotten and then was abandoned to miscarriages, cavemen, and liedown comedians . . .

– Why does anything exist?

– Because God's evil.

– What's the true order of the universe?

– Chaos . . .

Grandpa made a sign that the séance was over. He took out his gold watch and saw it was a quarter to four. The day darkened and the wind whistled and wet snow covered the terrace and extinguished the torches.

– It's just going to be you and me, boy . . .

– I don't know why they didn't come . . . they said they'd come . . .

– It is what it is, we'll just have to make the best of it . . . You've got no friends, that much is obvious . . . you're too small and insignificant . . . you've never had luck when they're picking the lottonumbers . . . you'll just have to live with the menu as is . . . Don't pout or the boohooboogieman will come and take you away . . .

So we ate and drank and sang and played . . . We played Jews and Nazis . . . kicked shiprats to the curb . . . suffered . . . The seas stormed . . . the earth burned . . . all Sweden must go . . . Then Blind

Man's Bluff, Where's the Penny, and The Pot's Boiling Over . . .
We played Watch Your Tail, Guess the Jew, and Find Your Pain
Threshhold . . . Mark My Words, Lose Face, and Hang Your Lip . . .
Charades, Monads, and Doodads . . . Hang Out, Cast Stones, and
Crack a Grin . . . Hawk and Dove, Ratcatchers, and Face to the
Wall . . . Dodge the Louse, Ormen Lange, and Chainsmoker Tag . . .
Pull a Tarzan, Roll the Foreskin, and Hide the Salami . . . We
played Trashpoker, Sink the Boatpeople, and Jago . . . Khmerchess,
Dominance and Submission, and Amnesia-Memory . . . Starve
the Bengals, Solitaire, and Stylite . . . Grandpa made noises like
howler monkeys and hyenas . . . Holmér and Lönnå . . . There's
a lot you can come up with on the fly . . . We sang "It Was so
Funny I Had to Laugh" . . the one about the baker and the little
frogs . . . about Mother's little Olle and the priest's little crow . . .
"Gulligullan Koko" and "Zum Gali Gali" . . . "Follow Me to Syra-
cuse" . . . about the raindrops falling on my head . . . And last of
all, I opened my presents from Grandpa. There were two books
wrapped in old waxpaper: *The Most Clever Jewish Ritual Murders:
Adapted for Children* and *Moomins Run Amok* . . . a puzzle showing the bombing of Dresden . . . some pajamas Lenin had pissed
in . . . and a pitbullterrier that unfortunately had suffocated in the
package . . .

Then the party was over . . . we froze so our bones rattled and
our joints squeaked . . . neither of us had the energy to clean up . . .
I'd never had a nicer party . . . But it didn't make me happy. I lay
awake a long time . . . Thinking of all that had been . . . memory is
a maggotinfested dump . . . I've only seen the sea once and it was
gray and roared . . . I've only seen the mountains once and they

were floating in a soup of fog as thick as rootmash . . . I've only been happy once and it gave me fevershock . . . If you're not up and coming, you're down and out . . . In the end, all you can do is sit and chew your nails . . . How will I live if Satan won't teach me to laugh at suffering . . . I wonder if I'll ever do anything worthwhile . . . like Gavrilo Princip . . . or Paul Tibbets . . . Life is a rebus no one can solve . . . a hairsplitter . . . a cruel pun . . . Before I slept, I prayed I wouldn't have any more birthdays . . . Forgive me . . . then forget . . .

AROM—Artificial Rupture of Membranes

STRESSGUT—lit. translation of Swedish *stresstarm*: Irritable Bowel Syndrome

LO AND SAF—the Swedish Trade Union Confederation (*Landsorganisationen*) and the Swedish Employers Association (*Svenska Arbetsgivareförening*)

STRESSHUNT—lit. translation of Swedish *stressjakt*: when the hunter gives his prey no respite and so wears it out

KAL-LUKÄ—clear-cut

KHARLAMOV—Valeri: great Soviet hockey player

OSKAR ERNST BERNHARDT—an imprisoned merchant in Weimar Germany who founded the Grail Movement and claimed he was the Messiah

GAZIN OR ARISTOV—see *The House of the Dead* by Fyodor . . .

HOLMÉR—Hans: Swedish police chief responsible for the (botched) investigation after the murder of prime minister Olof Palme

LÖNNÅ—Kjell: Christian choir leader and TV host

MOOMINS RUN AMOK—Moomintrolls, characters in various comic strips and books by Tove Jansson

GAVRILO PRINCIP—assassinated Franz Ferdinand in Sarajevo and started WWI

PAUL TIBBETS—dropped the Hiroshima bomb

XXXIV

– As I live and breathe! Hugo Silvergran exclaimed, gawking through a crack in the door, who's this illustrious person standing on my doorstep? Is it Grandpa out trolling for quarry?

– Ah, Hugo, Grandpa coughed, by the Goat Lord, how I've missed you!

– Listen, friend, I thought it was just the opposite, Silvergran smiled coquettishly. You weren't so eager the last time you stopped by.

– Can you ever forgive me? Grandpa sobbed and lit a purpleciggi in a hipgirdleholder, I'd give anything to undo the past.

– That all depends, Hugo declared. In my heart of hearts I know you're gooey as a baby's ass, Grandpageezer, but dear Lord you've got a mouth on you.

– I'm begging you on my knees, Grandpa blubbered and folded up like a prayingmantis. You know it hurts me, he wailed, we know each other inside and out and we've had so many beautiful times together!

– Yeah yeah, so we might as well make up, Hugo laughed dryly. Quit your groveling, you'll ruin your fancy clothes.

Grandpa had on a sulphurcolored smokingjacket, a nice shock-pink pullover, his pissyellow, flared gabardinepants, and a pair of saffron pumps. His SS-cap was set at a jaunty angle. I was dressed for going out in my comfy leather and rubber getup. It was elk-matingseason and the hunters were out in fullforce. Volleys of bullets echoed through the marshes of Drängsmark. A cow with leadpeppered flanks drug herself into a bramblesnarl only to be met by a flamethrower. Since cock-, cunt-, and bellyshots give hunters the most prestige, a swarm gathered around the wounded animal, which bellowed in pain and heat.

– I've got something on the stove, you might as well come in and have a bite, Silvergran offered. The boy can come too, he added graciously, arranging his moldy features in what was meant to be a smile. It just looked like he'd swilled some sperm and lost all his money, though.

– Thanks for the offer, I'm just overwhelmed, Grandpa gushed, cuddletousling his hairwisps.

Then he strutted into the peatwalled entrancehall and pushed his way through a thicket of homespun paraphernalia. Finally, he shouldered his way into Hugo's kitchen. I followed with a lump of oldcum in my throat, and last came Hugo, waddling along on gangrenous legs. Grandpa swept off his coat and hat elegantly and threw himself down at the kitchentable. He spit in my face and made me climb into the gynechair normally reserved for Hugo's clientele. Silvergran wasn't looking too good. He wrapped a spermflecked angorasweater around his bumblebee waist and adjusted his Lovikkasuspenders. His varicoseveiny legs were bare and thick socks swallowed his feet. He had some nasty suckscars on his tits and turquoise curlers in what was left of his hair. His skull was carrionyellow, his hairlipped mouth was an angryred, and those frogspawn eyes of his were cataractwhite. As soon as he got into the kitchen, he stuck a sheet of newborn babyheads into the gas oven.

– You know, it fucking sucks, he complained; to get these right, you have to grease the sheet with cuntjuice from gigglygirls.

– The hell you say, Grandpa exclaimed and injected his temple with a cannula of heroine. How do you come by it, and how in the name of Mary Mother of God's gnarly anus can you handle that stuff?

– I know this Afrochap, who's bi. And, you know, that crazyass mofo fucks so many of the lesserbreed that he's getting swaybacked. So when the cows are grimacing and writhing, he's usually able to milk them for a couple of deciliters. I trade him some cartilageporridge for it and then I suck his salami.

– That just makes me want to puke, Grandpa moaned sybaritically. Still, I don't begrudge you your babyheads, Hugoito. What do you use to stuff them?

– A homemade mixture of boogerstew, steelwool, conductoreyeballs, carbuncles, and sulfuricacid.

– Have you ever thought about using luespurée?

– Nah, that's way too hoitytoity, Hugo said defensively.

Grandpa took dainty girlypuffs from his ciggi. Then he cleaned his Ahnenerbe glasses and stared illnaturedly at Silvergran's plumpass. Hugo was tinkering at the stove, brushing a sauce made from syrup, ketchup, and sawdust over some tumoraspic. Grandpa began to flip through an issue of the *Svensk*

Damtidning, absentmindedly dribbling a spitblob on Princess Victoria and, sansanima, playing with my stiff little cock.

– So how are things with you, he finally said, mostly to break the silence, which was starting to writhe in agony. Are you just wasting time and jacking off or do you see a little cock every now and then?

– Ah, you know how it is: you have to be around and about to get something on and in yourself, he joked, swallowing a snotcube.

– I'm just so goddamned happy to see you again, Uno, Grandpa gushed. Fuck me, but I think I'll just whip it out and go.

– God, you're making me blush, Hugo said, going red and digging out a handful of dingleberries to garnish the aspic with.

– You know, I never thought fornication was a waste of time. In fact you might say it's been my life's calling, Grandpa declared. If I do say so myself, Master Hämmerlein has been good to me. The fact is, I'm the fairest one in all of Kågedalen. My cock was forged in martyr's blood and it's never forsaken its lord and master! Not once!

– You're about as fair as an outfucked old pigfart's gut, Grandpa, and your cock's stiff as a maggot! a gruff voice bellowed from the door.

Two giants pushed themselves into the kitchen. The one who had spoken was clearly the leader, on account of his age and hardheadedness. He was none other than Kågeträsk's firechief, Johan Westermark. He sank heavily onto the pigskinsofa, fixed Grandpa with a malignant stare, and pressed the barrel of his moosehunting rifle against Grandpa's forehead.

– How should we do this, he asked arrogantly, swelling with selfsatisfaction and twisting his pigbristle mustache with legendary, agile lips.

– But Johan, whimpered Grandpa, who was really beginning to sweat now, why are you being so nasty? Are you just trying to make yourself unhappy?

– You're so fucking smart, you old devil! the other man cackled in schadenfreude.

He was Ralf "Slurpykiss" Markland of Norrlångträsk, a hard MBD-geezer in a gray persianhat, a cottonsweater, and rainpants. His great passion was dynamitehunting burrowinganimals. However, he'd happily toss handgrenades at anything from ungulates to handitards on wheels. He had a stooped figure and his eyes were like snuffedout ciggibutts.

– Just tell me what I did to you, boss, Grandpa whined, twisting slender hands encased in blackvelvet, onanist's gloves.

– Let's not waste words on that, Johan declared and then laid the gun across his grannylap. I just wanted to see if you got scared, you homomofo! he roared and took off his shabbyhat, revealing a scrubby thicket of grayhair. Then the firechief unbuttoned his hamsterfurtrimmed wolfskincoat to reveal his shaggy breast. His powerful, huge prick was, however, still partly obscured by a handmade weave of boyscoutprickdown, with balls that dangled like coconuts over the back of the couch. Johan Westermark was a weatherbeaten, bowlegged charmer straight from the marsh's edge. He had crocodilohumor, a potashheart, a certificate in childtampering, and a potatodumpling nose. It was anyone's guess, even his, how many times he'd won the Finnish Thousand Fags Rally. In sports like smokinginbed and selfinflictedfailure he was unparalleled.

– By the fuckers that made mincemeat of Ernst Röhm, Grandpa swore and lit a ciggibutt with trembling fingers. I couldn't tell if you were pulling my thirdleg or what, Johan, but there's one thing you should know, and it's this: I often think of you when I jerk off.

– Nice to hear, but it doesn't change anything. I never could stand you, Grandpa, I just don't know why.

– It isn't important, Slurpykiss broke in, to spray cream into a Belsenqueen like that.

– Ah Ralf, Grandpa smiled and took a drag of his ciggi, go suck your own damn cock before you pucker up for others.

It was silent for a moment and the kitchen grew inhospitable as a womb. We blinked at each other like lizards in the shadow of a corpse, and I thought I was going to die. Darkness was about to lie down with our recalcitrant countryside. The only thing you could hear was the occasional accidental shot from some automaticweapon.

– How about some grub, boys! Hugo chirped. He took the babygratiné out of the oven with a shrunken, smokestained ovenmit. Then he unlocked the pantry and started setting out this and that.

– You know, I haven't been able to keep anything but fattysperm down this year. When business gets slow, stores get low. Anyway, I hope I can find something tasty, even if it's from year before last.

He divvied up a bag of sores, a dryplacenta, and a clairvoyantumbilicalcord. That was followed by a plate of rats floating in sphincterjelly, a live Turkishkidney, two cold labiacroustades, each with a deepfriedclitoris on top, and a bowl of Inuitforeskins sprinkled with powderedsugar.

– Come and get it! he announced, an idiotic expression on his eructated, liferavaged face. He set out a jug of Kool Aid and a bottle of muskratschnapps. After the meal was over, he served up coffee with a shot of Bhopalacid. Each person also got a niggerball with skin and hair still attached. All told, it was pretty satisfying.

Of course, Grandpa and Ralf came to blows over the Turkishkidney, which gave a heartrending shriek when they both speared it with their forks, but otherwise everything was peaceful.

It wasn't until afterward that it all went to hell.

– To be honest, that meal amounted to highwayrobbery. What a disappointment. You had to gnaw the shit out of the Eskimoskin just to get it down, Grandpa growled, picking the few rottenstingers he had left with a pimp's stilettoheel.

At that, Hugo turned gray as Fru Öberg. He was a housewife to the tip of his cock and one harshword was enough to crush him, especially when it came to his mushmash. He covered his eyes with rheumatic hands and cried silently, the livingdead incarnation of reproach, a smoking Kekkonencigar stuck fast between his cichlidlips.

– I just don't understand why you didn't serve up the babygratiné and tumoraspic, Grandpa continued, sour as a cunt. A nice man like yourself must be ass-deep in greedy little buggers the whole year, you said as much yourself. Cum on a kisser, then stuff your tummy, as Per Albin always said.

– Hell, you old sow, Ralf Marklund swore for Hugo, who was speechless. You're the nastiest thing to ever straddle a cockhorse in all of Kågedalen!

– Ugh, Tiddly-Om-Pom-Pom, I can't believe all the things you pull out of your ass, you old bastard, Grandpa exclaimed. I'll never forget the time Pattaya-Uri tricked you into fucking Slag-Inez. The whole time you thought it was a seven year-old's milky-white marzipanass.

– You know, everyone wonders how you lived with Grandma all those years without your cock slipping inside her jellybelly sometime or other, Slurpykiss threw out, trying to hide his old shame.

– Sure as Henry Rinnan really wrote *Emil of Lönneberga*, Grandma was all man! Grandpa declared. She had whiskers and the strength of a cavetroll. I swear by the Impotent One that she had one hole down there and one hole up here. As Nietzsche said: a whorehag grows not a meatsausage in her crotch, nor can she drink a Lappishshaman under the table. But Grandma had a hangman's cock and she drank like a mongoswine under the butcher's knife!

– Don't fight over my Grandma's sex. He Who Rules Over Piepel and Animals is the only one who knows for sure, I said . . . the boy with the Neeskenssideburns.

– Shut your hole! Grandpa shrieked until his voice cracked. By Satan's gut, I wish I'd choked you as soon as you were squeezed out of your papa's ass!

– The scamp is right, Johan declared. Grandma's been dead for a good many years and it's neither here nor there what she had or didn't have between the legs.

– But children shouldn't talk back, Grandpa whined.

– You can't help feeling sorry for him, though, Ralf said. The kid looks like hell.

– Maybe his growth got stunted or something, Johan suggested.

– Someone needs to take the bullshit out of him, Grandpa admitted, but I'm at my wit's end.

Then he sighed like an honest Jew.

– Anyway, boys, we need to skedaddle on home before the homoheadbashers start camping on the forestpaths, he said to no one in particular.

– You seem worried, Johan observed, and emptied his bottle of muskratschnapps.

Grandpa's face said he wanted nothing more than to be gone, but he'd been brusquely put in his place by the feral, grunting Kågeträsker.

– Assbackwardtwat, Slurpykiss exclaimed, baring his inflamedgums.

Then he grabbed the SS-cap and fingered the silver deathhead with his nimble apefingers.

– So you're a bonafide Nazi, eh Grandpa? he asked and tried to hold Grandpa's iceblue eyes with his yellow ones.

Grandpa contemptuously lit a marikacracker and blew the heliotropic smoke out of his nostrils. It was obvious, though, that he was scared. He fiddled with a glassjar where a walkingaddictstick was climbing the walls, and examined the neglected warts on his wrist with obscene focus. He glanced out the window and asked how the elkhunt was going, good or—

– We'll come back to that, Johan interrupted him harshly, wrenching the stiletto out of Grandpa's Barbiehand.

– Right now we're going to find out whether you're really a Nazi or not.

– You bet your ass I am! Grandpa howled, suddenly beside himself. And I'm proud as Satan of it!

– You deny the gassing of over 600 million Jews!? Johan Westermark screamed, grabbing Grandpa's lacefrill and shaking him like a prostheticcock.

– Hearthisyouyouyou sweet thing, Grandpa mocked, those Jews I skinned in the war were infamous for setting themselves on fire with their own farts and that's the only gassing I ever heard of, I swear by all that's dear and holy.

– Lord have mercy, whispered Silvergran and stubbed his ciggi out on a fire- and asheating geranium. If you knew how you sound, Grandpa, you'd flay yourself to death with a cheesegrater rather than live with the shame.

– Hey, Huga-Hugo, Grandpa said with a grimace, caught fast in Johan's grip like a fart in a bag, I think you should know that I want to puke every time I see you! Why, you're so ugly, the sperm turns sour every time someone cums inside you!

– Ah, woe is me, Grandpa, you shouldn't have said that, Silvergran informed him. Because now you're our bitch, whether you like it or not. Take him to the bedroom, he added and nodded to Mademoiselle Westermark.

Grandpa hooted and hollered like those hawkers who drove Jesus out of the temple, but it didn't help. Johan carried him like a defiantchild into Hugo's dingy, smoky, cumsoiled fuckcubby. My Grandpa hissed and spat like a sexstarved cunt; he tried to bite, but a knee in the mouth sent the rottenstumps of his teeth flying.

– I learned that from Tommy Alexandersson, Westermark said conversationally, tossing Grandpa facedown onto the bed and wrenching back his arms and legs. Then Hugo took a mouseskinstrip from his jockstrap and hogtied him.

– Come in, boy, because this is the last you'll see of your Grandpa.

I went in and sat down on the bidet. Johan whipped out his ramcock and made me flick it with my tongue.

– Now look here, Grandpa, Ralf said with a sneer, we're about to do the most beautiful thing two people can do together. Keep his head still, he ordered and whipped out a razorblade. Hugo grabbed Grandpa by the ears and beat his cursing, dolichocephalic head against the headboard until he was beyond reason.

– I became an expert in what I'm about to do when I was with the Tonton Macoute, Slurpykiss boasted, slipping his free hand under Grandpa's chin.

With two elegant sweeps he cut off his eyelids.

– Now you can't go beddybye when things get rough.

– Help me, mite, Grandpa moaned, can't you see that they're hurting me?

– I can't do anything, I said, not to these types.

– I think I'm just about ripe for some loving, the firechief informed us, swaggering around the room with his salivadrenched homobeatstick held high. And by Satan, I'm getting mad, he hissed, fingering Grandpa's little hardon.

– Why, he's hornier than a hog, Hugo laughed, gripping Grandpa's sprucecone as hard as he could.

And when Grandpa opened his mouth to holler, Ralf Marklund shoved his halflimp stoolpress into Grandpa's gaping mouth.

– God help you if you don't suck like Jesus unmanning the three wise men, he threatened, because I'll come down on you like a herd of lunchladies gone wild!

Grandpa obediently puckered up his little mouth and started taking long, deep, luscious pulls. He worked so hard he had twin gaps in his cheeks. Johan smeared his bullcock with Kabylemustard and brutally ripped open Grandpa's hinterhillocks. Then, with a girlychirp he crammed his bluebaton into Grandpa's bruisedandlubed sewerpipe. He started off slow. Ralf tenderly cradled Grandpa's laboring head, controlling the tempo, while Johan too kept it nice and easy so he could reach the cerebralhemorrhage he was aiming for. Grandpa bobbed up and down like a buoy, eyes wide and staring, and it was a wonder his brittle skeleton held up as well as it did.

– Surely you can see how much better it is to be tame than troublesome, Ralf declared for the sake of the show. I'm betting that before long we'll bleed the Nazi right out of you.

– You a proud Aryan now? Hugo barked and crept forward on his knees to shove himself awkwardly in Grandpa's bloody, aristocratic face.

Grandpa tried to shake his head, but this disturbed Ralf, who was just about to reach the Big O. He dug his nails into Grandpa's skull and stuck his thumbs into Grandpa's ears, pulling and twisting until Grandpa's ostrichneck cracked dangerously.

– By the saltycream stuck up Sven Wollter's numbertwofunnel, it'll be down the hatch, he declared angrily.

By this time, Johan was in his own world. He looked like he was suffocating, panting and puffing and generally carrying on. Each thrust took his whole twelve inches. His balls thudded heavily on Grandpa's emaciated hams; the tempo approached eighty beats a minute. Hugo stared at me with unfocused eyes and played with his raw sausage.

– What do you think, fuckmite, he asked hoarsely and gave a deep sigh of contentment as a fist went up his ass, can you make your head go like a yoyo? If so, you can have a taste of my magnificent hotrod.

– You horngeezer, I snorted dismissively.

– You're as foulmouthed as a washedupwhore, he growled, but as you're about to find out, nothing can help you now, not the skin of your teeth nor the milk in your breasts.

– Why don't you bend over and lick your own pussy, cuntface!

– Hellfireandbrimstone! he roared and lunged at me with his pants down around his ankles. You devil, I'll kill you!

Unfortunately, he tripped and fell headlong to the ground. And while he was down, I kicked his wildrasperrysized testies black-andblue and bit off his left eyebrow. Panting, Hugo dragged himself into a corner.

– No fucking diva gypsyboy's going to suck my magnificent batteringram anyway, he moaned and chafed and coddled his brokenpride. He probably sucks worse than a socialfuckingdemocrat with mumps, so it's not like I'm missing anything.

In the meantime, the Big Bosses had begun to cum.

– Iiiihh! howled Ralf Marklund, pulling his infected, wartyrod out of Grandpa's throat so he could mess on his face.

The lidless mirrors to Grandpa's soul dripped with spermpus and urethraslop.

– Uuuuhh! roared Johan Westermark, dragging his pimply trollpole out of Grandpa's betterhalf. Slimecoated sperm pumped from its tip like foam from a fireextinguisher and covered Grandpa's atrophied, writhing flesh.

– Lord Jesus and those fuckhungry cribbiters, Ralf whispered and wiped himself on Grandpa's nicotinestained wisps of hair, that hit the spot, you bastards.

Johan shut his eyes and swallowed a little of his own seed.

– Hey Ralf, Grandpageezer may be evil as Snoddas and ugly as my old ma, but his mouth and ass are open 24/7. Ume-Eskil once told me that Grandpa sucks like Ebbe and backbumps like Sighsten, Johan said and untied the mouseskinstrip.

– Eskil's a lovely old spermburping cumbag, Grandpa said in a choked voice and stretched his creaky danceofdeathcarcass. Then he propped himself gingerly on the potbellypillows and lit a methtartciggi.

– But I'll never forgive him for being crazy enough to compare me to those epicenequeens. Fact is, I'm the tastiest asswipe to ever suck on a pissrag.

Grandpa sat there and smoked like a lady, a coquettish smile gloomily playing across his ravaged features.

– I've gotta thank you, he finally mumbled in servile embarrassment, placing his hands on his rapists' limp dicks. By Satan, you boys know how to make someone feel like a real woman.

– Ugachaka! Hugo shrieked and crept to the edge of the bed on all fours.

– Why, Hugo baby, Slurpykiss laughed scornfully, what the hell happened to you? You're a bloody mess from the top of your head to the tip of your fountainpen.

– Furry critters with cunts! Silvergran swore. The boy went apeshit and tried to jump me. But look here, he exclaimed and dipped his bottomfeeding finger into Grandpa's own vomithued spermpuddle, which formed a glaring contrast to the palegray fucksauce the steers had pumped out.

– Fuck me, you've sexed up your last retardchild, dirtbag!

– You're about to see how it feels when the priestmeat burns, Ralf declared dramatically. The fact that you enjoyed yourself just now like a ditz on a pizzle really irks me, he added and disappeared into the kitchen.

He came back with a fryingpan and bashed Grandpa's head with it until his right eyeball popped out and dangled against his cheek.

– Easy there, old dame, Johan laughed, let Hugo torture him a bit before he's too far gone to feel any pain.

– Devil in my pants! I promise to be cruel, Siljabloo, you can count on me, Hugo said and stuck his prick in Grandpa's empty eyesocket.

– Too bad Elisha Burr Myregg isn't here, Johan sighed, he likes theroughstuff. I remember how he tormented that pair of Jehovah's witnesses to death at the intestinalfest in Lauker.

– Ralf and I will get the job done, Hugo said. But keep him still, oh my lord and master.

He waddled to the garderobe and took out a roll of barbedwire, some pipecleaners, a pair of sheepsheers, a kerosenelamp, a tub of glue, and a hose.

– When we're done with you, not even the corpsefucking fibromyalgic moose that Gunnar Grönland shot the balls off will want to shag you, he said. Being beautiful is a pain in the ass, he gigged and fed a strand of barbedwire into Grandpa's moistoyster.

At the same time, Ralf prodded a pipecleaner up Grandpa's urethra.

– You're just an old kinkyminky, growled Frau Westermark when Grandpa struggled like a Gadareneswine and shrieked like an almightybaby. Hugo stuffed barb after barb into my howling Grandpa, and auntie Ralf crowned him with more barbedwire still. Johan held him a little tighter as Hugo ripped out what he'd just pushed in. Grandpa fainted. He was as broken and bloody as a beaten shiprat.

– I have a nasty pisshardon, Ralf declared and stuck his bloatedtumor into Grandpa's sweet ass. You look like you could use some fertilizer, he scoffed and pissed in Grandpa's gut.

Hugo smeared diarrhea between Grandpa's lips when he started to come around.

– Time to beat him blackandblue, boys, and then I'm going to flambé him, Ralf said.

– You're a real joker, tittycrusher, Johan sneered and grabbed Grandpa again.

– Struggle and fuss as much as you want, buggerdevil, because you're about to get what you're begging for!

Slurpykiss lit the kerosenelamp and smiled like a pious girlchild swallowing a severeddick.

– Say something nasty about Hitler, he commanded.

– He licks pussy!

– More! Worse!

– He was born of a woman!

– Oh, you naughty little cockgobbler! You don't really think you're going escape the fires of hell just because you badmouthed Amos Hitler, do you?

Ralf moved the hissing, purple flame toward Grandpa's spread cheeks. The flames licked his soiled tangle of hair and turned it to ash in a second. Slurpykiss pressed the mouth of the kerosenelamp tight against Grandpa's analopening and let the flame eat into his gut. Grandpa squealed like Holy Berndt when the Lardskinleague was strapping on the slaughtermask. It smoked like the ovens of Arschwitz and reeked like boymeetsgirl. Grandpa's voice broke, his body shook with spasms, and his cock spurted sludge.

– Stop horsing around! Johan cried, You'll kill him!

– Yeah, for Gunde's sake, don't off him while he's still having fun, Hugo agreed.

Ralf turned off the gas with the expression of a fermentedherring who wakes up in its own juice.

– So what the fuck now? he asked listlessly and slunk toward the window, which looked out on Ethanol Hooker Street. In the meantime, the firechief put out the fire in Grandpa's ass with the hose, and Hugo hesitated between the sheepsheers and the gluetub.

– Hey look, there goes Olga Saur! Ralf exclaimed suddenly. And Pirjo Propp! Invite them in, Hugosatan, so they can catch a ride on Grandpa!

Wild with schadenfreude, Hugo dashed out, breasts bobbing, while the other oldboys prepared Grandpa for what was sure to be the most degrading thing to ever happen to him.

– You, so proud you'd never touched a whatthefuckaretheycalled, oh yeah, woman!

– You bragging about how you knew Immanuel Cunt's *Critique of the Unclean Pussy* inside and out!

– We'll teach you to like three holes, and may God have mercy on you if you don't stay hard, pisscunt!

– This'll be the funniest thing to happen since Moses and Aaron held their wankoff contest!

Grandpa couldn't make a sound, but he looked so pathetic I started to cry. The oldbags came strutting in with Hugo in tow. Olga Saur was small and dry and had teddybeareyes, Pirjo Propp was big and juicy and listed to the side.

– So this is Grandpa, Olga confirmed to herself. Hugo said you're drooling for some cunt.

– He's always ready and willing, Ralf assured them.

– Then the old cock's about to get sweaty, Pirjo said and bared her bloody cloaca.

Grandpa shook like a lickedclit, and his cracked lips parted with the devil's own groan. Hugo and Johan each grabbed one of his arms, and Ralf laid himself across his skinny legs. Pirjo took out her dentures, squatted down and took Grandpa's balls into her cavernous flytrap. Her supporthose was mended with nailpolish. Grandpa gave a brainpiercing shriek and then fainted. Johan earboxed him back to life. Olga unbuttoned her official countrycouncilwoman-jacket, folded up her prostheticleg, and began to lick Grandpa's withered hobbyhorse. The women worked up a froth with their saliva, but his cock stayed limp. Grandpa prayed in Hebrew and Ralf gestured to Pirjo to try kissing him. No matter how hard they tried, though, his dick remained down. Finally, they took a smokebreak.

– He's one nasty devil all right, Propp said in a horrified voice, snuffing out her cigar.

– You hear such things about him.

– Irma had a helluva time with him.

– I know what we could do! Ralf exclaimed, brightening up. I'll fuck the kid, that'll put some juice in old Grandpa's bag.

He forced me to my knees and made me take him in my mouth. I greedily sucked his pamperedcock and kneaded his lankyballs, but he was as hard to get going as Grandpa had been.

– Satan's leech! Slurpykiss exploded and gave me a fist between the eyes. When I tumbled to the ground, he kicked me in the back of the head with his safetyshoes until I passed out.

When I came around, Johan was prying open my shitseat. He pulled me hard against his calloused fist, and then slowly forced in his navvyprick.

– It won't help to pout and fuss, Hugo told me and scalped me with the sheepsheers, while Johan burst my gut.

I was swallowed by the creepingdark and met the light that never warms.

– Hate and suffer, it commanded me. You're the Grandpa now.

It showed me the whole world and then the ovenuniverse, and I learned Kågedalen was everywhere. And that there must always be a Grandpa. From up above I suddenly saw Drängsmark and Hugo's house. Then I was floating in a corner and I saw myself being Arabfucked by Master Westermark so hard that the bedclothes steamed. I was feverish, but I looked dead. Grandpa was convulsing on his back on the floor. Hugo and Ralf had him by the shoulders and were forcing him to watch Johan's raw murderfuck. Pirjo Propp had Grandpa's legs and Olga Saur rode his shamefaced cock. She panted and labored with her festeringcrack snug around my Grandpa's tarnished joystick. Grandpa's mouth was open like he was shrieking, but I couldn't hear a thing. Olga worked him with all the frenzy only deadestrus can give. Pirjo piddled his balls with a retardedgrin. Ralf laughed unshedtears and greedily jacked off. Hugo alone had hold of Grandpa's head and shoulders now and was still forcing him to watch as Johan violated my little body. Grandpa's hands were nailed to the floor and he had a batteryoperated Luciacrown on his head. His upper body was naked, but he'd kept his chaps.

– Grandpa looks like a god, I said to myself, then his remaining eye popped out of its socket. He trembled and quaked and turned red as a lobster. His colostomybag burst, his dinner came up. I saw in and through him. His heart broke, his brain burned, his soul shriveled down to nothing.

Olga rolled off Grandpa with sperm dripping from her sick cunt. Then I was pulled away and woke up with evil still muttering in my flesh. I lay on a big offalheap about a gallstone's throw from Silvergran's yard. I was burned, scraped, and stung, but I was impossible to subdue. My ass ached and my crown smarted, but Grandpa had fared far worse. He was on his stomach next to me. I turned over and saw he was dead. They'd cut off his balls and nipples and sliced off his cock. He had it in his mouth.

I stole Hugo's wheelbarrow and wrestled Grandpa into it. Then I plowed my way through bogs and pinemoors, shrouded by night, frozen by wind, whipped by rain. When dawn finally poked a hole in night's hoary pupil, the freezing rain turned to sleet. I huddled naked under a logdump in Ersmarksbodarna, took a catnap, and ate a rat. When evening came, I shoved off again. The capercailliewoods were like a thousand bombedout cathedrals. The night entered my bones and whispered lewd propositions. Firs brooded over an ancient evil, they'd wandered down from Siberia to spread darkness over the Aryan heartland. They had to be sure they settled close enough to suffocate each other, though. The tufts of grass were springy, but groves of berrybushes made a stand, and stones and roots lashed out. Fallen trunks barred the way, mud turned slick as ice. The darkness had no heart, the paths had forgotten why they existed. But I trudged on and made good time; well after nightfall I was there. I stole into the Lansförsamlingen churchyard and found a good resting place next to an old conifer, maybe a black- or turpentinepine. I grabbed a spade and dug a hole and tipped my Grandpa in. Then I went to the mortuarychapel and dragged out a reinforcedconcreteslab. I scratched the word "Grandpa" into it with a nail. Then I read a Mass. Since I had a cold and was frozen to the bone, though, I tried to fill in the hole as quick as I could.

I leaned the gravestone against an ashtray and then sat down on a treeroot. Kama-Mara came by and babbled about violence and sex, and I promised to do my best, since I owed Grandpa that much. He bellowed, full of hatred and lust . . . the Kali Yuga will ramble on . . . And then I was alone . . . As it was ordained from the beginning. As it has always been. When the light finally forced its way through night's hymen, slow but stubborn, I stood up.

– I loved you, I mumbled and pissed a few salty drops on Grandpa's grave.

I wanted home.

I'm Grandpa now.

LUES—an old name for syphilis

SVENSK DAMTIDNING—Swedish equivalent of the *Ladies' Home Journal*

MASTER HÄMMERLEIN—the Devil

MBD-GEEZER—MBD stands for Minimal Brain Dysfunction, now known as ADHD

ERNST RÖHM—Nazi leader, well-known homosexual

KEKKONENCIGAR—Urho Kekkonen, a former Finnish president

PER ALBIN—former leader of the Swedish Social Democrats and four-time prime minister

FRU ÖBERG—an old, weird, quarrelsome pipesmoking woman

HENRY RINNAN—Gestapo agent

PIEPEL—young ass in a concentration camp

TOMMY ALEXANDERSSON—killed five people in 1989, nicknamed "The Butcher"

TONTON MACOUTE—Haitian paramilitary force

SVEN WOLLTER—Swedish actor

SIGHSTEN—Herrgård: Swedish fashion designer, well known for his unisex clothing designs; he is credited with "giving AIDS a face" in Sweden

EBBE—Nils "Ebbe" Knut Carlsson; Swedish journalist and publisher who revealed his homosexuality, and the fact that he had contracted HIV, on television in 1991

SILJABLOO—Gunnar "Siljabloo" Nilsson, popular Swedish jazz musician and renowned scat singer

GADARENE SWINE—the herd of pigs Jesus cast demons into

GUNDE—Gunde Svan, Swedish cross country skier and oddball

cloaca—old term for sewer

KAMA-MARA—Siddhartha Gautama's adversaries, the demons of desire and death

KALI YUGA—worst of the cosmological cycles

XXXV

It's been a week since they killed Grandpa . . . Eons . . . I can't stay here alone . . . I'm going to Skellefteå . . .

Skellefteå . . . I live in a garbageroom again . . . nothing but sourdough and mustardseeds to eat . . . I wander around like the dead . . . I remember all we did together . . . Drink my cares away and stare into the black empty heavens, the soul's darknight . . . That's all there is left . . . nothing else to tell . . . just fragments . . . "Do I alone hear this melody, which so wonderfully and softly . . ."

> If anyone ever reads what I've written, they'll wonder who I was . . .
> Just a nameless boy who was forced to be a Grandpa, but couldn't do it . . .
> Just another animal in the chaos . . .

Christmas . . . I visited the grave last night and talked to Grandpa . . . Begged to go to him . . . Said I couldn't do it anymore . . . He said it'll all be over soon . . . Abaddon's angels will take me away . . . He knows I've written about him, but he's forgiven me . . .

I'm sick and crazy . . .

Death take me . . .

Grandpa, I'm not worthy . . .

Eloi . . . Eloi . . . lama sabachtani? . . .

Do I ALONE, ETC . . .—from Wagner's *Tristan and Isolde*.

ELOI . . . ELOI . . . ETC.—My God, my God, why have you forsaken me?

Appendix: Memories of Grandpa

André Sundlund, 91 years old, childhood friend
– You bet I knew poor Holger. We went to school together and during the last few crappy years we'd shoot the shit about God, Satan, nearlife experiences, and the foundations of agrarpriapism.

Holger was always a handful, everyone says so. Even before his eyes opened and he'd stopped babbling babynonsense, he was off on a crookedpath. He was raised by a man who lived only for death. Holger's own Grandpa was named Holger Holmlund and he'd been the devil's bitch for as long as any forcepsdelivered oldfuck could remember. Old Grandpa was said to be cruel as they come, a savage to everyone he met, he worshipped the devil and scorned men who lay with women and weren't brave enough to sow the darkground. Anyway, he eventually called forth and then fanned the flames of forces he couldn't master, and they took him just as little Holger learned the noble art of selfgratification.

But let me tell you what I remember about Holger from our elementaryschooldays. It was a crime to be alive back then, that's a lesson we all learned early on. Up at three every morning to

pack a lunch of stalebreadcrusts and moldyleftovers, then haul ass
forty kilometers to school for a quickie on Mistress's chair. Sex
didn't matter, most kids were usersandabusers, getting drugs was
easy, all you had to do was lift your skirts and bat your eyes at the
sextons and old eccentrics. Holger was the worst of us all, but he
knew how to play his cards right. The teachers were devils in the
flesh, anorexic beanstalks. They held out as long as they could, and
then it was off to the loonybin with them. Either that, or they'd
hang themselves with the guts of unwantedchildren. I especially
remember one, a retarded hunchback we used to call the Spider.
He was wordblind and proud of it, and he wouldn't tolerate us kids
using words that weren't his. We probably had him about a year,
and every class he'd drone on about how Joyce from Dublin died
for our cysts' sake and how no matter how much we moaned and
groaned, we could never make it goodygoodygood. One time he
wanted Holger, the quickest of us peatbog children, to read a sentence out loud. The problem was, Holger was so drunk he couldn't
see straight, so he just said: "Man was created in God's image."
     At that the Spider cooed:

> Brown guu, if only there were more like you!
> Words should fly, but they just sneak on by!
> You ugly hog, you'll be top dog!
> Life's divine, but death's devilishly fine!

Then he stuck a pointer up his nose and into his brain.
     At recess, we pegged kiddos with pebbles or blew frogs and
toads up with straws and then poked them full of holes. Halfwits

had to pay with their balls. If someone fell, the herd was on him lightningquick, set to kick him while he was down. Suddenly, tattoos were all the rage. Most kids chose scenes from the Acts of the Apostles, but I remember that Holger got three sixes tattooed on his crown. Still, he was sweet, and how sweet he was to the bosses and other bigwigs! He was never stingy with compliments, even if they only got halfway inside! Back then, though, times could be tough. When you got home, it was just wipe your ass and off to bed, pronto! You knew you were alive, and what a damn shame that was. Not just for your mom and dad, but for your family and friends, race and kind, material and energy! Superstrings and subquarks!

"I was just wondering," . . . my dad said when he finally noticed me, "if we should let the calf live."

Mom had been stuck in the kitchen for the past few years. She looked up and you could tell she'd been pretty before she'd eaten it all away.

"Nah, you know, Papa, he's had his time in the sun . . . he's had his chance, but he didn't take it . . ."

Grandma saved me, though, because she wanted to do me. But Holger kept mostly to himself. After three years, we were fully trained, we knew all about making our rumps blush in the bath and why everything under the sun gets up and off. One time Holger and I hung out after school, we were going to go hunting with slingshots. There was this oldcunt who wrote shitbooks and lived in a carwreck out near Dire Straights. She was the one we were gunning for. Holger had always been real outdoorsy and so he found us a willowbed beside the path that gave us an open fieldoffire. It had rained and so it was pretty slick when she finally came huffing along. There was nothing special about her . . . she was just annoying . . . that was enough . . . we were fed up . . . She put on airs, pretended to be a fortune-teller, made herself out to be a psychic. And you know what, she looked right at where we were hiding and shouted at us, even though there was no way she could've seen us. It wasn't what you'd call the perfect shot, but Holger wasn't going to lose any time. He aimed and sent that ball flying. It took her eye out! And before she could get a real fire going in her pipes, he'd put her other eye out! Then we rushed out and talked some sense into her! Guess if we were proud!

HENNING MIKAELSSON, 87 YEARS OLD, FARM OWNER, FORMER COMRADE OF HOLGER HOLMLUND
– I hung out with out with him in the fifties, back when Irma was still alive and kicking. She was a piece of work all right: sleeping higgledypiggledy with the livestock and creeping beneath the bingotable to suck on any blowhard she could find.

Holger was pretty stylish back then, even though his hair was going thin and his ass was getting bony. He wasn't nearly as interested in sex as he was later in life, though. If you want someone to blame for the fact it was all downhill for Holger Holmlund, it's Irma. She'd go to town on any old pieceofmeat, but she wouldn't touch Holger's with a pair of sugartongs. I don't know how Holger took it. We didn't talk cunt. We massacred bugs with modeltrains, and every now and again I'd play the accordion and Holger would sing spirituals. Sometimes the devil would take him and he'd lock himself in his room and work like a hellion on his Biblecommentary, which was so horrible that just thinking about it made you want to scrape your foreskin right off.

Sometimes he'd recite whole passages from memory, and I'd weep and pray for him. He read up a storm, and he knew every language under the sun.

He borrowed thousands of books a year, a lot of them musty and gray and from far away places. And man, how he wrote! Up one side and down the other, roll after roll of cheap toiletpaper, while the devil sat on his left shoulder and dictated.

"If only the apemen don't off me before I'm done," he'd say. He hated Judeobolshevism, but he was totally crushed when Stalin died in '53.

"He really gave them hell," he sobbed.

And he'd say, "Everyone's a devil," every now and again.

He stayed out of the sun, so his skin wouldn't get dark. He thought shampoo made your hair black and curly, so he washed his with sagopearls. He was afraid snuff would make his nose crooked and his lips thick, so he smoked twice as much.

"What are you going to do if you get rikscancer, Holger?" I asked him once.

"Kill them all," he answered, catching a blowfly in his mouth and swallowing it.

MARGOT SANDMARK, 81 YEARS OLD, GRANDMA IRMA'S FRIEND
– Holger Holmlund was the nastiest wretch to ever dirty up a cunt!

The fact that there were ever people like him in the world is un-believable. I've seen some things in my day, but he took the cake . . . He murdered Irma, I'd swear it on my husband's grave! And Doris, too! He was so ugly, it was a disgrace . . . And what's more: if a spe-cialevent was happening, a party or a wedding, say, he'd make sure to humiliate Irma in front of everyone . . . He lied to her when they got married . . . Said he was polite, charming, virile, and rich . . . Promised her Happily Ever After . . . He was a shitbag! Emergency-rations were all he had to offer! He pretended to work in the church congregation . . . consoling survivors . . . crying over new-borns . . . He brought people nothing but grief! Longwinded as he was, you'd go into metestrus just listening to him . . . He said God was invisible! that there's more than one sun! that it's bad to tor-ture livestock to death! that movies aren't real! You've heard it all yourself! Toys in the attic! gadfly! galorum! gawd! grainworm! An abomination! He was sick! What a wastrel! A donothing! I felt so sorry for Irma, I nearly drank myself to death . . . I don't know how many times I stuck my hands between her thighs, looked her in the eye, and said: "You've got to put an end to him . . . he'll make you crazy . . . he may seem like he's been good and tamed, but I know the type . . . he's out of his mind, Irma! . . . listenhere! beagood-girl! there'snootherway! it'syouorhim! he'sgotmurderinhiseyes! dowhatI'masking! hellsbellsIrmadon'tyouseewhathe'sdoingtoyou! nobody'llbreatheasyuntilhe'sgone!"

But Irma wanted him . . . on a shortleash, of course . . . She needed the money, poor thing . . . Holger threw a fit every week-end, Irma had to whip him back into shape . . . Damn, he was difficult! Irma loved to dance, you know, but boy you should've seen him fuss when we were getting ready to go out! Just begging and hollering and making a scene! "Irmadon'tyoudaredoit, you'llbethedeathofme!" and "Iloveyoumorethanfinalvictorypetyouknowthat" and "Youcandowhatyouwantwithmejustsolongasyoudon'tleavemeIneedyoudamnit!" and "Forgivemeforlovingyousomuch I'mgoingtoburst!" He'd grab her around the knees, but Irma knew enough not to give in . . . She just made herself up even bolder than before, she didn't bother to wear underwear under her dress and she made fun of him when our girlfriends came by . . . If she found some tasty morsels at the bar, she'd bring them home, work them up, tie Holger down, and force him to watch . . . Irma was the finest woman you can imagine . . . homely, surly, portly . . . It was never the same without her . . . She loved a good romp in the sack . . . What stamina! From dawn to dusk! Up and down, front and back! She knew everything about everyone! and she could talk your ear off, that's something anyone'll you! With a smile on her lips the whole time! She had Doris in fifty-six . . . The girl got along fine . . . she was unbelievably like Irma, both in her attitude and around the mouth . . . Holger wasn't allowed anywhere near her . . . He read like a maniac . . . Irma burned his books, but he always got new ones . . .

I told her: "Put his eyes out, that'll stop him from reading those wicked books . . ." All for nothing! She was too sweet and kind to make it when the prince of this world kicks up a rumba with Conway Twitty. . . What I'd been telling her was going to happen finally happened . . . thank God, Doris was at her Grandma's, Permesiva, who lived out in Gråberg . . . Irma had got the cockshivers . . . They found her in a ditch . . . he'd used a vacuumcleanerpipe to force meltedlead into her cunt . . . They never arrested him for it! the buggerfucks! Three old friends swore he'd been with them all weekend making pineconeanimals . . . So they left him free to wreak havoc . . . A wolf in the flesh, that's what he was . . . a leftist . . . He held nothing sacred, he left nothing in peace . . . They took Doris from him, but he murdered her, too! And then he took her boy, Helge! How that boy's going to make it now that Holger has so obligingly up and kicked it, is something I don't even want to think about . . . All you can do is hope he doesn't understand too much about what's going on . . . he always was feebleminded . . .

LILLEMOR LUNDBERG, 38 YEARS OLD, SOCIAL WORKER
– Holger Holmlund needed a lot of support, but he was extremely difficult to help. He never came to us, we always had to go to him. You never felt welcome, though.

"Jabbercunt!" he'd spit right between your eyes. "Scurfbag! Cloacalwhore! Cancernode!" he'd keep on going. He'd been on disabilitypension since childhood, on account of rectalcancer. And in the last thirty to thirty-five years, he received economicsupport in the form of incestbenefits and a BSDM-subsidy. And he also got a widowager's pension after his wife died. He made a bit by volefarming in the bakery, and every now and again he earned a couple of kronor by writing letters for the town's old neverwed analphabetic geezers. He had a severe drinking problem, but all he did was laugh scornfully when someone tried to set him straight. I remember this one time Mari and I visited him. His answeringmachine was just one long, awful string of abuse, so we drove out to Hebbershålet unannounced. It was spring, the sap was rising in every cunt, but Holger's yard loomed dark amidst the suninseminated forestglade. The shutters were closed tight, and from inside the stereo was thundering forth a weird Mass. Hard, heavy primevalsounds were drowned out by bestialhowls, children's tears, and women's wails. Metallic cadences and insane choralstanzas, unnatural sybariticgroans, and piercing cries of pain. Mari pushed the doorbell, which by the way was shaped like a penis. I could tell by her nipples that she was scared. All at once the soulshriveling music stopped. We waited a couple of minutes, and then I pushed the dickhead myself. A piercing sound like the matingcall of the pale sprucebarkbeetle echoed through the tired house, which had already witnessed so much misery. Grumbling, Holger wrenched open the door, and I asked him how he was and if we could come in.

"New deal, God," he babbled. "You won't get me, you Satan you!"

He was barechested and had on a pair of brightyellow long underpants. He was bleeding from deep gashes on his stomach and breast. As usual, he stank of alcohol. His knotty hands held an Arabian deck of pornocards. His goateyes stared shrewdly out at nothing. Mari tried a little kindness, but he kneed her in the mons pubis and she fell back off the porch.

"Sorry, what did you say?" Holger asked, cupping his ear with his hand. "If it's about the offer to teach Sundayschool for the kiddies, I'm still interested. But I want free booze and lubricant."

"I was just asking how you were and if we can do anything for you—"

"Aren't you old Suctionpump Desiré?"

"No, Holger, it's Lillemor from socialservices. Now you listen here, you have to stop drinking—"

"I've had more than enough of you, you slimeball. Get out of here before I sic the boy on you!"

"Actually, we'd like to talk to you about how it's going with Helge—"

"Go to hell, harpy!" the boy shrieked, peering out between Holger's legs with a blackandblue, bonetired face.

"If you don't cooperate, Holger, we'll have to call the cops."

"I'm so fucking fed up," he sighed and slammed the door again.

I stuck Mari in the trunk and drove away. When we got to town, my boss called the police. When they stormed Holger's place, though, he was so wellgroomed it was almost sickening, he was just as friendly and hospitable as any GB-Gubbe. Besides that, we didn't really have any real proof that Helge had suffered at Holger's hands. In the fall of '88, we got a report alleging that Holger had repeatedly abused his grandson, Helge, whose parents were found raped and beaten to bloodypulps in the Skellefteå museum's movietheater. I think it was a documentary called *Skellefteårs: The Missing Link* that was showing while the two of them were getting their justdesserts. They died of their wounds before regaining consciousness. Helge was delivered by chancelloreansection at seven months and spent his first extrauterine year in a clinic for relapsed pederasts. After that, he spent two years with his grandmother in Kåge, until she succumbed to gardenhosemasturbation. He spent a few weeks in a garbageroom, because nobody gave a shit. Then one fine day Holger Holmlund swept into the office, ready to do business.

"I want to abort the boy," he said.

"You mean adopt."

"Yeah, I want him. What do you want for him?" he asked, fingering a wad of Monopolymoney.

"Excuse me?" Lisbeth, who ran the whole shebang, asked.

"How much do I have to shell out, already!?"

She blushed furiously and clung firmly to the letter of the law, because he was a stately man, and you could tell that there was something slightly "off" about him. He had no barriers left, so to speak.

"To adopt a child, you have to fill out this form first. Then a committee of rejects will be appointed to decide if you're a fit guardian. After that, the matter is in the hands of the local omnipotents."

"Superb, cuntskunk," he said, "I've got my thumbs in the local powersthatbe, and I don't just mean in the eyes."

He stood and filled out the paperwork, while he sang Hans Sachs's last piece in the *The Mastersingers of Nuremburg*, the one that begins with "Verachtet mir die Meister nicht, und ehrt mir ihre Kunst!" The laying on of hands went recordquick, and the next Monday that came around, Holger thundered in, banging open the entryway door so hard it splintered.

"I have an appointment with a three-year-old!"

I lifted up the boy in a blanket. Small, woolly, yellow lambs were leaping in a meadow, and one corner had been sucked to scraps. He was an alert little rascal, his eyes followed everything that moved. Skittish and mute. But I'll never forget the expression on Holger's face when he took that bundle into his arms. The child looked up at the old man—and, suddenly, everything was good, just like it was meant to be. The boy laughed for the first time, and it sounded horrible. He stuck his small fist between Holger's cracked lips. The old man pretended to bite, and the child just about died. The sounds he made seemed to stand for all the miracles of joy, love, and safety. He was beside himself, he whimpered and yowled, as if everything before now had been a nightmare, but today there was healing, hope, and forgetfulness at last. Holger was like a vortex of pure light. I saw that he was the Madonna with child. Neither before nor since have I seen a face so twisted by purelove. The rest of us didn't exist any longer, the whole fucking world had burst like a troll in the sun. He flew off, glided out, people melted in his presence, melted in the face of his heartcoremeltdown, and God existed, and goodness, and mercy. Death and the Devil stood by in shame, Holger was Creation's champion. It was a good while before everything went back to normal again, and we could smoke and chat and think about other things. And as for the accusations of incest, well, nothing was ever proven, none of the powersthatbe bothered to launch an investigation. Sometimes it seems like I dreamed the whole thing . . .

Harald Holst, 79 years old, drinking companion
– Holger Holmlund was a real pal, I wanted to say that first off. Anyone who knew him knows he wouldn't harm a louse. But there are always those awful busybodies who have to insist that a person was so and so, a dib and a daub, little by little, this and that after they're dead. Holger, though, was really the salt of the earth. Neat and calm. Generous with the gifts our Grouse who art in Heaven gave him, whether you're talking about spirit, the way

he had of telling a story, or just your runofthemill paltry human compassion. He always had a word or two for you, no matter how tedious it was for him. And he reaped what he sowed. He'd been married to a crackwhore who fucked two, three thousand guys a year. I heard about Irma from other people. Holger never said boo about it, though. So now I understand better why he wouldn't get together with women. Still, the idea that he liked men is, I think, an outandout lie! I never saw hide nor hair of it.

Holger lived pretty reclusively and kept to himself. He pissed on his own ground, if you know what I mean . . . He never drank more than one schnapps with a meal and he smelled fresh as a maid in heat. I can see him there in front of me now, spinning wool in the corner of his kitchen with a succulent bratwurst between his lips. He had thick, round glasses in slender frames and was extremely educated, without being cocky. It made him unhappy to hear anyone using spiteful words. And his boy, Helge, was raised in a strict Lutheran way. Just mess with those who are weaker than yourself and all that. They had it rough, but they killed time as best they could. We mostly hung out during the dark months, and a lot of what he said could creep you out. He had a low, rough voice for telling tales, and you sat there like a rat before a snake, mouth open wide. He was a great preacher, but so humble that the vermin finally got the better of him. He left a big, blackhole behind him.

RIGMOR MORTIS, 63 YEARS OLD, NEIGHBOR
– Holger was terribly hard to deal with, that I'll say straight out. We were terrified of him, and we hoped they'd come and take

him away and lock him up and throw away the key. He was in and out of the loonybin, of course, but he always came back worse than before.

He was already pretty foul and rotten when Irma was alive, but after she died he was just plain batty. Holger was always drunk, and he smoked like a chimney, oh-me-oh-my! Our children wouldn't play outside if Leif-Örjan wasn't with them the whole while. One time I was out getting the mail, and Holger came traveling along on a kicksled, and my wetcunt began to bubble like a hotspring.

"Aren't you dead yet?" he hollered and swept a cuddlecushion at me, so that I was suddenly up to my ears in mud. I was wearing my beige overalls and brown rubberboots, and I prayed to my Maker that he'd take me as I was.

"Well, is that how you treat people, then?!" I babbled. "Are you just going to leave me here in the muck, cunt bared?"

"I'd rather hump a lopsided electricaloutlet than that rancid grannyhole of yours!" he scoffed and went on his way. I lay there for a while. Then I rolled up North Västerbotten and stuck it clean up my wetcunt, which was just aching for a little attention. There's nothing better than using your Kegelmuscles to squeeze out the last few drops of sperm. But that homospecter thought he was too good to cream it up in my uterine mouth. He was always an idol to us, and it's a good thing that he's dead. It was a shame, though, for that boy he was raising. To this day it baffles me down to my whitehot cunt why social services didn't take poor Helge away from him! How they got by, only Uri knows. He probably had a homosubsidy. Holger talked so strangely, like he had a hotpotato in his mouth.

I remember Irma saying that he had books with letters and numbers in them, and that's enough to make anyone real suspicious. Oftentimes there was an awful racket coming from his house, even though it's a good kilometer from here. Laughter and merrymaking and then a sudden shriek that made you think someone was getting themselves a threewaysandwich. I hope he's burning in hell, and that when I've gone to my heavenlyhome, I can drop by and pour cookingoil all over him.

SAMUEL MÖRK, 62 YEARS OLD, FARM OWNER
– Holger Holmlund was always welcome in our house.

He was just skinandbones, you know, so the meals that Mama would whip out of her cunt were put to good use. We'd usually offer a bag of crispy cheeserot for dinner, and if we weren't too full, we'd have frozensoda ices for dessert. Then we'd settle in front of the TV and have a drink. Holger liked to munch on snails and shrews, while we watched *Nygammalt* or *Here's Your Death*. I usually ate lefse and pancakes. Around half nine Mama would fall sleep, and I'd carry her out to the shed. Holger was incredibly restless, his eyes were constantly roaming around and he was always fiddling with something or other. And what a talker! He'd just warble on in a high, shrill voice, and sometimes he'd also act like he was hard of hearing, he thought it was cool. He'd seen a lot, Holger had, and that's the truth, but you only understood a fraction of what he actually said. Sometimes he'd sing a psalm, and it would make your heart want to burst. If he got excited, he'd rattle off invocations in Babylonian or whatever it was, and his eyes would roll like a niggertroll's. He admired the ancient

Assyrians and Aztecs for their reckless cruelty and wanted to be jettisoned from the Earth on an endless trip through the cosmos when he died. Of course, I only knew him for the last twenty years or so, what he'd gone through before that is anyone's guess. But maybe it ain't so fuckin' cozy for us either! He said so many strange things: one evening he claimed he'd been a slave in a tribe of Jewniggers in Burkina Fashoda, another that he'd created the HIV virus in Staffan and Bengt's home lab, and when he was really plastered, he'd say that he'd gotten a taste of Mao's littleredbook, that he'd been Fritz Haarmann's apprentice, but that he'd surpassed his master early on. He also praised the Sambia tribe in New Guinea, where little boys are taught to suck mancock early on, something they'd be doing for the next ten to fifteen years: "The more sperm they swallow, the fiercer they'll be as warriors!"

And then, "Shut the fuck up, milksop!" he'd roar, whenever anyone had any objections. "You don't know a thing!"

One time he was raving about a couple of hockeyplayers or something, who he'd known real well and had had a few laughs with. I think their names were Freisler and Vyshinsky. Usually you got next to nothing out of his whining, though, since mostly he'd just babble on like a badbook. But he was a nice, standup guy and he always gave me a good schtuping before he went home.

GUNIVAR ISRAELSSON, 68 YEARS OLD, TRADESMAN, NIGHT-BALROG IN THE IRON PRISON OF ANGBANDT
– I'll always remember Holger Holmund as a bonafide, outandout rejected member of society . . . He never raised his voice!! He was

prudent in all his purchases . . . once a quarter he'd come bumping along on his velocipede with the boy on the handlebars . . . sugar, coffee, saltedherring, jam, not to mention some of the best falukorv, thank you very much, just like you find in Bullerby . . . that was it . . . well, that and every cigarette I had . . . he was a pleasure to deal with . . . never an unkind word . . . never a violent gesture . . . never even a salty expression . . . he had real understanding, he was a nutandbolts kind of guy . . . he leapt ahead of his time with a leper's jinglejangle . . . he was downright civil, thank you, thank you very much . . . and aryosophic . . . he supported the racewar against the Lapps . . . you know what he said, he said, just think, Gunsan, of all we have to thank industry for! Capitalism brings such good with it that it destroys all the supposed glories of life! Ravage the forests, I say! Make every town a new Norilsk! God bless supervisors and manufacturers! lostsouls and ruinedbodies! the hoipolloi shouldn't get uppity! Who isn't fed up with freshair and cleanwater! I hung on his every word . . .

Just think! he ordered . . . where would Skellefteå be without Boliden and Rönnskär! They're the best thing that could've happened to us! Where would we be without heavymetals! We never would've enjoyed the Skellefteåsickness! the Västerbottensyndrome! the Kågespew! Thousands of tons of sulphurdioxide a year! dozens of tons of copper! zinc! lead! arsenic! cadmium! We would've had PMS! migraines and discharge and badtempers in the morning! like Kikewhores! Rapers of the earth! industrytycoons! profiteers! Thank God for them! consortiums and investmentcompanies! concerns and financialtrusts! all our age's heroicdeeds take place on the stockexchange! No more wildanimals! No more freefantasy! Just commerce and industry! profit and production! exploitation and consumption! Conformism and narcissism! Hedonism and mammonism! Dollar, yen, and mark! They're the Holy Trinity! He sounded like an auctioneer! . . . he was meek and mild, so long as we were left in peace . . . he knew what he wanted and he knew how to get it . . . he was a firstrate customer . . . I'd offer the boy a raisin, and for Christmas a saltcone . . . But if a woman came in and started blathering, then it was different story altogether . . . you saw he was a shaman . . . without further ado they went out to settle the score . . . once and for all . . . no more niceties, no more chitchat . . . he lashed out with his walkingstick . . . slipped . . . they went down. . . bit the dust . . . made snowangels . . . rolled around . . . sent the snow flying . . . but Holger knew how to use his elbows and knees . . . and he had the kiddo . . . he always won . . . came in again, paid up . . . bitched and moaned . . . but if there was a crowd, he left . . . He'd been married, and I can remember how Irma looked . . . tall and skinny . . . on the pretty side, if the lighting was bad . . . reddishblonde . . . bony hips and a limp ass . . . a bitter, lewd expression . . . big nose, but not so much that it was offputting . . . shrewd, frightened eyes . . . she sounded like a National Bolshevik when she came . . .

HEMMING FORSLUND, 64 YEARS OLD, VILLAGER
– I can see them in front of me when I close my eyes . . . the little kid and the old geezer . . . always together . . . always underway . . . off on unknown errands . . .

310

Holger was a demon . . . apparently he'd been scandalously handsome once, but had decided to do something about that . . . he hated everything established, obvious, and unequivocal . . . He wrote a tract, *Concerning the Difference in Our Conceptual Worldviews*, and then something called *Anesthetic Breviarium* . . . He cast neither shadow nor reflection . . . he was terrified of bidets . . . he was loud and lustful . . . But it never turned out the way you expected . . . it was terrible . . . they were like Grendel and his mother . . . satrap and hierodule . . . You might've felt sorry for them, but they were so disgusting . . . complete outsiders . . . no one could help them . . . they were beyond all aid . . . utterly disgraceful . . . they knew what was what . . . reduction and regression . . . They lived alone . . . back behind where Zakri had his pasture . . . the house was a two-and-a-half story mass . . . darkred with black corners . . . all the upper and lower windows were nailed shut . . . They had a Christmasstar and Easterdecorations up all year round . . . their yard was wild and overgrown . . . sunflowers, marigolds, and rhubarbs . . . hops, touchmenots, and bilberries . . . rowans and birches . . . huge, ancient aspens and yews . . . and an ash . . . Nettles, ferns, and mandrakes . . . navelwort, hoodedskullcap, and bugleweed . . . Moses's burningbush . . . They didn't till the ground . . . the area was overgrown with tall grass . . . Old plows, a harvester, and a cowskeleton dotted the hayfence . . . Two hundred meters from the house flowed a troutstream . . . The fish found in the deepest pools were unnaturally large and bitegreedy . . . Wolves howled in the midwinter twilight . . . a lot of superstition and queerness . . . the entropicforest whispered esotericsecrets . . . it wasn't a good place . . .

The boy's name was Helge . . . ninjirkilkin . . . you didn't notice him at first . . . on account of Holger's flair and flamboyance . . . He seemed easily startled . . . a little slow . . . never said hello . . . had trouble even with small tasks . . . a lively imagination . . . the nearest other kid was in Kusmark . . . Holger wouldn't let Helger go to school . . . forged a doctor's certificate . . . eczema and gastriculcers . . . otitis and skin cancer . . . hoofandmouthdisease . . . Holger wasn't exactly tonguetied . . . no one can accuse him of that . . . he founded the French Anal Annales school and analytical philosophy too . . . wrote the *Analects* . . . He was intense and haughty . . . sublime . . . beyond good and evil . . . he had an extremist's smile and a kind of Paleolithic charm . . . If you rubbed him the right way, he was as gentle as you please . . . But if he felt he'd been insulted, and he always felt that way, there was no end to it . . . For us who had to live nearby and stay on our guard, it's a relief that he's gone . . . we feel refreshed and reassured, like after a bad wetdream . . . I don't know where the boy got off to . . . Holger slurped up earthworms . . . stole salt off the roads . . . there was always a swarm of flies around him . . . like Beelzebub . . . Holger Heresiarch . . . Mister Malibog . . .

Now that he's departed this life, we can begin to ponder the great, eternal questions again . . . though they may always go unanswered. . . why they stopped showing the *The Forsyte Saga* . . . and *A Family at War* . . . how I could've missed that minigolf putt . . . who in the hell stole those unripe apples in the fall of fifty-five . . .

– You bet your ass the police knew all about Holger Holmlund. He was a serious alcoholic and even went in for narcotics. We could never pin anything on him, though, not until a couple of days before his death, when I got him for having the handlebars on his packmoped too high. His fine was a five-kronor gift card made out to the dwarves in Kåge.

Still, he was often a suspected of serious crimes: I remember a few years ago, it was Easter Eve, when a chubby oldbat in Sandfors discovered three little boys crucified on the chapelwall. They were dressed up like Jesus and the two thieves. Scattered on the sand were ciggibutts with sepiacolored lipstick on them, which we know that Holmlund used for his blacksabbaths. But we could never connect him to the crime: several Biblethumping Buggers swore themselves sweaty that they'd seen him gambling away his pension at the pecarirodeo in Norra Bastuträsk on Good Friday evening.

Another couple of examples of vile, unexplained events that Holger Holmlund was very likely responsible for: In the wartwinter of seventy-nine, six or seven pious oldwhores disappeared from the nursing home in Rökgroven. A glassblower who sucked like a kissinggourami found their remains a year later in the trunk of an abandoned dieselthresher on the tractorroad south of Gustav Gustavsson Grönlund's skunkfarm. In the trunk was also: 1 surgicalbag, whose contents were used to skillfully torture the hags to death, 1 copy of *The Vivisection of Cripples* by the queen's mother, and 1 *Children's Bible*, with notes written in Holger's ornate hand: terrifying curses, gamasch, damasch or something like that—enough to make the cock of any ordinary mensch stand on end. Too bad fingerprint-

313

ing hadn't been invented yet, then we could've tied him directly to the murder, as well as to the collection of priestlygear that we also found in the trunk. We took Grandpa, the devilspawn Holmlund, in for questioning. Some bonehead had burst his eardrums, though, so it was difficult to make yourself understood. He shrieked deafly until he was blue in the face that nowaynohow did he bluesuck any bluenigger's bluerod. An officer, who shall remain nameless, but who liked to dip his sideburns in peasoup and then suck on them, lied to Holmlund and said the boy had already confessed to everything.

"Hohahah!" Holger cackled and licked his glasses clean.

He knew you couldn't get a single sensible word out of Helge, his orphaned grandson, and besides, the boy loved his Grandpa. I said: Holger, we know you killed the oldwhores. You're so crazy, not even the lice will have you. Be that as it may: if you'll just admit that you stole the thresher from poor Aron and scribbled nasty words in the *Children's Bible*, we'll temper justice with mercy and let you go home, right after we've lit up your ass with our paddywackers. Everything we said was recorded quick as fuck on a tripewriter by some little touslehead who tasted like cinnamon between the thighs. Pursing his lips, Holger saw right through my bullshit. It was obvious, though, that the sap had started rising when I promised him a spanking. Still, he was sly, the old pike, and just shook his head and waved his hands dismissively.

"I didn't do a thing!" he shrieked, at the same time semaphoring like the deaf homos on Novaya Zemlya. "I never went near the oldbags and I'm sad and scared!"

He grinned, so we shivered, and a seasoned chiropracticconstable puked up some undigested buggratin on the coffeeandnookiegirl's knee.

"There are witnesses, Holmlund, who saw you dressed in sexy lingerie at the old folk's home in Rökgroven on the same day the urwhores disappeared!"

"Who's been badmouthing me?"

"Oskar Lindkvist from Kåge, Norrland's largest soap- and sundrydealer."

"He's lying! May his balls shrivel to two raisins and his dick get stuck in a waffleiron!"

"We want what's best for you, Holmlund. You need help and you know it. Take the chance we're offering!"

His freshlaid lawyer sat there apathetically pulling hairtufts from his downy forelock. His name was Erika Åmärg and he'd lost his cock in a foxtrap. But he was educated. Holmlund elbowed him in the side and shouted that he wanted to leave.

"Hell, you've got no evidence against him!" Erika said abruptly. "Let him go, before I start swinging!"

And there wasn't much else we could do, because Grandpa was too smart for us.

Also, not too long ago, some jackass mixed woodalcohol in the communionrum at Kusmark's church, so that two people died and five were declared braindead. Holger Holmlund had run a couple of small errands to the pigchurchsty the day before, and left the priest—who was gullible as a girl after his cerebralhemorrhage—with the impression that he was newlysaved and hungry for a round with Jesus. But we came up emptyhanded, because Holger produced a testimonial from the districtnurse.

And then, in the mid-sixties, some firebrand had wholeroasted an oldfogey on a stake on the edge of the garbagedump in Kåge. Holger was passed out just a pissthrow from there and had burns on his lips to boot. Still, some crackpot claimed responsibility and was electroshocked to death before we could find out who else was in on it.

Pentecost day of '87, a tallshit and a littlelump, each wearing homemade eggcarton and potatostamp masks, which were supposed to look like Auntie Anita and Televinken, stole a deliveryvan full of bakedgoods, although they tossed out everything but the tastiest pastries. Then they drove to Anderstorp's *dascenter* and lured eighteen retards into the van before the personnel there could do anything about it. A couple of days later, a groggy sourpuss found the van on Kyrkvägen between Kåge and Ersmark. Inside it were the CP-kids, who'd been gassed to death. The porky ones had had the ham sliced off them while they were still alive. And when we paid a little visit to Holmlund, he offered us rimsugared bacon. He even cried cobalt tears when we told him about the massmurder.

"God, it's so terrible," he moaned. "How those lardbags must've suffered!"

We didn't press him any further and left with our errand unfinished. However, it's as certain as my raging hardon that me and Kent-Håkan got a taste of freshsmoked mongoflesh that day.

Holger was also the prime suspect in an incident at the beginning of the eighties: a railthin man kidnapped a playschool group of about a dozen three to four year olds. He nabbed them while the teacher was getting some in a lilacbush, then took them to the sulfurmine in Appojaure under the false pretense that they were going to learn how to hunt for fossilized cocks. Apparently he started by forcing the tiny tykes to stick cactuses up the little girls' downy muffs until they fainted from the pain. Then he stuck his veiny furuncle into each tykes' mouth, laid a spermdab on every tongue, and recited Satanic oaths. After that, he made them take each other under his expert supervision, and the most proficient at it got themselves a pair of lacehose, a French tickler, and, after he'd shaved their hair off, a skullbrand. He burned in three sixes, so they'd be sure of a place at the Lord's left hand. The kids said the tall, mean geezer took off on a scooter to the south. After questioning some wellrespected Norrbotten pedophiles, we got the order: pick up Holmlund and grill him like a fucksick broiler. So that's what we did, and if memory serves, those noobconstables were downright optimistic, because this time they had something to go on. The thing was, the perpetrator had bit a couple of the children pretty bad in the face, so they thought that all they had to do was take a dentalimpression from Holmlund and it'd be case closed. We caught Holmlund at the home of C-H Midlothian. Grumbling and half-naked, he came along to the station, playing the part of the indignant elderly gentleman. Then he bit into a piece of modelclay and then I told him to answer some questions.

This is how an interrogation with Holger Holmlund can sound. I'm reading right from the record:

"So, Holmlund . . . let's start at the beginning . . . what were you doing on the tenth of June?"

"I don't remember."

"But you just said . . ."

"Yeahyeahyeah! Me and Helge were celebrating Eilert's seventy-fifth birthday, and what a day. On that day, God dressed in pink crinoline and drank himself silly. Greatgrayshrikes quipped, wagtails climaxed, and wolf's foot and valerian grew so that it was a delight to behold. Eilert got a nightrajah and a lacy blouse, just perfect for when suitors come a-calling, and he looked so damn good I couldn't control myself. I tore off his skirt and started licking him like a cat laps milk. Before I could say *heil*, though . . ."

"That's enough! If I had my way, old buggerfucks like you would get nailed in your stinking assholes with icecold monsterdildos of steel."

"But Ubbe, you're scaring me! Aoww! Are people supposed to strike their elders?"

"Hold your tongue before I beat it with crushedglass into a pyttepanna! Where were we . . . oh yes. Now, you know very well what we're investigating, and I don't think you understand the mess you're in . . ."

"Pigcunt! Aaaoojojojoj! . . . You've gone wild!"

"Now Holger, calm yourself! How many hectoliters of soap would it take to wash your mouth out?!"

At this point I took a wankbreak, then resumed the interrogation.

"You had a book on you when you were picked up."

"Mmm."

"It's in a foreign language, the title seems to be *The Compleat Child Molester*. What does that mean?"

"Imitation of Christ."

"I see. But how do you explain the fact that you've got a lot of teeth here that are exactly like the teeth of the one who committed this crime?"

"I didn't do it, lovey, I swear it on Holy Simon's hanky."

He spent the night, and we kept that boy of his leashed up in a fuckcubby. But that evening, one of the kids he'd attacked, a boy named Urban, just like myself, screamed when he saw that singer Lasse Berghagen making a fool of himself on TV: "That's him! He's the one who was mean to us!" And the other kids all said the same thing. But Lasse had an alibi, so it was either someone who looked just like him or someone who was wearing a mask. When it came time to identify Holmlund, the kids were terrified, but they all agreed that he was too old to be the culprit.

"He was even younger than you," they said in chorus and laughed at me.

So Holger wandered out into the fresh June morning a free man. I tried one last time to appeal to his pride.

"Can't you just go ahead and confess?" I said at the exit.

"Things to do and places to be, Ubbe! I'd just love to, but I don't have the time."

"Oh, come on, Holger, what harm would it do, you're the last of your old rotten line . . ."

"There are more of us than you think."

"But you're the vilest man I've ever met or heard about."

"Flattery will get you nowhere."

"Clearly not. But would you tell me something that I've been wondering?"

"Mmhm?"

"How come everyone but gypsy Allan Schwarz calls you Grandpa?"

"Well, I mean, I'm the Grandpa, after all."

With that he toddled away, and sunbeams licked his neckdown and the pollen swirled around his gangly form. And what do you know, a dumpsterdiver found a guttapercha Lasse Berghagen mask in a bin for those who don't have what it takes to lead a normal life. It's located in central Kusmark. The only thing the lab was certain of, in the end, was that whomever had used the mask had probably had fingers.

One time Holmlund was caught redhanded emptying a kiddietrap in a playground in Ersmark. But he swore up and down that he was just happening by, when he got curious about what in tarnation the trap could be. He was horrible to children, but it took quite a few years before the folk in town got suspicious of him. One Midsummer's Eve, it must've been in the fifties, the geezers of Hebbers organized a kiddieparty with a fishingpond, an Indiantrail, a mobcourse, and electroplay. However, there were certain irregularities. One smallfry was so impressed by mancock that he cut his mama with a pair of scissors right in her whorecunt, another kept on about how God was a little dopefiend, and a pair of twins disappeared without a trace in the tunnelofhorrors. Holmlund was pretty brilliant, in his way. He was so devilishly clever, he knew how to dandle a boy on his knee and slowly increase the tempo until they were, you know, riding the cockhorse. He'd gradually he'd let his pole glide in, and they'd never even notice a thing. But a couple of parents sensed that something was amiss: the geezers seemed happy, the children were shouting, and the mothers and fathers were downing free booze—but wasn't it really carrion chuckling, stillborns screaming, and corpseeaters swilling the foamy brew? The children were redeyed and panting too heavily, and those who walked the Indiantrail came back with a grownup's worldweary gaze and voices gone thin. So a couple of loudmouth gossipcunts kept an extra eye on Holmlund and his closest cronies, Eilert and Wolrad. Wolrad was sullen and stupid and lived to tangle and tussle. He was obese and obscene, dimwitted but quicktempered. He was in charge of the tunnelofhorrors. He got his, though, in the end. Fucked a two-year-old tyke in the mouth, foaming with rage all the while. The little shaver survived and tattled and he's a policeman here in Skellefteå to this day. Wolfrad was sent to the nuthouse, where he committed suicide by driving an electricwhisk, which he'd managed to smuggle in, up his hiney, at which point he bled to death. Holger, Eilert, Henning, Herbert, Hilding, Larry, Hardy, and Tony all knew enough to pretend shock and outrage, so that they could escape punishment themselves.

Well I remember how Holger looked and sounded when I broke the news to him. He was even paler than usual and was weepy as an orgasm.

"My Nordic brain just can't wrap itself around the fact that Wolrad could behave in such a despicable way toward an innocent child."

"So it's certain that you don't know anything else about the matter?"

"Just as certain as the sun rises in the north."

None of the men could be convinced of his guilt. But the sexual-offense wasn't the only serious charge. For example, Holger was cited several times for the persecution of minorities. I sat down with him a couple of years later, when he came sauntering in on a charge that he'd been trying to instigate a pogrom.

I'm reading directly from the interrogation report:

"So, Holger . . . perhaps you know why you're here?"

"You call, I come a-runnin', massa."

"Stop right there! Now, a pious little auntie called in and told us that you were bragging outside Bauta Gym in Kusmark about how you bathed in Jewblood during the war and how much you'd like to relive those good old evil days."

"What?! You think I have anything against Jewdevils? Me, who's always preached circumcision and bloody offerings! Besides, one of the best lovers I've ever had was a hooknosed, curlyhaired kosherslaughterer, whateverthe- fuck his name was."

"You're supposed to have said that they should be roasted in their own fat."

"All I might've said about Jeeeews, is that they're nice and greasy . . . Shit, I got my Weltanschauung from Lukács, Jiminy Cricket, and Marcuse!"

"Here's the deal, Holger. If we get another report that you're threatening the inferior races with beatings and gassings, we'll have to set you straight in court, that's just the way it is. Agda Meir isn't the first we've heard from."

"Lots of people are envious that I've got the gift of gab, the eyes of a serpent, and the body of a mannequin."

"You've sworn to call down sorrow and damnation on everything from Samis to niggers, and a lot of it reminds me of that German character . . . you know . . . ummm . . . what the hell's his name . . ."

"Heini Hemmi?"

"That's the one . . . but what I wanted to say is that you have to hold your tongue about how the swarthyhost must be exterminated, and so forth, because this here is a Free Church district, and people have enough trouble just keeping their privates clean . . ."

Otherwise, Holger Holmlund was usually too drunk and horny to give a damn about politics and religion. As to drugs, we never could pin anything on him when it came to moonshine and dope. If I call to mind all the fruitless accusations against and investigations of Holmlund, it's striking how skillful he was at squirming his way out of them—there were hardly ever any reliable witnesses and he usually had someone who'd vouch for him. If nothing else, Henning Sjöström always backed him up. If we just take the second half of the sixties, we have: Sex with a minor . . . pettytheft . . . misappropriation of moviestarphotos . . . misuse of difficult words . . . coitusinterruptus . . . exposing a slackcock . . . serving foreign spiritual powers . . . subversion . . . scootertheft . . . prankcalling . . . arson . . . genocide . . . needless neediness . . . badmouthing popularlyelectedofficials . . . elitism . . . enginetampering . . . murderfucking . . . unlawful giggling . . . scandalous braggadocio . . . blasphemy . . . bestiality . . . disturbing the peace of the grave . . . cannibalism . . . serious assault . . . incest . . . loquaciousness . . . failure to commit suicide . . . sex with the overaged . . . drunkenness . . . melancholy . . . lightheartedness . . . hermaphroditism . . . failure to move beyond the analstage . . . indigestion . . . hightreason . . . making rudegestures at the grievanceofficer . . . violentresistance . . . poorgrooming . . . instigation of Satanic sadism . . . possession of a forbidden analstimulator . . . massmurder . . .

That last one makes for a strange story. Holmlund and some southern queerbeard nailed together a house of worship in Gran, where they subsequently lured old and decrepit shrews by promising them spiritual guidance and Extreme Unction. In and of itself, that wasn't illegal, but when a roving shiteater by the name of Assar Lalla happened by and saw Holger and the foreigner performing a shitfaced bloodeagle on a crookbacked oldcunt, he sprang over to the policestation and we drove off in a riotcontroltruck. It was a lovely September day, when nature's at death's door. Sirens blaring, we screeched to the turnaround. Holger and the other geezer came out on the bridge to see what was up.

"So, Holmlund," said a respectable old inspector, who used raw porkshanks instead of diapers, "where've you stashed all the poor wretches you've offed?"

"But Hugglund!" Holger twittered and bravely struggled to wipe away his Polish grin, "surely you know me well enough to see how gaga I am about my fellow man? The women who came to my and Poglavnik's chapel were saved, ask them yourself!"

"We'll get to that, but now why don't you be good boys and take your clothes off."

They did that and the inspector paid their orifices a little visit. The queerbeard looked ancient, but he rasped out some perverse rubbish when the inspector started poking around in his outstretched asshole. He got a baton to the nose, which sent him to the ground.

"You aren't thinking about beating up an oldgeezer who doesn't even know if God exists or not?!" Holmlund objected.

A pimply subordinate kneed him in the crotch.

"Holger and Ante, I wanted to let you know that you're suspected of torture and murder. So why don't you hang around for a coffee and a chat," the inspector rumbled.

"Whatthefuck," the queerbeard jabbered.

"Alrighty," Grampa said and put out his cigarette with his tongue.

We held them for three days and three nights, and we put clamps on their urethras so they couldn't piss. They weren't allowed to sleep and were forced to listen to Barry Manilow while they were in their cells. But the oldcows in the rootcellars around the synagogue unanimously insisted that Holger and Ante were virile and sweet, and that they could preach the shorthairs right off you. None of them had witnessed any violence. At the same time, Assar Lalla, the only witness, disappeared for good in the unexplored mangroveforests in the innermost part of the Bay of Bothnia. Since we hadn't found any graves or bodyparts in Gran, the two reprobates got off. Not too many days passed before the satanicsynagogue burned down and a dozen invalids perished . . .

"Do you know anything about this, Holmlund?" the inspector asked over the telephone.

"Even less than I know about the femaleorgasm and the origin of the ovenuniverse!" he answered.

So the matter was dropped.

There were hundreds of accusations against him, but none of them ever got to court. If I pick up the list again at the start of the seventies, we have: molestation of elkhunters . . . premature ejacu-

lation... excessive wit... implausibility... mimicry... shyness...
vampirism... teratology... reevaluation of all values...

RIKSCANCER—play on the title *Reichskanzler*

METESTRUS—period of sexual inactivity that follows estrus

GAWD—nutso

GALORUM—totally wrong

PRINCE OF THIS WORLD—the devil

GB-GUBBE—mascot in ads for the Swedish ice-cream company GB
Glace: a pudgy clown with a sickeningly sweet smile tipping his hat to
the world

KICKSLED—a sled consisting of a chair mounted on flexible metal runners; the sled is driven by kicking the ground as you go

LEFSE—thin, unleavened bread of Norwegian origin. Called *klådda* in
Sweden

STEFFAN AND BENGT—characters on a Swedish television series

FRITZ HAARMANN—"The Vampire of Hanover"; serial killer of adolescent
boys in Germany during the years immediately following World War I

VYSHINSKY—Andrey: Prosecutor General of the USSR and considered
to be the legal mastermind behind Stalin's Great Purge. He was also a
prosecutor during the Nuremberg trials

FREISLER—Roland: acted as judge, jury and executioner in Hitler's People's Court (*Volksgerichtshof*). During his tenure, there was a dramatic
rise in the number of death sentences handed out

FALUKORV—traditional Swedish sausage

BULLERBY—refers to the *Six Bullerby Children* series by Astrid Lingren,
which take place in the small Swedish village of Bullerby (Bullerbyn in
Swedish)

ARYOSOPHIC—member of an Aryosophic order created by Guido von List at the beginning of the nineteenth century

NORILSK—infamous contaminated industrial town in Russia

BOLIDEN AND RÖNNSKÄR—mining and smelting operations located near Skellefteå

SATRAP AND HIERODULE—satrap: general name given to a governor of a province in ancient Persia; hierodule: temple slave in ancient Greece, often associated with prostitution in service to a deity

NINJIRKILKIN—"the shy one"; apprentice shaman among the Chukchi

MISTER MALIBOG—or else, Mister Horny

FORSYTE SAGA—British television series based on *The Forsyte Saga* by John Galsworthy

A FAMILY AT WAR—British television series

PECARIRODEA—a rodeo conducted with a *Pecari tajacu*, a "collared peccary": a type of swine native to Central and South America

PADDYWACKER—police baton

AUNTIE ANITA AND TELEVINKEN—Anita Lindman, who starred in the Swedish children's television show *Anita och Televinken*; Televinken is a marionette

DASCENTER—Swedish play on words, lit. *dass* (toilet) + *dase* (dick) + *center*, instead of *dagscenter* (day center)

NIGHTRAJAH—hip-long jacket

PYTTEPANNA—(also pyttipanna), traditional Scandinavian dish; usually consists of potatoes, onions and meat, which are diced-up and then pan-fried

LASSE BERGHAGEN—Swedish singer-songwriter

POGLAVNIK—Ante Pavelic's title when he ruled over Nazi-controlled Croatia during World War II

Afterword

Assisted Living has a rare quality: even when approached by relatively experienced readers, and people with strong stomachs in general, evidence shows that the novel has the power to give us at least a glimpse of that incredulity and confusion and delightful shock that a few of our first unsettling (and unsettling mainly because they were our first) reading experiences gave us. To be disturbed by a book is something that belongs to the childhood of our reading. Only as an exception, only very rarely are we blessed with being exposed to something similar later on in life. As we gradually put the years behind us, as we gradually see more, hear more, experience more, and read more, our chances of suffering a literary ambush are also reduced. We become situated, establish an overview, develop tastes, follow our preferences, know more or less what to expect if we go here or there; know pretty much what to expect as we embark upon page five or page seven. I, for my part, have to return to my youthful encounters with Burroughs/Miller/Genet to trump the almost puerile kick I got when I read Teratologen for the first time. "Chuckling at his impudence, weeping at his tender sentiment, trembling with sorrow, paralyzed by hate": he's already summed it up pretty well himself, I think.

Assisted Living, with its surplus of violence and obscenity, is, of course, not unique in literary history. Forerunners can be found in works by Rabelais, Lautréamont, de Sade, Apollinaire, Céline, Bataille, and Burroughs, to name just a few. Nonetheless, I believe that the novel has something truly original, especially in the way it combines the fairy tale with the surreal and the learned with the poetic, which in turn are mixed with a gruff, biting, and in many ways typical Nordic "rural realism." The most striking thing about the novel is how complex it is, and how all-encompassing. In a mass of seemingly incompatible vegetation, it blooms explosively, evading most attempts to categorize it. It's a rough-cut and vulgar trash comedy. It's a classic epic, with roots going back to the Middle Ages and Antiquity. It's a poetic hymn with some of the most beautiful descriptions of nature in Scandinavian postwar prose. It's an exhaustive study in perversion and taboo-breaking. And it's a radically experimental novel, which in a crossfire of wordplay, allusions, and quotations, converses with (and makes sport of) the entirety of world literature. As such, *Assisted Living* is a book that contradicts itself at just about every turn. And it's in this odd polysubstance abuse, in this wellspring of self-contradiction, that Teratologen has developed his distinct voice.

The fairy-tale tone, the grotesque exaggerations, the over-the-top fantasies, which, on the one hand, make it easy to distance oneself—my God, this is *too* wild!—are, at the same time, that unpredictable force in the text which puts us in direct contact with the harsh living conditions from which it (the text) springs. When

Grandpa and the boy creep into Paul Holm's cow barn and are ambushed by a monster with greedy cunts all over its body, or when stuffed authors and hydrocephalic skulls appear among the trophies in the rightwing Maoist's [sic] rumpus room, it's clear that, realistically speaking, plausibility has been discarded long ago and that the perfidious details are, therefore, not to be taken seriously. At the same time, it's precisely because it's all been laid on so thick, precisely because the details so thoroughly exceed the boundaries of probability and plausibility (and because they do so throughout the entire novel)—it's precisely by virtue of these lunatic premises that the novel creates a version of reality that demands credibility. Obviously, the moment that the light from the seven-branch candelabra makes the rumpus room come to life "like a blood-clot," it's no longer a real space that we're entering, but rather an all the more clearly defined *space of possibility*. In this way, a door is opened into the mental and emotional depths in us all. This is actually conceivable, it's possible to imagine it, and, therefore, the possibility exists—in the individual, in us, in everyone.

One could say, using Kundera's words on Kafka, that the Upper Kåge Valley—*Övre Kågedalen*—is "an extreme and unrealized possibility" (*The Art of the Novel*). It's the world according to the boy, and either we accept it or we don't. Nonetheless, Grandpa's relentless boasting and the first-person narrator's tendency to distort anything and everything can be read as the last, desperate (read: literary) attempt of two degenerate and outcast souls to overcome their unbearable loneliness. The "dear friend's" introductory comments regarding the appendix ("Memories of Grandpa") supports this reading. And yes, perhaps it really is just the two of them making it all up . . . ? Perhaps the enchanted, devilish landscape is, in reality, nothing more than a gloomy, northern, deindustrialized, remote sort of place where nothing much happens . . . ? Perhaps the beastly murders and gory violence really are simply the quixotic daydreams of an old man and a boy the world forgot . . . ? It's at this point that the endless transgressions and boundary-crossings of Teratologen's tall tale takes on a tragic dimension, despite whatever wild and unbelievable hyperbolic heights the novel may reach. This idea invites a "realistic" interpretation of the novel, in which every character seems to have an aura of insane wishful thinking about them, an aura that, in the boy's story, materializes in the form of real characteristics, real features, real artifacts in an obscene white-trash theater of dreams.

In *Downfall* (*Nedstörtad angel*; literally, "Fallen Angel"), Per Olov Enquist writes of the monsters in the first Satanic church in California that "They found themselves on humanity's outermost edge: there, on the edge, they set up camp." And: "They were themselves touchstones: deformed human beings showing on whose side one stood: perfect God's, or imperfect man's."[1] I believe that it wouldn't be far-fetched to give this perspective renewed validity in the case of Grandpa and the boy. It's for this reason that the relationship between these two moral freaks makes such a strong impression, despite all conceivable forms of depravity and degradation. They're isolated in their outcast state, they seek out isolation and cultivate it, they—or at least Grandpa, to the extent we can take him at his word—finds in being cast-out and isolated

---

1   My translation. —KAP

from the general community a last dormant possibility to truly exist in the midst of a corrupted, late-capitalistic, affluent society.

Grandpa and the boy's political stance is, therefore, more ambiguous than that which might derive from their alienation alone. With their ruthless destruction of life and value, they break with all norms of investment, production, and profit. The creation of value is replaced, in their case, with raw destruction and waste. Given their absolute violation of any existing formal or social law, then, they seem to have something heroic about them after all. They represent a freedom we can't tolerate, a self-realization there's no place for. And from their camping ground on humanity's outermost edge, they sing (they screech and shout) the song of great irrevocable loneliness. Which isn't a pretty song. But how could it be?

When faced with offensive literature, or literature that's ethically problematic in some other way, it's a common strategy first to praise it for its amoral or immoral attitude, and then conclude that the author's project is, in reality, *deeply moral*. To wit: "Don't worry, he's one of us after all!" With Teratologen, however, it's more difficult than that, since his books—in addition to *Assisted Living* (*Äldreomsorgen i Övre Kågedalen*, 1992), the novels *Förensligandet i det egentliga Västerbotten* (Alienation in True Vasterbötten, 1998), *Hebberhålsapokryferna* (Hebberlhål's Apocrypha, 2003) and *Att hata allt mänskligt liv* (To Hate All Human Life, 2009), as well as a collection of aphorisms, *Apsefiston* (2002)—are all permeated by such an obvious enjoyment of and delight in the incessant dwelling upon that which, obeying whatever prevailing standard, must count as unacceptable and intolerable human behavior. And it's precisely this maliciousness, this genuine anti-humanism, this heartfelt cynical and nihilistic attitude toward life and literature that gives *Assisted Living* its remarkable power. There's an affinity for the perverted and degenerate that one can't escape, that one can't ignore, when reading this book. It's there, all that we're used to keeping our distance from, imparted with such poetic joy that anyone and everyone can ask themselves what it's good for. And perhaps the answer is, it's not good for anything. And perhaps that's the real reason that the novel has proven so difficult for so many to swallow. And, presumably, the reader has a single choice before him or herself: turn away in disgust, or be swept along for all you're worth. Those who choose the latter are forced to look death in its white eye and laugh. Without this laughter, *Assisted Living* remains an unreadable book.

STIG SÆTERBAKKEN

NIKANOR TERATOLOGEN (a pseudonym), born in 1964, is widely recognized as one of the most original and shocking young writers working in Sweden, where his *Assisted Living* is a famous—and infamous—bestseller, provoking scandal, hatred, and veneration in equal measure.

KERRI A. PIERCE is the translator of Lars Svendsen's *A Philosophy of Evil*, Mela Hartwig's *Am I a Redundant Human Being?*, and other novels available from Dalkey Archive Press.

PETROS ABATZOGLOU, *What Does Mrs. Freeman Want?*
MICHAL AJVAZ, *The Golden Age.*
The Other City.
PIERRE ALBERT-BIROT, *Grabinoulor.*
YUZ ALESHKOVSKY, *Kangaroo.*
FELIPE ALFAU, *Chromos.*
Locos.
JOÃO ALMINO, *The Book of Emotions.*
IVAN ÂNGELO, *The Celebration.*
The Tower of Glass.
DAVID ANTIN, *Talking.*
ANTÓNIO LOBO ANTUNES, *Knowledge of Hell.*
The Splendor of Portugal.
ALAIN ARIAS-MISSON, *Theatre of Incest.*
IFTIKHAR ARIF AND WAQAS KHWAJA, EDS., *Modern Poetry of Pakistan.*
JOHN ASHBERY AND JAMES SCHUYLER, *A Nest of Ninnies.*
ROBERT ASHLEY, *Perfect Lives.*
GABRIELA AVIGUR-ROTEM, *Heatwave and Crazy Birds.*
HEIMRAD BÄCKER, *transcript.*
DJUNA BARNES, *Ladies Almanack.*
Ryder.
JOHN BARTH, *LETTERS.*
Sabbatical.
DONALD BARTHELME, *The King.*
Paradise.
SVETISLAV BASARA, *Chinese Letter.*
RENÉ BELLETTO, *Dying.*
MARK BINELLI, *Sacco and Vanzetti Must Die!*
ANDREI BITOV, *Pushkin House.*
ANDREJ BLATNIK, *You Do Understand.*
LOUIS PAUL BOON, *Chapel Road.*
My Little War.
Summer in Termuren.
ROGER BOYLAN, *Killoyle.*
IGNÁCIO DE LOYOLA BRANDÃO, *Anonymous Celebrity.*
The Good-Bye Angel.
Teeth under the Sun.
Zero.
BONNIE BREMSER, *Troia: Mexican Memoirs.*
CHRISTINE BROOKE-ROSE, *Amalgamemnon.*
BRIGID BROPHY, *In Transit.*
MEREDITH BROSNAN, *Mr. Dynamite.*
GERALD L. BRUNS, *Modern Poetry and the Idea of Language.*
EVGENY BUNIMOVICH AND J. KATES, EDS., *Contemporary Russian Poetry: An Anthology.*
GABRIELLE BURTON, *Heartbreak Hotel.*
MICHEL BUTOR, *Degrees.*
Mobile.
Portrait of the Artist as a Young Ape.
G. CABRERA INFANTE, *Infante's Inferno.*
Three Trapped Tigers.
JULIETA CAMPOS, *The Fear of Losing Eurydice.*
ANNE CARSON, *Eros the Bittersweet.*
ORLY CASTEL-BLOOM, *Dolly City.*
CAMILO JOSÉ CELA, *Christ versus Arizona.*
The Family of Pascual Duarte.
The Hive.
LOUIS-FERDINAND CÉLINE, *Castle to Castle.*
Conversations with Professor Y.
London Bridge.
Normance.
North.
Rigadoon.
HUGO CHARTERIS, *The Tide Is Right.*
JEROME CHARYN, *The Tar Baby.*
ERIC CHEVILLARD, *Demolishing Nisard.*
MARC CHOLODENKO, *Mordechai Schamz.*
JOSHUA COHEN, *Witz.*
EMILY HOLMES COLEMAN, *The Shutter of Snow.*
ROBERT COOVER, *A Night at the Movies.*
STANLEY CRAWFORD, *Log of the S.S. The Mrs Unguentine.*
Some Instructions to My Wife.
ROBERT CREELEY, *Collected Prose.*
RENÉ CREVEL, *Putting My Foot in It.*
RALPH CUSACK, *Cadenza.*
SUSAN DAITCH, *L.C.*
Storytown.
NICHOLAS DELBANCO, *The Count of Concord.*
Sherbrookes.
NIGEL DENNIS, *Cards of Identity.*
PETER DIMOCK, *A Short Rhetoric for Leaving the Family.*
ARIEL DORFMAN, *Konfidenz.*
COLEMAN DOWELL, *The Houses of Children.*
Island People.
Too Much Flesh and Jabez.
ARKADII DRAGOMOSHCHENKO, *Dust.*
RIKKI DUCORNET, *The Complete Butcher's Tales.*
The Fountains of Neptune.
The Jade Cabinet.
The One Marvelous Thing.
Phosphor in Dreamland.
The Stain.
The Word "Desire."
WILLIAM EASTLAKE, *The Bamboo Bed.*
Castle Keep.
Lyric of the Circle Heart.
JEAN ECHENOZ, *Chopin's Move.*
STANLEY ELKIN, *A Bad Man.*
Boswell: A Modern Comedy.
Criers and Kibitzers, Kibitzers and Criers.
The Dick Gibson Show.
The Franchiser.
George Mills.
The Living End.
The MacGuffin.
The Magic Kingdom.
Mrs. Ted Bliss.
The Rabbi of Lud.
Van Gogh's Room at Arles.
FRANÇOIS EMMANUEL, *Invitation to a Voyage.*
ANNIE ERNAUX, *Cleaned Out.*
LAUREN FAIRBANKS, *Muzzle Thyself.*
Sister Carrie.
LESLIE A. FIEDLER, *Love and Death in the American Novel.*
JUAN FILLOY, *Op Oloop.*
GUSTAVE FLAUBERT, *Bouvard and Pécuchet.*
KASS FLEISHER, *Talking out of School.*
FORD MADOX FORD, *The March of Literature.*
JON FOSSE, *Aliss at the Fire.*
Melancholy.
MAX FRISCH, *I'm Not Stiller.*

SELECTED DALKEY ARCHIVE PAPERBACKS